THE HEART OF MEMORY will linger in your memory long after you turn the last page. Alison Strobel plumbs the depths of lost faith and the loss of self in this amazing book. I couldn't put it down.

ANE MULLIGAN
editor of Novel Journey

THE HEART OF MEMORY is a heartfelt journey through secrets and loss, through fame and faith, and past all that is skin deep to what lies deep within. Alison Strobel aptly captures the breakdown of a family and one woman's struggle to reinvent both her faith and herself.

LISA WINGATE
national bestselling author of Larkspur Cove
and Dandelion Summer

ALSO BY ALISON STROBEL

THE WEIGHT OF SHADOWS

THE HEART OF MEMORY

ALISON STROBEL

ZONDERVAN®

ZONDERVAN.com/
AUTHORTRACKER
follow your favorite authors

ZONDERVAN

The Heart of Memory
Copyright © 2011 by Alison Strobel Morrow

This title is also available as a Zondervan ebook. Visit www.zondervan.com/ebooks.

This title is also available in a Zondervan audio edition. Visit www.zondervan.fm.

Requests for information should be addressed to:
Zondervan, *Grand Rapids, Michigan 49530*

Library of Congress Cataloging-in-Publication Data

Strobel, Alison.
    The heart of memory : a novel / Alison Strobel.
      p. cm.
    ISBN 978-0-310-28947-0 (pbk.)
    1. Christians — Fiction. 2. Self-realization in women — Fiction. I. Title.
    PS3619.T754H43 2011
    813'.6 — dc22   2010040503

Cover design: Curt Diepenhorst
Cover photography or illustration: Robert Swiderski/Trevillion Images
Interior design: Publication Services, Inc.

Printed in the United States of America

11 12 13 14 15 16 /DCI/ 20 19 18 17 16 15 14 13 12 11 10 9 8 7 6 5 4 3 2 1

THE HEART OF MEMORY

CHAPTER 1

KNOWING THERE WAS ALWAYS SOMEONE WATCHING HER AT these conferences, Savannah Trover kept her mouth moving as the crowd sang along with the worship band. She wasn't on stage yet, but sitting on deck with the other speakers made her nearly as visible. She was just glad no one had heard when her voice had given out with a squeak on the last verse, and hopefully no one around her noticed she wasn't actually singing anymore.

Lousy timing, God she prayed as she took a casual glance to the door behind her. Where was Marisa? Savannah went on in ten minutes and wouldn't have a voice to teach with if she didn't get some Ricola and water soon.

The song ended and a new one began, admonishing her to trust in the Lord. *Shame on me. Thanks for the reminder.* She straightened her shoulders and mouthed the words to save her voice while she tried not to panic that she'd bomb when she took the stage.

A hand on her arm startled her from her thoughts. Marisa held out a bottle of water and an unwrapped lozenge. "Sorry it took so long," she whispered. Savannah smiled and waved away the apology as she took the lozenge. Marisa always knew exactly what she needed. Savannah wished the ministry could afford to give her a raise; she certainly deserved one.

Marisa pulled Savannah's phone from her pocket and handed it to her. "Shaun texted three times while I was in the dressing room. I figured it must be important if he was trying to reach you when he knows you're teaching this morning."

Savannah drained half the water, then popped the lozenge and took the phone.

Leather bound exec checkbook — can't find it.

Know where it is?

She frowned.

Didn't know we had one. Sorry.

She handed it back to Marisa with a shrug. "I don't even know what he's talking about."

Marisa pulled a small bag from her purse. "I've got one dose each of zinc, Echinacea, vitamins C and D, and garlic. Want any of them?"

Savannah glanced at her water, then held out her hand. "I'll take them all. Might as well." She chewed down the Ricola, then swallowed the handful of capsules. The band reached the final chorus, and she quickly reapplied the lipstick Marisa offered her, then closed her eyes and took a deep breath. Adrenaline was kicking in, soothing the dull ache behind her eyes and chasing away the feeling of uneasiness that came with knowing her immune system was being hacked.

The song ended, and a moment later the lights dimmed and the opening video illuminated the screen behind the stage. Savannah closed her eyes again, centering herself and spending one last minute in prayer. *Just get me through the day, Lord. Keep my voice and body strong. I don't care if I'm sick for the rest of the month, just keep me healthy today.*

She stood and straightened the ruby red jacket of her pantsuit before climbing the stairs to the stage. The video ended, the audience burst into applause, and the lights came up, activating the performer in her. "Thank you, ladies," she called out, waving and basking in the heat of the lights and the attention of five thousand women hanging on her every word, "and welcome to the last day of this summer's Women of the Word conference."

More applause, and her impending cold was forgotten. For the next forty minutes, Savannah was home.

SHAUN TROVER RAN A HAND through his hair and stared hard at the floor. "Think," he muttered. "Come on, think." He walked back to his den and pulled open the bottom drawer of his desk, the spot where the checkbook should be and where he had already looked three times. Still empty. *Of course it is. Come on, think.*

He sat down and scrolled through his online calendar, looking for something that might remind him of the last check he'd written. And there it was. He closed his eyes, walking step by step through that afternoon. *The phone rang, just as I pulled it out of the drawer.* The sudden memory made him smile—finally, some hope. *I remember taking that message on the kitchen counter—*

He'd brought the checkbook with him as he left the office to track down the cordless that was not on its base on his desk. He went back to the kitchen to look again.

"Hey, Dad." Jessie jerked open the fridge.

Shaun jumped. "I thought you were at work."

She smiled as she opened the orange juice. "I don't leave for another five. I'm sorry. I didn't mean to scare you."

"It's alright. Hey—you haven't seen a big leather binder, have you? About this big." He held out his hands, indicating the size as he scanned the room again.

When Jessie nodded, relief was followed quickly by fear. She wouldn't open it, would she?

"You have?"

"Yeah, I think so. It was here on the phone desk last week, on Mom's study Bible. I put them both in her office."

Shaun bounded upstairs. "Left-hand side of the credenza," Jessie called after him. Shaun let out a shaky breath as he pulled out the binder from beneath the tattered Bible. He'd have to be more careful. This couldn't happen again.

"Sorry about that," Jessie said when he returned. "Is that for A&A? I thought you guys had an accountant now."

"We do. But this isn't for A&A; it's for our personal account. I just don't like those smaller checkbooks—too easy to lose." They laughed at the irony and Shaun took the binder back to his office, locking it in its proper place before rejoining Jessie in the kitchen. "So Mom comes back tomorrow. I was thinking we could do a family dinner; you could bring Adam."

Jessie's face went dark. "No, thanks. Adam and I already have plans."

"Come on, Jess. It's your mother. She's been gone for three weeks."

"It's not that different from when she's here. I don't see what the big deal is."

Shaun offered a fatherly look, but Jessie returned it with a stony stare. He tried a different approach. "Maybe you two should do something together before classes start up. Take a road trip to Estes Park, maybe."

Jessie let out a flat laugh. "We wouldn't have enough to talk about to fill a fifteen-minute coffee break, much less a whole day. No, thanks." She shifted on her feet and raised her eyes to Shaun's. "But speaking of school, would you drive up with me when I move back and help me cart my stuff to my dorm room? It'll go so much faster with two of us, and Adam and I are helping to throw the freshman dinner that night. It would be great to have it done before that."

"Of course, Jess. As long as Mom doesn't need—"

"Oh, right, unless Mom *needs* something." She spun around and grabbed her keys from the counter. "I forgot she's the center of the universe."

Shaun winced when the door slammed shut. He should have known better than to try to throw them together like that. He just kept hoping things would change. *Not that they can when Savannah's never here.* He shook his head and went back to his office, then groaned when he remembered why he'd been racing around the house in a panic ten minutes ago. He pulled out the checkbook binder and removed a smaller checkbook from the back, then opened his email, his gut clenching as he scanned the inbox for the letter. His hand shook as he wrote the check, and by the time the envelope was addressed his handwriting was chicken scratch. He pushed a stamp onto the corner and walked to the kitchen for his keys, then grabbed the shopping list from the counter. He'd go grocery shopping after stopping at the post office. At least he and Savannah would have a nice dinner.

JESSIE ROLLED THE WINDOWS DOWN and cranked up the stereo. She sang along with the Brad Paisley tune, loudly and off key as usual, to try to cleanse her mind of the conversation with Shaun. When was her father ever going to learn?

At least school was starting soon. She missed seeing Adam every day, and having her friends around all the time. She'd miss seeing her dad so much, but at least they could meet for coffee halfway between A&A and campus now and then. She preferred that to being home and having to put up with Savannah's paradoxical attention. How someone could appear to not care at all about what Jessie did while simultaneously criticizing every move she made was beyond her psych 101 education.

Jessie pounded a fist lightly on the steering wheel as guilt nagged her. She had a mother—that was more than a lot of people had. And, though annoying, her mother was relatively healthy on all levels—didn't abuse or neglect her, was successful, and provided for her family. Jessie wished they could just get along.

She pulled into the parking lot of the strip mall and took a spot in the back row. After affixing her name tag to her shirt and brushing her wind-tangled hair, she took a deep breath and prayed her pre-work prayer. *Make me gracious and squelch my bias, God.*

The bell above the door chimed as she entered the bookstore. She waved to her manager, Torrie, who was working the register, and walked back to the offices to stash her wallet and keys before taking her place on the floor. A cart of new arrivals stood outside the stockroom; she wheeled it to the fiction section and read the back of each one before placing them on the shelves. She loved that she had a job that required her to read. Fiction was her specialty, though her growing interest in child development had her perusing the parenting section these days as well. She'd thought about trying to write a book, even had some decent ideas, but she worried everyone would compare her to Savannah or think she was trying to ride her mother's Sak's Fifth Avenue coattails. That was the absolute last thing she'd ever want anyone to think about her.

"Hey, Jess—oh good, you've got the cart." Torrie appeared at her side and slouched against the bookshelf. "There's a couple boxes of returns in the stockroom, too."

"Okay, I'll do those next."

"Do you know your schedule yet for next term? I'm going to start working out the shifts for the fall this week."

"Oh, yeah, I'll bring that tomorrow. I should be able to keep the same number of hours, though."

"Good. Between you and Dagne we should be set then, assuming your availability doesn't overlap too much." Torrie pulled a book from the cart and read the back, then handed it to Jessie. "Did you see the numbers for last month's sales? Your mom's book went through the roof after her conference in Denver."

"Oh, really?" Jessie clenched her teeth briefly as she pushed a book on the shelf. "Well, that's good."

"She's such an inspiration. My parents aren't believers, so I didn't have much of a role model when I became a Christian." Torrie sighed, looking wistful. "You're so lucky."

Live in my head for a day and see if you don't change your mind. "Yeah, she's really ... helped a lot of people."

"Is she back from the tour yet?"

"Tomorrow night."

"Know if she has any other books in the works?"

Jessie swallowed back a snarky comment. "I don't know. I haven't talked to her much this summer; she's been gone so much."

"Ah, true. Probably no time to write when she's touring. Well, I hope she comes out with something soon—she's great for business."

Torrie grinned, then pushed away from the bookshelf. "Gonna go work on the books. You've got the register."

"Okay." She watched Torrie disappear into the office and let out a deep breath. Nothing made her want to vent more than hearing other people paint her mother as some kind of hero. She could just hear people thinking, "And what are *you* going to do with *your* life?" Everyone's expectations were so high—including Savannah's. Jessie dreaded the day when they all realized she would never live up to them.

She finished stocking the books and began straightening the shelves. The front door chimed and she peeked around the bookshelf to greet the customer. "Welcome to Grace Notes," she said. "Can I help you find anything?"

The young woman pushed her sunglasses up and held out a sticky note. "Um, yeah. I'm looking for this book—*A Jewel of a Woman* by Savannah Trover. I caught the title at the end of a radio show, but didn't get to hear much about it. Would you recommend it?"

Jessie turned on her saleswoman smile and tried not to feel like a hypocrite. "Oh, definitely. Follow me. Savannah's books are over here." She led the woman to Savannah's section of the Christian Living shelves, smile frozen to her face, her insides smoldering. She rattled off her sales pitch for the book, then left the customer to skim it on her own. A few minutes later she closed the sale, then went back to work on the cart of books. She may not be thrilled with the author, but she had to admit, the lady sure could sell books.

SAVANNAH TOOK ADVANTAGE OF THE audience's laughter to take a sip from the water bottle that sat beside her Bible on the small podium. She could feel her immune system breaking down, in spite of the adrenaline. Three doses of various supplements over the course of the day had done nothing but push off the inevitable, and now, as she faced the last few minutes of her final talk, she knew she would just barely finish in time to keep a smile on her face as she spoke.

"So tomorrow, when you get ready to start your day, look in the mirror and see the whole you. Not just a single woman. Not just a wife. Not just a mom. Not just a … whatever it is you use to label yourself. See the woman God put here for this time in history. See the change agent whose community is waiting for her to step up and reach out. See the image of God that the Lord wants to use to shine his light and love into this dark, tumultuous world. You are more. And together, we are more. More than the lies, more than the pain, more than the fear and the busyness and the complacency that Satan uses to oppress those who don't know the Father. Don't listen to the voices that tell you you are less. Grab the day by the neck and don't let it go until you've wrung out of it every last opportunity to change this world for the better, in the name of Jesus."

The worship band began to play behind her, and she picked up her Bible and water from the table as the singers broke into the first song of the final worship set. Savannah walked down to her seat and released a deep breath as Marisa held out another handful of vitamin C capsules. "You made it."

"Just barely." She swallowed the pills with the last of her water. The music lulled her; she closed her eyes and let her body relax. Her head began to hurt as her adrenaline drained away, and she could feel her muscles and joints stating to ache.

The final worship set lasted for fifteen minutes. When the lights came up and the applause began, Savannah forced her heavy eyelids open and stood with the other presenters. They walked down the aisle and back to their dressing room, where all but Savannah began to chat about the evening's wrap-up dinner. Savannah sank onto the sofa and closed her eyes again. "Marisa, what time is our flight tomorrow?"

"Not until ten-thirty. But I'm going to try changing it to tonight. I'm worried about you being too sick tomorrow to fly."

"Wise woman." She pried her eyes open and hoisted herself from the couch to pack her things. Marisa called the airline, and Savannah eavesdropped until it was clear she had secured a new flight.

Marisa hung up a few minutes later. "We're booked for an 8:35."

Savannah glanced at the clock. "We'd better hustle then."

"Right—you ready to go?"

Savannah looked around the room for stray items. "I think so."

She hugged each of the other presenters she'd traveled with for most of the last three months, sad to miss out on the celebration dinner, and then left with Marisa for the hotel to pack.

Savannah felt like she was moving in slow motion as she folded pajamas and reclaimed her personal items from the nightstand. "I just know I'm going to forget something."

"That's why I'm here, silly." Marisa chuckled. "I know we're good friends and all, but this is my job, remember? So don't worry; I've got your back."

Savannah flashed her a weary smile. "Thanks, girl." Savannah zipped her bag closed and lay back on the bed. "When do we leave for the airport?"

"About half an hour."

"I can't wait to be on the plane so I can sleep."

"Unfortunately we're not flying direct to Colorado Springs. We'll go into Denver, and then drive down from there. Connecting to the Springs would have taken about the same amount of time, but at least this way you don't have to race through the airport to make a connecting flight."

"Good thinking. I'm sorry you'll have to do all that driving. And at night too." She groaned. "I hate being sick."

"Knowing you, you'll be back on your feet in a few days. Me, I get sick and I'm wiped out for a week, minimum. Oh—do you want to call Shaun or do you want me to?"

Savannah rolled over and sat up, rubbing a hand across her face. "I will." She pulled her cell from her purse and dialed, then flopped back onto the bed. She gave him the update when he answered, and he didn't like the thought of Marisa having to drive that far at night.

"Give me your flight info and I'll pick you up."

"Are you sure?"

"Of course. Might as well save the expense, since I'm sure the budget was blown with the rescheduled flight."

"I'm sorry—"

"No, don't be. She was right, you need to come home tonight in case you're too sick tomorrow. That's life. Besides, it just means I get to see you that much sooner."

Savannah smiled. "Thank you, Shaun. I'll tell her."

"Take care. I'll see you in a few hours."

"Okay, babe. Bye."

Savannah hung up and tossed her phone back into her purse. "Shaun will pick us up in Denver. Let's go now, before I fall asleep."

It was another two hours before she was settled into her seat on the plane, but she was asleep before takeoff. Marisa woke her just before they landed in Denver, and by then Savannah felt far worse. A fever had kicked in. Her teeth chattered and her skin prickled beneath her clothes. She groaned as she climbed into the car.

Shaun laid a quilt over her, the one she kept on the back of their couch at home. "Brilliant," she said to him as he kissed her cheek. "Thank you."

The next thing she knew, they were pulling into the parking lot at Marisa's apartment complex. "Are your expense receipts easily accessible?" she heard Shaun ask Marisa.

"Right here in my purse. Why?"

"If you want, I'll take those in tomorrow and file your expense report for you. You're not going to want to come in this week just to do paperwork."

"Thanks, Shaun. I appreciate that."

"Thanks again, Marisa," Savannah mumbled, eyes still shut against the pain in her head.

"Of course. I'll give you a call in a couple days, see how you're doing. Let me know if I can do anything."

Shaun walked Marisa to her apartment, then drove them home. "Have you eaten? Do you want me to make you some soup, or tea?"

"No, love. I just want to go to bed."

"You've got it."

He followed her into the house, carrying her bag and purse, and she made a beeline for the bedroom. Not bothering to change from her traveling clothes, she pulled the covers up to her chin and prayed she'd feel better in the morning.

CHAPTER 2

Shaun was ready to leave for work by the time Savannah finally awoke on her second day at home. "How are you—oh." Looking closely gave him his answer. "Still that bad, huh?" She nodded silently as she shuffled into the kitchen. "Can I get you something to eat before I leave?"

She gingerly eased herself onto a barstool. "Some tea?" Her voice was raspy and weak, no different from when she'd awoken yesterday. After spending the day on the couch, mostly sleeping, he'd have thought she'd be doing at least a little better.

He filled the kettle. "Did you sleep alright?"

"Mostly. Up for water once, but that was it."

"Are you going to be okay today? Do you want me to stay home? Jessie is working today, I think."

Her hand gave a small wave. "No, go to work. I'll probably just sleep all day anyway."

He pulled out a can of chicken noodle soup and set it on the stove beside a pot. "In case you get hungry later."

"Thanks."

He made the tea, then kissed her on the forehead. "I'm sorry you're miserable."

"Thanks. Me too. Hopefully it won't last long."

"You'll kick it quick, I'm sure." He pocketed his wallet and grabbed his keys and cell. "Call me if you need me to come home, okay? I can work from here if I need to."

"Thanks. Say hi to everyone."

Five minutes out, the gas light lit on the dash. He groaned, having forgotten about Saturday night's jaunt up to Denver that ruined his fuel budget, and backtracked to the gas station a block from home. The lost time was worth the money he'd save filling up there versus the station closer to the ministry office.

Shaun opened his wallet and considered his array of credit cards. He chose one toward the back, figuring it was time to add it into the rotation, just to be safe. He tried not to think too much about the price of the gas as he swiped his card and punched in his zip code. *Highway robbery.* Every tick of the price on the pump display made him want to wince. Picking up Savannah and Marisa had been cheaper than a rental, but it still meant taking money from somewhere else. He'd have to forgo lunch the rest of the month to make up for it.

A few minutes later he was parking in his usual spot in front of Abide & Abound's office. A banner announcing their tenth anniversary hung in the front window, and a little rush of pride made him smile as he pulled his briefcase from the front seat. This humble endeavor of theirs had grown so much in the last decade. Once upon a time it had been him and Savannah cooped up in his home den, but now they boasted six employees on the payroll and a proper, though nondescript, industrial park office just outside of downtown Colorado Springs. He had an office here, the only one amidst the maze of cubicles, and Savannah would pop in once a week to "greet the troops" before heading out to a coffee shop to work and have meetings.

It's a heck of an accomplishment, he thought as he locked the car. *Though not without its trials.* He tried not to think about the trials currently dogging him as he entered through the smoky glass door.

"Good morning, Shaun," said Brenda, their receptionist and customer service representative. "Savannah get home alright last night? How did the last stop on the tour go?"

"It went well—but Savannah's got the flu. She and Marisa actually came back Saturday night because she could feel herself getting worse and she didn't want to get stuck unable to fly."

Brenda's face fell. "Oh no! Can I pick anything up for her, or you?

I can stop at Vitamin Cottage over lunch, get her some of that immune booster tea she likes."

Shaun smiled, but shook his head. "She's fine. Marisa bought a bunch of stuff while they were in Omaha, so she's set. I appreciate the offer, though. Thank you."

"Not a problem. I'll add her to the prayer chain."

"Good idea. Thanks."

Brenda was an example of why he loved this ministry so much. They all cared about each other. It was like working with family.

Though that wasn't always a good thing.

He greeted their resource director and their accountant, the only other two staff members currently in. Savannah insisted on letting people set their own hours, within reason. "No point in making people drag themselves here at nine if they're completely unproductive until eleven," she'd say, and as long as things got done properly and on time, Shaun supported that. Monday mornings held one small exception: the ten a.m. staff meeting. It was Shaun's favorite part of the week.

He turned on his computer and opened the blinds a fraction, letting in slivers of the blinding August sunshine. He unloaded his briefcase, thanked Brenda when she appeared with a cup of coffee, and then sat down to orchestrate his day.

A quick look at the calendar reminded him of the two speaking engagements Savannah had early next week. It was a good thing she tended to get over illnesses quickly. It would kill him to cancel those gigs, knowing how well they paid. Thank goodness she never took anything the week after a tour.

He pulled out the receipts Marisa had given him and began to separate Marisa's from Savannah's. He was grateful for Marisa's thrifty nature and Savannah's Scottish roots; there were never receipts for steak dinners or fancy designer water. He itemized Marisa's reimbursement report and set it aside for her to sign later. Before itemizing Savannah's report, he pulled an envelope from his desk drawer and rummaged through it a moment, then pulled out a receipt for a haircut dated the week before Savannah had left for the tour. He added in the receipt from this morning's gas purchase, crumpled them all, then smoothed and crumpled them again before examining them for legibility. Three of the totals were now much more difficult to decipher. He itemized everything on the report, changing a couple 3's to 9's and one 5 to an 8 before photocopying all the receipts and attaching the copies to the reports.

His conscience twinged, but he tried to ignore it.

He spent the remaining forty-five minutes preparing his notes for the staff meeting, and at just a few minutes before ten, left his office for the conference room.

Brenda had already placed a platter of donuts in the center of the table and flanked it with a pitcher of water and a pot of coffee. Shaun opened the window to let in some air and took his place at the head of the table. The other staff trickled in, each of them asking about Savannah as they entered.

"The tour went very well. I'll give a quick rundown of the numbers and what we need to do for follow-up in a minute," he said when the meeting officially started. "And thanks for all your concern for Savannah. She's still feeling pretty sick, but you guys know how she is; she'll bounce back quickly. Darlene," he said, turning to their resource director and resident prayer warrior, "would you please open us in prayer, and ask for healing for Savannah?"

"Certainly, Shaun." The staff joined hands and Darlene brought them all to tears with her praises and supplication like she always did. Shaun allowed himself a peek at the others as she spoke, reveling in the community he and Savannah—and God, of course—had built over the last decade. Knowing the dividends coming in from the conference boosted his spirits even more.

When "Amen" was finally uttered, Shaun launched into the agenda as napkins were dabbed to cheeks and the donut platter passed around. "Final numbers from the conference aren't in to me yet, but from Savannah's book table we netted nearly 25% more than we did on the last tour, so that's a blessing. She prayed personally with about thirty-four women to receive the Lord, and with nearly eighty to rededicate themselves, and Marisa prayed with a bunch too."

"Amen" rang out from multiple people at once.

"So, Brenda, you've got your work cut out for you there. Let Marisa know if you'll need some help following up with those women; she's on vacation this week but I'm sure she wouldn't mind helping with those when she comes back.

"Alright then, moving right along ..." Shaun exhausted the agenda in less than the usual hour and led them in prayer again before everyone left for their cubicles. He caught the new accountant, Nick, before he could leave. "Here is Savannah's reimbursement report. I meant to do this at home this weekend so Savannah could sign off on it, but I forgot to bring home the form. You can call her if you want to go over it, or I can take it tonight and have her sign it."

"Oh, not a problem," Nick said as he scanned the report. Shaun had counted on him saying that. "I'd hate to bother her when she's feeling so lousy. I'll just ask you if I have any questions."

"Great, Nick. Thanks." Shaun went back to his office, high on the feeling of a meeting well run and the knowledge that checks from the conference book tables would soon be in the mail. His to-do list for the day was long, but he was energized now to tackle it. He woke his computer monitor from sleep mode and pulled up his email. *Time to pare down that inbox.*

Six new messages sat at the top, but it was the third that caught his eye and made his gorge rise. *No, please. Not again.* He clicked away from the list of new messages, bringing up instead a page of the oldest of the 264 emails he needed to sort through.

She would have to wait. He couldn't handle that right now.

SAVANNAH AWOKE FROM HER NAP on the couch feeling worse than when she'd first laid down. She whimpered as she sat up, every joint and muscle screaming, and dragged the quilt up over her shoulders.

A soap opera now played on the TV, and she changed it over to the country music video station just to have something on in the background. She really needed something to eat. And some water. Definitely some more water.

She slowly rose from the couch, quilt still clutched around her, and hobbled to the kitchen to refill the giant water bottle she always carried. The can of soup Shaun had left beckoned to her from the counter as she waited for the bottle to fill. What she really craved was her mother's homemade chicken noodle soup, the recipe for which she had once memorized but now could scarcely remember. At one time she'd made that soup nearly once a month, freezing some for when illness might strike, and bringing the rest to the person whose illness had inspired her to cook it in the first place. The sorry can of soup wouldn't cut it, but she was in no shape to attempt reawakening her culinary skills at the moment. She sighed and pulled out the can opener from the utensil drawer.

Once the soup was ready she sat back down on the couch with a steaming mug of it. The heat barely seemed to permeate the chill in her fingertips. She stared at the television, letting video after video play without comprehending anything. Her mind was elsewhere—assessing every body system, cataloging every pain and complaint, and thanking God that she didn't have to go through this often.

The dregs of her soup were stone cold when the doorbell jolted her from her thoughts. She ignored it until the sound of familiar laughter caught her ears. Her girlfriends. She'd forgotten about their lunch.

She set down the mug and shuffled as quickly as she could to the front door. The faces of her friends fell in unison when she opened the door. "Oh, hon," said Mary. "You look like death warmed over."

"I feel worse than that, if you can believe it." She stood aside as Mary, Andi, Colleen, and Bethany filed in, each carrying a potluck item. "I forgot, girls. Just completely forgot. All I have left is soup."

"Do you even want company?" asked Colleen. "We can leave if you just want to sleep."

"No, come on in—if you don't mind exposing yourself to my germs."

Andi grinned. "Hey, you're the germaphobe of the group. You know we don't care."

"Oh good. My mind just—" She waved a hand. "Never mind. I could use the company, that's all. I hate being here alone."

"You hate being anywhere alone." Bethany led the procession to the kitchen, then nodded to the pot on the stove. "Is that your homemade chicken noodle soup in there?"

"Don't I wish. It's just a can."

"Oh, bummer. I remember you made that for me when I had that terrible flu the year Riley was born. Do you remember that? Man, that was good soup."

"I think between the four of us you've probably made that soup twenty times," said Mary.

"I think it's the only thing that made me sad when you started working at A&A full-time," Colleen admitted. "No more homemade chicken noodle."

"Yeah, we really sacrificed for you, Van. I hope you can appreciate what we gave up when you started working." The women all laughed, and Savannah rolled her eyes and managed a grin. Their company was healing. She was glad they'd been willing to stay.

"Are you hungry, or was the Campbell's enough for you?" Bethany asked as she uncovered the dish she'd brought in. "I have twice-baked potatoes."

Savannah shuddered. "The soup was enough. Thanks, though. You all dish up what you want and come into the family room. Help yourself to drinks, too."

She moved to the cupboard for plates, but Mary beat her there. "Go sit down. We know where everything is."

She left them chuckling at her relief and reclaimed her place on the couch. They all came in together, plates heaped with side dishes and desserts. Savannah was supposed to have supplied the main dish. "Sorry again, girls."

"No worries." Mary sat on the opposite end of the couch and set her drink on the end table. "More room for Colleen's cheesecake."

"So what's your diagnosis, Van?" asked Andi.

"I don't know. Just the flu, I guess."

"Weird time of year for the flu."

She shrugged. "Leave it to me to pick it up on the off-season."

"When was the last time you were sick? I mean, seriously, in the twenty years I've known you I think I've only seen you sick, like, twice."

"I had a cold right before my second tour with Women of the Word."

"I remember that!" Colleen snapped her fingers. "You were worried you wouldn't be well in time."

"But you were over that in, like, three days. I remember calling to see if I could bring dinner for Shaun and Jessie, and you were already past the worst of it."

"Yeah, you're so good to your body, you'll be over this by Friday, easy." Mary grinned. "Now, if it were me," she said, waving a hand to indicate her ample figure, "I'd be bedridden for a week. I wish I had your self-discipline at the gym—and the kitchen. And the grocery store." The others laughed, but Savannah shook her head.

"This isn't going to be as easy to get rid of, I don't think. I've never felt this awful in my life. Honestly, it's kind of disconcerting."

"Well, I hate to bring it up, Van, but you are getting older."

"Mary!" Andi laughed.

"Well, it's true! You're, what, nearly forty-seven, you work like a maniac, you just got back from nearly three months on the road. Your body is just plain worn out, sister. Of course you feel the worst you've ever felt. When was the last time you got sick at the tail end of so much activity?"

"That's true," Colleen said.

Savannah pouted. "Not that it makes me feel any better."

"I know." Mary gave her a sympathetic smile. "But seriously, you're going to be fine. The flu can be pretty dangerous, though.

Go to your doctor if you're really and truly worried. Just don't be surprised if he tells you you need to relax a little. Like you said, it's been a long time since you got sick. You're just due for a good hard knock to the immune system."

The conversation turned to homeopathic flu treatments, and Savannah let the others chat and eat while she sat back and sipped her water. Mary was probably right. Just a flu, maybe a bad one, but nothing she couldn't handle. *Right?*

She just couldn't shake the feeling, though, that she was wrong.

JESSIE WAS ON HER WAY to turn off the *Open* sign when Torrie grabbed her elbow as she walked past the Bibles. "Jess, this customer is looking for Lutton's *Biblical Parenting.* Could you check the shelves? I've got a customer on hold on the office phone."

Jessie smiled at the woman and tilted her head towards Marriage & Family. "Sure, it's right over here."

The woman fell in step behind her. "I looked once but didn't see it. The computer said you had it, though."

"Someone might have mis-shelved it; happens all the time. I'm pretty sure we had at least a couple copies, though." She ran a finger along the spines, then knelt to check the bottom shelf. "Ah ha! Here we go." She pulled a copy and handed it to the customer. "Great book, too. Can I help you with anything else?"

"No, that's all."

Jessie walked her to the front and rang up her purchase. Once the customer was gone, she flipped the switch on the sign and locked the door. Closing didn't take her long, and when she finished her job she poked her head in the stockroom where Torrie was doing inventory. "I'm outta here. See you tomorrow."

"Will do—oh, wait a minute." Torrie nodded to an open-top box on the floor. "Copies of your mom's books for that fundraiser we're helping with. Think you could take them home and have her sign them?"

Jessie had forgotten all about those, but being reminded made her question whether she'd gotten this job solely because of the access it would give Torrie to Savannah. It was the kind of thing she'd hoped to avoid. Were it not for her love of books, she wouldn't have applied at all. She hoisted the box with a grimace. "Yeah. Sure."

"Tell her thanks for me."

"Will do."

Jessie backed out of the front door, grimacing under the weight of the box. Hardbacks were a pain to move—but they made great gifts. The private Christian school where they were helping with the fundraiser would make a mint selling the autographed copies.

She dropped the box into the front seat of her car, and the inventory list blew off the top. Her mother's face smiled up at her from the book's cover. She tossed her purse over it and shut the door.

Once home, she was not at all surprised to see her mother asleep on the couch. The first few times she'd found her that way, Jessie had been stunned. She'd never seen her mother nap. Savannah never had the time. But this flu she had was really kicking her butt. Jessie wasn't happy that her mother was miserable, but she did feel a teensy bit smug at seeing her laid out as badly as Jessie had been when she'd had the flu last year.

Human after all.

The uncharitable thought burned in her spirit. It had been a particularly bad day for the kindness of her thoughts toward her mother. She'd overheard one customer gushing to another about Savannah's talk at the conference, which had then segued into a hearsay-based discussion of her marriage and family life. Jessie had bitten back a correction, not wanting to reveal her own identity. But hearing her mother nearly sainted by two total strangers had really gotten under her skin.

Seeing her mother curled beneath the quilt kicked her guilt into high gear. Savannah couldn't help what people said about her or control other people's motives. Jessie knew her anger was misplaced, but it had turned in Savannah's direction for so long that she channeled it toward her practically out of habit.

Time for penance. Jessie left the books by the door and went to the kitchen. It was nearly seven-thirty already, but she was hungry and could tell by the lack of dirty dishes that her mother likely hadn't eaten much that day. She decided to go all-out and make her mother's chicken soup.

Standing on tiptoes, she pulled the wooden recipe box from the cabinet above the stove. She hadn't cooked anything from scratch in ages—but then again, neither had Savannah. Before she'd started working, Savannah had always made everything by hand—even bread. Jessie could remember coming home to the most amazing smells when she was in elementary school. But the bigger A&A got, and the more writing Savannah was contracted to do and the more speaking engagements she received, the less time she spent in the kitchen, until the only one who cooked anything anymore was Shaun. And his repertoire was limited to the basics; everything else came from a can or box.

Jessie flipped through the index cards until she found the soup recipe that had nourished her through countless childhood ailments. How long had it been since she'd had it? Eight years, easily. She read the ingredients, mouth watering at the memories of the taste, and began pulling items from the fridge and pantry. She'd never made anything more complex than pancakes from scratch when the boxed mix had run out—she hoped she wouldn't mess up the soup. She was a lousy cook and she knew it; she seemed to be missing the domestic gene, and by the time she'd been old enough to start helping in the kitchen Savannah had been wrapped up in A&A and book tours and hadn't had time to teach her anything. *But it's not rocket science, right? I can totally do this. So what if the recipe is two cards long?*

She had the chicken boiling in a pot when Savannah wandered in, her short hair sticking out in crazy directions and her eyes droopy with sleep. "What's going on in here?"

Jessie summoned her compassion. "I'm making you chicken noodle soup."

"Well, that's sweet, Jessie. Thank you." Savannah glanced into the pot. "What's in here?"

"The chicken."

"What did you use?"

Jessie held up the card. "Well, it said to use a whole chicken, but we didn't have one so I just used a bunch of chicken breasts. I looked up the amounts to make sure I'd have enough—"

"It's not the amount so much as the taste that's going to be affected. Without the dark meat the flavoring will be all wrong."

Jessie's compassion left her in a single breath huffed in irritation. "How was I supposed to know that? The card didn't say that, and it's not like anyone ever taught me that kind of thing."

She instantly regretted the words, but Savannah didn't appear to notice the dig. "Oh well, better than nothing, I suppose. Just add some stock and rosemary." She set the top back on the pot and said, "I'm sure you'll figure it out," and wandered out again.

Jessie focused on the carrots she was dicing, trying not to let her thoughts darken again. For once she'd love a reason to *not* resent her mother. Savannah had had the chance right then. Had she come alongside Jessie and walked her through the recipe—explaining the difference chicken breasts would make compared to a whole chicken, showing her the best way to prep the vegetables and explaining how to make sure everything was done at the right time— Jessie would have gladly shelved years of hurt. But instead she'd done what she always did—swooped in, dropped a confidence-destroying bomb, and then retreated, leaving Jessie to figure it out herself.

Blinking away tears, Jessie consulted the recipe card again, but didn't really comprehend it. For years she'd longed to have a mom who took her under her wing instead of assuming she was smart enough to work everything out on her own, a mom who knew how to offer suggestions without making it sound like criticism. But her hope of ever having that had all but died out. Savannah would always be Savannah; there was no point in wishing she'd change.

Jessie turned off the burner beneath the pot and swept the vegetables into a bowl, then covered them in plastic wrap and stuck them in the fridge. Her enthusiasm was gone. She'd make mac n' cheese from a box instead.

Shaun was just finishing his bag lunch the next day when a knock came on his door. "It's open," he called.

Nick entered, holding an expense report. Shaun's heart went into panic mode, beating like Morse code.

"Hey, Shaun—oh, you're eating. I'm sorry."

"No, not a problem. I was almost done. Come on in."

Nick walked to the desk and held up a piece of paper. "I was going over Savannah's reimbursement form and found an error in your math." He pointed out the total he'd come up with, written next to the total Shaun had recorded. Instantly Shaun saw his mistake. "It's not a big deal. I just wanted to show you so you didn't wonder why the amount was different when you got the check."

"Thanks, Nick. I appreciate it. You'd think I'd be able to operate a calculator, huh?"

Nick shrugged. "Hey, it happens. At least you're getting more than you were expecting."

"Ha, yeah."

"I'll get you the check by the end of the day. Come see me if you don't have it before you leave, in case you want to go early to take care of Savannah."

"I will. Thanks." Nick left, closing the door behind him, and Shaun let out a breath and rubbed a hand over his eyes. He'd done this dozens of times, but he'd never forgotten to check his math. What had he been thinking? The last thing he needed was to give Nick a reason to start checking those forms more closely.

His appetite gone, Shaun stuffed the rest of his lunch back into the sack and shoved it into the trash can beneath his desk. Now he felt jumpy. He couldn't concentrate, and his thoughts kept going back to the second he saw the report in Nick's hand and was sure he'd finally been caught. How much longer until his luck ran out? He'd been under the impression that Nick rubber-stamped whatever Shaun turned in, but apparently he was more diligent than Shaun had realized.

He stood and paced the small office for a second, trying to dissipate some of the adrenaline, then headed for the front door. "I'm going out for a bit," he told Brenda. "I'll be back in an hour." Slipping on sunglasses, he set out towards the small park a couple blocks away. The noon sun seared him through his golf shirt, but the shade above his favorite park bench when he arrived made up for the heat. He sat down beneath the cottonwood and closed his eyes. The adrenaline was mostly gone now, but the problem still remained.

He'd have to do something about Nick.

CHAPTER 3

Savannah had been awake for ten minutes, but still hadn't opened her eyes. She'd listened as Shaun had showered and shaved and left for the kitchen, planning to get up after he went downstairs. But instead, she was still beneath the covers, her mind vacillating between cataloging her current ills and throwing herself a pity party.

She'd been home for over a week, and she still felt about as sick as she had that first day after the tour. The only improvement so far had been when her fever had broken four days ago. It removed some of the aches, but not all of them, and sleeping still took up most of her day. She was resolved—in her head, anyway—that today would be the last day she just sat around. It was time to start figuring out what was going on with her body.

Ten minutes later she dragged herself from bed and into the shower. The improvement in mood that usually came with a hot shower eluded her yet again. She combed out her hair but skipped styling it, then dressed in yoga pants and a T-shirt before going downstairs. She'd start with a good breakfast; she hadn't had one since she'd been home. She knew she needed to eat, despite the fact that she had no appetite. But once she faced the refrigerator, all inspiration left her. She shut it and slumped onto the couch instead.

"I thought I heard you down here." Shaun came out of his office and kissed the top of her head. "Just getting ready to go. Can I make you something to eat?"

"That's sweet, but I don't know what to have. Just make me anything."

"You've got it." He disappeared into the kitchen, leaving Savannah to stare out the window at the stand of trees at the back of their property. After a week spent this way, she had every tree just about memorized.

Shaun set a plate with toast and grapes on the table beside her, and held out a mug of tea. "Anything else I can do for you before I leave?"

"No, but do you think I should go to the doctor?"

"That's your call, hon. I know how you are about doctors."

She sighed. "I know. I'm just afraid something is really wrong."

He sat beside her. "Like what?"

"I don't know. This just doesn't seem right, though. No one else is sick; it's not like this is going around."

"Maybe not here, but maybe it is in Omaha, or wherever you were before that stop."

She sighed. "Maybe. But ..."

He wrapped an arm around her shoulders and drew her against his chest. "Look, Van, you need to listen to your gut. If you think it's serious, then make an appointment with Dr. Helms. But if you're just discouraged because it's taking so long, then look for something to do today that will keep your mind busy so you're not dwelling on it. It's not like you're not improving at all; your fever is gone and you don't hurt as much, right?"

"Yes, you're right." She sat up. "Go to work, honey. I'll talk to you later."

He gave her another kiss, then left her with her breakfast. She opened her Bible and read while she ate, though her mind was only half engaged with the text. The other half was thinking about her symptoms. When she realized she wasn't comprehending anything she read, she shut her Bible and opened her journal to the back page and wrote "Symptoms." She followed it with a bullet-point list.

- Weakness
- Exhaustion
- Melancholia

Writing them down made her realize she didn't have as many symptoms as she thought she did. The ones she did have didn't seem as concerning when she wrote them out. Shaun was probably right, she was just discouraged.

Although ...

She went to the bookshelf in their bedroom and pulled a medical encyclopedia from the lower shelf. She'd purchased the thick volume when Jessie was born, paranoid that her daughter might be sick one day and she wouldn't know what to do for her, though in the end it had rarely been used. She flipped to the flow charts that helped diagnose based on symptoms and checked each one until she found the one she wanted. She moved her finger along the page, following the path from box to box, until she reached the end.

Possible Diagnoses:

Anemia

Underactive Thyroid

Pregnancy

She shut the book. *Pregnancy?*

She laughed out loud for a brief moment, then moved more quickly than she had in a week to her Daytimer. She flipped the pages back until she saw the red circle, then wracked her brain for a memory of the last time she and Shaun had been intimate. She'd been on the tour for three months ... but made a stop at home in July. She looked again at the date and did the math.

"Oh my goodness."

It wasn't possible, was it? She was forty-seven years old, for heaven's sake. Underactive thyroid made much more sense—but would that hit as fast as this had? She wondered the same about anemia. Whereas pregnancy symptoms *could* hit strong out of nowhere. She'd been pregnant three times, and each time the signs had turned on as though flipped by a switch.

She thought back to her pregnancies, looking for similarities between how she felt then and now. The exhaustion, the lethargy, even the blue mood—she'd experienced all of them. Granted, she hadn't had a fever. *But what if I really did have the flu first?*

It was possible. She could hardly believe it, but it was definitely possible.

She crawled back under the covers, seeking a safe place to let her emotions unravel. A baby, at this age, with their only other child already halfway through college—talk about completely un-ideal. They'd never know each other, Jessie and the baby. Jessie would be more like an aunt than a sister. And at her age, Savannah would certainly be considered high-risk, which would mean frequent appointments, ultrasounds, and other medical interventions she was not a fan of. Not to mention the toll it would take on her ministry. The timing was, in all ways, absolutely horrible.

She pulled the sheets to her chin and curled on her side, eyes squeezed shut. What was the point of even thinking about the effects of a baby on her life? If she really was pregnant, then the likelihood of her carrying it to term was small. She couldn't bear the thought of going through another miscarriage—the dreams dashed, the hopeless labor, the raging emotions with no baby to hold on to and anchor her. *Please, God, not again.*

She stayed in bed, overwhelmed at the possibility, until the sun shifted and shone on her face. She sat up and forced herself from bed. She knew it was ridiculous to let her imagination run like that when it was possible to confirm—or rule out—the pregnancy with a home test. She just had to go buy one.

She hadn't left the house in a week. The idea of going out was enough to distract her. She pulled a baseball cap over her head and tied on her gym shoes, focusing her thoughts on where she would go to buy a test and not on what it might tell her.

She drove to the pharmacy six blocks from their house, then turned around and left. It would not be a good idea to risk being seen by someone who knew her. The last thing she wanted was for anyone to know this might be happening. She got on the freeway and went south, then took the last exit before leaving Colorado

Springs and stopped at the closest gas station to get directions to a pharmacy. She still might be seen, but it was much less likely.

It felt good to be out. She spotted a coffee shop and nearly stopped, but then remembered caffeine wasn't good for the baby. *Not that it matters. It's not like it will live long.*

The callousness of her thoughts surprised her. That wasn't like her — even if it were true. *And what if this is the one that sticks? God could work a miracle, right?*

She pulled into the pharmacy parking lot and shut off the car, dwelling on that last thought. He *could* work a miracle. She really could have another baby, if God willed it. And to get pregnant now, after all this time, even though they used protection — that really would be God, wouldn't it? He wouldn't help her conceive only to put her through the same pain yet again, would he?

She entered the store, eyes peeled for familiar faces, and sought out the right aisle. She was stunned when she found it. It had been fifteen years since the last time she'd been pregnant, and the home pregnancy test industry had exploded since then. With so many choices — and having taxed her mental energy too much already just by driving — she couldn't discern which test was the best. She grabbed the most expensive box, reasoning that it must be the most accurate, then grabbed one more just to be safe.

She went through the check out, feeling oddly embarrassed with her purchase, then went back to the car with her hat pulled low. Once safe inside, she ripped open a box to read the instructions. Her heart sank when she read that it was better to wait until first thing in the morning. How would she ever make it that long?

She drove home, frustrated and utterly spent from all the activity. After stashing the boxes in her bathroom drawer, she crawled back into bed to try to sleep. But for the first time all week, sleep eluded her. She couldn't stop thinking about the chance to hold a newborn again.

THE SLAM OF THE DOOR awoke her. She opened one eye to check the clock and sighed; she had just fallen asleep. She pulled the sheet up to her chin and shut her eyes again, but a knock at the door brought them back open. "Come in."

Jessie appeared in the doorway, looking sheepish. "I woke you up; I'm sorry."

"No, baby, that's okay." Savannah pushed herself upright and winced at the thudding that commenced in her head. "Did you need something?"

"I'm packing for school but can't find my bedding. I went to the cleaners, thinking it was still there from when we brought it in back in May, but they didn't have it. Do you know where it is?"

"Bedding, bedding ..." Savannah swung her legs off the edge of the bed and stood. "I think I got it when I picked up some of my speaking suits. Let me check the closet." Jessie followed her in, and Savannah glanced around to make sure there were no traces of her pregnancy test packaging around. The thought brought another to mind: Jessie was in her first real relationship, and while Adam was an upstanding young man, and Jessie herself had a smart head on her shoulders, Savannah knew there was no difference in hormones between them and any other twenty-year-olds.

And with that, Savannah realized in a panic she'd never talked to her daughter about sex. The public school had beaten her to it, and since Jessie hadn't dated in junior high or high school, Savannah hadn't seen the point in bringing up such an awkward subject. But now, with Jessie and Adam so serious, and heaven only knew what kind of supervision was going on at the college, Savannah knew she should probably bring it up.

She'd been lucky so far — Jessie had grown up just fine even though Savannah hadn't been able to spend all the time with her during those years that she'd planned. But who knew what disasters might be avoided if she did the motherly thing and brought up the topic now, uncomfortable as it may be? It had been a long time since she and Jessie had engaged in a good heart-to-heart, and these opportunities came less and less frequently; she should grab this one while she still could.

"So, Jessie," Savannah began, trying to sound casual as she examined the contents of her closet, "you and Adam are pretty serious, I know.... May I ask what the two of you are doing to keep your relationship pure?"

Jessie's eyes went wide before she sputtered, "What—*pure?* Oh my gosh, Mom, are you asking if we're having sex?"

"No, no, no—I'm asking what you're doing to make sure you *don't* have sex."

"No way, Mom. I am not having this conversation." Jessie's face was red. "I totally can't believe you just went there."

"Honey, listen, I was dating your father at your age, and I vividly remember wanting—"

"So help me, if you talk to me about having sex with Dad—"

"Good gracious, no!" Savannah was flustered. "I wasn't going to give any details. I'm just saying I remember the temptation and how difficult it was to handle sometimes, and I wanted to make sure you had a plan in place to handle that temptation when it came your way."

Jessie's hands covered her face. "Gross, gross, gross. I cannot believe we're having this conversation." Her hands slid down her cheeks. "We're not gonna have sex, Mom, okay?"

"Alright, honey, I'm glad you're resolved not to. But listen, if you find yourself struggling you can always come and talk to me, okay?"

Jessie let out a snort. "Yeah, okay."

"What do you mean, 'Yeah, okay'?"

Jessie rolled her eyes. "Nothing."

Savannah pulled the bedding, still in plastic, from the bottom of a pile of off-season clothing. "Not nothing. What?"

Her daughter's eyes were focused on the striped duvet cover. "No offense, Mom, but you and I don't really talk about that kind of thing."

"Well, no, we haven't—but we haven't needed to, either."

"That's not what—never mind." She took the bedding from Savannah's arms. "Thanks for picking this up for me. Sorry I woke you up."

"Honey, wait," she said to Jessie's retreating back. But she was out the door before Savannah could think of what else to say.

Jessie was inching further and further away. It hurt Savannah to see it, though in her heart she knew she was partly to blame. She just wasn't around enough. She liked to think she was justified, at least somewhat—she did what she did for Jessie and her generation, for the Christian women they would become. They needed good role models, a culture that would allow them to be who God wanted them to be; Savannah was just trying to do her part to provide that for them.

The reasoning rang hollow when she tried to sort it out, so she didn't often try, and she wasn't going to attempt it now. Instead, she crawled back into bed and closed her eyes, fighting against the new maternal concerns that blossomed now for Jessie, and wondering who she *would* go to when she needed to talk.

JESSIE FELT THE FLAMES RISE in her cheeks as she shut herself in her bedroom. Sex was dead last on the list of things she'd ever want to discuss with her mother. Where on earth had that conversation come from? Were her thoughts that plain on her face? She'd never have expected her mother to be able to read her that well. *It must just be coincidence. It's got to be.*

Regardless, it gave her that much more incentive to be more careful. Way more careful. The last person she'd want to find her out would be Savannah.

Not that there will be anything else to find out, Jessie reminded herself. Last night had been a total fluke; she and Adam had already agreed it wouldn't happen again. Had the other couple they'd been doubling with not canceled, they wouldn't have been alone at the drive-in, and they wouldn't have started the make-out session that nearly claimed her chastity. It was why they never went out alone, why they limited themselves to holding hands after dark and always crammed a pillow between them when they were sitting together on the couch. Typically the fear of headlines screaming that Savannah Trover's wanton daughter had gotten pregnant was motivation enough to abstain, but last night her thoughts had been very, very far away from her mother's reputation.

Angie had fixed that the minute Jessie had called her for advice. "You guys what?! Girl, are you out of your mind? What if you got pregnant? Can you just imagine what that would look like for your mom?"

Jessie hadn't taken her best friend's admonishment very well. "Seriously? You're bringing my mother up? Have you not been my friend for the past fifteen years? Do you really not know that she is the last person I want to think about right now? Thanks a lot, Ang. That's just why I called you, so you could read me the riot act and make me feel even worse than I already do."

"I'm sorry! I'm sorry, Jess. Really. I'm just surprised; it's so not like you to lose control like that."

"Yeah, I know. It's just that I'm sick of always having to be in control for someone else and not for myself. Maybe *I'm* really *not* all that self-controlled. Maybe, if I didn't have to worry about how someone else would be affected, I'd go totally nuts, be all crazy like that girl in Footloose."

"Straddling the freeway in the face of oncoming semis, you mean?"

That made Jessie laugh. "Yes. Exactly. I'm totally the road-straddling type."

"You're not, though — you know that, right? Even if it weren't for your mom, you wouldn't be the kind to go wild. It's just not who you are."

Jessie let out a snort. "Thanks for the reality check. *Of course* I know. But sometimes I wish I were. I just want my own life, and I don't feel like I'll ever have it. I'll always be 'Savannah's daughter.'

I can't wait to get married and drop 'Trover.' At least that dead giveaway will be gone."

"Gonna do plastic surgery to change your eyes and cheekbones and mouth, too? Because with your hair pulled back you're a dead-ringer."

"Gah, don't remind me." She fingered the cross Adam had given her for her birthday. The guilt returned, and with it, the anger. "I'm just so tired of being shadowed by her all the freaking time. I'm twenty years old, for pete's sake. My mother should be the last person on my mind when I'm with my boyfriend. Even if it *does* keep me from going too far." She groaned. "But man, Angie, it was dicey for a minute there. Seriously, I was *this close* to just throwing myself at him. And I'm seriously scared that we won't be able to go back to the little boundaries we put up before to keep ourselves from going too far."

"Extra vigilance, extra boundaries, extra company all the time. Do whatever you've gotta do. You *do* know that it's not just your mother's life that would be ruined if you got pregnant, right?"

"Well, to be totally honest, I don't think my life *would* be ruined. Children are a blessing from God, right?"

"Seriously? You're questioning the 'no sex out of wedlock' standard?"

"No, I'm not questioning it—I'm just saying I think it's sad to say that a beautiful miracle like a baby 'ruins' your life. It doesn't ruin it; it just changes it."

"Uh, yeah—for the worse when you're not married and still in college. Don't try to make it okay, Jess."

"I'm not, I'm just playing devil's advocate." But truthfully she did want to find a loophole, something that would give her a reason to chuck caution just once and do something on a whim and not worry about it.

Her phone buzzed with an incoming text from Adam.

Bowling 2nite?

OK.

She set the duvet in the corner atop the box that held her bedding. Bowling was a safe choice. She appreciated that he was looking out for them, too. But what would they do afterwards? What if they went back to his house? To the basement where they watched movies and played Cranium with their friends? If no one else was with them ...

Jessie sighed and continued to pack as she prayed a simple request. *Give me strength, God. Give me strength.*

SHAUN DROPPED HIS KEYS ON the counter and gave Savannah a hug. "Hey, babe. How was your day?"

She thought of the conversation with Jessie and decided not to share it. "Same old, same old, mostly."

"Find anything to keep your mind busy?"

Savannah made a face. "You could say that."

He eyed her carefully. "I hear a tone."

"Well ..." She smiled. "I have a theory."

"A theory?"

"About why I'm still sick."

"What's that?"

She sat on a barstool at the kitchen island and motioned for him to do the same. "I think I might be pregnant."

His eyes went wide as the color drained from his face. "You're kidding."

"No."

"You can't be—"

"I can, actually. I checked the calendar."

He slumped in his seat and rubbed a hand over his face. "But you're not sure, right? When will you be sure?"

"I can take a test in the morning."

He shook his head as he stood, then walked from the room without another word. Savannah followed him to the bedroom. "I've been thinking about it all day, and I'm not as worried now as I was. I mean, we use two forms of protection. The chances of both failing at the same time have got to be close to nil."

"Your point?" His voice was terse.

"That it's God's doing. And if he made me pregnant, then he wouldn't just take it away; that wouldn't make sense. What else do I have to learn from a miscarriage that I haven't learned already?"

Shaun snorted. "That we should be using three forms of protection?" He pulled off his khakis and replaced them with a pair of shorts. "Savannah, the last miscarriage almost killed you emotionally. I can't believe you're not upset about this."

"But I just told you, if God—"

"You learned a lot from the first miscarriage, right? And you still had another one. I wouldn't count on God's will being only for pleasant things." He pulled on a T-shirt and took his running shoes from the rack on the floor. "This is bad on so many levels."

His words stung. "Shaun—"

"What are the odds of two people our age producing a healthy baby after two miscarriages? And second-trimester miscarriages at that." He tied the shoes, yanking on the laces with more force than necessary. "The timing is just—" He shook his head as he straightened and moved past her, leaving the room. She followed him to the front door. "I'm glad you're not a panicky mess, Van, but I can't be happy about this. I'm sorry. If it turns out you are ..." He shrugged. "We just need to pray you aren't."

He left the house, taking off down the driveway at a near sprint. Savannah watched him go as the little light of hope that had bloomed in her chest snuffed out.

SAVANNAH WOKE AT FOUR AND couldn't get back to sleep. Getting to sleep in the first place had taken longer than usual, and she dreaded the thought of a day wasted catching up on sleep. But that thought didn't last long as she remembered the little plastic stick waiting for her on the bathroom counter.

She rolled quietly from bed, not wanting to wake Shaun. He'd been shortchanged on sleep, too. She'd wanted to talk to him in the middle of the night, knowing they were both faking sleep for the benefit of the other person, but the chasm that had opened between them seemed too wide to cross. He'd been in a foul mood all night after his run, and she hadn't had the energy to spar.

She shut the bathroom door and turned on the light. Squinting, she read the instructions one more time, then took the test.

Three minutes never felt so long. She brushed her teeth and flossed, her back to the test where it sat on the bathtub ledge. She checked her watch continuously, not wanting to wait a second longer than necessary, and when the second hand completed its third trip around the dial she checked the instructions once more, took a deep breath, and turned around.

Negative.

She checked again, looking more closely, but the digital readout was too clear to be mistaken. *Not Pregnant.*

She sat on the ledge, tears gathering in her eyes. She'd convinced herself this was it, that God was going to finally and miraculously grant a long-abandoned wish. It made sense of her symptoms, and now, without that explanation, she was right back to where she'd been before: anxious and sick and sick of being sick.

She took a shower, allowing herself a good cry as the warm water brought a bit of relief to the muscles that still ached. By the time she got out and dressed, Shaun was already downstairs. She could see anxiety in his features when she joined him in the kitchen.

"Negative."

He let out a deep breath and gave her a hug. "Thank God."

"Easy for you to say." She took a mug of coffee into the living room and took her place on the sofa, not wanting to discuss it any more than that.

"I'm sorry, Van." He sat beside her, rested his hand on her knee. "I know you were getting excited about that. But it just wouldn't—"

"I know, I know." She waved a hand, batting away the discussion without making eye contact. "I'll call Dr. Helms today."

Shaun left for work and Savannah stared at the trees until her coffee was cold. She made that her excuse to finally get up, then grudgingly pulled out the address book where the doctor's number was recorded. It had been so long since she'd used it, she couldn't remember if it was filed under the D's or the H's.

The receptionist said it was her lucky day—a cancellation had just been made, and she could come in at eleven. She killed time with a snack and mindless television, then left for the appointment. A small measure of her worry abated, knowing she'd likely leave with at least some kind of diagnosis, even if it required waiting for tests to confirm it. She was almost to the point where she didn't care what was wrong, she just wanted to know for sure.

"That does seem like a long time for the flu, but in actuality the flu can last for quite a while," Dr. Helms told her as he marked her chart. "But since you no longer have a fever, I doubt you still have it, if that's what it was. Let's take a listen." He held the chest piece of his stethoscope between her shoulder blades and asked her to breathe deeply. He moved it to the back and she breathed again. He asked her to breathe deeply three more times as he moved the chest piece lower, finally settling it around her ribs. "Well, I am hearing something in there."

"'Something'? Like what?"

He marked on his chart. "They're called rales. Noises in the lungs." His eyes narrowed. "Do you have any chest pain?"

"No, I don't think so—I mean, I've been achy all over, including in my chest, but not heart-attack pain or anything like that. Nothing serious, really."

He was silent for a moment, then nodded. "I'm going to write you a script for a chest x-ray; I want you to go up to the third floor where the imaging center is and have them do this right now. Once we get the results of that and some blood tests we'll figure out what our next step is. We can do a hemoglobin test here for the anemia, but I'll have to send the blood samples to the lab for the rest."

"How long will that take?"

"I'll put a rush on it; we should get it back tomorrow."

She asked him about the other diagnoses she'd read in the medical book at home. He agreed her symptoms were consistent with hypothyroidism, but because she lacked so many other symptoms and the onset had been so quick, he doubted that was it. He also mentioned mononucleosis, but had been reluctant to guess beyond that, especially given the sounds in her chest.

Savannah left the office three vials of blood lighter and significantly more worried. The hemoglobin test had come back normal, so anemia was off the list. But the list of possibilities was daunting. Savannah's longing for an answer now clashed with her fear of just how serious that answer might be.

The imaging center squeezed her in an hour later, and she drove home afterwards feeling rattled and frustrated. The doctor was supposed to have written her a script for an antibiotic and tell her to rest for a few more days, not send her into a panic with talk of blood tests and X-rays.

When Dr. Helms called the next day, Savannah's fears grew. Hypothyroidism and mono had been ruled out by the blood tests. "And the X-rays confirmed what I was thinking—there's fluid in your lungs and your heart has me concerned as well."

Her gut seized. "So what does that mean?"

"Well, I don't know yet. I'm going to fax a script over to the echocardiogram lab at the hospital. I want you to call them and make an appointment to get an echo done."

She went clammy with nerves. "Oh. Okay. Give me the number and I'll call right now." She took down the number he gave her, then hung up and stared at it. She really had expected the blood tests to give them an answer. But now that the answer would be more serious than she'd expected, she was afraid to know what was really going on.

She glanced at the clock. Quarter after four. They probably weren't there after four. She'd call first thing in the morning.

SHAUN WAS ANTSY THAT EVENING, trying to keep his mind off the possible results of tomorrow's echo but not wanting his concern to show. When Savannah had given him the rundown of her blood tests and Dr. Helms' insistence on getting the echo, he'd waved it off to diffuse her obvious anxiety. "Seriously, how bad could it be?" he said. "You're normally healthy as a horse. It's a precaution, I'm sure. It'll be fine and he'll go to the next test on the flow chart." But he knew the possibilities were limited, and something less serious would have been found by now.

His mind was a mess. He wanted to hide in his office or go for a run, but he knew Savannah needed him and his false confidence nearby. He feigned interest in the paper to keep from having to engage too much, turning the pages at appropriate intervals and pretending to read while she lay on the couch and stared out the window. Maybe she'd fall asleep and he could sneak out...

"So, how are things at A&A?"

Or not. He gave her a sympathetic smile. "I know it's killing you to not be there."

She rolled to her back, adjusting the throw pillow behind her head. "Torturing me, actually."

Shaun gave her foot a squeeze. "It's fine, just like it was yesterday, and the day before that. We're not going to fall apart without you, you know."

She sighed. "I know. I just get so tired of sitting here thinking. I almost wish A&A *was* falling apart, so I had something else to focus on besides what might be wrong with me."

"Heh, bite your tongue." *Though the thought of being free from the weight of the financial responsibility is bliss.*

She nudged him with her foot. "Come on. We must have something to discuss. Any big decision you want to hash out? Any new curriculum ideas? Anything at all?" He chuckled, shaking his head. "Oh—what about the feedback from the tour? Marisa told me on Monday the info cards had come in, but she hadn't had time to go through them yet."

He nodded. "Yes, they did come back, and Marisa just gave me the report yesterday. All very positive; no surprise there. Only one case of books was left, so you set a personal sales record."

She gave a half-hearted pump of her fist. "Yay."

Shaun thought for a moment, debating whether or not to mention the one issue he actually could bring up to her. "I am a little concerned with one thing." Her face lit up with interest. "Remember Nick Albright, the accountant we hired back in April?"

"Of course."

Shaun set aside his newspaper so Savannah wouldn't see his hands shaking. He'd never been able to keep his cool while lying. "I've got a really bad feeling he's been stealing."

She raised her brows. "Office supplies?"

"Money."

Savannah sat up. "Oh Shaun, seriously? He doesn't seem the type! What happened to make you think that?"

"I was checking the bank statement, going over some things, and the numbers weren't reconciling with the monthly reports he's been giving me. I started going back over previous statements and reports, and I noticed a trend." He shrugged, giving her a brief look before averting his eyes again. "I thought maybe I was the one making the mistake, but I did them all at least twice, and got the same discrepancies. I think he's taking money from the ministry."

Savannah shook her head as her hand massaged her chest. "Oh Shaun, what are we going to do? He seemed like such a nice young man."

He chuckled. "You'd have expected him to come to the job interview with a ski mask?"

She gave a mirthless chuckle and lay back down. "That just breaks my heart."

"I know; that's why I haven't said anything yet. I knew you'd take it hard. I didn't want to worry you with things you couldn't fix."

"So now what?"

"Well, I think it's clear we need to replace him."

"What? No—we need to confront him, Shaun. What good are we doing for him if we don't call him on it and do what we can to help him? Who knows what his motivation is. For all we know he's got some awful financial trouble and doesn't know what else to do. Taking away his income might make him even more desperate. I just can't believe he's doing it to be malicious."

"Sweetheart, I know you like to assign positive intent to everyone, and overall that's a good policy. But when we have proof that someone has been blatantly stealing from the ministry, I don't think trying to make excuses for that behavior is helpful to anyone."

She frowned, sitting up again. "I'm not making excuses, Shaun. I'm not saying it's alright that he's stealing. I'm saying we don't know what is going on behind the scenes, and we need to consider the possibility that our brother in Christ—" her brows arched "—is just in dire need of help. How can we, in good conscience, just send him on his way to steal from someone else and not even try to get to the bottom of things?"

Shaun mentally kicked himself for opening his mouth. After twenty-two years he knew how her mind and heart worked. How would he get himself out of this mess? "I'm just trying to help us avoid a scandal, Van. If anyone got wind of the fact that we knew about this and didn't deal with it—"

"Oh, for pete's sake, Shaun, are you listening to me at all?" Savannah pushed herself from the couch, glaring at him as she swayed on her feet. "We *should* deal with it, of course we should. But dealing with it doesn't have to be—" She reached out a hand to the back of the couch, grasping it tightly as her other hand flew to her chest. "Oh …"

Shaun, frozen in shock, watched as Savannah seemed to fall in slow motion, her legs folding beneath her and her body settling in a heap on the floor.

CHAPTER 4

SAVANNAH HADN'T BEEN TO THE EMERGENCY ROOM SINCE HER last miscarriage. She welcomed the distraction of a new environment, letting herself stare unapologetically at the nurses and doctors as they walked or ran past her room. It kept her mind off her own troubles — like how much harder it was to breathe, and how much more her chest ached.

Shaun looked about as awful as she felt. He sat beside her bed in a plastic chair, shoulders hunched and features etched with worry. She'd never forget the look on his face when she'd regained consciousness — it still hadn't faded entirely. The intake nurse had asked him twice if he was alright.

The time passed slowly. The ER didn't seem full, but apparently it was still busy. She had nothing to compare it to, other than the rare episode of hospital dramas she'd seen on TV, and who knew how accurate those were. Regardless, it took half an hour for a doctor to finally come to Savannah's bed and pick up the chart; when she did Savannah's nerves kicked up a notch for fear of what she might say. Shaun straightened in the chair and they reached simultaneously for each other's hands.

"Hi there, Mrs. Trover. I'm Dr. Rockwell." She pulled over a stool, lips pursed, and looked over Savannah's chart. "Weakness and fatigue for two weeks?"

"Yes."

"And the fainting spell this evening."

"Yes, that's never happened before."

Dr. Rockwell pulled her stethoscope from her neck and settled it into place. "You told the nurse your chest ached. For how long?"

"I don't know—three or four days, maybe? But not as badly as it does now."

"Have you had shortness of breath, vomiting, diarrhea?"

Savannah blinked at the rapid-fire questions. "Um—short of breath, yes. It used to be just when I'd go up the stairs, but it's a lot harder to breathe now than it was before I fainted."

Dr. Rockwell moved the chest piece to a new place, eyes trained somewhere above Savannah's head as she listened. "Have you ever had a stress test, heart catheterization, echocardiogram?"

"No, never—I'm usually very healthy."

"Do you have high blood pressure, diabetes, high cholesterol, or do you smoke?"

"No."

"Have you ever been told you have a weak heart?"

The questions were becoming unnerving. "No. No to all of it. Like I said, I'm usually really healthy. Although ..." She rubbed a hand to her chest. Talking so much was making it hurt more. "My doctor told me today to get an echo done. I was going to make the appointment tomorrow."

The doctor helped Savannah sit up, then pushed her hair behind her ears and settled the chest piece between Savannah's shoulder blades. "Deep breath in, please."

It was more difficult than she expected it to be. She bit her lip, trying not to jump to any conclusions.

"Your doctor didn't hear anything amiss in your lungs?"

"Rales—he said he heard rales."

"Did you get a chest X-ray?"

"Yes, at the imaging center in his medical building. He said he saw fluid in my lungs and told me to get an echo done because my heart didn't look right."

Dr. Rockwell removed the stethoscope and laid it around her neck. "That's consistent with what I'm hearing. I'm sending you up for an X-ray, we're going to check your lungs again, and your heart."

Shaun's hand tightened on hers. "Any idea what it might be?" His voice sounded strained.

"I don't want to say anything until I've had a chance to look at the X-rays." She pulled back the sheets and continued her examination. After a moment she pressed on Savannah's ankles. "Do you get swelling very often?"

Savannah pushed herself up on her elbows and gasped. Her ankles had swollen considerably. "No," she said, her voice small. "Never."

The doctor gave them a sympathetic look as she draped the sheets back over Savannah's legs. "Don't worry; we'll figure this out. But first things first. I'll order that X-ray, and someone will be with you in a bit to take you up to radiology. As soon as I get a chance to look at the results I'll come back here and tell you what we've found."

She made some notes on the chart, then left them staring at each other.

"'What we've found'—she didn't tack on an 'if anything.'" Savannah lay back again.

"Noises in the lungs—that could just be pneumonia. Walking pneumonia, maybe."

"That's pretty common, though. Dr. Helms would have picked that up. And my ankles ... what on earth would cause that?"

They both fell silent, staring once again at the activity outside their little room. Savannah tried not to let her imagination run wild, but it was an exercise in futility. She thanked the nurse with more gusto than necessary when they were finally taken up to radiology; she was grateful for the change of scenery and another new experience to keep her mind occupied.

By the time they got back down to the ER—and placed in a curtain-walled cubicle room, which did nothing to calm her anxiety since now the noises and drama of the place were more easily heard— Shaun was looking almost worse than Savannah felt. "Honey, you need to get something to eat, or ... something. Coffee—go get yourself some coffee. It's past ten o'clock; who knows how much longer we're going to be here."

"I don't want to leave in case the doctor comes back."

"I promise I'll make her wait until you're back. Seriously, they're going to think you're the one that's sick pretty soon."

He gave her a weak smile, then reached for her hand and brought it to his lips. "I love you, Van."

"I love you, too. Don't get all emotional on me, Shaun. I won't be able to take it."

He chuckled and stood, kissing her hand once more. "Alright, alright. Make sure she waits for me."

"I promise."

It turned out there was no need; it took another hour before Dr. Rockwell came back. When Shaun roused Savannah from her nap to hear the news, the dull ache of too little sleep pulsed in every muscle. She prayed she'd be able to rest again soon.

The look of tension in Shaun's face was at odds with the gentle way he clasped her hand. Savannah was grateful for his strength; she didn't know how she'd make it otherwise. "So what's the story, doctor?" he asked. "Do you have any theories?"

"I do, yes. And I think it was a very good thing you came in tonight." Dr. Rockwell uploaded the X-rays onto the computer beside the bed and took out her pen. She used it to point to the hazy image of Savannah's lungs. "You can see the somewhat cloudy appearance of the lungs here—as though the film didn't develop all the way. That's called pulmonary edema, which basically means fluid in the lungs." Then she traced a bulbous shape that ballooned out to the right from the center of the chest. "This is your heart. A healthy heart would only come out to here or so—" She indicated a space about half an inch closer to the center. "Yours is enlarged."

Savannah felt like the breath was pulled from her lungs. She fought out the words. "Enlarged heart?"

"So what does all that mean?" Shaun's voice belied his fear, as did the way his hand tightened on hers.

"I believe we're looking at heart failure."

Savannah almost laughed. "Heart failure? I'm the healthiest person I know. How is that possible? It can't be right. Right, Shaun?"

Shaun's eyes never left the doctor. "You can fix this, right? What do we do now?"

"We're going to admit you for an echocardiogram and a cardiology consult. But I'm encouraged by the fact that you're still as active and alert as you are. I think we caught this just in the nick of time."

THE NEXT TWENTY-FOUR HOURS WERE like a roller coaster that only went down.

It was past midnight when she was finally brought up to the room. She insisted Shaun go home and sleep since the night nurse assured her nothing else would be done until the morning. "I'll call you as soon as they tell me when things will get going again."

"I won't be able to sleep knowing you're here alone."

"You're exhausted. You'll sleep. Believe me. You definitely won't if you're here, at least not well. Better chances in your own bed. Just go."

She slept on and off, woken frequently by unfamiliar noises, vitals checks by the night nurse, and runaway dreams that left her breathless when she woke. Her breakfast was brought in at seven-thirty, and she gave up trying to sleep after that.

In the new semi-private room—which she shared with a woman whose heart monitor beep drove Savannah batty—the television with limited channels was her only source of entertainment, and nothing on the airwaves was interesting enough to hold her attention for long. As a result, her thoughts ran wild, dreaming up scenarios that all ended with her wishing she had pen and paper to write down her wishes for her funeral. She felt worse than she had when they'd first arrived in the ER. True fear was starting to set in.

She was taken after breakfast to the echo lab, Shaun arriving just minutes before the appointment, and underwent the echocardiogram. After that it was back to her room, where Shaun settled in to the chair beside her bed with a book and Savannah tried to take a nap. It was a pointless attempt — her keyed-up nerves were enough to override her exhaustion.

"Jessie wanted to know if she should come," he said out of nowhere.

"What did you tell her?"

"That we would let her know when we found out anything, but that she didn't need to come unless she really wanted to."

"When does she leave for school again?"

Shaun thought a moment. "The 27th."

"She's got a lot on her plate with work and getting ready for the next semester. No sense in her wasting time here. Besides, anytime you visit someone in the hospital they always look worse than they really are. I wouldn't want her getting scared when things aren't really that bad."

"Aren't that bad?"

She kept her eyes to the ceiling. "I'm working on positive thinking." She sighed and looked to the window, but the sunlight that snuck in through the cracks between the curtains and the walls hurt her eyes. "I should have asked you to bring my Bible."

"Want me to find you one?"

"Would you?"

"Of course. I'm sure we've got one in the car. Give me a minute."

He returned a bit later with a flimsy paperback version that had seen better days. "I should have thought of that when I came this morning. I'm sorry."

"No, don't worry about it. I'm not really in the mood to read. I wanted it more for the comfort." She held it in her hands and frowned, disappointed. The unfamiliar feel of the cover couldn't compare with the soft, worn leather of her personal Bible. She flipped to the Psalms and let her eyes skim the page until they caught a familiar verse:

Why are you downcast, O my soul?
Why so disturbed within me?
Put your hope in God,
for I will yet praise him,
my Savior and my God.

She had written out those lines after her first miscarriage and taped them to the bathroom mirror. The verse had still been there when she'd had her second miscarriage, but sometime in the years after she'd removed it; the paper had curled from shower humidity and the words were ingrained on her heart and memory. Why hadn't they come to mind during the last two weeks?

A disturbing thought came to her as she stared at the Scripture. She hadn't prayed once—besides the brief and panicky, "Dear God, don't let my heart go out!" after seeing the X-ray—since coming to the ER. Shaun hadn't even suggested they pray together.

What had happened to her faith?

Like a panoramic movie, the last ten years of her life scrolled through her mind, revealing the incremental decline of her spiritual life. She saw herself on stages across the country, at the head of endless lines of fans wanting her signature in their books, at planning meetings and publisher meetings and marketing meetings. She didn't see herself in church, or hidden away in prayer, or reading Scripture. She'd become a businesswoman for God, selling the promise of a meaningful life and cashing in on the desperate longings of harried mothers who wondered if their existence amounted to anything more than carpool schedules and menu planning to stretch a buck.

"Shaun, we need to pray."

He looked up from his book, concern clouding his face. "Why, what's wrong?"

"We haven't prayed at all since we came in. We haven't prayed together at all since I've been home, even. And before the tour ..." She shook her head. "I can't believe I haven't seen it. I've been so

caught up in the … the business of ministry. I feel like such a cliché."
A humorless laugh escaped, and her chest burned with the effort.
"What if all this is meant to be a wake-up call? We've lost our pas-
sion, we've lost sight of our — our *need* for God."

Shaun's face was sympathetic. "Oh babe, I'm sorry you're feeling
like that."

"But you see it too, right? It's not just me imagining this? I
mean, when was the last time you and I were really on our knees
together? It's both of us. We're going through the motions like this
is just our career and not a ministry, not a mission."

Shaun nodded slowly, his eyes trained on the Bible in her lap
and his expression unreadable. "No, you're right. You're absolutely
right."

"We need to repent. Now."

Shaun looked to the doorway, then took her hands as she bowed
her head. Tears slipped from her cheeks as she asked forgiveness
for their prideful independence and lack of desire. Her spirit ached
almost as much as her chest as she cataloged all the ways she'd
turned Abide & Abound into just another job, all the ways her relationship with Christ had been reduced to a business contract, and
Shaun mumbled his agreement along with her. As she prayed she
felt a renewed sense of connectedness not only with God, but with
Shaun. They'd been more like coworkers than man and wife for a
while now; maybe this would reignite the flame they'd once had.

They murmured their amens, Savannah wiping the tears from
her face and Shaun giving her hands a brief squeeze before sitting
back down in the chair beside her bed. A lightness in her soul gave
her a surge of hope. No wonder her body was in revolt. Her spirit
had been sick. But maybe now that they were back on track, she'd
begin to heal.

Savannah began reading the Psalms again. Now the words were
leaping off the page and into her heart. A mix of remorse and relief
had her alternately thanking God and confessing her sin as she read
for the next hour. After a nurse interrupted her to check her vitals,

she looked to Shaun. "Listen, regardless of what we find out today, I want you to call Pastor John and see if he can come over tomorrow. I think we'd really benefit from praying with him. Maybe we should start meeting with him once in a while, to keep us accountable. What do you think?"

"Accountable? What do you mean?"

Savannah was disappointed by his defensive tone. "Just ... I don't know, making sure we don't slip back into that rut again. You don't think that would be helpful?"

"That makes me feel like you don't think I can be trusted to do the right thing without someone breathing down my neck."

The comment was out of character. Savannah gaped in surprise. "Shaun, what on earth would make you think that? That's not what I said at all, and it's certainly not what I meant." He had always been more private than she when it came to his faith, but she never would have expected him to respond like this. "You used to meet with Alex and Kurt and William once a month for breakfast— that's the kind of thing I'm thinking of, just a checking-in now and then, someone to 'report' to besides just each other. That obviously isn't working."

Shaun shook his head and waved a hand to dismiss the idea. "Look, when you're out of here and we're back to normal, then we can talk about that kind of thing. For now I don't even want to think about A&A. I just want us to focus on getting you better." He sat back in his seat and reopened the book he'd been reading, effectively ending the conversation whether she was finished or not.

Hurt but too tired to fight, Savannah flipped back to the Psalms, but instead of reading she closed her eyes and began to pray.

She awoke with a start, unsure of how long she'd been sleeping. The cardiologist stood at the foot of her bed. "I'm sorry to have interrupted your nap, Mrs. Trover," he said, his deep voice soothing her. "But I wanted to talk to you about our next step."

Savannah clutched the Bible tightly with one hand. Shaun grabbed the other. "So you know what's wrong?" Shaun asked.

"Well, yes and no." The doctor pulled the curtain as far to the other wall as it would go, giving them the most privacy they'd get in a shared room. He perched himself on the edge of the bed and consulted the printout he held. "Based on a lack of indicators for congenital issues, we're guessing a virus has attacked your heart—which would make sense, given the flu you had. We just don't know what virus, though honestly it doesn't matter at this point. It's the result that we're concerned about—namely myocarditis. Heart failure, in layman's terms. We're going to keep you here, get you started on some medications that will hopefully help slow down the failure, monitor you for a few days to track your heart's efficiency, and that will help us determine what the next step is. Typically we can't do a lot for the myocarditis; we'll treat the symptoms and give your body the rest and support it needs to heal the heart itself. To that end, we'll keep you on the heart monitor to watch for arrhythmias, put you on a restricted diet, start you on digoxin and Lasix, and see how things go for the next week or so."

"A week?" Savannah rubbed a hand over her eyes. "That's so long."

"Well, honestly, it may be longer than that. We just have to see what happens."

Shaun sat on the edge of his seat. "So what are you looking for over this next week then? And what are the options at that point, the possibilities?"

"Well, if things go the way we hope they do, then your heart will begin to strengthen, we'll see some improvements in energy and strength, and your heart's efficiency will recover to where it should be. Most patients do recover from myocarditis with standard supportive treatment, and your previous health is a good indicator that you will."

Savannah was afraid to ask what was on her mind, but more afraid of the unknown. "And if I don't improve? What then?"

"Hopefully it won't get to that. But depending on how things go, we may have to try some other medications, see if they slow the failure and help turn things around. A pacemaker may be necessary, if your heart's rhythm gets out of sync. But if you continue to worsen at the pace you have so far, it's possible you'll need a heart transplant."

Savannah feared her heart would stop right then. She couldn't even bring herself to look at Shaun, knowing she'd break down. "A transplant? It could get that bad?"

"There is a possibility, yes." He stood and hung the chart back on the foot of her bed. "But don't dwell on that. Your chances for a full recovery are good."

He gave them a parting smile and nod, then left them to sit with the reality of a heart so broken it might never heal.

SHAUN WOKE DISORIENTED, THE LAST of his dream still playing out in his mind as he opened his eyes to a room with too much light. He shook the disturbing images from his head and checked the clock, then groaned when he saw he'd overslept.

By the time he got downstairs for breakfast it was almost nine o'clock. He heard Jessie in her room, talking on the phone, and realized he couldn't leave for work until he told her what was going on with Savannah. She'd already been asleep when he'd gotten home the night before, and he'd been reluctant to wake her since he wasn't sure if she had a morning shift. Apparently she did not, which meant she was probably on the phone with Adam; that conversation could go on for hours. Shaun decided to have his breakfast and then ask her to hang up so they could talk.

" ... And then we could do a sundae bar for dessert, maybe see if The Sweet Shoppe would be willing to donate — oh wait, my dad's here, hold on a sec." She covered the mouthpiece of her cell with her hand. "Hey, Dad, what's up? I didn't know you were still here."

"I overslept this morning. Can we talk for a minute before I leave for work?"

Her face clouded. "Yeah, hold on." She went back to her phone.

"Hey, let me call you back. My dad needs me for a minute. Cool?...
Okay, love you too. Bye." She hung up and tossed the phone on the
bed. "It's about Mom, isn't it?"

"Yes, it is." He sat across from her on the bed, their knees touch-
ing over the floral bedspread as he laid out the details, starting
with Savannah's collapse. "They've started her on some medications that might help—in fact, they seem fairly confident that they
will. But she's going to be in the hospital for at least another week,
possibly more."

Her eyes got big. "Wow. That's a long time."

He huffed out a chuckle. "Yes, it is."

"But then what?"

"Well, hopefully the medications will help take some of the
pressure off her heart and let it heal. Once it does ..." he shrugged.
"She'll be back to normal."

Jessie nodded slowly. "That's good."

"Yeah."

"So ... anything else?"

"Well, she asked me to get her laptop to her sometime today. I
was hoping you could take it to her."

She made a face. "I don't know if I'll have time. Adam and I have
to finish planning the freshman welcome dinner, and I'm working
until five—"

"Jessie, this is your mother. She's lonely in there."

Jessie rolled her eyes. "Come on, Dad, we both know she's not
desperate for *me* to visit."

He arched his brows in reproach. "You're her daughter. Of course
she wants to see you."

She sighed, slumping back against the pillows. "Come on, Dad.
You know we don't get along."

"I know—and that's why I think you ought to go in and see her.
How often do you two spend time alone together? Your relationship
will never improve if you're never together."

"But, Dad, hanging out with someone and hanging out in the

ICU are completely different. Seriously, it's just going to feel forced. She'll know it, and I'll know it, and it'll be totally uncomfortable."

He remembered yesterday afternoon, when Savannah had gone off about them not being spiritual enough lately. Maybe with that personal awakening her eyes would be opened to how distant she was from her own daughter. "She may be a little ... easier to relate to." He put up his hands in surrender. "Look, you're an adult; you can make your own decisions. Just bring her the laptop and leave if you want to."

"Oh, right, that would be really nice." She narrowed her eyes at him. "You're telling me everything, right? They didn't give her only a month to live or anything?"

"Well, no. They think it's serious, but they seem to think they'll be able to get it under control."

"But what if they can't?"

He hadn't wanted to get into the what if's. He let out a long breath. "If they can't, she might need a heart transplant."

Her eyes went wide. "Oh—oh wow."

"Yeah. But really, they don't seem to think it will get that bad. Although being cooped up in there by herself might be enough to do her in," he said, attempting a joke.

Jessie looked at the clock, then back at him with a look of resignation. "I work at noon; I'll go see her before then."

He stood and planted a kiss on her forehead. "You're a good daughter."

"You're a good dad. And guilt-tripper."

He laughed for the first time in two days. "Thanks, I think."

Shaun got in the car and headed for A&A. He hadn't planned on working today, but Savannah had insisted. "The only thing you can do here is sit in an uncomfortable chair all day and read while I nap." She was right, of course, but he still felt like he should be there—if for no other reason than to monitor how her spirits were doing. He hadn't said anything to her before leaving, but by the time he was finally kicked out of the ICU, he was concerned at how much she'd slept and how much more drawn she looked. Certainly it was just the shock of the previous 24 hours of tests and news and constantly being awakened by nurses when she was trying to nap. But still …

He shook the thoughts from his head. No use borrowing trouble. She was in the best place possible if she truly was deteriorating, and dwelling on it wouldn't fix anything. He had other things to think about, like the hospital bills that would be rolling in soon. A&A had decent insurance, but it didn't cover anything 100%, and he knew hospitals were notorious for gouging you on even the small est items, like ten bucks for an aspirin. He needed to start planning now for when those statements came, because they had no money right now to pay them.

He could think of a few ways to save some money here and there, like not going grocery shopping while she was away and just eating what they had in the house. Jessie usually had one meal at home, sometimes two, and he could skip breakfast. Over a week that wouldn't amount to much, but he could get used to it now and then keep it up when Savannah came home. Over the long run it would help a little.

But not nearly enough. He knew that for sure. The only way he could think to get more would be to skim more from A&A. And in order to do that, he'd need to get rid of Nick.

Savannah would be mad when she found out. But he had to do it. What choice was there? If Nick was as conscientious as he appeared to be, it wouldn't take long before he figured out Shaun's scheme.

He didn't anticipate any pushback; one of the reasons he'd hired Nick was because one of his references mentioned something about Nick's avoidance of confrontation. As long as Shaun stayed firm, chances were Nick would slink away and never come back.

Shaun pulled into the parking lot and sat in his car for a minute, psyching himself up. He wished he could just get it over with, but he didn't want to do it at the beginning of the day when everyone was around to see Nick pack up. He'd catch him around 4, ask him to stop by Shaun's office before he left for the evening.

As for what Shaun would do until then, he had his work cut out for him. Time to start reacquainting himself with how to do the job of an accountant.

JESSIE TOOK THE LONG WAY to the hospital, giving herself time to let her emotions sort themselves out before facing her mother. She was angry with Shaun for guilting her into going. But mostly she was scared. Scared to go to the hospital, a place she'd only been one other time, to say goodbye to a dying friend in high school. Scared to see her normally vibrant and healthy mother in the stark white bed. And, despite her chronic irritation with Savannah, she was scared her mother might die.

Yes, Savannah drove her nuts, with her critical view of everything Jessie did and her disinterest in building a more solid relationship with her daughter. Yes, she was sick of being in Savannah's shadow, of hearing someone's squeal of excitement when first meeting Jessie and discovering she was the daughter of "*that* Savannah Trover." Yes, she was tired of being an involuntary spokesperson for A&A. But a girl needs her mother, and Jessie was no exception.

Knowing there was a chance, even a slim one, that Savannah might pass brought Jessie to tears. A tiny sliver of her heart still held to the dream of their relationship changing. Maybe it was time to start doing whatever she could to make that dream happen. It would have to be a two-way street, but if she didn't get things going she might lose her chance.

But how?

Jessie parked the car in the visitor's lot but kept it running as she analyzed her typical reactions with Savannah. She didn't usually engage much, choosing instead to do whatever needed to be done with Savannah as quickly as possible and then retreating. And when Savannah said something that irked her, or hurt, or insulted, Jesse's typical response was sarcasm or anger or passive-aggressiveness. She winced at the realization. Maybe their poor relationship wasn't completely her mother's fault after all.

"Okay, so what do I do differently?" She drummed her fingers on the steering wheel, staring at the lobby doors, waiting for inspiration. "A little help?" she prayed aloud, glancing to the sky and then frowning when it dawned on her that she'd never really prayed about her relationship with her mom. *Figures it would take the possibility of death for me to finally start. I'm sorry I'm such a dunce, God.*

She was about to give up and just go in when the word *honesty* came to her. "But I've been honest before. Haven't I?" She sat with that thought for a moment, waiting to see if God revealed anything else. *Honest in my responses to her, yes. Honest with my feelings, no.*

She'd never told Savannah flat-out how their messed-up relationship bothered her, or how Savannah's criticism hurt, or how Savannah's lack of interest in Jessie's life made her feel like her mother didn't really care about her as a person. It was time to lay it all out on the table — or, at least, to stop biting back her true feelings and opting instead for snark and sarcasm. If she didn't start it now, she might never get the chance; and if, God forbid, Savannah really did die, Jessie didn't want to spend the rest of her life wondering how different things might have been if she'd just spoken her mind.

But could she do it?

"Oh boy," she sighed. "God, help me." The prayer seemed to be her new mantra. She turned off the car, pulled the laptop case from the front seat, and headed for the hospital.

Savannah was woken by yet another nurse checking her vitals. She groaned but didn't have the energy to open her eyes and administer a glare of annoyance. "Again? You have got to be kidding me."

The nurse chuckled. "Oh honey, you'll go right back to sleep. Not like there's anything else for you to do."

"You're telling me." Savannah sighed, then jumped when the phone rang. "Hallelujah, conversation." She pried open her eyes and saw the nurse smirking as she handed Savannah the receiver. "Hello?"

"Hey, Mom, it's me."

Savannah warmed at the voice. "Oh, sweetheart, hello."

"I'm downstairs, but if you don't want visitors it's totally okay—"

"Of course I'd like to see you. Come on up." Savannah handed back the receiver with a smile. That was a pleasant surprise. Hopefully it would be pleasant, anyway. They hadn't talked much since Savannah's failed attempt at emotional intimacy with her daughter. Maybe this would give her a chance to redeem herself. She wouldn't be out of the hospital before Jessie went back to school, and then her opportunities for conversations would be even more scarce.

Jessie's face peeked in the door a few minutes later, just as Savannah was about to close her eyes again. "Sweetheart, come in," Savannah said. "Thanks for coming. Oh, my laptop, wonderful. Just set the bag on the floor. I'll get it later." She reached out her hands to give Jessie a hug, noting with an ache the way the girl hesitated, eyeing the heart monitor before leaning down to her. Savannah hadn't seen a mirror in two days; no doubt she looked awful.

"Did I wake you up? You look really tired. Like, *really* tired."

Savannah gave her a wan smile. "I am. But I can sleep all day, so don't worry. If I could get more than an hour's sleep at a time I might feel better. They poke and prod you at all hours here. It's ridiculous."

Jessie's eyes slid back to the machine. Savannah couldn't blame her. It was almost eerie, seeing the little green line jumping like the stock market chart, just like in the movies. "It's mesmerizing," Savannah admitted. "I spend way too much time staring at it, like it's going to do something different all of a sudden. Or stop."

Jessie's gaze snapped to hers, and Savannah winced.

"Sorry. Didn't mean to be so noir."

Jessie turned her back to the machine and looked around the room. "So, Dad said you're stuck here for a week?"

"Yes. A very long week. But the laptop will help, if I can find the stamina to use it. Sit down, if you want." She nodded to the chair beside the bed and smiled. "Terribly uncomfortable, I'll tell you right now. So are you working today?"

"At noon, yeah; I'll have to leave in half an hour."

"That's fine, I understand. You were sweet to come in; I appreciate it."

Jessie smiled slightly. "Sure."

"So when do you go back to campus?"

Jessie smiled. Savannah loved how Jessie's face lit up like Shaun's when she was excited about something. "The 27th. That's the day before the freshmen orientation starts, and Adam and I are in charge of the welcome dinner. In the past it's been this casual thing, right? But we decided to make it sort of like a formal, with the jazz combo doing background music and some of the upperclassmen— "

"You know, when I started there in '79, they held a separate welcome party for the women. So few women enrolled they just set up a table in the kitchen. They gave us a welcome tea, with doilies on the table, like we were a bunch of grannies or something. We all just died laughing."

The memory came from nowhere, and made her want to laugh again, if only she had the energy. That was the first day she'd met Tabitha. She hadn't thought of her in years. She knew how sad it was to admit that. "I had that great Farrah Fawcett feathered 'do and used half a can of Aqua Net to get it to stay."

She caught Jessie's unreadable expression and gave a weak chuckle. "My gosh, I *sound* like a granny. Actually, I feel like one today, too." She closed her eyes briefly, trying to summon the strength to keep up the conversation without feeling like her chest was going to explode. "So, you must have your classes picked out, then?"

"We did that before school ended in May. I told you the classes I was taking when I got back, remember?"

"You did? Oh, that was right before I left for the tour, wasn't it? I was probably distracted; tell me again."

Jessie was silent for a moment, then said with a sigh, "Child psych, worldviews, 21st Century Issues, and language arts."

"That's an interesting load. I think my junior year I took six classes both semesters. It was the one year I really put the pedal to the metal. You should consider picking up a fifth class. You don't want your senior year to be—"

"I've got all my semesters already planned out, Mom. I know what I'm doing."

"I didn't say you didn't, Jess. I just don't want you to be overwhelmed your senior year, that's all. Leave space to enjoy it."

"I'm not planning on graduating next year anyway, Mom. Dad and I talked about this, remember? I'm going to take an extra semester so I don't have to kill myself with school and work." She huffed out a breath. "I know he told you, you just don't remember. As usual."

Savannah frowned. "I'm sorry, sweetheart. It must be this stupid heart thing—"

"No, it's not, Mom." Jessie rolled her eyes. "This is how you always are. If it doesn't pertain to you, you don't remember and you just plain don't care."

Horror dawned on Jessie's face. Before Savannah could think of a response to the completely unexpected accusation, Jessie hopped up from her seat as though electrocuted. "I should go; there was traffic."

Savannah watched Jessie disappear, her heart wounded in another way. She and Jessie had never connected; she knew she wasn't always the most attentive mother, but to insinuate that she was self-centered to the point of ignoring her only child—that was ridiculous.

She hit the call button, and a nurse arrived a moment later and pulled the laptop from its case and set it on Savannah's lap. Her thoughts hummed around in her head, though her body barely had the strength to type. She opened her mind-mapping brainstorming program and began to slowly take notes. Surely she had a book somewhere in this mess. Certainly that's what God was expecting her to do with this experience—turn it into a way to minister to other Christian women facing hardship.

Scripture re: illness/hardship/suffering. Comforting the afflicted. Other ppl's stories, not just mine? She stopped frequently to let her thoughts play out or her mind wander, but also to rest her hands and eyes. She had fatigue in every muscle. She tried to be patient with herself and her limitations, but finally during yet another break she slapped the laptop shut with a grunt of anger.

Frustrated, she closed her eyes and fought tears. She hated crying when people might see her. She also hated being so weak, a prisoner to the strength-sucking heart disease that was hindering her from living the life she loved. She couldn't remember the last time she'd been so still and unproductive.

The light bulb in her spirit went off again, just as it had the day before. She was doing it again—trying to do, do, do instead of just abiding with God and letting their time together overflow from her heart and into the way she ministered. That's how A&A—*Abide and Abound*—had gotten its start. She was embarrassed to see how few hours it had taken to fall back into the trap of treating her relationship with God like a means to a career.

Savannah reached for the Bible that was still sitting on the bed beside her. She set it on the laptop and opened it to the Psalms again, her new favorite book. After sitting still for a moment to catch the breath that was stolen from her nearly every time she moved, she began to read, soaking up the words and trying to focus on God alone instead of the noise of the hospital and the urge in her head to keep *doing*. She didn't last long before her eyes closed against her will, the muscles too spent to continue. Prayer became her next outlet, and occupied her until she fell asleep again.

SHAUN DIALED NICK'S EXTENSION, IGNORING the fist in his gut. "Hey, it's Shaun. Listen, I'm tied up for pretty much the rest of the day, but could you stop by my office before you leave this evening?"

Nick was amiable, as always, and Shaun indulged in a brief moment of self-hate before going back to the budget he'd been reviewing. At least Nick was single—no family to support, no girlfriend to disappoint, at least not that Shaun knew of. He tended not to get too close to his accountants.

Shaun had spent most of the day combing through the budget, thinking the stingiest, most miserly thoughts he could to try to find more places to cut back. The biggest possibility was in relocating to a cheaper building. If they could slice off at least a quarter of their rent, he'd feel a lot better. And with one less cubicle needed, they'd fit in a smaller space. The fact that he was about to get a whole salary back into the coffers helped, too, though he didn't feel nearly as good about that.

Nick knocked on Shaun's door at five o'clock. Shaun felt the tremble start in his hands as he waved him in. He began to clean up the mess of papers on his desk to give them something to do for a moment. "Hey, Nick, take a seat."

Nick sat just in time to catch the container of pens that teetered off the back edge of Shaun's desk when it was pushed by a mound of paper. "Didn't get a chance to ask you today, how's Savannah?"

"Ah—still hanging in there. Thanks for asking," he said with a terse smile. Why did Nick have to be such a nice guy? "Nick, I— I'm going to just get right down to it, and I hope you'll forgive me for not giving you a little more warning. With Savannah and all, I've been a bit distracted, but I knew I had to get on with this." He cleared his throat, clutched his trembling hands out of sight in his lap. "You're the accountant, so you know that our budget is tight, and this economy is struggling." Nick nodded along with him, a politely curious look on his face. "You haven't been here long, and I know I never went over with you the trends in giving this organization has seen since its inception ten years ago, but I'm confident, unfortunately, that the resource and book purchases are going to continue to decrease as our economy continues to struggle. I don't know if I ever told you this, but I'm a stock-market-playing kind of guy, and I make it my job to know what the market is doing so I know how to best invest and sell. Everything is pointing to things getting much worse before they get any better."

Nick cocked his head. "Really? I thought things were already starting to get better."

Shaun shook his head. "No. It looks that way on the surface, but the foundation of the market is cracking. Point being, we as a ministry need to start planning now, while we're still in the black and not in crisis mode. We need to prepare for the day our giving and sales drop off so we can stay afloat. I've been trying to think of ways we can tighten our belts here, start stashing more into our savings, and one of the ways I can help make that happen is by taking on more responsibilities. One of the jobs I'm qualified to do here is the accounting."

Understanding dawned in Nick's eyes. "Ah ... I see."

"You've done an excellent job in the short time you've been here, Nick, and I can't tell you how awful I feel letting you go. But we'll give you a month's severance and a glowing recommendation, which I hope will get you back into the job force somewhere soon." Shaun slid a confidentiality notice across the now-cleared desk, then held out a pen to Nick. "I'll stay late; you can take whatever time you need to clean out your desk."

Nick's expression clouded as he took the pen. "Oh, so — today?"

Shaun held his gaze steady. "I'm afraid so."

Nick studied the confidentiality notice for a moment, then opened his mouth as though to speak, but quickly shut it again and signed. "I'm sorry I won't get to see Savannah before I leave. Please let her know Christy and I are praying for her."

"Christy?"

"My girlfriend."

Dang it. "Oh. Well, thank you, to you and Christy, and I will definitely let Savannah know." He stood and shook Nick's hand before he left, then waited for the door to close and Nick to disappear from view before vomiting his lunch into the trash.

THREE DAYS LATER, THE LAPTOP and the book both lay forgotten on the table beside her bed. She spent most of her time sleeping now, partly to escape the pain that was worsening in her torso, but mostly because she simply couldn't stay awake.

Her mind was having a heyday, however, playing out in dreams all the things she couldn't do in reality. This time it was a marathon. She'd never run a marathon before, never even had the inclination, but here she was, flying past the cheering crowds that lined the street in some nameless city. They were shouting her name in unison, urging her on; she could see the ribbon stretched across the lanes in the distance. *Van. Van. Van.*

"Van? Van? Hey, babe, it's me. Wake up."

The scene faded away as Savannah came back to consciousness in slow motion, her senses awakening one at a time. She opened her eyes and saw not only Shaun, but the cardiologist as well. Neither knew how to keep their thoughts off their faces.

She smiled at Shaun and lifted a finger in greeting. "Hey." Her voice was barely a whisper.

Shaun kissed her forehead. "Hey, babe. I'm sorry to wake you up, but Dr. Wells wanted to talk to us; I knew you'd want to hear everything firsthand."

She nodded, then raised her brows at the doctor whose lousy poker face made her aching heart sink. "Your face … gives you away."

He gave her a faint smile. "One of these days I'll have to take an acting class." He held her file, which had grown thick in the five days since she'd been admitted, but didn't look through it like he usually did as he spoke. "I wish I had better news—or at least an explanation. But I don't. Your body just isn't responding like we'd expected to the medications. Your ejection fraction is still dropping; the last reading was 18%. For it to get back up to 60% now would be a miracle; I've never seen a recovery that major. We think it's time for a transfer to University Hospital up in Aurora."

Savannah felt Shaun's hand tighten around hers. The sound of his breathing changed; she knew he was fighting back tears. She tried to squeeze back and hoped he could feel her feeble attempt.

"They're very experienced there; you'll be in excellent hands. They've got more resources for this kind of illness than we do; and if you need a transplant, they can get you on the list and handle the surgery. Your nurse will be in with the transfer paperwork shortly; once we get that done we'll get you into an ambulance and they'll take you up." He looked to Shaun, then Savannah. "Do you have any questions?"

Questions? Savannah wanted to laugh. Of course she had questions. But she didn't have the mental strength to line them all up. She looked up to Shaun. Shaun coughed then said with a strangled voice, "What are the chances ... I mean, how long will it be before she gets a new heart?"

"They'll be able to give you that kind of information in Aurora."

"Will a new heart fix everything?"

The doctor's face brightened. "It should, yes. That's the source of all the trouble right now. If we get that fixed, you should be good as new, barring any rejection complications. I don't know the stats on that, either—another question Aurora can help you with. But they'll go over all that with you when you get there."

Dr. Wells took Savannah's hand. "I'm sorry things are working out this way, Savannah. You've been a pleasure to work with. Come back and visit us when you're back to your old self." He nodded to them both, then left.

Shaun sank into the chair beside her. "It's not like we didn't see it coming. But having it all official ..." He coughed again, his way of covering for his breaking voice. She squeezed his hand again, and he squeezed back, which made her smile. "Okay, time for the really awkward conversation." He looked up from his lap, but still not into her eyes. "It's been ten years since we looked at our will, Savannah. We should do that ... soon."

She blinked at him. "Seriously? Don't jinx things!"

"I'm not jinxing them; I just want to make sure we're prepared.

It's the Boy Scout in me. Our life now is nothing like it was a decade ago; we need to account for that, make sure everything is covered. Think of it this way—if we do it, we won't need it, right? It's a law of nature. You prepare for the worst so that the worst doesn't happen."

She turned her head away, her gaze going to the unremarkable view beyond her second-floor window. She knew in her heart he was right, but still, the thought of making those kinds of preparations ... actually, the more she thought about it, the more she realized she should probably make some other preparations as well. Just in case.

"Memorial service, too. So we don't need it."

"Oh, Van." Shaun's voice cracked. She took his hand as tears came to her own eyes. She didn't have the strength to fight them back, or to even cry them out. They slipped down her cheeks, and she conjured the image of her dream, her body bounding through the street, her hair long—though she'd had it short for years—flowing behind her. She imagined handing the dream to God as she prayed, flat-out begging that this not be the end.

CHAPTER 5

Shaun popped another pretzel in his mouth as he sat at
the red light. They were stale, but washed down with water they
weren't too bad. He'd found them that morning in the back of the
pantry, a forgotten snack from the Fourth of July picnic he and Jessie had thrown while Savannah had been on tour. Lately he'd been
skipping both breakfast and lunch, but he'd worked up an appetite
helping Jessie pack up her car that morning. She'd been torn on
whether or not to go back to campus, but he'd insisted she leave,
since they had no idea when a heart might become available. "No
use sitting around here," he'd said. "Might as well go and keep
yourself busy."

He hadn't admitted how jealous he was that she had somewhere
to go, an excuse for not going up to the hospital every day to do
nothing but read and watch TV while Savannah wasted away on
the bed beside him. It was depressing, to be honest. Depressing
and scary. When she was awake—which wasn't often—she was
confident God wasn't ready to take her yet. He wouldn't have been
surprised to hear God had told her that himself. He could see in
her eyes that she had changed, had tapped back into that connection with him that Shaun had never really had. He was a little
jealous.

The drive from A&A's office, where he spent the mornings, to
the hospital in Aurora took nearly an hour and a half. Savannah
tried to talk him into getting a hotel room and working remotely,
but he couldn't bear to spend the money—though the gas wasn't
all that much cheaper. Instead, he did everything he needed to do in
the mornings, foregoing business and staff meetings since he knew

he wouldn't be able to concentrate, and then went to the hospital in the afternoon to wait for good news.

He was late today, however. He'd left work at lunch, like always, then had headed for home to scrape together some lunch from what was left in the fridge and pantry. He'd been slowed by a funeral procession that crossed in front of him at a stoplight, and the view of the hearse was like a kick to the solar plexus.

He'd been doing pretty well up until then. He had so much else to worry about—the medical bills, the fact that they had no savings, the email threats he was getting—that he'd been able to effectively lose himself in those issues and not confront the fact that his wife was dying. But as the gray car slid past him, his fear of losing Savannah and the pain he'd been burying erupted to the surface. As the slow parade of cars drove through the intersection, he choked out sobs that shook his whole body and left his throat raw.

The uncorking of his emotions sent him into a tailspin. He couldn't get a grip. A life without Savannah ... it was unfathomable. No one could ever love him like Savannah did. And no one in the world was like her. No one made him laugh so hard or love so much. Everything he did was for her, and he liked it that way. And after twenty-two years of marriage, he still thought she was as sexy and beautiful as she'd been when they'd met in college. Without her, the capstone of his world was gone. Everything would crumble to dust.

Once home, he stood in the shower and prayed aloud in the steam, alternately begging God for Savannah's life and railing at him for the mess he found himself in. When the water went cold, he forced himself to dress and find food, though all he wanted to do was crawl into bed and sleep for a week. He just had too much to face, too much to worry over and try to solve. Too much he could do nothing about. The thought of escape was bliss, though what form of escape he was unable to let himself ponder. Too many details and he might actually attempt it.

Back at the hospital he pulled into the parking lot and checked his reflection in the rear view mirror. The shower had removed the outward traces of his breakdown, but he wondered if the ever-perceptive Savannah would see it in his eyes.

He let himself daydream, as he crossed the blacktop to the hospital doors, about what it would be like when they finally got The Call. How hope would bring the light back to Savannah's weary face, how he would be fully consumed—for the meantime, anyway—by the fact that his wife would soon be back to normal. He hadn't thought much about what that day would be like. It actually made him smile.

The one problem was that the good news they were hoping for would soon be irrelevant. With her condition declining at this rate, Savannah would eventually be too sick to withstand the stresses of the surgery. It was a race against time now, a race he didn't usually acknowledge because the reality of it was too much to shoulder. He knew Savannah was convinced a heart would come in time, but God sure was cutting it close.

He was halfway to the elevator when his phone *dinged* to alert him of an incoming email. He tapped a button, then glanced at the screen and nearly choked on a pretzel. *No, no, no...*

He slumped against the wall and stared at his inbox, his stomach roiling with anxiety. He didn't want to open the email, but he was afraid not to. "I can't deal with this right now," he muttered through clenched teeth. Did this woman not pay any attention to the news? Savannah's story had been all over the local media this past week; certainly she knew what he was dealing with.

Unless that's the point—she knows she has me over a barrel.

He shook his head and exited the email program, then pocketed the phone. It didn't matter either way; he couldn't do anything about it now.

Savannah was actually awake when he arrived. He thought she looked a little better—not much, but a little—but it might have just been wishful thinking. "Hey, babe, sorry I'm late," he said, then kissed her forehead as he prayed she didn't see the worry in his face. "How've you been?"

"Okay," she said, her voice barely above a whisper. "Jessie gone?"

"Left this morning, yes — but she made me promise to call her if we wanted her to come. She almost didn't go, but I made her."

Savannah nodded her approval. "Can I do anything for you?"

She shook her head. "Gonna sleep."

"Okay. I'll be here until tonight, okay?"

"Okay." She closed her eyes, and sleep seemed to take her immediately. He was jealous of that, too. Half his night was spent staring at the ceiling.

Shaun reached into the bag where he'd stashed his book, sack dinner, and the mail from the last three days. He removed the latter, all rubber-banded together thanks to a conscientious Jessie. It had been piling up on the counter because he hadn't had the energy to go through it, but he knew he couldn't avoid it forever. Might as well go through it now while Savannah slept.

He threw out the sales flyers and business ads, then wasted some time thumbing through the Christian ministry magazine that came every month. He couldn't concentrate on the articles, though he tried; really he just didn't want to look at what was inside the envelopes that looked like bills. He looked at every article and even read the classifieds in the back before returning it to the bag and drawing a fortifying breath. *It's just mail, it can't kill you.* At least not directly.

A new insurance card for the car. The gas bill — lower than usual. So far this wasn't too bad.

An envelope from their health insurance company. His shoulders sagged. He felt defeated already.

He slowly ripped it open and pulled out the pages. Eight of them in all, filled front and back with a mess of confusing tables and codes and procedure names he couldn't decipher. The last page ended with a total due to each provider. Their combined total had five digits before the decimal.

His vision began to swim. Maybe he wouldn't have been so devastated if he hadn't gotten that email first. But now...

"Babe?"

Savannah's voice startled him, despite how quiet it was. He sniffed, tried to blink away the tears standing in his eyes. "Hey, I thought you were sleeping."

"You okay?"

"I'm fine, babe. I'm fine." He gave her a smile, but she shook her head.

"What's wrong?"

"Nothing, seriously. I'm just ... tired. I'm sorry if I woke you up. I didn't mean to."

She lifted a hand and he took it in his own. Her eyes were bright despite the rest of her face looking so drawn. "I'll be okay."

"I know you will. I believe you."

"Believe God."

He hated that his gut reaction was one of cynicism. "I do, babe. You're going to be fine. Everything is going to work out, I know."

She smiled and her eyes drifted shut. He waited until her hand was limp in his, then lowered it back to the bed.

He wanted so badly to believe what he'd said. He wanted to trust that God had a plan that involved Savannah recovering and Shaun winning the lottery, or discovering buried treasure behind the trees in their backyard, or anything that would allow him to finally get out from under the crushing financial struggle that was sucking both him and their bank account dry. But all he felt was despair, and no amount of praying seemed to help.

JESSIE FELT LIKE A POSTER child for Murphy's Law.

She'd been back on campus for less than 24 hours, and it had been one lousy break after another. For obvious reasons Shaun hadn't been able to help her move in, so she'd been stuck moving her belongings herself. That in and of itself wouldn't have been too bad, but because so many others were vying for the moving carts and the elevators were so packed, it had taken her way longer than she'd had time for, given all the details that still needed to be dealt with for the freshman dinner. Then she'd made the mistake of stacking too much on the cart once she got one, and a bump in the sidewalk had sent her desktop computer crashing to the pavement. The accidental damage insurance would take care of it; but she'd have to find time to file the claim — and until that was all sorted she was without her music or internet or email.

With so much time taken up with moving in, she'd had no time to start getting her room in order before having to abandon it for the dinner prep. That meant she had no idea where the shoes were that matched the outfit she'd planned on wearing that night, or where her bathroom caddy was so she could shower before the evening's event. And apparently she had "customer service representative" tattooed on her forehead, because any time she ventured outside her room she got stopped by a freshman or parent asking her questions she had no idea how to answer. The resident advisor still hadn't arrived, and as one of the few upperclassmen in the dorm, she was like a beacon to all the new students who were trying to figure out how to get their beds de-bunked or their computers set up to the internet.

And as if all that weren't enough to stress her out, her mother was going to die and no one wanted to admit it.

Savannah's decline since her admittance to the hospital had been frighteningly quick. Jessie had gone back to say goodbye the day before, and her mother had been so weak she could barely hold a conversation. It had only been a handful of days since Jessie had brought Savannah's laptop to the hospital in the Springs. It was hard to believe someone could deteriorate that fast. It was harder to believe they'd then be able to recover.

And yet Shaun — and Savannah herself — seemed convinced that she would. Jessie wanted to believe them, and to have the same faith they did, but she was unable to muster the confidence they seemed to share. So she checked her phone obsessively to make sure she hadn't missed a text or call, and found herself unable to concentrate on anything for long before her thoughts turned to funeral plans and wondering how she'd handle the grief once the inevitable occurred.

Jessie shook the dark thoughts from her head and consulted her checklist. *Tablecloths—check. Centerpieces—check. Decorations*... She looked around the gym for the box Adam was to have dropped off. She didn't see it. She pulled her phone from her pocket and texted him, then checked the next item on the list. *Sundae bar items.* She groaned aloud. She'd forgotten to confirm the sundae bar with The Sweet Shoppe.

Their contact info wasn't in her phone or on her checklist. Berating herself with mumbled insults, she dropped the checklist on a nearby table and headed for her dorm room.

On the sidewalk outside her dorm's front door stood a new student and her parents. Tears glistened on all their faces, and she ducked her head in embarrassment when they engaged in a family hug that brought a lump to her throat. As she passed them she overheard the father praying aloud and saw the girl's head resting on her mother's shoulder.

Nothing like when I moved in. Savannah had spent more time talking to people who recognized her from her books and speaking tours than she had with helping Jessie move in. Granted she was less than an hour from home and they all knew they'd see each other often, but not even the milestone of beginning college had created a soft spot in Savannah's heart. After her boxes had been moved in they'd gone to dinner, where Savannah had dominated the conversation with unsolicited advice about time management and not-so-subtle hints at the kinds of classes she thought Jessie should take.

When the time had come for her parents to leave, she'd gotten a giant hug from Shaun—who also pressed a wad of cash into her hand—and a peck on the cheek from Savannah when she took a break from the list she'd been dictating of activities she thought Jessie should check into. It would have been different if Jessie could have written off the behavior as her mother's attempt to control her emotions over the thought of her baby girl growing up and moving on in life, but she'd known Savannah too well to even pretend that was the reason. It had been just another example of Savannah wanting to steer Jessie the way she thought she should go, and not taking into account the fact that Jessie had no interest in writing for the school newspaper or trying to join the honor society.

Jessie turned her back on the family whose experience highlighted the deficiencies of her own and swiped her card to unlock the door. She kept her head down and avoided making eye contact with the people who swarmed through the hall as she pushed her way through to her room. Once there, she grabbed the folder of freshman dinner info from her desk and looked up the number for The Sweet Shoppe. She called and asked the employee who answered to confirm the ice cream and toppings delivery for that evening.

"Gosh ... I'm sorry. I don't see that order in our computer. When did you say this event was?"

"Know what? Never mind." Jessie hung up the phone, flopped to her bed, and cried.

SAVANNAH AWOKE TO FAMILIAR VOICES. It took a moment for her to get her eyes open, but by the time she did she was already smiling. "Hey," she croaked.

"Ah, Sleeping Beauty awakens!" Mary gave Savannah a gentle hug, then frowned. "Okay, so, I had no idea you weren't eating anything anymore. The nurse just told me. That really sucks — I brought brownies."

Savannah smiled. "Make more ... when I'm better ... and I'll forgive you."

Colleen held up a stack of DVD cases. "Shaun said you were sleeping a lot, but we brought these just in case you find yourself awake and bored. All the good ones are here — *Sleepless in Seattle*, *Shakespeare in Love*, *When Harry Met Sally*, and *Dirty Dancing*."

"Just don't, you know, get any ideas," said Bethany, waving a hand to the machines beside the bed. "All those cords and tubes would really get in the way."

Andi took Savannah's hand. "Listen, just let us know if you need peace and quiet. Or just take a nap when you want to and we can stick around until you're awake again. We don't want to impose, we just wanted to see you and pray with you and make sure you knew we were all here for you."

"Love you all … you're angels."

"Let's pray now — get the important stuff out of the way," Mary said with a grin.

Savannah didn't dare close her eyes, for fear she'd fall asleep. She stared instead at each of the women holding hands around her bed, their eyes closed and heads bowed as they interceded for her and Shaun. She was moved beyond words by their faithful friendship and sacrifice — she knew how long that drive was from the Springs — and as they spoke over her she thanked God for them and prayed that this ordeal would end in a way that encouraged everyone in their faith.

When they finished, Colleen began straightening the stack of cards and letters from fans that Shaun had brought a few days ago and now cluttered the bedside table. "So, are you really okay with visitors right now? Or do you want to sleep?"

"No sleeping," she said. "Later. Tell me … what's up."

"What's up, let's see …" She began to regale Savannah with a dramatic retelling of the senior lunch she and Mary had helped host at church for the retirees. "I swear, I *will* get Alfred Collins and Helen Grable together by Christmas."

"Girl, there's got to be a better way to spend your time than playing matchmaker with senior citizens," Bethany said with a laugh.

"They'd be … cute together," Savannah said.

"See? Savannah agrees with me."

"Savannah is not operating on all cylinders."

Savannah gave a minute shrug. "She's right."

"Any news on when those cylinders might all be up and running?"

She shook her head. "When God's ... good and ready."

Mary pulled a knitting project from a bag at her feet and began to unwind purple yarn. "Alex has been trying to get ahold of Shaun to go out for breakfast or something, but Shaun hasn't returned his calls. How is he doing?"

Shaun hadn't mentioned this to her, though she wasn't surprised. "Not well. It's hard on him ... all the driving ... me like this. I think he's scared."

"I would be too, if it were me. I just wish he'd get together with Alex so he could go vent, or play golf, or whatever it is men do to feel better."

"I'll tell him ... to call ... but you know Shaun ... he's private."

"Yeah, I know. But still. He needs someone to talk to through all of this, someone that isn't you."

"I wanted to organize some meals for him and Jessie," said Bethany. "Or is Jessie back at school now?"

"Left yesterday ... Shaun's always here. Not many ... meals at home."

"Well, he's got to eat sometime. Maybe I'll just hunt him down at A&A and bring him some sandwiches or something."

Savannah smiled. "You're sweet."

"How about you?" Andi asked. "How are you doing? Like, *really* doing."

She nodded slowly. "I know ... God will ... heal me ... but ... still scary. Pain scares me."

Andi squeezed her hand. "Oh, Van. It breaks my heart that you have to go through this."

Savannah shook her head. "No ... it's good ... God ... renewed me through this ... broken body but ... mountaintop faith." She glanced at the clock on the wall. "Lots of prayer time ... listen to worship music ... I needed to ... slow down."

Colleen snorted. "He couldn't have just broken your leg?"

The others laughed as Savannah smiled. "Guess that wouldn't ... have done the trick."

"Is there anything you need, Van?" Mary asked. "Besides the obvious, which I would gladly donate to you myself if it were possible."

"Prayer for us … and the donor's family."

Mary's face fell. "Oh, gosh. Yeah."

"Will you know who they are?" asked Bethany. "Do they tell you that kind of thing?"

"You can … correspond … anonymously … of course I will."

Andi chuckled. "That's a heck of a thank-you card to write."

Savannah's head nodded a fraction. "You're telling me."

Suddenly exhaustion hit her like a fist. "Gotta sleep. But stay … if you want … watch a movie."

"We don't want to keep you up."

"You won't." She smiled. "Hopefully I can … chat more … before you leave. Shaun comes … around one. Hound him then, Mary."

She grinned. "Perfect."

Savannah closed her eyes, worn out from the effort of conversation, and fell asleep to a soundtrack starting in the background.

SHAUN JUMPED AS A CLAP of thunder took him by surprise. He hadn't noticed the lightning with the kitchen light on. He moved the pancakes to his plate and poured two more onto the griddle, then checked the salmon in the countertop grill. He'd managed to feed himself without a single trip to the grocery store since Savannah's hospitalization, but this was definitely scraping the bottom of the barrel. He conceded he'd need to go shopping tomorrow.

One of the nurses had called on behalf of Savannah that morning to tell him not to come up because of the storm that was expected to roll across the state. It had been sunny when she'd called, but by lunch the clouds had begun to darken. He'd almost blown off the warning and gone up anyway; but now that the rain was pouring in buckets, he was glad he hadn't.

Instead, he was eating an entirely unappetizing dinner and reviewing some stocks he was considering buying. It had been awhile since he'd actively played the market, but it was one of the few ways he could think of that might bring in some extra money. He'd taken out everything he could when the IRS had come calling a few years back, and hadn't had the time to research stock picks thoroughly enough to make any moves since then. But with two more bills from the insurance company and Jessie's tuition due, he knew it was time to get back into it.

He ate his pancakes as he made them and took the salmon to his office to eat while he read up on the two stocks he was interested in. The seed money was the one problem. He could get it if he went into their retirement, but he'd get penalized, which meant losing some of the money they desperately needed. But what choice was there?

By the time the salmon was gone his choice was made. All he had to do was bite the bullet and pull the money out of his 403b. He was about to pick up his cell to call his investment company when it surprised him by ringing.

"Hello?"

"Shaun, it's Tammy—Savannah's transplant coordinator."

His blood iced in his veins. "Oh God—she's not—"

"No, no, Shaun—we have a heart."

It took a second for his emotions to put the brakes on his grief. "Wait—a heart—for Savannah?"

She laughed. "If it were for someone else I wouldn't be calling you."

He darted for the kitchen where his car keys sat. "I don't know when I'll get there with the rain. Oh man—I never packed a bag."

"That's alright, just get here when you can. The heart isn't here yet, and it probably won't get here for another couple hours anyway; it's up in Fort Collins right now."

"Okay, okay. I'll be there as soon as I can."

"Drive safely now—no speeding."

"Right, right. No speeding." He hung up and ran back into the bedroom to grab a change of clothes, then shoved them into the computer bag that held his laptop.

He was on the road before he realized he ought to call people. But who? Jessie first, of course. He dialed, praying God would protect him from crashing as he drove through the storm. "They've got a heart," he said when she picked up. "They said it'll get there in a couple hours. I'm guessing she'll go straight into surgery once it's there. I'm on my way up now."

"Oh my gosh! Okay, okay ... we'll finish up dinner and hit the road in about ten minutes."

He called Alex after that, who promised to get the word out to their friends and Pastor John. Then he dialed Marisa, who had just gotten back two days prior from a visit to her boyfriend in New York. "They got a heart; it's on its way."

"Hallelujah! I can't believe it! That was so fast."

"Fast?"

"It's only been, what, twelve days since she was admitted to the hospital the first time? Some people are on the list for months."

Shaun had to do the math himself to believe it. Less than two weeks? It felt like a lifetime. "She wouldn't have lasted months. God knew what he was doing."

"Are you on your way?"

"Just left ten minutes ago."

"I'll call the staff and let them know. Is it okay if people come up?"

"As long as they promise to pray like crazy while they're here, sure."

She laughed. "You got it. See you as soon as I can make it up."

The rain lessened as he drove, and by the time he was half-way there it had stopped completely. Without the weather to worry about, his mind was free to wander. They had a heart. Savannah had been right; God was going to heal her. Why had he doubted?

His thoughts turned to the surgery, and then to the bill that would be coming. Hopefully he'd be able to grab those stocks beforehand. If he had a minute alone, he'd leave a voicemail for the investor who handled A&A's retirement program to find out about pulling out the funds.

Between the rush hour traffic he'd hit and the weather, it took him almost two hours to get to the hospital. It was just after eight when he ran at full-tilt from the car to the building and up the two flights of stairs to Savannah's room. Two nurses were preparing to take her to the operating room. "I'm here, Van!" he said, squeezing her foot. She opened her eyes and smiled bigger than he'd seen in weeks. "Jessie's on her way; Marisa's coming up, too. I called Alex; not sure who will come up but he's calling everyone."

"Tell them all hi."

He laughed. "I will."

Tammy entered and threw an arm around Shaun's shoulder. "You made it! What a night, huh?"

"You can say that again."

"They'll take her down in a minute; the heart is about half an hour away. I'll walk you down to the waiting room and we can go over any questions you have about the surgery."

"We're done here, Tammy," said one of the nurses.

"Alright then — Shaun, you and Savannah can have a minute alone." She and the nurses left, and Shaun moved beside Savannah and held her hand.

"You okay, babe?"

She nodded. "You?"

"Better than I have been."

"Pray for me."

He closed his eyes and found himself speechless. Words couldn't convey the desperation he felt for this surgery to go right. He stumbled through a prayer he was sure would make Savannah roll her eyes, but when he opened his own she was smiling wide. "See you tomorrow."

He felt his throat threatening to close. "Promise?"

"Promise." She squeezed his hand and he kissed her as hard as he dared.

Tammy returned. "Ready to go?"

Shaun let Savannah go and stepped back. "Not really."

She chuckled. "Savannah?"

"Let's get this ... show on the road."

"You've got it. Off we go!" The nurses wheeled the bed into the hall, and Shaun and Tammy followed them as far as the swinging double doors that led to the OR. He kissed her once more, then let Tammy lead him to the spacious waiting room lined with couches and dotted with tables and chairs.

"Will anyone else be coming?"

"Our daughter and her boyfriend, Savannah's assistant ... possibly some others, but I don't know for sure."

"I'll let reception know and they'll send them all here. Do you want to wait for your daughter before we go over the surgery?"

"No, I'm not sure when she'll get here. Let's just do it now while I can still concentrate."

They sat at a table and Tammy went over the sequence of events that would begin with the arrival of the heart, but Shaun barely paid attention. All he could think about was his wife in the OR, chest splayed open, her life in the hands of a team of mere mortals. *Well, and God, too.* But that didn't comfort him as much as it comforted Savannah.

"Dad!"

He turned in his seat and saw Jessie and Adam coming down the hall. She wrapped her arms around his neck. "Is she okay?"

"She just went in a few minutes ago for prep. The heart should be here soon. This is Tammy, the transplant coordinator. Tammy, this is our daughter, Jessie, and her boyfriend, Adam."

"Nice to meet you. Boy, aren't you the spitting image of your mother."

Jessie smiled a little. "Thank you."

"I just finished explaining the next twenty-four hours to your dad, but I'll leave these papers here so you can read over them. Feel free to page me if you have any questions. I'll be here until she's out of surgery."

"How long will that be?" Jessie asked.

"Around nine hours, assuming there are no hitches."

She blew out a breath. "Wow."

Shaun stood and shook Tammy's hand. "Thanks again."

"You're welcome. Let me know if you need anything and I'll see what I can do."

She disappeared down the hall. Shaun sat back down and rubbed a hand over his face. "I can't believe this is happening."

"How did she look before she went in?"

"Not great, but obviously she wasn't bad enough for them to not do the surgery. I have a feeling this was an eleventh hour save, though. At the rate she was going ..." He shook his head. "Anyway, we just have to pray this goes okay." He took the hand Jessie stretched out to him.

"So ... what now?"

He shrugged. "Now we wait."

THEY DIDN'T HAVE TO WAIT alone, however. Not long after Jessie and Adam arrived, Mary and Alex did as well, followed by Adam's mother and two other A&A staff members, including Marisa. Then Andi and Colleen showed up with their husbands, bringing four pizzas with them, and Pastor John arrived with his wife an hour into the surgery. The impromptu party in the waiting room made Shaun both happy and edgy. It was good to know how many people cared about them—and cared enough to trek for nearly two hours through rotten weather. But it was overwhelming as well—all the praying and worshiping (John had brought his guitar), all the concerned faces close to his asking how he was holding up. A couple hours into the surgery he told Jessie he was going for a walk, and left the group for the quiet of the chapel.

He stared at the stained glass picture of a hilly countryside at sunset, trying to capture some of the peace the image depicted. He was scared Savannah would die, and he couldn't shake it. He was afraid to consider the details he'd have to face if the surgery didn't work. He didn't want to jinx it, or make God think that he was prepared enough for it that he would decide to go ahead and take her. But at the same time, he was afraid not to plan, knowing that he would never think of all the details in the throes of grief; better to have things figured out just in case.

He'd sell the house, for sure. He'd never be able to stay there without his wife, and it was too much space for just him and Jessie—especially since Jessie would likely never really move back. He knew how serious she and Adam were; surely a wedding would follow on the heels of graduation.

A&A would shut down, certainly. It was built around Savannah; without her at the helm it was pointless. It was a ministry for women; Shaun would not be able to do what she did, and Jessie had no interest in being involved—had no interest in the ministry at all, period.

Though at least with A&A gone and the house sold the debts would all go away. What a relief that would be, to have that monkey off his—

"What am I doing?" He said the words aloud, shocked at the turn of his thoughts. "God, I didn't mean it. I would never trade Savannah just to get out from under this mess. It's all my own fault. She shouldn't have to pay for it."

Another thought ignited panic. "This isn't all because of me, is it? God, I'm sorry. Please, don't take her. Don't let her die."

A noise behind him made him turn. A chaplain stood at the back, and Shaun's chest tightened with embarrassment. How much had he heard?

"I'm sorry to disturb you. I did a service in here earlier and think I left my glasses on the podium." He gave Shaun a friendly smile as he passed him on the way up to the simple wooden podium at the front of the chapel. "Ah, bingo." He pocketed the glasses and walked back to Shaun. "I'm Reverend Hutchinson. Is there anything I can do for you?"

"My wife—she just went in for a heart transplant, and I'm—" Shaun didn't know what to say. *I'm cheating her ministry out of money at every turn so I can keep someone quiet and keep my kid in college?* "I'm feeling ... desperate."

The reverend sat in the pew in front of Shaun and turned to face him. "Can I pray for you?"

He'd gotten plenty of prayer in the waiting room. He didn't deserve any more. "No thanks," he said as he stood. "Just pray for my wife."

He left the chapel and headed back to the waiting room, but the strains of everyone singing made him turn around. He was definitely not in a worshipful mood. He followed the signs to the foyer where a bank of vending machines provided snacks and drinks. He could still hear the music, but hearing it wasn't as bad as having to participate in it. He slotted some change for a coffee, then sat at one of the tables and let the minutes tick by as he chanted *Don't let her die, don't let her die* in his head.

He rested his head on his folded arms and eventually began to doze, only to awaken with a start sometime later, panicked that he'd missed something. The music down the hall was gone. He checked his phone for the time and saw that the surgery had been going for four hours. He took his coffee, now cold, back to the waiting room and found most of the visitors had crashed out on the couches. Jessie and Adam were playing cards; Mary was knitting in the corner, a blanket with various shades of purple cascading from the needles; and John sat at a table with his Bible and a notebook. Those who were awake acknowledged him when he returned, but thankfully said nothing to him as he made his way to an empty couch and settled into its corner. The chant picked up again in his mind as he closed his eyes, and for the next few hours he dozed off and on before finally succumbing to a deep sleep.

He was awakened by Tammy gently calling his name and shaking his shoulder. His eyes flew open when it finally registered who she was.

He jumped to his feet. "What's happening?"

She smiled. "Surgery is done, and she did great. It's over now. Savannah has a new heart."

CHAPTER 6

SAVANNAH SAT ON THE COUCH, HANDS WRAPPED AROUND A MUG of tea as she stared at the trees. It was all she'd done since coming home three days ago, and she was frustrated by how little things had changed. Hadn't she been doing this before going into the hospital? When was the new heart going to kick in and give her some energy?

She had been warned about the emotional roller coaster that came along with a new lease on life, about the depression that came with knowing someone had to die so you could live. She'd known it beforehand, of course, but with the evidence housed in her chest, she had trouble not dwelling on it. The concept was obviously familiar, and she'd expected to feel a lot more gratefulness toward Jesus for his sacrifice after this experience, but instead she just felt … angry.

She tried not to overanalyze her emotions. "Everyone processes their transplants differently," Tammy had assured her at a recent checkup. "Just go with it, let yourself feel what you feel. It'll all even out eventually. But it takes time." It had been a relief to hear she wasn't some emotional freak; but even so, she had expected to feel like herself again, and she didn't — and that was maddening.

Her Bible sat beside her on the end table, the bookmark still in the Psalms. She'd picked it up every day, even opened it a few times, but reading felt like a chore and the verses weren't alive for her like they had been before the surgery. Every now and then she'd imagine herself approaching the throne of Heaven, the image she'd often used in her younger years to get her mind in the right state for prayer, but later she'd realize her thoughts had wandered and she'd never actually prayed anything. She'd center herself and try again, but "thank you" didn't seem strong enough given the magnitude of the gift, and she felt guilty praying about anything else. She longed for that brilliance she'd felt in the days before the transplant, when God had been as real and close as her own self. Now she just felt alone, and she resented that the mountaintop experience had been so short-lived.

She took a slow sip of the tea after waiting just long enough that she wouldn't scald her tongue. The heat streaked down her throat but died in her chest, as though swallowed up by ice—which is what her chest felt like these days: as though a snowball sat in its center. Her cardiologist chuckled when she described it. "I haven't heard that one before." She didn't appreciate that he didn't seem to take it seriously.

She thought she'd feel a lot better if she could just get the energy to *do* something. She'd lost so much time during her illness; it was driving her crazy to lose so much more. She'd envisioned the new heart being like a new engine in a run-down car, thinking she'd jump back into life and make up for all the days she'd spent on the sofa and in the hospital. But here she was, almost three weeks post-op and only slightly less sluggish than she'd been in the days before her collapse. The problem was that her brain was ready to get back in the game; it was her body that didn't have the stamina.

Shaun kept telling her to get her laptop out and get back to work on the book she'd started to brainstorm in the hospital. She'd managed to get the whole book's outline done before growing too weak to work, and at the time she'd been quite pleased with its depth. But she'd made the mistake of mentioning it to her agent when talking to her the week after her surgery, and the agent had called two days ago to tell her they had a contract for the book. "Didn't even need to see a proposal," he said with a laugh. "Just happened to mention it to the publisher over lunch and they begged for it. Now, they don't want to set a deadline for you, because they know you're still recovering and don't want you stressing out over finishing it. But the sooner the better, of course, to capitalize on the buzz. It would be ideal if we could get it on the shelves by the end of October."

She knew her agent didn't mean to sound heartless. But she couldn't help feeling hurt by him and her publisher taking such a materialistic view of her personal suffering. She understood the nature of the business, but it didn't change the fact that it made her mad. Maybe that was why she was balking at working on the manuscript.

Savannah made another cup of tea, then opened her laptop. She briefly thought of launching the word processing program, but clicked instead on the internet browser. She never spent much time online, save for doing email; she'd never felt comfortable navigating the nebulous World Wide Web. But on a whim she went to a search engine and entered "heart transplant support" just to see what would happen.

She hadn't expected over seven million returns for the search, and laughed aloud when she saw the number. This would certainly keep her busy.

She scanned the first ten returns and clicked on one that said something about a forum. She found herself at a message board, something she'd never interacted with before. It took her a minute to figure out what it was, but once she made it into the forum and saw the list of threads, a smile spread wide across her face. Post after post from people just like herself filled the screen. She began to click each one in turn, reading them voraciously. Finally, people who understood what she felt, what she'd gone through! People who didn't keep telling her how blessed she was, which made her feel horrible for not feeling more happy. She lost track of time as she read, and jumped when the doorbell rang.

"Surprise!" Her girlfriends stood on the front porch with balloons and a cake. Their festive mood mirrored the refreshing lightness she felt after reading the forum, and she welcomed them in with far more gratefulness and joviality than she would have had they come before she'd gotten online.

"You guys are sweet, thanks. Oh — that cake is too funny!"

Andi set the two-tiered, heart-shaped cake on the kitchen counter. "It's strawberry, and none of us could recall if we'd ever seen you eat strawberry cake, so we decided to take a chance."

"Oh, I'm sure it will be delicious." Honestly, she wasn't a fan of the flavor, but she wasn't going to admit that after all the trouble they'd gone through. She got a knife from the drawer and wielded it above the frosting. "I much prefer being on this end of the slicing." They laughed as she cut pieces for everyone, then Mary poured sparkling cider for everyone and they toasted to Savannah's health.

When she took a bite of the cake, she was stunned at how delicious it was. "Oh my gosh, this is heaven."

Colleen grinned. "So you do like strawberry cake."

Savannah took another bite. "Well, I'll confess I usually don't. But this is … wow."

"I'll give you the recipe."

"So how is it to finally be home?" Bethany asked between bites.

"Good. Not like I was expecting, but better than being in the hospital."

"How is it not like you expected?"

"I just thought I'd be back in the swing of things sooner. I didn't think I'd still be feeling this blah."

"How long is it supposed to be until you're back to normal?"

She shrugged. "They don't know. Some people have more energy, some people never really get back to how they were. It's just a waiting game to see which way I'll go. Though these days I have my fears that I'll fall in with the latter."

Andi set her plate aside. "So is it weird, knowing a piece of someone else is inside you?"

The question made her squirm. "Um, well … yes." Though these were her closest friends, she still had trouble talking about the details of the surgery. Even Shaun hadn't asked questions like that yet. And if he had, she wasn't sure she'd have answered honestly.

"Can you tell it's someone else's? Does it feel different?"

Bethany rolled her eyes. "It's a heart, Andi. How many ways can it feel?"

"Well, I don't know, maybe it's one of those things that you don't notice until someone goes messing around with it."

Savannah wasn't about to admit that yes, it did feel different, and she was acutely aware of it every minute of the day. "I notice it … sometimes … but it might just be the healing from the surgery."

Mary nodded. "That would make sense. How are you healing up?"

"Just fine, according to the doctor." She didn't want to get into how she felt like she was still laid open on the table, at least emotionally, or how the scar running the entire length of her torso would never allow her to forget, no matter how much she wanted to.

Colleen gave Savannah's shoulder a squeeze. "So the only thing left is to get you back to regular speed and everything will be fine."

Andi put an arm around her shoulder. "God will take care of you. We'll start praying that you're renewed to your old self, or better."

The comment rubbed her the wrong way, though she didn't know why. She forced a smile. "Thanks."

"You know," Mary said to the others, "maybe the four of us could organize a little prayer team for Savannah. We should have started one back when she first got sick, but I don't think any of us realized how bad it was going to get. Like you, Savannah, we all figured it was just the flu. And then things went downhill so fast …" She waved away the memory. "Anyway, the four of us, let's do it. Once a week, we'll pray over you, and commit to praying for you every day until you're back to how you were."

"That's really sweet, but—"

"I love it!" Bethany said. "How about we meet at my place for coffee next Thursday around ten? Does that work for you, Savannah?"

"Um, I'll have to check—"

"Why don't we all check and email Bethany with our availability," Colleen suggested.

"Perfect," said Bethany.

"You know who we should invite in on this?" said Mary. "Arlene Wilkins at church."

Andi nodded. "Oh, yes, she's such a prayer warrior."

"I'll give her a call tonight and see if she'd be able to make it."

"Great idea!"

Savannah withdrew from the conversation, irritated and feeling like a project for them to pounce on. She thought back to the conversation with Shaun when she'd suggested having Pastor John meet with them for accountability. Now she understood why he'd been so opposed to it. Hearing people talking about her in a spiritual way made her feel exposed.

She kept herself busy eating cake so she wouldn't have to talk. A second slice came in handy for that—though admittedly she'd have taken another one anyway, it was so good—and she contributed noncommittal "Mm-hmms" for the next ten minutes while hoping they'd all leave. The goodwill she'd been feeling when they arrived wore off quickly, and now she was just eager for them to go so she could get back to reading her support forum.

After half an hour they still showed no signs of leaving, so Savannah made the decision for them. "Well, I have a doctor's appointment in twenty minutes, so I should start cleaning up and get going for that."

"Oh, of course," Mary said as they all stood. "I'll bet you're at the doctor a lot these days."

"Yeah, they're keeping close tabs, as you can imagine."

They took turns giving Savannah hugs, then filed out the door. "Thursday at ten, don't forget," Bethany said as she walked down the porch stairs.

"Yes, I'll let you know about that." She stayed at the door for a moment, not wanting to look impolite, then shut it and sagged onto the couch, exhausted.

She loved her friends, she really did, but this was beyond the scope of their understanding. They couldn't possibly fathom the way this experience had turned her inside out in every possible way.

She could barely understand it herself, and she was the one living it. They couldn't know how personal those questions were, and how disturbed she was by their answers.

But the people on the forum could.

She continued to read, indulging in another slice of cake, until Shaun came home. "That looks like it was good," he said, eyeing the crumbs on the empty cake plate.

"It was. Sorry I didn't save any for you. I couldn't stop eating it."

"That's alright. Guess I'm on my own for dinner then?"

She smiled. "I think so, yes."

"I take it you had a visitor today, then? Who brought it?"

"The girls."

"All four of them? That was sweet."

"Yes. All four of them."

He raised an eyebrow. "Did it not go well?"

She shrugged. "It's not that it didn't go well ... I just don't think I was ready for so many visitors asking so many questions."

He nodded and gently wrapped his arms around her. "I'm sorry."

"That's alright."

"So did you find any time to start working on the book again?"

She fought the defensiveness that rose in her chest. "No. I was busy."

"How long were the women here for?"

"Not with them—I found an online support group for transplant recipients. It's been really wonderful reading all their stories, hearing how much we all have in common with our recoveries—"

He chuckled. "You're not going to become an internet junkie now, are you?"

"Well, if spending time trying to help myself understand what I'm thinking and feeling and trying to get back to my life before all this happened constitutes being a junkie, then yes, I might."

He gave her a look. "I was just playing, Van. I wasn't being serious."

She deflated a bit. "I'm sorry. I'm just feeling ..." She shook her head and shrugged. "Never mind. I don't know what I'm feeling." She left the kitchen for the sofa and pulled the computer back onto her lap.

"Honey, I'm sorry." Shaun followed her and sat beside her. "Maybe tomorrow you'll get a chance to start writing. I really think it will help if you get back in the saddle. It'll all come back to you. You're wallowing a bit, I think, and it's totally understandable; but maybe if you start focusing outward instead of inward you'll start feeling better."

She shut the laptop with more force than she intended. "Quit trying to diagnose me. You're no psychologist, and you have no idea what it's like to be me right now." She pushed herself to her feet, shaking off Shaun's attempt at helping her stand, and headed to her office with more speed than she'd managed since coming home.

She was dying to tell him what she was really thinking, to finally get it off her chest, but she couldn't voice those thoughts aloud. How could a ministry president like herself admit how angry she was with God right now, how the very thought of his goodness and provision made her want to laugh? Especially when she didn't understand it herself. Knowing a book was expected from her on the subject made her panicky; she fought that by simply not thinking about it and hoping she'd wake one of these mornings and find those feelings gone.

But so far the mornings only brought more anger and confusion.

Jessie zipped her duffel and texted Adam.

Ready when u r.

Her stomach fluttered; she took another bite of the sandwich she'd brought back from the cafeteria at lunch and hoped it would give her insides something to do besides reflect her anxiety. This was a new experience, being nervous about going home.

Savannah's transplant had happened three weeks ago, and Jessie hadn't been back to visit since that night. She'd almost gone a number of times, but something always stopped her—a project she needed to work on, a meeting she couldn't miss. Her own nerves. She knew she was being a terrible daughter by not going to visit her mother in the hospital, and now that Savannah was home the guilt was even worse. But Jessie's remorse over their last conversation held her back.

She should have just kept her mouth shut. What had led her to believe it was wise to try changing the past by confronting a dying woman with her shortcomings? It had solved nothing, had led to no reconciliation, and had only added to the stress her mother was already dealing with as her body betrayed her. Jessie had planned on at least apologizing when she'd visited Savannah before moving to campus, but her mother had only lasted a few minutes before falling asleep, and Jessie had been so disturbed by Savannah's deterioration that she'd left rather than wait for her to wake. And now she had to go back home and face her again, knowing she'd been selfish in the face of her mother's decline.

Her phone buzzed.

Ready in 20 or so. Will txt u.

Her nose wrinkled as she looked for something to keep her occupied and her mind off the impending visit. Not enough time to start homework, and too much time to just sit around. She woke her computer instead and tapped in a URL.

Last week she'd stumbled across this website while doing research for her child development class. It was a forum for Christian moms, and while she was nowhere near motherhood, she'd found herself sucked into the message board and had gone so far as to apply for membership. An entire subforum was devoted to developing the parent-child relationship, and reading it was like applying antibiotic to a wound: painful, but healing.

Ever since her relationship with Adam had gotten serious, she'd had motherhood on the brain. Not because she was looking forward to it, but because it scared her. What if she passed on the brokenness of her own mother-daughter relationship to her children? What if she didn't know how to be the kind of mom she'd always wanted Savannah to be, precisely because Savannah hadn't been able to model it for her? The posts she read in the forums eased some of her fears, because so many of the other women were doing what she'd eventually have to do—working out from scratch what it meant to be the kind of mother they'd never had.

The forum also gave her something she rarely had: anonymity. All they knew was what she told them, and so far she hadn't told them much. Her screen name—Mom-In-Training—gave nothing away, and instead of her own picture she posted an image of a sunflower on her profile. The best part was being able to post her frustrations about her relationship with her mom without worrying about how it affected Savannah's reputation. She hadn't gone into much detail, but what little she'd shared had been met with encouragement and messages of commiseration, and with the help of some other women who had weathered similar struggles she'd made a plan for this weekend.

Coming as close as she had to losing her mother had convinced her she needed to make things better between them—she just had to work a bit on how she went about it. Honesty was important, yes, but her own response and attitude was even more so. It was unrealistic to think that one vulnerable and emotionally open conversation on her part was going to make Savannah change her tune. She had to be consistent with her honesty but also grace-filled in her acceptance of her mother's response; after all, Jessie knew what to expect from her mother. Rather than fighting against Savannah all the time, Jessie was going to try to model the kind of responses she hoped to get from Savannah and not let herself get worked up when her mother's reaction wasn't what she wanted.

It was an approach that looked good on paper. She just wasn't sure how it would actually play out.

She posted to various threads on the message board until her phone buzzed again and going 2 car now

showed up on the screen. She added a brief prayer request for her weekend to the prayer forum, then shut down the computer and grabbed her backpack and duffel. *Ready or not*, she prayed, *here we go ...*

JESSIE CAME IN JUST AS Savannah was making herself a mid-morning snack after having spent the last two hours on the transplant forum. Her mind was still engaged in the conversations she'd read about the emotional component of organ transplants, and Jessie's arrival disrupted her thoughts.

"Didn't know you were coming home," she said when Jessie appeared in the kitchen.

"It was a last-minute thing. Adam's mom needed help with some stuff. That poor house of theirs is just falling apart; they seriously need to apply for that home makeover show."

"Mmm." Savannah spread strawberry jam on her toast. "So how are things?"

"They're fine. How are you? Healing up okay?"

It was a topic she was getting tired of addressing with every person who saw her these days. "Yes, fine, thank you."

Jessie began to fix herself some toast as well. "That's good. I can't imagine what it must be like. But, I'm sure you don't want to talk about that with me."

Savannah was relieved by her daughter's unexpected empathy. "Thank you."

A cloud passed over Jessie's face, but her voice was still light when she spoke. "So the freshman welcome dinner went off without a hitch. I told some of the girls about the doily story you'd told me; they all want to make next year's dinner a throwback thing and cover everything with doilies. Isn't that a riot?"

"Mmm." Savannah eyed her computer as she bit into her toast. "Yes, funny." She thought of something one of the other transplant recipients had written about, and she was struck with a sudden insight into the man's struggle. She began to form her reply in her head as she blew over the top of her tea mug.

" ... children's home on Tuesday afternoons. It's been such an incredible experience. I've only done it twice but I have a feeling this is really going to affect the way I go with my career."

Career. Savannah certainly wished these days that hers had gone in a different direction. "Well, don't be surprised if it doesn't go the way you're expecting."

"What's that supposed to mean?"

Jessie's tone snapped Savannah out of her own thoughts. "I — just that, your career — "

"Is this more about my major? I thought we were done with this conversation, Mom. I love the options I'll have in education."

Savannah set down her tea, bewildered by Jessie's reaction. "I'm not sure why you're so angry, sweetheart."

"Gosh, could it be because you have once again shown that you have no respect at all for me and my choices? I could be the home-coming queen and valedictorian and you'd still think I'm inadequate." Jessie popped the toast prematurely from the toaster and spread a sloppy layer of peanut butter over the still-soft bread. "I don't know why I keep trying to show you how wrong you are. You never see what I've accomplished, only that it's not what you'd choose to do. I'm really sorry I didn't turn out to be a mini Savannah, but I am who God made me to be; and if it's good enough for him it should be good enough for you."

Savannah stared at Jessie, shocked. "Look, Jessica, I wasn't try-ing to criticize with my comment. My mind was elsewhere — "

"Of course it was. It's always been elsewhere. I don't think I've ever had a conversation with you where you were fully present. This wasn't some momentary lapse of focus, Mom. This is an issue ten years in the making. You have no idea what it's like to be Savannah Trover's daughter — her *only* daughter — no, worse, her only child. Not only do I get to live with everyone's expectations of what your daughter should be like, but I have to live with *your* expectations all concentrated on one person. I really wish you'd at least had another kid so I'd have someone to commiserate with."

Savannah stared open-mouthed at her daughter. The comment hurt more than Jessie knew. "I'm serious, I've never meant to be hard on you. And any criticism I might have made was only to try to push you to consider other options instead of just blindly following what some guidance counselor made you think was your best bet. I never realized you were taking it *that* hard."

Jessie sniffed and rolled her eyes as she pulled a napkin from the stack on the counter. "Of course you didn't. You never think about anyone else. You never notice anyone else's feelings. You never consider how what you say might hurt someone. You're totally self-centered, but you excuse it as ministry. 'Oh, I'm sorry, I don't have time for you because I need to work on my book.' 'Gosh, I'd love to help you out, but I really need to devote my time to my ministry.' One excuse after another. Thank God I had Dad."

The words were a slap in the face. Savannah watched Jessie storm off to her room, heard the door slam shut, and wandered in a daze back to the couch to try to figure out what just happened. She'd been called focused, and driven, and passionate, but never self-centered. Surely this was just Jessie spouting Psychology 101 insights that were completely off-base.

But as the sting wore off, Savannah couldn't help noticing how accurate Jessie's accusations were. She'd considered her ministry to be A&A and *only* A&A. She'd considered herself ... not *above* serving in other ways, but *excused* from it. Her ministry was writing books and speaking, not feeding the homeless or praying with the sick. Savannah ministered to the people who did those kinds of things, and when someone invited her into the trenches she'd politely decline.

And when it came to Jessie ... well, she had never meant to come off the way she apparently had. Yes, she did have high expectations for her, but she'd never disapproved of what she was doing — she'd merely thought other avenues might yield more fruit for her.

Though by not explicitly approving her choices, wasn't I disapproving of them?

Jessie was so smart, had so much potential, Savannah was afraid she'd end up unappreciated in some overcrowded school working for pittance. And, if she was brutally honest with herself, she had to admit she'd often hoped Jessie would want to join Savannah in her ministry to women, helping them to reach out and grab the life God had for them.

It had all been for Jessie, really. For Jessie and her generation and the generations after her. All she'd wanted was to make the Christian subculture a place where women's contributions were just as valued as the men's, where the jobs mothers did were held in the same esteem as the pastors and teachers of the church. She'd been trying to strengthen and empower Christian moms to see the worth in what they did—and in doing so, she had checked out of her own mothering role and left her daughter to fend for herself.

She now saw the irony.

Savannah went to Jessie's room and knocked. She opened the door when "come in" was muttered, and leaned against the door-frame. "I'm ... I'm sorry, Jessie."

"Thanks." Her daughter's tone suggested she didn't think the apology very heartfelt.

"Listen—why don't we do something this weekend, since Adam is going to be tied up anyway. Why don't we go somewhere—like a spa."

Jessie's breath left her like a deflating balloon. "A spa? Seriously? I never even paint my nails, Mom. Not that you've probably ever noticed."

She was right.

It was obvious Jessie had no intention of letting this smooth over and be done with. Their problems had been a decade in the making; one spa invitation wouldn't make things right, but Savannah had no idea what to do. She shut the door and went back to her computer to lose herself on the forums.

SHAUN COULDN'T SLEEP. HE'D BEEN staring at the ceiling for over an hour when he finally got up and tiptoed from the bedroom so as not to wake Savannah. She'd told him about her conversation with Jessie, and it had broken his heart to see Savannah so wounded by the realizations she'd come to. He'd been unable to answer her, however, when she'd asked why he'd never said anything to her about her attitude.

"We've been doing this for ten years and you never once told me I was turning into a prima donna. Why didn't you stop me, speak some sense into me?"

He'd squirmed beneath her stare, unwilling to confront his own shortcomings. He already had enough to hate himself for. He'd made up some excuse about not wanting to encroach on her personal approach to ministry, but she hadn't bought it. Thankfully she hadn't pushed him for a better answer.

Sure, maybe he should have challenged her more in regards to Jessie's and her relationship — but what did he know about mothers and daughters? He'd been raised in a houseful of boys. When Jessie had been born, dads at church with daughters had warned him of the teen years. He'd just assumed a rocky relationship was par for the course. And the few times he'd spoken up on Jessie's behalf, Savannah had countered with what sounded to him like a perfectly reasonable excuse for whatever it was she'd said or done to send Jessie crying to him.

He sympathized with Jessie's frustration; he just wished she had picked a different weekend to dump all this on Savannah. She had enough on her mind without facing the damage she'd done to her daughter. But trying to untangle it now was not going to make her any more confident in writing that book, and that book *needed* to get written. They needed the advance. Jessie's tuition bill was past due; he'd written a letter to the financial department asking for grace given the unexpected financial hardship they were facing, but he hadn't heard back yet on whether or not they would be willing to give him some more time.

What frustrated him more was that Savannah wasn't even trying to write the book. Twice he'd snuck a peek on her laptop to see
if she'd started the manuscript, but found no new documents in
the word processing program. The file for the outline hadn't been
opened in weeks.

He sat in his office with the lights out, staring at the moon and
trying to figure out how to get that book done. Maybe he could
hire a ghost writer. It would kill him to have to split the advance,
but part of an advance would be better than none at all. Savannah
could just write out notes, rather than having to worry about craft-
ing them into something readable; maybe she could go through the
finished manuscript and add her own touches here and there so it
sounded more like her voice. All it really needed was her name on
the front to be a bestseller.

And if they arranged a small book tour to promote it—just ten
cities, perhaps, to guard her from exhaustion and overexertion—
they'd really be in the clear. That would bring in all they needed,
certainly. Savannah could sell hamburgers to a vegan if given the
chance; she could easily get this book on the top of the New York
Bestseller List if she was able to get in front of people. He knew
how important a personal connection with the author could be in
increasing sales; maybe if they arranged for signings that didn't
include a presentation and held those in other cities—

The light switched on and he let out a yelp of surprise. Savannah
stood in the doorway, looking sheepish. "I'm sorry. I didn't mean
to scare you."

Shaun rubbed a hand over his face as the adrenaline settled.
"That's alright. I was just lost in thought and didn't hear you
come in."

"It's two in the morning. You're not still working, are you?"

"No, just couldn't sleep. Figured I'd come in here rather than
risk waking you up."

She sat in the chair across from his desk. "What's on your
mind?"

Had he been thinking, he wouldn't have answered the way he did. But instead he made the mistake of being honest. "I was thinking about your book. Maybe we should hire a ghost writer, just to take some of the pressure off you."

"A ghost writer? Are you serious? What—you think I can't write anymore?"

"No, Van, it's not that at all. Just, like I said, to help take the pressure off. I don't doubt your ability, but I've seen how difficult it's been for you to get going on it. We have a lot riding on this one; we have lots of bills to pay. The sooner we get it done, the better."

She waved her hand. "That's what savings are for, Shaun. I know you like to have that safety net; this is when it's okay to dip into it."

"Well, between the medical bills and Jessie's tuition, our savings aren't going to cut it." He knew better than to tell her they had none.

"So this is all on me then? It's up to me to save us, is that what you're saying? Ha—no pressure or anything."

He winced at the bitterness in her tone. "No, Van, that's not how I meant it. I'm just saying that ... that God brought you this contract. He's trying to provide a means for us to deal with these expenses, but we need to do our part."

"You mean *I* have to do *my* part, as in, this is all on me—just like I said." She crossed her arms, her expression steely. "So God throws an 'opportunity' at me and I don't have a choice? I just have to take it? What if I don't want it?"

"What do you mean, 'throws' an opportunity at you? You started the book on your own; it's not like God was twisting your arm. If you didn't want to write it you shouldn't have told your agent about it."

She pushed herself to her feet. "Well, regardless, I don't feel like dealing with God and his opportunities right now."

Shaun was confused. "What does that mean?"

But she was already halfway out the door, and if she heard him, she didn't let on.

He stared at the doorway with his mouth hanging open. What was that about? He knew writing books wasn't always her favorite thing to do — it was too solitary a task, and she hated the time it took away from relating face-to-face with people. But she knew it was part and parcel with being a speaker, and had always managed to soldier her way through the process anyway. Why was this book any different?

He certainly couldn't go to bed now; he didn't want to risk running into a steaming Savannah. He woke his computer, planning on returning a few emails he'd been putting off, but when he opened the program his mouth turned to cotton. Another email from her sat in the inbox. Fear won out and he closed the program without looking at the message. That was the last thing he wanted to think about. He'd read it tomorrow.

Maybe.

WHAT'S THAT AXIOM ABOUT THE best-laid plans? Or, even better — Man plans, God laughs. Well, if he's laughing at this then he's pretty cruel.

Those were the thoughts in Jessie's head as Adam drove them back to school Sunday night. The weekend had been an absolute disaster. All her self-analyzing and resolutions aimed at improving things with Savannah had flown right out of her head during their first conversation. It was as though her mouth worked on autopilot. She hadn't really wanted to fight, but the accusations came almost without her thinking them. *Years of practice, I suppose. An unfortunate form of muscle memory.*

She'd kept herself out of sight for the rest of the weekend, spending as much time at Adam's as she could. They needed the extra hands anyway, and it wasn't like she was needed at home. Her dad worked most of the time, even on the weekend, and all her mother did was sit around on the computer — a new hobby, apparently. Jessie wondered if Savannah enjoyed the anonymity of internet forums as much as she did. She had actually been really curious about the forum Savannah was on, and would have liked to have talked with her about it. For once they had something in common. But she'd wrecked any chance of that with her opening salvo. *Old habits die hard. Another fitting cliché.*

She'd just finished unpacking when her cell rang. Shaun's name was on the screen. "Hey, Dad."

"Hey yourself. Back at school?"

"Yeah, just a bit ago."

"Didn't get to see you much this weekend."

Guilt tugged at her gut. "Yeah, I know. Adam's family needed some help."

"Well, I'm glad you could help them out. But I was hoping we'd get a chance to talk. I, um, heard you and your mother had an interesting conversation."

Her defenses rose. "We talked, yes."

"Sounds more like you ranted."

"Seriously? You're going to judge our whole conversation just from her view? That's not fair."

"I don't really think it matters whose view it's from, your mother doesn't deserve to be called self-centered."

"Even when it's true?"

"Your mother is *not* self-centered. She's focused."

"Semantics, Dad."

"Mind your tone, Jessie."

She winced. "Sorry. But really, Dad, it's not like I haven't told you this stuff before. She just ... I don't know. And honestly, I was trying so hard to be agreeable, but it's like my brain has these ruts from years of us butting heads, and the minute she says something that rubs me the wrong way I fall right into them and can't get out. I end up arguing even though I don't want to. Believe me—" She swallowed back the lump that was forming in her throat. "I don't want to fight with her. I don't. And I really do want for us to get along. But it's like it doesn't matter what I do; it's not gonna happen."

His voice was softer when he spoke. "I understand, sweetheart. And I'm glad to hear that you're trying and that you want things to change. They will. Change is hard, especially when the old way of doing things is so ingrained. Keep working at it, keep praying for a change of heart—it'll come."

"Thanks."

"You're welcome. And in the meantime, I think an apology would be a good idea."

Her jaw dropped. "What?"

"You were pretty disrespectful, Jessie. And your mom is having a hard enough time right now."

"Is she going to apologize to me?"

"Should we only apologize when we're receiving an apology as well?"

"No, but that's not the point."

"Don't worry about what your mother does or doesn't do. Just do what *you* need to do."

Anger made the tears start. "Yeah, I'll think about it. Gotta go. Bye." She ended the call and choked back a sob of frustration. This was not how she'd wanted to end her weekend.

She dialed Angie's number. "Talk me down."

"Uh oh. What happened?"

"Mom and I had a fight and Dad is totally taking her side and insisting I apologize, even though *she* isn't going to apologize, as usual."

"Oy. Details?"

Jessie laid out the conversation, sniffing her way through it and hating how hard it was to talk while crying.

"I'm so sorry, Jess," Angie said when she finished her story. "I totally get why you're so upset. But I think your dad is right."

"What?!"

"Put on the big-girl panties and apologize. You know, that whole fifth commandment thing about honoring your parents."

"I can't believe you're siding with my dad."

"Oh, come on, Jess, you know I'm not siding with anyone. I really do get how angry you are, and I totally agree that your mom was out of line. But seriously, if you're wanting to make things better with you guys and break out of the pattern you're stuck in, then this is a good way to do it."

Jessie rubbed her eyes and sniffed. "I hate it when you're right."

Angie chuckled. "Sorry."

"I just ... seriously, I feel like it's all a lost cause. She's never going to change. And I know I really tried only once to make things better, but I feel like it's always going to be an uphill battle and that it's not going to work in the end anyway, so why keep trying?"

"That's uncharacteristically pessimistic of you."

"I know. But I can't help it."

"Keep praying about it."

Jessie sniffed again. "Yeah, I know. Hey, I gotta run. Dinner ends in twenty minutes and I haven't eaten yet."

"Okay, keep me posted."

"Will do." Jessie ended the call and mopped up her face with a tissue. She knew Angie was right, but she also felt like it was all for naught. It wasn't like she hadn't tried in the past to make things better. What had she been thinking? It hadn't worked then, and she had no reason to think it would work now.

She thought about her life in ten years, about having her own children and what their relationship with Savannah would be like. Would Savannah treat them any differently? If she didn't change, Jessie didn't want to subject them to the same kind of subtle and not-so-subtle criticism that she'd lived with. And Savannah's criticism of her wouldn't suddenly end—it would just shift from her personal choices to her child-rearing choices. She'd read posts on the mothering forum about how some of those moms had to deal with their own parents butting in when it came to discipline and parenting and how damaging it was, to the point where they'd chosen to limit, or cut out altogether, the time their children spent with their grandparents. Granted, other circumstances were often at play that Jessie didn't have to worry about—past abuse, mental health issues—but the thought of having the stress and arguments out of her life sure sounded appealing.

Though that would mean Mom was out of my life as well. That wasn't possible without something extreme happening, and almost losing her mother had shown her she didn't *really* want that. But if the expectation of seeing her as often as she currently did was removed, Jessie had a feeling she'd be a lot happier.

Her stomach rumbled. Tossing the tissue to the trash, she rolled off the bed and onto her feet. Out of habit she began to text Adam about meeting her for dinner, then erased the message. Better to eat alone. She had some thinking she had to do.

SAVANNAH WAS JUST OVER THREE weeks past her transplant when Shaun finally convinced her to come in to A&A and see everyone. "You haven't been there in four months," he reminded her. "These people are like our family. They miss you. And as their leader, you really should reconnect with them, even if it's just a brief drop-in."

Guilt was the only thing motivating her to go. She knew it was bad form not to at least go and say thank you in person—their cards and flowers had filled her room at the hospital, and they'd provided meals and encouragement for Shaun throughout her post-op hospitalization. But save for her frequent doctor visits, she hadn't left the house since coming home, and the idea of being out in public—exposed to germs and feeling like a freak show on display, not to mention interacting with people—felt monumental.

She stood in her closet and surveyed her wardrobe. She'd been living in pajamas and sweats, and now none of her normal clothes appealed to her at all. All the jewel-toned pantsuits and blouses looked gaudy—why hadn't she noticed that before? She flipped through the hangers until she found a simple white blouse and a faded pair of jeans. She couldn't remember the last time she'd worn either one, and they weren't the most interesting ensemble. But at least it didn't make her look like a limelight-seeking attention hog.

She pulled on the blouse and tried to button it, but it wouldn't fit across her stomach. Frowning, she pulled on the jeans, but came nowhere near close to being able to button them. She yanked them both off and stared at herself in the full-length mirror behind the door. She hadn't taken a good look at her body since well before her illness, and she was stunned to see how different she looked. It wasn't just the red line that bisected her body from neck to navel, though that was disturbing in and of itself. It was the way she had filled out—or, more accurately, swollen. She'd been warned of this side effect of one of her medications, and had put away her wedding and engagement rings the previous week when she noticed how difficult it had become to remove them. But her roomy pajamas had hidden the truth, and she'd excused the tightness of her yoga pants and T-shirts as being the result of not exercising regularly like she had before her illness. But this was not just muscle going to flab. This was honest to goodness weight gain. A lot of it.

She pulled another pair of jeans from a drawer and tried them on. No luck. She tried an elastic-waisted pair of slacks, though they were technically too heavy for the September heat. No luck again. She began to panic. She hadn't been more than a size 8 since having Jessie.

Jessie! She pulled on her robe and went into Jessie's room. Surely she hadn't taken all her clothes with her to college. She opened the closet and breathed a sigh of relief. Not much was there, but certainly something here would fit. Jessie had inherited her father's bigger bones and owned mostly 10's and 12's.

Savannah found a pair of jeans with a rip in the knee and pulled them on with figurative fingers crossed. *Bingo!* Encouraged, she took a little time to see what else was there. Her daughter's style definitely ran more towards the outdoorsy Coloradan side of the spectrum than Savannah's smart businesswoman attire. She now found herself drawn to the subdued, natural colors that Jessie favored—slate blues, hunter greens, grays, and browns. She selected a long-sleeved T-shirt in a mossy color and reveled in how comfortable it was. She'd have to get some of these. She looked dressed for October more than September, but at least the clothes fit. And maybe the extra warmth would help with the perpetual chill in her chest.

THE DRIVE TO A&A FELT longer than it used to. She found herself wishing something would happen to divert them. It used to be that she loved going in, chumming around with the women, taking everyone out for an impromptu coffee break. Being there always made her feel like she was a part of something bigger than herself.

But when she walked into the office now, that feeling eluded her. Instead, as everyone dropped their work to smother her with "Welcome back" and "We missed you so much," she saw things as though the veneer had been sanded off: how needy they were for her approval, how desperate to please her, how they ignored Shaun in favor of kissing up to her despite the fact that he really ran things. Even the decor struck her wrong—the cheesy Scripture-laden prints in poster frames on the wall, the plastic plants in the corner, the depressing gray cubicles. She couldn't believe she'd ever felt at home here.

"I'll be in my office," Shaun said with a smile that looked forced and left her to handle the staff on her own. Only Marisa appeared to be unfazed by her return. They hadn't had a true conversation yet, however, and Savannah was nervous about being alone with her. Savannah had often joked that Marisa knew her better than Shaun—but now she felt like no one knew her, not even herself.

After a few minutes Marisa was the one who stepped in and said, "Let's not overwhelm her—plus she has to be mindful of germs, since her meds suppress her immune system. Right?"

Grateful for Marisa's cautious thinking, Savannah nodded. "Yes, right, exactly—to ward off the possibility of rejection." It was her most cherished excuse these days. Why else would she avoid her own ministry for so long, or skip church Sunday after Sunday?

The others fell back like chastised children, and Marisa led her by the elbow to the front door. "Let's go get some coffee and go over some things."

Savannah was grateful for the rescue, though she didn't really want to go talk, either. She wasn't sure which would be worse: to be one-on-one with Marisa and have her seeing right through her, or to stay at A&A and have the rest of her staff nipping at her heels like hungry puppies. She followed Marisa to her car and tried not to look as conflicted as she felt.

Marisa wasted no time. The car was barely out of the parking lot when, voice tinged with concern, she asked, "So what's up with you? It's like you got a personality transplant with that heart."

Savannah's heart sank. Not even any small talk before digging in. She tried to put her off, though she knew it was only a matter of time before Marisa figured everything out. "What on earth are you talking about?"

"You're one of the most social people I've ever met, but it looked in there like you were about to have a panic attack."

"That's not how I felt," Savannah lied.

"Then how did you feel?"

Marisa might be her closest friend, but that didn't mean Savannah was ready to fully open up about the doubts and fear and inexplicable anger that were eating her up inside. "I don't feel like myself anymore," she finally offered.

Marisa nodded, eyes on the road. "That's understandable. Regardless of the physical effects of having a new heart, I can imagine the mental and emotional impact would be pretty profound."

"Yes, exactly." Savannah appreciated the refreshing lack of Christianese platitudes in Marisa's response. "I didn't expect this. They told me I might be depressed, but I'm not. I'm ..." She hesitated, not wanting to reveal too much about how she seemed to have changed. "I'm sure it'll all settle down eventually and I'll be back to the old Savannah."

Marisa gave her a sidelong look but said nothing.

They went to their usual coffee hangout, where Marisa presented Savannah with an impressive and overwhelming backlog of mail. Together they crafted responses for the various kinds of letters — a thank you message for those sending notes of encouragement and prayers for her recovery, gentle letters of decline to those asking her to come speak to their church/women's ministry/mom's ministry — then Savannah signed bookplates requested by readers. They weren't there long, but it was enough time for Savannah to feel like she could handle going back into the fray at A&A without snapping. Marisa said nothing else about how she had changed, though Savannah knew she wouldn't drop the subject completely. Maybe the next time she asked Savannah would be ready to open up.

After finishing their business, Marisa gave Savannah an almost shy look. "I wanted to talk to you about something — but I feel badly bringing it up."

She groaned inside. "Why? What is it?"

"Well . . ." Marisa plucked invisible lint from her skirt. "I'm feeling really conflicted about something. Normally I'd come straight to you to hash it out, but my frustrations feel so petty compared to what you're going through."

Savannah let out a genuine laugh. "Marisa, I can't tell you how nice it would be to think about someone else's problems for a while. Not that I'm glad you've got them, of course. But seriously, your issues are no less important to you just because I've got my own thing going on. Spill it."

Marisa chuckled. "Okay, good." She took a deep breath and blew it out slowly before starting. "Well, here's the deal. The time I was in New York with Jeremy was amazing. I never thought I'd love that city, but I'm really starting to. And things with Jeremy . . . they're so wonderful when we're actually in the same time zone. This long-distance thing is really starting to get hard." She stilled her fidgety hands in her lap and finally made eye contact with Savannah. "He wants to marry me."

Savannah smiled. "That's wonderful! Right?"

Marisa smiled, looking slightly less nervous. "Yes, it's wonderful. But definitely not doable while we're still so far apart. Neither of us can just up and transfer our jobs. I *could* find work out there, but I don't want to just leave you and A&A. I mean, this is so much more than just a job to me — you're my friend, this is my ministry ..." She sighed. "I'm feeling really stuck."

Savannah nodded slowly as the words sunk in. Marisa had been her closest friend for years now — it was hard to imagine life without her. Not even Shaun knew some of the things about her that Marisa did. But if Marisa moved, it would mean one less person she had to try to fool into thinking she was the same person she'd always been — and Marisa would be the hardest of them all to keep in the dark.

"Listen, Marisa — if you love this man, and he loves you, then you need to do whatever needs to be done to make sure you don't lose this opportunity. And if that means leaving A&A and moving on to New York, I'm okay with that."

Marisa blinked. "You — you are?"

"Yes, I am. This might be ... confirmation, you might say, that things are going to be changing for me, in terms of ministry. And I'm okay with that."

"Oh." Marisa shook her head, eyes wide with surprise. "I wasn't expecting that. Thank you for being so understanding. I really can't imagine leaving, but maybe this is God's way of confirming that Jeremy and I really are meant to be together."

"Ah, yes, there you go."

"Still ..." Marisa frowned. "It's hard to imagine. You and I are so close, and this ministry means so much to me ..." She looked to Savannah. "Would you mind praying for me?"

Savannah was taken aback. "What, now?"

Marisa gave her a puzzled smile. "If you don't mind. Just for some peace and clarity."

"Oh ... sure." Savannah closed her eyes as Marisa did, scrambling for the words to say.

It was then she realized she hadn't prayed once since the surgery.

She fumbled through what she hoped was a coherent prayer that wouldn't make Marisa think she'd lost her mind. But if Marisa was concerned, she didn't say anything, and they drove back to A&A without much conversation. Savannah thought back over the weeks, sure she was forgetting something, but no, she really hadn't prayed. She'd *tried*, but only a handful of times, and always unsuccessfully. She wasn't sure what concerned her more — the fact that she hadn't prayed, or the fact that she hadn't noticed.

Once back at the office Marisa went to work on the letters, leaving Savannah to sit and chat with Brenda at the front desk and with whatever other staff members came up to talk to her. Thankfully the excitement of her return seemed to have worn off, though nearly everyone came to her for just a moment to give a hug and offer once more to help however they could. The one exception was Adam's mother, Ginny. Savannah and Ginny had developed a comfortable bond since their children had begun to date, and while they didn't often spend much time together, they always got along like friends and not just friendly co-workers. Ginny came over and gave Savannah a hug, then said, "Could we talk for a minute, maybe outside?"

They went out into the sunshine and walked down a couple storefronts to a bench that sat outside a used bookstore. "I wasn't sure if I should bring this up or not," Ginny finally said. "But I just keep getting this troubled feeling and didn't feel right not saying something."

Savannah swallowed hard. "Alright," she said, feeling suddenly on the defensive. Her mind raced to think of where this conversation might be going.

Ginny took a deep breath. "Well, some of us are a little worried. We feel like maybe we're not getting the whole story on how A&A is doing, financially speaking. Brenda talked to Nick after he was let go, and he said Shaun made him sign a confidentiality notice, so he couldn't say much, but he hinted at A&A's financial situation as playing a part in why he was terminated. But whenever someone asks Shaun about our outlook he makes it sound like we're firmly in the black and have nothing to worry about. Now, maybe Shaun just doesn't want to worry us before there actually is a problem, but if there's the potential for the ministry to go under I need to start looking for a new position sooner rather than later. You know how it is with Carl on disability."

It took a minute for Ginny's words to sink in. Once they did, Savannah's blood began to boil. "Wait a minute. Nick was fired?"

"Last month, yes."

"Because of our finances?"

"That's what Shaun told him, apparently. Shaun didn't actually tell anyone about any of it, which I thought was a little weird." She shrugged. "But it wasn't really my business, so I didn't say anything."

Savannah didn't know what to say. "He probably just didn't want to worry me with the details," she finally said. "A month ago . . . that would have been right before the surgery."

"That makes sense. And I doubt Shaun would lie to us — what reason would he have? So I'm sure everything is fine. But the appearance of double talk is troubling some people. If things really are okay, I think it would ease a lot of minds to hear you say it. If it comes from you, they'll believe it."

Savannah cringed. That was just the kind of pressure she did not need right now.

She placated Ginny with a promise to talk to Shaun, then followed her back into the building and made a beeline for Shaun's office. She shut the door and glared at him. "You fired Nick."

Shaun's jaw clenched and she could practically see the wheels turning in his head. She didn't give him a chance to respond before launching her own assault. "I told you how I felt, and you not only completely disregarded my wishes but then lied to him about why he was being let go! The staff knows something isn't right; Nick hinted to Brenda that it had to do with A&A's financial health, so now they're all panicked that we're going to shut our doors and they'll be left out in the cold. What is wrong with you?"

"Look, I had no solid evidence that he was stealing. I couldn't confront him with that and risk being slapped with a wrongful termination suit. But I really felt like that's what God was telling me to do. I think we dodged a bullet here."

Savannah scoffed in disbelief. "If God was telling you that, then why didn't he tell me?" She shook her head, eyes riveted on Shaun who seemed to wilt somewhat under her scrutiny. "You're lying, either to your staff or to your wife. Neither one is good."

She didn't press him to admit who was getting the wrong story, though. Instead, she took his keys from the corner of the desk. "I'm leaving. Call when you want a ride home." With a brief wave to Brenda she left the building, then started for home, seething.

Her thoughts were racing. What was Shaun hiding? And how could he do it in such a small organization, when everyone was so close? Certainly he hadn't expected to never be found out. She didn't buy his excuse, regardless of what opinion of God's he was trying to invoke. Honestly, it was the comment about God telling him to fire Nick that made her even more doubtful.

But she wasn't far from A&A's campus when she realized that she was as guilty as he. She was harboring her own secrets. And it was the fact that she had her own secrets now — the doubts and anger involving God that got stronger every day — that made her even more worried. She knew just how bad things might get if she admitted how she truly felt.

She was afraid to even imagine what Shaun's secrets might lead to.

CHAPTER 7

IT WAS FRIDAY NIGHT, AND A&A WAS CLOSED FOR THE WEEK-
end. Despite this, Shaun was in his office, the budget printed out
and its pages strewn across his desk. He clutched a highlighter as
he poured over every line item, considering each carefully before
moving to the next. When he found something he could eliminate,
he dragged the squeaky marker over it, relishing the sound. He
hadn't heard it much since starting the exercise.

When he finished going through the budget, he pulled out a
list of the positions held in the ministry. Each description outlined
the responsibilities of that job, and he began to scrutinize each one,
looking for ways to consolidate them. Having Nick gone helped, but
if he could cut at least one more position, he'd easily be able to move
them to a smaller office space.

It was almost eight by the time he locked A&A's doors behind
him. He felt bad for staying late, but it was easier than trying to
mull these issues over at home where Savannah might get nosy
about why he couldn't keep focused on anything. His mind wandered to the issue of money at the slightest provocation these days.
It didn't help that getting the mail every day almost always meant
receiving another bill — mortgage, insurance, utilities, hospital
bills, hospital bills, and more hospital bills. And now on top of that
were Savannah's medications, of which she had a small pharmacy's
worth. Not exactly the kinds of things he could scale back on. He
was doing as much at home as he could to cut costs, but without
Savannah being on board his skimping didn't amount to much. And
he wasn't about to break it to her that they were broke.

The one thing they had going for them was an excellent credit rating, which meant high spending limits on their credit cards. He hadn't been much of a charger before, but he was lately out of sheer necessity. Of course, those bills came calling, too. He knew he could use them only so much before he dug himself into a far deeper hole.

He took the long way home, wanting just a few more minutes alone to think. He really wanted to downsize their home. They didn't need a house this size, especially now that Jessie was essentially gone. But Savannah loved it, loved the neighborhood, the proximity to good shopping. The only cheaper housing options in that area were condos and apartments, neither of which would fly with Savannah. And a move would be out of the question without opening up about just how badly they were in debt, and he just couldn't do it, not yet.

But when?

And on top of the stress was the guilt that squeezed his soul night and day. What kind of man had he become, who did the kinds of things he was doing? A desperate one, certainly. And a weak one. He hated himself a little more every time he fixed the books or messed with receipts.

Shaun felt more and more trapped with every day that passed. But what really scared him were the thoughts of escape that would form out of nowhere. A longing to just be ... gone. It didn't help that his marriage was not what it once was—nor was his wife. He'd thought crises were supposed to bring couples closer together, but this one seemed to be pushing them apart, even though it had a happy ending with Savannah's transplant. But it was the transplant that seemed to be causing all the problems. Ever since, she'd been ... harder. Like some of her Southern upbringing had been removed along with her damaged heart. She was constantly irritable, less gracious, not as warm. He kept hoping it was just part of the emotional flux they were told to expect, or maybe the medication. But what if it wasn't? What if this was who she was now, for good?

It was making working with her—and living with her—a lot more difficult.

SAVANNAH'S DEADLINE WAS TWENTY-FOUR HOURS away. Not that she technically had one, but the subtle pressure to get the book done quickly made it clear her publisher—and Shaun—wanted the book done *now*. For the last three days she had literally locked herself into her office to pound out the project she'd been pushing off and avoiding for the last month. She'd never written her books at home before—usually she took her laptop out somewhere so she was surrounded by people, even if she couldn't afford to stop working to interact with them. But this time she couldn't bear the thought of being recognized. Not just because she didn't have the time to chat, but because she felt like such a fraud, and she was afraid it would be obvious somehow.

When she'd read through the outline she'd been overwhelmed at the topics she'd been trying to address. God's goodness amidst suffering? Taking a "heaven's eye view" of pain? What had she been thinking? Had she really thought she'd be able to speak with authority on topics that scholars still wrestled with? What had made her think she could be at all convincing?

It had been a brutal seventy-two hours as she'd hammered out the text. Trying not to think too much about how thin her arguments appeared to her, she laced the manuscript with platitudes and sayings tweaked just enough to sound original, and leaned heavily on the narrative of her own experience to carry the book. But even the retelling of her revelation before the surgery—which was only slightly drawn-out and embellished—read as trite and unbelievable. And if it sounded that way to the person to whom it had happened, how would it sound to those in the midst of their own struggles?

The end was in sight when Shaun called to tell her he wouldn't be home for supper. She was relieved. She was so close to being done, she hadn't wanted to stop working to try to figure out a meal. She skipped dinner and pushed through, not allowing herself to question the marginally coherent metaphors and shoddy writing that her flying fingers produced. She just wanted the book done.

When she finished the last sentence she almost cried. She didn't care that the book was a fraction of the length of her others and hoped no one else would either. She emailed it to her editor with embarrassment, knowing the quality was nothing compared to her previous books, but the thrill of being done overpowered her regret over the poor quality. When the email was sent, she shoved her chair back from her desk and breathed in deep. She was *done*. Done and feeling almost happy. The chronic edginess abated somewhat with the weight of the book finally off her shoulders. She hadn't felt happy since before her surgery. She needed to do something to celebrate.

She considered the contents of her pantry and fridge. With so much time on her hands these days, she'd begun cooking again, reviving an old hobby that had been forgotten when the demands of A&A grew to a full-time position. She'd pulled out old family recipes a couple weeks ago and started working her way through them. They all needed to be scaled down so she wasn't swimming in leftovers, but even with that challenge she had been enjoying herself in the kitchen. It wasn't just the fun of rediscovering a buried skill that Savannah appreciated as she sautéed and measured. It was the comfort of a decidedly Old Savannah characteristic, of finding a piece of her previous self she could point to and say, "See? I'm still me."

But tonight the thought of recalculating a recipe to serve one instead of eight seemed too laborious. She wanted to be catered to, to sit back and let someone else prep and serve. She also wanted a drink. She hadn't had one in a long time—decades, even. Technically she wasn't supposed to drink alcohol now because of her medication, but one drink wouldn't be the end of the world. The only problem was that getting one would mean going out.

But who knew when Shaun would finally get home? He stayed at A&A so late sometimes that she was on her way to bed by the time he finally got in. She couldn't imagine what was keeping him so long, though honestly she wasn't sure she'd want to go celebrate with him, anyway. Things with Shaun were … not great. It was mostly her own fault, she knew; keeping secrets always resulted in relationships falling apart in one way or another. But she wasn't ready to spill this one, especially not with this book on its way to publication. She had to keep the image up at least until after the book's initial release and publicity push. Maybe after that she'd be able to let Shaun in on the truth. Though the fact that he was keeping his own secrets and that he'd fired Nick behind her back still burned her, too. And yes, she recognized the hypocrisy in being angry at him for keeping secrets, but hypocrisy was low on her list of concerns right now.

She went to Jessie's room to raid her closet again. She wasn't sure where she was going to go, or with whom; she just knew she wanted to get out. She sorted through Jessie's clothes, looking for something that didn't appear too young. She finally paired a blouse with black slacks and topped it off with one of her own vests that didn't have to be fastened closed to still look nice. As she did her makeup she tried to think of someone to call, but she couldn't handle any God talk tonight, and she was bound to get that with all of her friends, the lot of whom she'd dodged as much as possible lately—even to the point of all-out lying just to avoid getting together. By the time she was done with her hair, she had given up on finding a companion and decided instead to just go out alone.

She drove for ten minutes before deciding on the steakhouse she and Shaun had often gone to on date nights. She took a seat at the bar, the first time she'd ever done something like that in her life, and ordered a martini. She kept one eye on the door in case a familiar face walked in as she sipped the drink and willed the knots of tension to undo themselves in her shoulders.

She couldn't remember the last time she'd been alone and enjoyed herself. She'd spent plenty of time alone at home while she'd been sick, but it had been far from pleasant. Since her surgery she'd been alone quite a bit as well, but her thoughts were so tormented by anger and doubt that she'd been miserable pretty much the

whole time. Before getting sick, being alone had been torture—
she'd always wanted to be in a conversation, relating to someone,
engaging with people. Alone had equaled boring. But she found
herself relaxing and reveling in the experience now.

A gentleman in a suit and loosened tie sat down two seats from
her. They exchanged polite smiles, but after he got his drink he
leaned over and said, "I've never been here before—would you recommend any of their appetizers?"

"Oh … well, the shrimp cocktail is good. I've had that a few
times."

He nodded. "That does sound good. I'll try that; thanks."

She gave an approving nod, then went back to people watching
as the stranger ordered from a roving waitress. When she returned
with the appetizer a few minutes later, the man slid the plate down
the bar so it sat between them. "Care to share?"

It took a second for it to sink in that he was flirting with her.
She was about to get indignant when she realized she didn't have
her rings on. *Well, guess I can't blame him, then.* "That's sweet—
thank you. But I really shouldn't."

He tipped his head, a smile playing on his lips. "Are you sure? I
hear they're very good."

She laughed, enjoying the interplay. When had someone last
flirted with her? Decades ago, certainly. Wedding rings had a way
of deterring men—and well they should. But it was nice to know
she could still attract attention, especially given the way the medication had affected her once-trim figure.

"Well … maybe just one." She reached over and plucked a shrimp
from the rim of the glass.

"I'm David."

"I'm, um, Roberta." It was almost true—her middle name was
Robertson, her mother's maiden name. She wasn't about to give this
stranger her real name.

"Are you waiting for someone to join you, Roberta?" His eyes
were very green. She liked them.

"No, actually. Are you?"

"Savannah?"

The familiar voice sent an arrow of adrenaline through her. She straightened up, having been unaware just how close to David she'd been leaning, and saw Colleen and her husband at the front of the bar.

"Colleen, hi." She grabbed her purse and slid from her seat, avoiding eye contact with David. She was shaky with fear. How much had they seen?

"Long time no see, huh?" Colleen asked when Savannah reached them. "Where's Shaun?"

"Oh, he was working late—I finished my book and wanted to celebrate, so I just thought I'd go out for a drink."

"The book is done? That's great, congratulations." She smiled, but Savannah would have sworn she saw a glint in Colleen's eye that hinted at reproach. "Would you like to join us? We just came for some dessert."

"No, but thanks. I should be going anyway—Shaun will prob-ably be home soon." She gave them each a brief hug, then made a beeline for the car, burning with embarrassment.

What had she been thinking? Shame burned in her chest as she drove home. *Stupid, stupid, stupid.*

SAVANNAH LET HERSELF IN TO an empty house when she got back. She had hoped Shaun would be home so she could make herself feel better by doting on him a bit. But no, he was still at work, presum-ably, and that just made her mad. Well, even more mad than she already was.

This new person she was becoming was really making a mess of things. How could she have let herself be so careless—had she for-gotten people recognized her in Colorado Springs? How often did she ever go out without getting stopped by someone, either a friend, or someone from church, or someone who had read her books or seen her at a conference? The Old Savannah never would have made such a rookie mistake, and now one of her closest friends—at least, she used to be—had a good reason to come track her down and start insisting on answers.

And when she did, flanked by the other women and refusing to take the hint that Savannah didn't want to talk, what was she going to tell them? The Old Savannah had been characterized by her faith in God, her passion for ministering to women, and her energetic extroverted personality. They'd never believe her if she admitted she couldn't bear the thought of crowds, couldn't care less about how other women handled their lives, and didn't believe in God.

I don't believe in God ...

She froze before the mirror where she was washing the makeup from her face. It was true. The concept of God meant nothing to her now. She'd been telling herself it was just the depression, the baseless anger, that was clouding her love for God. But if she was brutally honest, her faith was gone.

She scrubbed her face clean and went to her laptop to log into the transplant forum. She started searching for posts about when people started feeling more like themselves. She scanned entry after entry, her heart sinking with each one that touched on the waning of the emotional rollercoaster. This was when most people started to improve, to emerge from the fog of depression or at least notice the depression coming in shorter, less intense spurts. The same seemed to be true for the anger some felt—and their anger was often easily traced to something.

Unlike hers. And hers was not only growing, it was ruling her life.

Savannah shut the laptop and pulled a notebook from her desk drawer. It was the journal where she'd recorded her prayers during the tour. Lists always brought order to her internal chaos—maybe a little self-examination would give her some insights. She flipped a few pages past the last entry and titled the page *Personal Inventory*. It was time to figure herself out.

Anger—why???

God— who is that? I don't even care.

She looked at what she had just written, eyes wide. She never thought she'd think such a thing. And it wasn't just an isolated thought. She hadn't been to church since coming home from the transplant, hadn't cracked open her Bible, hadn't prayed — well, except for that one afternoon with Marisa, but that had been coerced and not at all heartfelt. Frankly, she'd felt ridiculous doing it, as though Marisa had asked her to pray to a stuffed animal.

She took a deep breath, not quite ready to address the implications of revelation, and continued.

Introvert— and it's not that I just don't want to be with lots of people.

She tapped the pen to her chin. She wasn't sure how to end this sentence. It *wasn't* just classic introversion, feeling drained by groups but energized with people one-on-one. It was different somehow. She doodled on the page, letting her mind wander, then had a thought and wrote it down to see if it resonated with her or not.

… it's that I just don't feel like I can trust anyone.

This not only struck a chord, it was the one thing that made sense. Her husband's double-speak to the staff and the way he fired Nick really hurt and worried her. Plus she knew he was hiding something. And who else on this earth was she supposed to be able to trust the most besides her husband?

She stared at the list. It was short, but its effect on her life was both profound and terrifying. What was her life without A&A? Without writing books and doing speaking tours and creating women's ministry curriculum? Without A&A, her life collapsed like a house of cards, and so did Shaun's, and so did the lives of the staff that worked for her. Her faith was the linchpin in a lot of people's plans. And sometime in the last month, it had been pulled.

Panic began to bubble in her gut. She couldn't possibly admit this to anyone. She couldn't let herself be found out, or everything would fall apart. How would they pay their mortgage, Jessie's tuition — heck, how would they put food on the table? Their paychecks were dependent on her now-missing passion for God.

What would she do with her life? What purpose did it have outside that ministry? Surely she was good at something else. But even her college degrees reflected the faith she'd once had. She couldn't very well get a job with a master's in Christian education if she didn't actually believe anything she was teaching.

Would they stay here in Colorado Springs, where you couldn't throw a rock without hitting someone who knew Savannah or A&A in one way or another? How embarrassing would it be to run into Mary, or Brenda?

Would Shaun even stay with her?

What would Jessie think?

She stuffed the notebook back into the drawer and shut it hard, as though the list might come flying out after her. She was tense with fear. Her palms were damp. Her mind was a mess of what if's, each one more desperate and frightening.

And there wasn't a single person in the world she could tell.

SAVANNAH PULLED INTO THE PARKING LOT at A&A and popped another Rolaid. Ever since the night she'd taken a hard look at her new self, she'd had a bout of nervous stomach that she couldn't shake. Having to get back to work wasn't helping.

When Shaun had finally come home that night, he'd laid out a plan that the Old Savannah would have loved. A book launch party at the local bookstore they often partnered with, followed by a ten-city tour starting a week after the book's release. "We'll schedule them four days apart so you have plenty of time to rest," he'd said. "Five in a row, then a break, then five more. You'll be back by December and can take that whole month to rest. Then after that we'll schedule some smaller events with bookstores and churches, just a handful of dates in January and February, then a big push in May. You'll be fine by May, don't you think? The travel won't wear you out; you won't be high risk anymore. So, what do you think?"

He'd looked so excited, so proud of the idea. She'd mustered as much enthusiasm as she could, excusing the lack of effusiveness with how exhausted she was from writing nonstop and not sleeping well. She'd hoped to put off the planning until … well, until Shaun forgot about it, which she knew wouldn't happen. Really, she'd hoped something would come along before plans could be made that would render the whole scheme impossible. But no such luck. Their travel agent agreed to meet them at A&A two days later to plot out the tour.

So here she was. She sucked on the chalky tablet with her head bowed against the steering wheel, knowing no one would interrupt her if it looked like she was praying. In reality she was giving herself a pep talk, psyching herself up for the meeting. *You don't have to look thrilled. Just don't look sick over it. It's time to start contributing again and get your life back. Think of all the people who are depending on you. What other choice do you have?* She sat up straight, checked her hair in the mirror. She could do this. She had done it enough in the past, surely some kind of mental muscle memory would kick in and she'd be able to sail through the whole meeting — *and* the tour. *Don't think about it too much. Just do it. This is your job. It's what you do.*

And this wasn't the time or place to debate just who that "you" was.

Savannah walked into A&A and faked a smile for Brenda. The office repulsed her even more than the first time she'd come back. She walked quickly to the back where the agent was standing beside Marisa's cubicle as they chatted. "Hello ladies," she said, pasting the smile back on. "Why don't we take this down to Dazbog Coffee? I'll treat for lunch when we're done."

It was the kind of thing the Old Savannah would have done, and she could see the light in Marisa's eyes as she agreed. *Yes, that's right, Marisa. I'm back!* What was the saying — fake it 'til you make it? Well, she wouldn't fail from lack of trying.

Once they had their beverages in hand and calendars spread on a coffee shop table, Savannah was able to sit back and let Marisa and the agent do most of the work. Her input was only needed to ensure she had enough time between gigs to relax and that she was in town to meet with her doctors when appointments rolled around. She was glad the details were up to someone else, because even this small amount of planning was making her wish she could pop a handful of antacids. She kept spacing out, distancing herself from the discussion until Marisa would call her back to reality to ask her opinion on something. She tried to be more engaged, but then the panic would begin to rise and she'd have to shut herself down or else risk throwing the calendars to the floor and calling off the whole tour.

They finished just before lunch, and the agent declined the dining invitation in order to prepare for another meeting. "Just you and me, then," she said to Marisa, secretly hoping she'd bow out as well.

"Sounds good. Where to?"

After that morning, she was desperate for something soothing, and her new favorite comfort food was calling her name. "This might sound silly, but how about Village Inn? I'm dying for a slice of strawberry pie."

Small talk held them over until their orders were taken, but then Marisa ruined things. "Confession time, Savannah." Her expression put Savannah on the defensive. "I'm worried about you. I've never seen you so unfocused before. Are you sure you're alright?"

She knew she'd been spacey, but she hadn't realized it had been bad enough to cause concern. How would she ever keep up the facade through the tour if her own assistant kept questioning her?

She decided to let some of the simmering anger that burned daily beneath the surface work for her. "Yes, I was unfocused. I haven't had a decent night's sleep since before the surgery and the medication I'm on makes it hard to focus. Why does everyone seem so convinced something is wrong with me? I don't think anyone understands just how life-altering a transplant is. Of course I'm not the Old Savannah. I'll never be who I was, but that doesn't mean the new me is somehow worse. And it certainly doesn't mean something is *wrong*. This is who I am for now, and who knows how that may change as time goes on. But I really need for everyone to just be okay with that and stop being so blasted concerned all the time."

Marisa blinked, her face a mask of surprise. "I—I'm sorry, Savannah. I didn't know. I never thought of it that way."

Savannah took a deep, calculated breath and sighed, schooling her features to convey weary remorse. "I'm sorry, too, Marisa. I shouldn't have taken that out on you."

"No, no, I understand. Of course you're different, that's to be expected. I should have been more considerate of you and how difficult this must all be."

Savannah waved a hand, as though to erase Marisa's guilt. "Never mind. It's in the past." She smiled. "I think we need some pie, don't you?"

She worked hard to bring some normalcy back to their conversation, to foster the same sense of camaraderie she used to feel when she and Marisa were working together. It would be a very long and uncomfortable tour if she didn't feel comfortable with her traveling companion. She was already going to be miserable from forcing herself to perform for the thousands of women who would show up.

But by the time she finished her pie, she was itching to be alone again—away from people and especially away from Marisa and her concern. Claiming she had a doctor's appointment she needed to get to—a foolproof excuse she was cautious not to overuse—she took Marisa back to A&A rather than lingering over their coffee. "Give me your receipts and I'll file them for you," Marisa said when they pulled in. "That way you can just get going to your appointment."

"That's alright, I need to talk to Shaun a minute anyway. I'll go write them up myself." She followed Marisa in and turned into Shaun's office, which was empty. She poked her head out into the hall and glanced around. "Brenda, is Shaun in?"

"No, I'm sorry. Do you want me to call him for you?"

"No, that's alright." She'd been planning on asking when he'd be home that night, but she had a feeling she already knew the answer.

She pulled her receipts from Dazbog and Village Inn from her purse and sat down at his desk to hunt down a reimbursement form. She was about to start checking his drawers when she saw one of the forms on top of a pile. Her name was at the top.

"Oh, handy." She pulled it off and took a pen from the cup to write in the details, but then her eye caught a line item that looked unfamiliar. Then another.

Why are these under my name? She looked again at the form and wracked her brain. Maybe they were from her and she just didn't remember. Maybe memory loss was also a part of the new Savannah.

She gave up trying to place the expenses and wrote down the day's totals, then paper-clipped the receipts to the form. She'd ask him when he got home. If she was able to stay awake that long.

CHAPTER 8

SHAUN STOOD BESIDE HIS CAR AND TOOK A PICTURE OF THE building so he'd remember it. The Mountain View property was the second office suite he'd looked at that afternoon, but this one gave him a good vibe. It was only two exits further south on the freeway, so it wouldn't require a much farther commute for his staff, and the neighborhood wasn't nearly as sketchy as the first he'd visited. It would shave nearly three hundred dollars off their rent, which was as good as he was going to find. It was quite a bit smaller than their current location, but if he gave up his office for a cubicle, removed the sitting area in the reception space, and doubled up a couple people, they'd be fine. Or he could fire someone else. There *was* someone who wasn't really pulling her weight these days, but unfortunately it was the same person around whom the whole ministry was built.

Another positive was that it was only half an hour from Jessie's campus, and the halfway mark boasted a decent shopping area where they could meet. It was where he was headed now.

He shook hands with the Realtor again, then got back in his car with a smile on his face.

Jessie was already at the Caribou Coffee when Shaun pulled in. He ordered his drink and then joined her at the table she'd chosen by the window. "Well, this is fun, seeing you during the week," he said after giving her a hug. "Good classes today?"

"Totally fascinating, yes." He listened as she told him about her child development lecture. "And I had this huge revelation," she said, her eyes shining. "I just kept thinking, motherhood is so much more than just housework and babysitting. You're a mentor, you're a teacher, you're a nurse, you're a psychologist. And it totally hit me—I don't have to have a career just because I *can*. Being a full-time mother is a huge responsibility; you're responsible for shaping and teaching a person for their whole life. Sure, I'd be able to shape and teach if I taught elementary school, but my influence would be so brief compared to the influence you have as a parent. It really is okay if I want to stay home and be 'just' a mom." She raised her eyebrows, looking uncertain. "Right?"

He chuckled. "Of course. If that's what God is calling you to, then it's absolutely okay. And I'm really happy for you that you're figuring this out. I think you'll make a fantastic "'just" a mom'."

"Thanks." She sipped her drink and rolled her eyes. "I'm so glad *you* get how important this stuff is to me."

"Of course I do." Then he caught her meaning. "But your mom, it's not like she doesn't see the value—"

"No, she just thinks I should be doing something else. The stuff I want to do is never what *she* wants me to do. It's like she has this idea of who she thinks I'm supposed to be, but rather than just come out and say, 'I think you'd make a great XYZ,' she just shoots down everything I like and expects me to read her mind or something."

Shaun winced, knowing how accurate the description was. "There's a reason for that, Jessie." And he really wished Savannah had just come out and explained it to Jessie years ago—it might have saved them all a lot of heartache. "Your mom was raised in a culture that had a very narrow idea of what women should do and be. Anything outside of that was supposedly unbiblical. And she sees you moving toward teaching, which was the only career option she was allowed to consider outside of motherhood, and she's afraid you're going to short-change yourself; with your skills and talents you could go so many other directions."

"But I'm not short-changing myself if that's what I'm meant to be, right? So why can't she see that?" She took a sip of her drink, then set it down with a look of worry. "Oh, my gosh. She feels shortchanged because she had me, doesn't she? She didn't want to be a mom, is that it?"

"Oh, Jessie—no, that isn't true at all. A&A was born out of her experiences as a mother; she never would have had the ministry without you."

Jessie let out a snort. "That's a bit twisted, given how much that ministry short-changed *me* out of a mom." She gave Shaun a small grin. "You should have at least given me a sibling so I would have had someone to commiserate with—and someone else to help bear Mom's expectations."

"Well, we tried."

"Eww, Dad. Gross."

"No, no. I mean, your mom was pregnant, two other times. But she miscarried both times."

Jessie's eyes got wide. "Seriously? Why didn't anyone ever tell me this?"

"Your mom took it really hard. She was absolutely devastated. I don't think she's ever really gotten over it."

Jessie's face fell. "Well now I feel bad."

"Don't, honey. You couldn't have known. Anyway, that's when she started writing her first book, to help her process the grief of that second loss. And things just took off from there. It's not like she woke up one day and thought, 'I'm going to build a nationally known ministry!' She just had this idea for a book and wanted to use it to reach out to all the other women who were dealing with the same frustrations and confusions and fears that she had. And when it got bigger and bigger, she had no role model to look to for how to balance a job and motherhood. It just wasn't done in her family, or in the culture she grew up in. So she did the best she could, and she screwed up, because that's what parents do. She didn't want to push you toward teaching and motherhood the way she was pushed, but she went too far in the other direction and tried to push you into a big career so you wouldn't think teaching and motherhood were your only options. That's parenthood for you: you learn from the mistakes of your parents and try not to pass those on, but then you end up making other mistakes instead. The best you can do as a kid is recognize your parents aren't perfect and realize that you do in fact have your own opinion and destiny."

Jessie was quiet for a moment, stirring her blended mocha with her straw. "So what mistakes did your parents make?"

Shaun chuckled. "My dad was an absent professor type, minus the intellect and education. Frankly, he was a bit of a laughingstock. He'd dream up all sorts of schemes and try to patent them or sell them to companies, rather than apply himself to a steady job. So we were poor and our family was looked down on, and I grew up wanting to make sure my own family never felt like that."

Jessie smiled. "So, off I'll go into my own life to screw up my own kids in my own unique way."

He laughed. "Yes, exactly."

"Maybe I ought to charge you for the therapy I end up needing."

"Hey, if the money's there I'll gladly pay it." His heart ached as he said the words, knowing the chances were slim to none that he'd be able to pay for the rest of her semester, much less therapy.

They talked for a while more, but Shaun was only half there, his thoughts having been turned once again to money. He called the Realtor the minute he was back in his car. "I know we had other places on the list to look at," he said, "but I don't want to waste any time. I'll take the Mountain View suite."

SAVANNAH HAD BEEN HIDING OUT at home for the last few days. She knew it was silly—what were the chances, really, of running into David?—but since she had no real reason to go out anyway, she let herself cater to her irrational fear. But it had been four days already, and even a now-raging introvert had to get out of the house some time. Besides, she needed new clothes.

Once parked at the mall, she cinched one of Shaun's hats to a smaller size and pulled it low over her eyes, just to be safe. She headed on auto-pilot for Nordstrom's, then found herself balking as it came into view. She had grown fond of the comfortable long-sleeved T's and jeans she'd been borrowing from Jessie. The thought of going back to pantsuits made her twitchy.

She found a directory and scanned the list of stores, then found what she wanted and made her way to the next floor. She smiled when the Eddie Bauer came into view. The first rack of women's clothing she came to had thick wool sweaters that beckoned to her. She went slowly around the store, selecting things on a comfort scale rather than by the look it created. By the time she was ready to check out, she had enough clothing to last her a week.

She got in the line, which was moving slowly; soon there were people behind her. Suddenly she heard, "Savannah Trover? Is that you?"

Every muscle tensed. She turned and saw a woman she thought she recognized from church — what was her name again? "Oh hey, hi there."

"I thought that was you. How are you feeling?"

"Pretty well, thanks."

"Oh, I'm so glad. We were all so worried about you when all that heart business happened." She leaned in and her voice dropped a couple notches. "You know, I heard the other day that things weren't going so well for you and Shaun. Is everything alright? Is there anything we can do for you?"

Savannah hoped her fear wasn't plain on her face. She and Shaun were hardly out together anymore; who would have witnessed the way they could occupy close quarters without even interacting? "Not going well? What do you mean?"

"Well . . ." The woman looked uncomfortable and Savannah's irritation grew. "I'd heard you were out on the town with someone—"

"Oh, good Lord." The woman's eyebrows shot up, but Savannah was too mad to apologize. "I was *not* out on the town with anyone. I went out to get some dinner, I was by myself, and I got into a conversation with someone because it was more pleasant than sitting alone. That was it. And you can tell whoever you heard that from that they should be more careful about how they talk about other people."

"Next please."

Savannah turned her back on the woman and set her clothes on the counter, thoughts spinning. What if Shaun got wind of this? Who else had seen her that night? Colleen wouldn't have been the one to spread such a rumor—would she? Or was it the work of some busybody who happened to be in the right place at the right time?

She took her bag and headed for her car, her head not even turning to check out the window when she passed Ann Taylor. Divorce rumors—just what they needed. It looked like, one way or another, she was going to be responsible for the downfall of A&A.

She got in her car and pounded a fist on the steering wheel. How could she have been so stupid? What had she been thinking, going out alone like that? She hadn't dined out alone once since getting married, and this was one of the reasons why. She had to be above reproach for her ministry; she had to get back out there and be as normal as possible so people didn't get any ideas. It didn't matter if she thought God was a joke; she had a family to support, employees depending on her to bring in their income, and she had to do whatever it took—like the book tour—to make sure she didn't let them down.

She heaved a sigh and stashed her bag in the backseat, then headed back to the mall. She was going to need some new pantsuits. And after that she was going home, getting her laptop, and going to a coffee shop to work on her book tour talk. She was going to give her audience what they were expecting, even if it killed her.

SAVANNAH DROPPED HER LAPTOP BAG to the floor and allowed herself to collapse on the couch. Shopping and writing had drained her—yet another reality she never would have expected to encounter. Even though writing had always been difficult, doing it in public had always made it fun, and the conversations that broke up her time were always energizing. And shopping? Once upon a time it had been like a hobby. Now she felt like she could crawl into bed and not come out for a month.

After a catnap she brought her bags upstairs, then sat on the floor of the closet and cut the tags off her new clothes, frowning at each one. When was the last time she'd purchased anything larger than a size 8? Or anything that didn't say "Dry Clean Only" on the care label? Only her new blue pantsuit required that. Shaun would be glad to know her new wardrobe would need less maintenance. He was so edgy about money these days.

She was craving a piece of strawberry cake. *Who would have guessed chocolate would ever be replaced?* Yet another little quirk that separated her from her old self. It seemed that every day revealed yet another change that made her stop and wonder, or brought a new thought she never would have come up with before. At this rate she'd be a completely different person by the time her transplant anniversary rolled around. Either that or she'd be committed somewhere as being insane.

These were the weird little things no one told you about when you got a transplant. She didn't even see people on the forum talking about it. And because of that, she was afraid to bring it up. What if the surgery had triggered something psychological? What if she really was going crazy?

Or what if she truly was becoming another person? Could that really happen? What would that mean for her marriage, her relationship with Jessie? She chuckled to herself as she dropped another tag into the trash. That was the one relationship that might actually benefit from her being someone else. She and Jessie had nowhere to go but up.

But Shaun ... he'd married the Old Savannah. He hadn't banked on that woman waking up one day and being fundamentally different. Could she really expect him to stay with her? Could anyone fault him for wanting out?

She stood and heaved the mound of clothing into the laundry

basket, then pulled on her pajamas and crawled into bed. The stories she'd read and heard about transplant patients always made it sound like their lives started fresh after their surgery. No one ever talked about their life falling apart. But that was what was happening. She couldn't control the changes she was experiencing, and she couldn't figure out how to go back to being who she was. And she didn't want this new self any more than Shaun would. So where did that leave her?

SHAUN BRACED HIMSELF AS HE eased open the door and poked his head into the kitchen. It was dark, the sink empty, no smells of food. The tension in his shoulders remained as he cased out the lower level. All was silent, and he suspected Savannah may already be asleep. He heaved a deep breath and went back to the kitchen to fix himself a quick dinner before going to bed himself.

Ever since he'd realized Savannah had added receipts to his doctored reimbursement form, Shaun had lived in perpetual fear, just waiting for the day she'd confront him on it. So far she had not done anything to indicate that she'd noticed, but he wasn't about to let down his guard. It made him even more reluctant to come home in the evenings, and he'd taken to killing time in the empty office or at the library just to avoid any unnecessary face time.

After dinner, which he ate with one ear listening for signs of life upstairs, he decided to turn in and get up early so he could be out of the house before Savannah awoke. When he went to the closet to get his pajamas, he saw unfamiliar clothes in the laundry basket. He pulled out a few pieces—a plain dark green long-sleeved T-shirt, a pair of cargo pants. It was the kind of clothing he saw on Jessie, not Savannah. They smelled new. *She actually bought this stuff?*

I wonder how much it all cost...

He tried not to begrudge her the shopping trip. He hadn't said anything, but she had definitely gained weight thanks to the prednisone, and he knew she wasn't wearing Jessie's old clothes these days just for the heck of it. For someone who had always been so careful about her appearance, she was probably really bothered by the weight gain.

Or maybe she wasn't. Who could predict Savannah's reaction to anything these days?

At least she'd gone out. She'd been staying awfully close to home lately. He'd almost asked her, twice, why she wasn't at least going for a walk and getting the exercise her doctor recommended, but he'd stopped himself. He didn't feel like it was his business—didn't feel like he knew her well enough anymore to ask questions like that.

It was just one more bit of evidence that Savannah was not who she once was. He'd expected some depression, maybe some anxiety over getting sick. He'd known to watch for exhaustion, for overexertion when she tried to do things she'd been able to do without a problem before. Tammy had prepped them both well for those kinds of changes. But he hadn't expected her to suddenly turn into some hermit, or to come home from the mall with a wardrobe more suited to camping than to public speaking. He hadn't expected the loss of grace, both in movement and attitude. The bluntness, the brooding, the lack of focus. Or the anger. Even when she was engaged in a completely neutral activity—eating dinner, brushing her teeth—she had a furrow in her brow and a narrowness in her eyes. People who didn't know her well probably wouldn't see it, and he wondered if Marisa had even picked up on it. It was subtle, but clearly evident to him—as was the prickly energy that seemed to emanate from her like radiant heat.

She wasn't the woman he'd married. It was eerie, like an alien takeover of her body. She looked basically the same, save for the weight and the clothes. But when she talked, it was like a ventriloquist was throwing her voice and putting words in her mouth. When would it stop? When would she go back to being the sparkly, energetic, *happy* Savannah he'd always loved?

And what would happen if she didn't?

He didn't like to think about that, and not just because he'd never imagined being in a place where he'd actually consider a divorce. He didn't like to think about it because he was scared at how relieved the thought of divorce made him feel.

Jessie used to be able to sneak home and back to school without anyone knowing she'd been there. Not that she did it often, or really had any reason to—other than avoiding Savannah. But these days it was impossible to stop in undetected. Savannah was always there. Jessie had a feeling she'd spent more time in their house since her transplant than she had all the years before that put together. She didn't get it. Savannah usually went stir crazy after a day inside. Two solid weeks was unheard of.

She eased her key into the locked front door and turned it as quietly as she could. She winced at the thunk of the deadbolt, then at the sound of the weather stripping on the doorjamb giving up its hold on the door as she gently pushed it open. She had the door closed and was halfway up the stairs before her mother's voice called out, "Is that you, Jessie?"

She sighed. "Yeah, Mom," she called back. "Just grabbing a couple things." Stealth no longer necessary, she jogged up the stairs to her room and began rummaging through her closet, looking for the fall shirts she hadn't needed until this past week. She found two, but two were missing—her two favorites, in fact. *Are they back in the dorm and I just didn't see them?*

She went down to find her mom. Maybe she'd seen them.

Savannah was on the couch, legs crossed as a table for her laptop. She was wearing one of the shirts Jessie had been looking for. "Oh my gosh. You're wearing my clothes?"

Savannah jumped. "I, um—well, yes. They're comfortable."

"I know. That's why *I* wear them. But you always said they were unfeminine."

Was her mother actually blushing? "Well, I just … changed my mind. Besides, nothing of mine fits anymore. I had to buy new clothes but I didn't want to get too many, in case I figured out how to lose this weight. Your things fit me better."

"Glad my wardrobe comes in handy for you now, but I was hoping to bring all my long-sleeve stuff back to school with me. I don't suppose the plum one is in the wash somewhere, is it?"

"Um, yes—wore that yesterday."

"Alrighty then. Guess I'll just do some laundry tonight or something. I'll come back for that one some other time."

"No, no, that's alright. I'll go change and you can take it." She set the pillow and laptop on the couch and got up, leaving Jessie alone in the living room.

I cannot believe she's wearing my clothes. Jessie flopped on the sofa to wait for Savannah, and glanced at the computer screen to see what her mother had been working on. She expected to see email, or the text of a talk or book, but instead it was the message board her mother had been on the last time she was home. She turned the computer so she could see it better and checked the title of the page. *Transplant Connections ~ Support, Encouragement, and Resources for Transplant Recipients and Their Loved Ones.* Jessie's interest was piqued. The title of the current thread was, "What else changed after your transplant?"

"What are you doing?"

Savannah's sharp tone made Jessie jump. "Just looking at—"

"Do you have no concept of privacy?" Savannah slapped the laptop shut, nearly catching Jessie's fingertips in the process. "Since when is it appropriate to look through someone's computer?"

"I wasn't looking through it, you left it open. I was just curious!"

Savannah thrust the shirts at Jessie. "Here they are. Now get out of here and go find some manners."

Jessie's jaw hung slack. She'd never heard that type of tone from her mother before. She took the shirts, waiting for her brain to kick in with some kind of comeback, but nothing came to mind. Nonplussed, she turned and left for her car.

What was that? Jessie had chalked up her mother's less-than-diplomatic tone during their last conversation to being tired or distracted. But the way she spoke to her just now had been downright antagonistic and offensive. She shook her head, eyes glued to the road. "And she's wearing my clothes?!" It used to be her mother wouldn't be caught dead in anything that wasn't fashionable. Jessie had never cared about fashion — yet another bone of contention between the two of them. At least her mother had given up trying to influence her wardrobe choices after she left for college. But to actually start wearing Jessie's clothes was more than just a concession for comfort. It was ... well, she wasn't sure what it was. But she was sure it *wasn't* like her mother. At all.

And to get all secretive about those forums ... *What is she hiding?* Jessie's incredulousness morphed into a mix of curiosity and anger. *What would make her act like that?*

One thing was certain. She had a new forum to join — and some sleuthing to do.

It was Day Two of Operation Old Savannah. She thought she'd done pretty well yesterday. She'd brought homemade cookies to A&A and managed to stay and chat amiably with everyone for nearly an hour. After that she'd gone to the coffee shop to work some more on her book tour talk. She found it much easier to write if she didn't envision herself actually giving the talk. She pretended she was just a speechwriter, so it didn't matter if she believed the words or not. She just had to make them sound good for the person actually saying them. As long as she didn't think about that person being her, she was okay.

This morning she'd pulled on her new jeans and one of the blouses she'd gotten, then dressed it up with a blazer that still fit as long as she didn't try to close it. The jacket toned down the outdoorsy feel and brought the ensemble a little closer to the styles she used to wear. Her goal was to get the talk finished today, even if it meant staying all day at the corner table in the back of the shop. As an incentive, she'd promised herself a slice of strawberry pie from Village Inn when she was finished.

Savannah unpacked her laptop and set it on the table beside

her steaming mocha. After powering it up, she launched her word processor and then, stalling, her email. Her inbox filled as the messages were downloaded, and one of them caught her eye. She chewed her lip, finger twitching as it hovered above the trackpad.

The book edits from her publisher had arrived.

Hi Savannah—just finished these last night, and must say you pulled together a great book given how little time you had to write it. Speaking of time, we're hoping to get this to the typesetter by the end of next week, so if you could get the edits back to me by the 7th that would be ideal. I know that's incredibly short notice, but it will keep us on track for having typeset pages available by the end of the month. I understand from Marisa that your tour dates are tentatively set—we don't want to botch up the release date and mess that up for you. Let me know if you have any questions.

Her relief at knowing the editor liked the book was overshadowed by the fact that she had only three days to get the edits completed. So much for working on her tour talk. She opened the attached manuscript with her editor's notes and began to read.

I will do a good job. I will not let my reputation be tarnished with a poorly written book. I will protect the jobs of my employees and myself by not screwing this up. She chanted these thoughts to herself whenever she felt her focus and attention waning, and managed to make it through the first chapter in just a couple hours. The editor's notes made sense, and though many of them required that she rewrite large sections of the manuscript, they at least gave her some direction so she knew which way to go and roughly what needed to be said.

The success of the first chapter gave her the energy she needed to continue after a brief lunch. Unfortunately, the notes in the second chapter indicated even larger rewrites, as well as asking her to rethink and redo an entire six-page section. *You can do this. You can!* She fought to maintain a positive attitude, but as the hours wore on her mind began to wander to the what if's she'd been trying to avoid. *What if the book doesn't sell? What if my editor is just being nice and this is really just a huge piece of junk? What if people can tell I don't mean what I say anymore?*

She forced herself to stay until four, then packed up as though being timed and made a beeline for Village Inn. Once there she changed her mind and bought an entire pie instead of just a slice. She deserved it — and needed it.

She got home at 4:30 and, after one glance toward the dishes left in the sink from breakfast, decided to forgo dinner in favor of the pie. It was a given now that Shaun would be working late, and she just didn't have the energy today to prep an entire meal for only one person.

She was on her second slice when the door opened. "Shaun?" Why was he home so early?

He came into the kitchen and she could tell from the anger in his eyes that something was wrong. "What is it?"

He dropped his keys on the counter, then speared her with his stare. "I talked to Kurt today. He told me he and Colleen saw you at the steakhouse with some guy."

Oh no. "Shaun, it's not what it sounded like."

"No?" He looked unconvinced. "What was it then?"

"I had just sent off the book. I'd been in the house for three solid days trying to get that thing done. I just wanted to get out and celebrate a little. But you were gone, so I ... I just went. I was just going to get a drink, maybe some food, and enjoy not having that stupid book hanging over my head. But then this guy asked me a question, and we started talking, and he was by himself, and he got an appetizer because I told him it was good so when it came he offered me some." Shaun's expression hadn't changed. "Hand to God, Shaun, that was it. Nothing happened other than a nice conversation with someone. Whatever Colleen and Kurt saw could not have possibly been untoward, because nothing like that was going on. But I'm sorry. I'm sorry I didn't call you to ask you to come home, or wait to see when you'd get back, or at least tell you about it in case something like this happened. I am truly, truly sorry."

She braced herself for the inevitable we-need-to-talk-to-Pastor-John speech. If he pulled that card, she would confront him about the mysterious receipts; she'd been holding onto that tidbit for when she needed to divert a probing conversation away from her and her behavior, though honestly she was afraid to hear his response.

But he did not threaten to call in the pastor; he didn't even continue the conversation. Instead, without a word, Shaun walked past her and into his office, then shut the door.

She sank back onto the couch and held her head in her hands. She was glad he hadn't kept on her about her night out, but she was also worried about why he hadn't. Did their marriage not matter to him anymore? Did he not care that they were floating further and further apart, that they barely spoke anymore, that the air was thick with tension when they were alone together? The last time they'd struggled, back when A&A was first starting, he'd practically dragged Pastor John to their house after the service one Sunday, he was so desperate to start counseling and get things back on the right track. His ambivalence this time was disturbing.

She finished her piece of pie, then a third and fourth slice, ignoring the nausea in her stomach and going straight to bed when she was done. Wired from all the sugar, but physically exhausted from a day spent working so hard on the book, she lay unmoving in the bed and let her thoughts run wild. It took two hours for her to fall asleep. She never heard Shaun leave his office. She drifted into dreams making a checklist of ways she'd rebuild her life after he left her, because she was sure that was what he was going to do.

CHAPTER 9

THE REST OF OCTOBER PASSED MUCH LIKE SEPTEMBER HAD: awkwardly. Shaun spent as much time away from home as he could, and Savannah spent as much time away from A&A as she could without it looking as though she was avoiding the place. Operation Old Savannah lasted a couple weeks, but by the end of the month she was exhausted from all the acting. *And I didn't even get an Oscar nomination.*

She had successfully transitioned into a full-time loner. Marisa and Shaun were the only two people she spoke with anymore, and she avoided even that interaction as much as possible. Colleen, Andi, Mary, and Bethany had doggedly pursued her, and she had rebuffed them with equal perseverance. Doctor appointments, both real and fabricated, imaginary illnesses or threats of illnesses she'd "heard are going around," and convenient bouts of depression or insomnia that required long stretches of daytime sleeping had given her plenty of excuses to throw at them when they wanted to get together. They'd even tried showing up on her doorstep uninvited. She didn't answer the door. She'd banked on Shaun's recent reticence to socialize to keep their husbands at bay as well, and he had unwittingly come through. Eventually, to her immense relief, they'd finally gotten the hint.

She spent the bulk of her days on her laptop, reading the transplant forum. Or she'd lose herself in novels to escape her new reality. She chose books at the library based on their thickness, and finished even the 800 page tomes in a matter of days. She avoided anything that might make her think about the impending book tour, though the increased severity of her sour stomach — which stole her appetite and the desire to cook — told her that her subconscious was dwelling on it night and day. When the beginning of the tour was finally upon her, she was almost relieved — the sooner she started it the sooner it would end.

The night before the first gig in Colorado Springs, she slept less than three hours and spent most of her awake time dry heaving in the bathroom. She assured Shaun that it was just nerves, and though she was telling the truth, she still felt deceptive. When she awoke in the morning, feeling like death and almost wishing for it, she couldn't eat breakfast and worked herself into a panic — dropping her notes and scattering the unnumbered pages.

"Savannah, just breathe," Shaun said, holding her hands in his. They had hardly touched in weeks; the intimacy of the gesture made her feel even worse. "I've never seen you such a wreck. Why are you so nervous?"

"I ... I don't know, Shaun. I don't know. I just am."

He nodded as though this made sense, then made her sit down while he reassembled her talk. "Here," he said after setting down the stack of papers. He reached out for her hands again. "Let me pray for you."

"Please don't." The words were out before she could stop them. He looked at her, confused. "I just ... I'm afraid it will make me emotional. Even more emotional, that is. I don't want to start crying and mess up my makeup."

"Oh. Okay."

A knock on the door announced Marisa had arrived to pick up Savannah. "Break a leg," he said to her, giving her a kiss on the cheek. "I'm sure it'll all come back to you. You're a natural."

She gave him a look that said, "What's natural anymore?" His seemed to sadly agree.

"You ready?" Marisa asked when Savannah opened the door. Her face fell when Savannah's expression registered. "Oh dear. Are you okay?"

"I'm fine, I'm fine." She shut the door behind her, the folder of notes clutched tight in her hand. "Just nervous about getting back on the horse."

"Okay." Marisa sounded unconvinced. Savannah begged her telepathically not to comment further. She wasn't sure how long she'd be able to keep things together.

They didn't speak as they drove. When they arrived at the church that was hosting the event Savannah's hands began to shake. She held them tightly in her lap. *I can do this. I can do this. I can do this. Make a crack about being out of practice. They'll all understand. Just read the talk, get it over with, and you can go home.*

And do it nine more times.

Marisa gave her a sharp look when she groaned. "Savannah?"

"I'm alright, really."

They entered through the back door. She could hear her church's worship band warming up on the stage when they entered the green room. Marisa opened a water bottle and passed it to Savannah, eyeing her closely but saying nothing. Savannah sat down and took a long drink, keeping up the chant in her head. She had no choice; she had to make this work.

The band stopped playing and came down into the green room. It was the first time any of them had seen Savannah since before her illness; they crowded her with hugs and congratulations, and the smile she forced made her cheeks ache. Marisa rescued her with a call to the stage for sound check. She followed Marisa up to the podium, where the sound tech threaded the wireless lav through her blouse and clipped the mic to the lapel. She tried to settle her nerves with the familiarity of the routine, and began pacing the stage as she spoke, getting a feel for its size as the tech fiddled with the levels from the booth. The familiar motions were comforting. If this was all she had to do, she'd be fine. If only she could encapsulate this feeling and pop it in pill form before coming up to speak.

Sound check ended and she switched off the battery pack for her mic and went back to the green room. Some of the band tried to engage her in conversation, but she extricated herself as quickly as she could and escaped to the women's bathroom. The window there conjured movie scenes of people crawling out to freedom. She wondered briefly how far she'd get before Marisa came in to check on her.

She sat on a small stool with her back to the mirrors, not wanting to look at her own stricken face. Marisa, bless her, left her alone, and while she waited for her call she stared at a blank wall, trying to gather that blankness and superimpose it over the panic she was feeling. If she could just remove the emotion, the fear, she might get through this.

The sound of the band playing told her the event had begun. She had fifteen minutes left before her time came to speak. *You can do this. You can do this.*

"Five minutes!"

Marisa's call through the door broke the spell of her meditation. She took a deep breath and gave up trying to still her shaking hands. Back in the green room, Marisa gave her a bright smile. "You ready?"

"As I'll ever be." Her voice sounded strange to her ears — strained, quavery. She took another sip of water and squeezed the file in her hand. *You can do this.*

The band finished their set. The audience applauded. Marisa switched on the mic and held open the door for Savannah, and she ascended the stairs to the stage.

The applause erupted again as she walked across the stage to the podium on legs that felt like they might give out any second. Tears sprang to her eyes when the crowd stood, their applause still filling the room. How could she not want to face these fans that cared so much for her and her family and ministry? She had received literally hundreds of cards in the weeks following her transplant. She needed to do this for them, so they would continue to support A&A. She didn't care about her own role anymore. She just didn't want to let anyone down.

She set the file on the podium and opened it as the applause died down and people took their seats. She took a deep breath and found her mind completely blank. She stared at her notes, unwilling to face the crowd. *Say something!* "Thank you."

"You're welcome!" called out a couple voices, and the light laughter that followed from the audience gave her a moment to focus on her notes. *Make the crack about being rusty. Then just read the notes. You can do this.*

"You have excuse to—I mean, you have to excuse me," she began. Cleared her throat. "I'm a little russy—rusty." Why wouldn't her mouth work right?

Read the words, read the words. They swam before her and she froze. She couldn't do it.

Her heart was pounding. She put a hand to her chest, pursing her lips tight. She heard the intake of hundreds of concerned breaths, and released her own in a shaky sigh.

"I can't do this." The words slipped out before she could stop them. She clutched at her lapel, muffling the mic, and nearly ran off the stage as the murmuring of the crowd grew louder. Marisa was at the bottom of the stairs, her eyes wide in fear. "What's wrong? Is it your heart? Sit down, sit down." She grabbed Savannah's elbow and ushered her to a couch as she and the lingering band members began to pray aloud.

"Stop, just stop. I'm fine." Savannah shook off the steadying hands and gasped back a sob. "I just can't—I can't do it."

"It's okay, Savannah—"

"No, I can't do this anymore. I don't believe it, I don't—any of it. I'm just—" She blinked back tears. The stunned faces of the band and Marisa staring at her were more than she could bear. "It's over," she said, then began to weep. "I don't believe it anymore. I don't believe in God."

Savannah wrung a tissue in her hands as she listened to Marisa addressing the crowd. "... been through a lot, and is struggling a bit to get back on the horse, you might say. We're going to take a bit of an intermission, but we'll start again in about fifteen minutes. Would you join me in lifting Savannah to the Lord in prayer?"

She reached up and snapped off the speaker that projected the audio from the stage into the bathroom. Prayers were the last thing she wanted to hear, especially when they concerned her.

The enormity of what had just happened still hadn't sunk in. But she knew she wouldn't be going back up on that stage, no matter what Marisa said. She refused to consider anything beyond the next hour, beyond going home and changing out of the blue pantsuit and back into her flannel pajamas and hiding under the covers of her bed. Possibly forever.

The door behind her creaked as it opened. Marisa appeared, her face a mask Savannah had never seen before. She leaned against the wall, arms folded. Savannah felt like a child waiting for the principal's judgment to fall.

"We can figure this out, Savannah."

"There's nothing to figure out."

"Didn't the doctors say that post-op depression—"

"This isn't depression. It's ... it's hate, it's anger, and it's been with me since I woke up from the surgery. I don't know where it came from, and I can't shake it. I've tried, believe me."

Marisa was silent for a moment; Savannah could almost hear the wheels turning as she tried to concoct a way to get her through this. "So what do we do? What can I do to help you go back up there?"

Savannah gaped at her. "Did you not hear me just now? It's over. I'm not going back up there. I can't look five hundred women in the face and lie to them."

"You wouldn't be lying."

"I don't believe in God, Marisa. I don't believe a single thing I wrote in that book. I don't believe a single word in that speech. To tell them I did would be lying."

Marisa spread her hands in exasperation. "Then what am I supposed to tell them?"

"Tell them I'm sick. Tell them I thought I was ready for this, but I wasn't. Tell them my heart couldn't handle it."

"So you want *me* to lie?"

"Trust me. It's not a lie."

THE RIDE HOME WAS AGONY. Marisa's silence was unreadable, her face blank. Savannah stared out the window, avoiding Marisa as best she could and occasionally swiping a hand at the mascara-tinted tears that ran down her cheeks. Marisa had called Shaun before they left, to make sure he would be home when they arrived. Savannah could hear his panic through the cell phone. "Her heart is fine, her health is fine," Marisa had assured him. "Just ... we'll talk about it when we get there."

She could see Shaun's face in the front window when they pulled up. It hit her just how much damage this was going to do. Dread shrouded her soul as they walked up to the door that Shaun opened as they approached.

"What happened?"

"She couldn't —"

"I can speak for myself," Savannah snapped. Marisa's mouth shut tight. Guilt upon guilt piled onto Savannah's shoulders. "Let's go sit down."

She left Marisa and Shaun in the foyer and made her way to the living room, longing for the comfort of the familiar space, the calming view of the trees outside the window. Shaun and Marisa followed her in silence, and once they were all assembled she attempted to explain herself.

"Ever since the surgery — I don't know why — but God has meant nothing to me. I've tried so hard to conjure up those feelings again, that faith — to be who I was before, but nothing has worked. The thought of prayer, of the Bible, of the concept of Christianity itself is just ... foolishness to me."

Shaun's eyes were hard. "Be careful, Savannah. Don't blaspheme the Holy Spirit."

She met his stare with her own. "If there is a God, I'm guessing he'll appreciate my honesty."

"Do you have any idea what you're saying, Savannah? Do you—"

"Of course I do! And I'll thank you for not treating me like some petulant teen who's all reaction and no thinking. I'm not doing this for the drama, believe me."

"Then why are you doing it?"

"Because I can't pretend anymore! You have no idea what the last two months have been like, trying to find myself again and failing. You know—I know you do—that I'm not the same as I was. I can't do anything about all these little changes—or this one huge change."

"Have you prayed about it?" This from Marisa, who sat on the edge of the couch, her brow furrowed as though puzzling out algebra, as though enough thinking would bring out the answer.

"Of course not. Why would I? There's no one to pray to."

"But you know that's not true."

"No, I don't. In my heart I know God is gone."

"But you believed in him before."

"And maybe before I was wrong. Maybe this is the truth, and my life before was misguided."

"So we're all wrong?" Shaun's eyes flashed, she could feel his frustration. "Everything we've done at A&A for the last ten years was just chasing after a fairytale? The lives we've seen changed, the miracles we've witnessed—it's all just a joke?"

She spread her hands in surrender. "I don't know what to tell you. I just explained how I feel. I'm sorry I can't just snap my fingers and say what you want me to say and believe it. I just can't."

He slumped back in his seat, ran his hands through his hair. "So what do we do about the tour?"

"We'll just have to cancel it."

He went white. "The whole thing? Do you have any idea how much money we'll lose?"

"Classy, Shaun. So glad you're concerned about me."

"I *am* concerned about you. I'm concerned about how this will make you look to the almost 20,000 people who've bought this book. I'm concerned about the thousands of people who have already purchased their tickets, and what they're going to think of you when you tell them you think they're all a bunch of pitiful ignorants for believing in God."

"I never said I think that!"

"You might as well have."

Marisa waved her hands. "Stop, you two. This isn't getting us anywhere."

But Savannah wasn't stopping until everything was out that she'd been bottling up. "What would you have me do, Shaun? Get up there and lie to them about what I believe? Don't you think that's going to make everything worse when I quit the ministry?"

Shaun's jaw hung slack. "Wh-what? Quit?"

She held up her hands. "I don't know yet. I'm just speculating. I can't make any decisions right now. I'm a total wreck, emotionally, and I need to get all this stress out of my body before I explode."

"Oh, yes, by all means, go run yourself a nice bath while I try to figure out how I'm going to fix your mess."

She swore at him, saying words she'd never uttered in her life. Marisa and Shaun's shocked faces didn't make her feel any better. She left for her office, slamming the door behind her, and sank into her chair and cried.

SHAUN SHOOK HIMSELF AWAKE AND shifted in his desk chair. He knew he should get home soon, before he was unsafe to drive from exhaustion, but home was the last place he wanted to be. Maybe it was time to bring one of their old sleeping bags in, stash it under his desk. He'd rather sleep on the hard floor of his office than next to the stranger in his bed.

It had been five days since Savannah had come unglued. They had spoken less than three times since, both of them choosing to avoid each other as much as possible. He and Marisa had agreed not to tell A&A's staff the real reason why the tour had been canceled, which meant even more lying since everyone kept wanting to know how she was doing, if she was feeling better, if they were going to reschedule the tour. He thought maybe he'd try his hand at writing fiction when A&A crashed and burned; he'd gotten very good at making stuff up.

The numbers he'd been so happy to see in their bank account balance had dwindled further than he'd ever seen them dive after paying back the revenue they'd received from ticket sales. They'd been hovering at the low end of financially stable when he'd steeled his nerves and paid out the deposits to the ten locations where Savannah had been scheduled to speak, but now that those monies weren't being replenished by ticket and merchandise sales, they were about to dip into the red. He wasn't sure how much longer he could keep this ship afloat.

He jerked awake again and stretched. Definitely time to go home. He woke his computer to shut it off and saw a new email in his inbox. It was from one of the stock promoters he subscribed to, singing the praises of an investment opportunity the promoter believed was going to skyrocket. Shaun read the email and knew by the end of it that he needed to get in on this ground floor. It had the potential to pay off all their debts and get A&A safely back in the black. He just had to find the money to invest with.

The problem was that he had no time. This report would make the price rise for sure. If he waited until he'd spoken with their retirement rep about pulling the money from their 403b like he'd planned on doing before, he'd risk not being able to buy a decent amount of shares. He had to do this soon—very soon. More than 24 hours and it wouldn't be worth it.

He pulled up their banking software and examined the accounts. He'd drawn a line in the sand for himself months ago, vowing he wouldn't touch A&A's meager savings. But if this stock exploded like the promoter thought it would, he'd be able to replace what he borrowed before anyone knew it was gone.

He logged into their online banking account and withdrew half of A&A's savings, then deposited it into his personal account, which he'd linked to A&A's accounts last month to make such shuffling easier to do. His fingers flew across the keyboard as he made the arrangements to move the money into his stock market account and put in a buy order for fifty thousand shares. He could almost taste the financial freedom that was finally within reach—though it wasn't strong enough to overpower the bitter tang of self-loathing.

After ensuring his requests had gone through, he resolved to go home before he did any more damage. He was about to close down his computer when the *ding* of his email announced another new message. He clicked on the program and felt his gut plummet.

She had written again.

Not now. I can't take it.

He hesitated a moment, planning on just shutting down the computer without looking at the letter, then realized it was the fourth he'd received since Savannah had gotten sick and he hadn't opened a single one. Could he afford to keep his head in the sand? What if she made good on whatever threats she was undoubtedly making? He couldn't let her go public, not on top of all the other fires he had to put out.

He gathered his courage, then keyed her name into the search box and selected all four messages to open.

$5000 by August 15. Send it to this address. A PO box address in Denver followed.

You thought I was kidding? This won't go away. $6000 by September 7th.

Don't make me call the Denver Post. *$7000 by September 28.*

Last chance, Shaun. I'm tired of waiting. $10,000 by November 10 or I call Paula Zittner at the Denver Post *and tell her all the sordid details. Don't make me do it, Shaun. I just want what I deserve.* A link to the investigative reporter's contact information followed—her way, he assumed, of showing she was serious.

He slammed his fist on the desk and shouted a curse at the top of his lungs. She may as well have asked for ten million. He simply didn't have it, and wouldn't in less than a week.

Although ...

He shook his head. He couldn't dip into A&A's savings a second time. He was nervous enough about what he'd done tonight.

He thought she'd finally gotten the message, finally realized he wasn't going to send anything else when he'd stopped responding to her. She'd already milked him for four thousand; how much did she think she deserved? He'd honestly thought she'd understand, once news got out about Savannah's illness, that he didn't have any money left to throw at her for her silence. What made her think he was flush with cash?

Of course: Savannah's book.

Apparently she hadn't heard that the tour had been canceled—with a great financial loss to A&A. Though she apparently *had* seen that the book had gone straight to the bestseller list. She obviously underestimated how much authors got paid from their sales.

He banged out *I don't have any money!!!* and sent it before he could worry about it any more. He was getting to the point where he almost didn't care if she went to the press. It was all falling apart anyway, thanks to Savannah.

But if he could just get this stock, and if the stock performed like it was supposed to ... at least he'd be able to untangle one mess before anything was discovered.

SAVANNAH AWAKENED TO A RAINY day that perfectly matched the foul mood that had followed her from yesterday. And the day before that. And the day before that ... right back to the day she'd pulled the rug out from under her life.

It was going to be a cooped-up-tiger day, she could feel it in the way her muscles were twitching to do something else besides keep her upright on the couch. She wished she hadn't let Shaun sell their treadmill; she definitely could have used it today. Though the inside of the house was beginning to wear on her, too. She wanted to get out just for a bit, stretch her legs and walk a longer track than the upstairs hall where she was getting in what exercise she could to help her body heal from the surgery. But where could she go and not have to worry about being recognized? She'd had nightmares more than once about an angry mob chasing her down in public—which was silly, since they'd all gotten their money back when the tour had been canceled, and no one knew the real reason the plug had been pulled. But she was still nervous, afraid she'd have to lie to cover her tracks if someone were to recognize her and ask what happened.

She thought she'd feel better once she'd admitted to someone how she was feeling, but the weight of the book tour had been replaced by the weight of their future, now that it was certain everything was going to fall apart. Frankly, it was worse now than it had been before her major fail at the book tour kick-off.

And despite the development of her hermit-like tendencies, she was still the kind of person who needed to verbally hash out her thoughts, to process life through conversation. But who could she talk to now? Marisa was probably halfway out the door now that she knew how Savannah really felt. Jessie wasn't one of the people she usually talked to about life in the first place; she certainly wasn't going to start opening up now. Plus, Jessie was in the dark about Savannah's confession, as were the girlfriends she'd pushed away over the past weeks—not that she wanted to reestablish those lines of communication anyway. And Shaun ... well, you couldn't have a conversation with someone who refused to talk to you.

Savannah power-walked the hallway, trying to burn off some of the frustration. Fifteen steps and turn, fifteen steps and turn.

She had to get out of here. She had to talk to someone before she went crazy.

A name popped into her head. She stopped, hands on her hips as she considered it. She would be perfect, actually—provided she was willing to talk to Savannah. It had, after all, been two decades since the last time they'd spoken, and as their final conversation bobbed to the surface of her memory, she cringed with embarrassment over the things she'd said. She had a new perspective now, that was for sure.

Savannah began to walk again, mulling as she did. She was entirely to blame for how much time had passed, for the fact that she and her best friend—former, anyway—hadn't spoken in twenty years. It probably wouldn't be wise to try to fix things now; why dredge up that pain, for both of them?

Savannah ditched the hallway and began taking the stairs up and down to give her mind something else to focus on. She pushed herself to do one more flight, then one more, and one more again, until her heart was pounding like it had the day she'd taken the stage for the book tour. It took more effort to get it really going than she'd expected it to; this heart was certainly up to what few challenges Savannah had thrown at it.

She showered and took a nap, then spent the rest of the afternoon in front of the computer, reading the transplant forum and flirting with the idea of trying to track down her friend. Every time she opened Google she froze and shut the browser window before she could type anything.

She was staring at the search engine page once again that night when Shaun came home. She jumped at the sound of the door, having lost track of time. She settled into her seat again to give him time to get occupied somewhere before she snuck off to bed, but he passed her open office door and their eyes unexpectedly locked.

His face held a look of disgust. "On the computer, of course. What else would you do with your life while I'm trying to keep our family and ministry from crashing and burning?"

The attack took her by surprise, but she wasn't about to let him get away with insulting her. "Don't you dare judge how I deal with this—"

"Deal? You're not dealing with anything, Savannah. That's the problem. You're wallowing."

"How would you have any idea what I'm doing, Shaun? How much time have you spent in this house over the last month? If anyone is avoiding things, it's you. I'm dealing the best way I can, and I'm so very sorry if it's not fixing things the way you'd like them fixed."

"Hey, I'd be happy for any kind of fix! But what you're doing is changing nothing. You just sit on that computer and lose yourself in other people's problems instead of facing your own."

"Those people know what it's like to be in my shoes. You can't fathom the toll this has taken on me, Shaun. Not that you'd bother to even try."

Shaun ran a hand through his hair and looked about to respond when he waved her off and left from the doorway. Tears began to form as her adrenaline slowed, but then Shaun was back and her defenses rose again.

"You need therapy. How about spending your day doing *that* tomorrow. Find someone you can go to, since I know you won't go to John. I have no idea how we'll pay for it, but obviously you need help, so ..." He left before finishing his thought, though Savannah knew he had nothing left to say.

She stared at the search engine screen, knowing he was right, and dreading trying to explain to a counselor what she was experiencing. What were the odds of finding a therapist well-versed in the emotional trauma of organ transplant? She hadn't read many posts on the forum about people going to therapy, at least not long term. She had a feeling her issues would require a lot of time to untangle. The odds of it making a difference were slim, she was sure.

But what if this was Shaun's way of throwing her a bone, of giving her a lead on what might make at least their relationship a little better? Therapy couldn't hurt, right? And even if it didn't work, the fact that she was trying had to count for something.

It would probably take forever to find someone who didn't think she was nuts—but she had plenty of time to spend looking.

CHAPTER 10

"The last item of business is for me to announce we're going to be moving to a new location in January. It's not too far, just off West Uintah. I specifically tried to find something that would keep the change in your commute times at a minimum. It's a great location, nice neighborhood. I'm going to give up my office and join the rest of you in the cubes, and we may need to combine a couple of you in a cube together, but when we make the move we'll figure that out."

Shaun looked around at the blank faces of the staff. He'd expected some kind of a reaction, but they didn't seem to care. Unfortunately, these were the expressions he saw more often than not these days. "So ... when I finalize things with the management company I'll let you know when our moving date is. Any questions?" He was met again with silence. "Alright then, have a good Monday."

He followed them as they shuffled out, noting how conversation didn't begin between anyone until he was about to close his office door. He was losing them, he could tell. This did not bode well.

He set aside the notes from the meeting and woke his computer. He checked for new email, then clicked the icon on his desktop that opened his account with his online stock broker. It had been almost a week since he'd purchased that stock, and he just knew one of these mornings he'd open his account and see the little green line shooting up.

When it loaded, he almost had a heart attack. The little green line had plummeted. The amount listed as the worth of his purchase was a fraction of what it had been. He scrambled to open a web browser and look up the company's website, and once he was there he wanted to cry.

A lawsuit over patent infringement. *This can't be happening.*

He read the article listed on the website, which assured stockholders that the plaintiff in the case didn't have a leg to stand on, and once the case got to court it would certainly be thrown out.

But that did him no good if it took months to get that far. He needed to get that money back now.

He put a sell alert on his stock, hoping to recover at least part of what he'd spent. Something would be better than nothing—though not by much.

He grabbed his keys to leave, then sat back down. He couldn't afford to waste gas on aimless driving, even if it did help him think. He was stuck here.

He was stuck, period.

SAVANNAH'S KNEE BOUNCED AS SHE flipped through a six-month-old magazine without reading its contents. She'd gotten to Dr. Boxer's office with ten minutes to spare and was now wishing she'd spent them in the car. Knowing she was about to be analyzed made her nervous, and she began to wonder if choosing a non-Christian therapist had been a good idea. She'd wanted to avoid people who would likely tell her to just pray harder, and people who would likely know who she was, but at least their approach would be somewhat familiar. She had no idea what to expect here.

Dr. Boxer's office door opened and a young couple came out holding hands. That gave Savannah some hope. A few minutes later a woman about her own age popped her head out of the door and smiled at her. "Savannah Trover? Come on in."

Savannah smoothed her pantsuit as she stood. She wasn't sure why she'd felt compelled to dress up, but it seemed like a good idea. She was kicking herself now for not dressing in something more comfortable. The suit just added to her sense of unfamiliarity with her own self.

Dr. Boxer nodded to a couch set under the window. "Feel free to take a seat. I just need to switch my files around here." Savannah sat and looked around the office while the doctor fiddled with some papers on her desk. After a minute she sat across from Savannah with a notepad and pen. "So, Savannah, it's nice to meet you."

"Nice to meet you too."

"Why don't you start by telling me what brought you in today?"

Savannah took a deep breath to calm her nerves. "Well, I had a heart transplant about two and a half months ago." She explained the circumstances leading up to it, even though the details weren't pertinent; she needed time to acclimate to telling a complete stranger about her most intimate thoughts. "And I feel like every day when I wake up I discover something else that has changed about me, or my personality, or the things I liked or didn't like. And it's not just in my head; my family and coworkers have noticed it too. But the worst part is that I have this anger that I just can't shake. I don't know why I'm so mad, but I am, all the time, and it doesn't take a lot for me to really show it."

Dr. Boxer pulled a form from a desk drawer and handed it to Savannah. *Depression Inventory.* "Do any of these apply to you?"

Savannah scanned the list. *Are you often sad or irritable? Have you noticed changes in your sleep patterns? Have you lost interest in activities you once enjoyed?* Her frustration mounted as she saw where this would likely lead. "Well, yes," she said after reading all ten items. "They all apply, actually. But not because I'm depressed, because I'm *not.*"

Dr. Boxer nodded as she wrote on the notepad. "It's quite common for transplant recipients to experience a wide swing in moods after their operation. Depression is very common—"

"But this *isn't* depression; it's anger. I've counseled people with depression before. I know what it looks like. This is anger."

"Anger is very common as well."

"For people who lost out on a lot of their life waiting for a heart—yes, I've read about that. But that's not true in my case. I went from healthy to transplant in less than a month."

"Anger can also be a symptom of depression."

"But I'm not depressed!" She took a deep breath, trying not to let her anger get the best of her. "Depression and anger are obviously two different things, otherwise we wouldn't have two separate words for them. I'm *angry*. And more importantly, I'm angry at God, around whom my entire pre-transplant life revolved. A *little* anger would make sense, but not this much—and not at someone that I wouldn't have even considered blaming before. Now I don't think he's even there to be blamed. And that makes no sense. It scares me. I'm not *me* anymore. And I want to get back to who I was."

Dr. Boxer's even expression made Savannah want to slap her. "I understand that, Savannah. But until you're willing to work with me and with what I believe is your diagnosis, you're not going to get any better."

Savannah tried not to roll her eyes. "Alright, what is my diagnosis?"

"I believe you're suffering from clinical depression, and I propose that you see your doctor about starting an antidepressant. We can continue to meet, if you want to, to work through the underlying issues that are manifesting themselves as anger toward God."

Savannah slouched back in the couch, resigned to the fact that this woman had no idea what she was talking about. "Fine, fine— I'll call my doctor." She stood and gave Dr. Boxer's hand a brief shake, then left the appointment twenty minutes early.

She knew she'd never be able to explain it to the therapist, whose mind was obviously made up, but Savannah just knew she wasn't depressed. It made sense that no one would believe her, but she wasn't going to play along with a diagnosis that she knew was incorrect, and she certainly wasn't about to add yet another pill to her daily regimen.

She sat in the car and tried to decide her next move. She didn't want to, but she knew her best bet was likely going to be with Rose, the counselor to whom A&A often directed local women when they called for advice. She and Rose had known each other for almost ten years, and while they weren't close friends, Savannah hoped Rose knew her well enough to know she wasn't in denial about being depressed.

She called Marisa on her cell and got Rose's number, then called the counselor's office. "Rose? It's Savannah Trover."

"Savannah! Honey, how are you — I heard about the surgery."

"Well, you know ... I'm not that great, actually. I was wondering if I could come talk to you some time this week?"

"This week? Nonsense. Can you come at 5?"

She smiled in spite of herself. *Maybe this is a good omen.* "Tonight? Yes, absolutely."

"Wonderful. I'll carry in some sandwiches and we can chat."

Savannah hoped the encouragement she already felt wasn't misleading her. They rang off and she headed home to change out of the ridiculous pantsuit and into her new jeans.

Savannah pulled up to Rose's office at five and smiled when she saw the Jimmy John's Sandwich delivery car in the lot. She went in just as the delivery boy came out, and was quickly greeted with a hug from Rose. "Come on in, honey. I've got a sandwich right here for you. Just pull up a chair to my desk." Savannah did as she was told, then froze when Rose said, "Shall we pray?"

Deciding then and there to be completely transparent, Savannah said, "Actually, I'd prefer that we didn't."

Rose didn't even blink, but instead pointed to the sandwich in front of Savannah and said, "Turkey and swiss. I hope that's alright. I didn't even think to get your order when we were on the phone."

"That's perfect. Thank you."

"So you had your transplant back in August, correct?"

"Yes."

"Is the reason you're here today related to that?"

"I think so, yes."

"I don't have any first-hand experience counseling people who have gone through transplants, just so you know. I've read case studies in the past, but nothing recent."

"That's alright. From what I gather the things I'm experiencing aren't very common, so I don't know how much help extra experience would have been for you anyway."

Rose's eyebrows arched. "Well, now I'm curious. Do tell."

So she did, trying not to gloss over anything as often happened when telling a story for a second time in a day. Rose nodded along as she ate and listened, and when she finished Savannah sat back and gestured with her soda in a "voila" kind of way. "I don't need to tell you how devastating this is to my entire life, Rose. I need to figure out what's happened, and get it fixed."

Rose dabbed her mouth with a napkin, then sat back and gave Savannah the answer she'd been hoping not to hear. "I don't know what to tell you, honey. I agree it doesn't sound like depression, though. I've never heard of this kind of a reaction to a transplant, but I can tell you that God created us in such a way as for all our facets to be integrated — the physical affects the emotional and the spiritual, and vise versa. You sound pretty well-versed in the basics of the emotional effects, but I'm just as clueless as you when it comes to the spiritual. If you don't mind, I'd like to consult with a few other professionals who might have a little more experience with this, see what they have to say. I won't use your name, of course."

Savannah nodded, though her spirits sank. "That would be fine, Rose. I appreciate your trying to help."

"Of course, honey. Just wish I could offer you more right now."

Savannah gave her a small smile. "Me too."

BACK AT HOME, SAVANNAH DECIDED it was time to pull out the big guns. It wasn't the approach Shaun was likely to approve of, but it was the only option left she could think of. She wasn't about to waste her time bouncing from clueless therapist to clueless therapist, rehashing her personal life over and over and getting the same response. She needed to talk to someone who had lived through at least some of what she was experiencing. She woke her computer and brought up a search engine, then typed in the name of her old college roommate, her former best friend, the woman she hadn't talked to in twenty years. *Tabitha Vaughn.*

Google returned only seven pages of links. She scanned the first page, then the second, wondering if she should save herself some time and trouble and just pay for the people finder website that came up as the top hit. Then her eye caught something familiar: the name of Christ College of Colorado, their alma mater. She clicked the link and found Tabitha's bio on the college's alumni page. It hadn't been updated in about six years, but it listed her location as Georgia. She went to one of the social networking sites Shaun had bugged her to join once and typed *"Tabitha Vaughn"* + *Georgia* into the search box. Only two profiles appeared, including one that was marked as private, but the picture next to the name was definitely her.

Seeing Tabitha's face after so long brought back a deluge of memories. Double dates, sneaking out — and back in — after curfew, studying for finals and envying how easily Tabitha's straight A's came to her. She was reminded yet again of the falling out that had come right after their graduation. She chewed her lip, debating. Was this worth it?

No harm in trying — or at least, not much. She clicked a link beneath Tabitha's name and began writing her a message.

Dear Tabitha,

She stopped, thinking. What did one say to someone after twenty years? Should she ease into things, not explain right away her reasons for tracking her down? Should she apologize? An apology over email didn't seem appropriate, given how harsh she'd been the last day they'd spoken. But then what *should* she say?

She agonized for a few minutes before giving up on propriety.

I know this is out of nowhere, and I hope you'll forgive me for being so forward, but I'm desperate for some help and you're the only person I can think of that might understand what I'm going through. If you'd be willing to talk to me — and I'll understand if you aren't — please call me.

She ended with her name and phone number, then her email address in case Tabitha couldn't handle such an intimate exchange. She waited expectantly, watching her inbox for a new message, then chided herself for her impatience and went to the kitchen for tea.

The phone rang as she was stirring in the sugar. Her nerves jangled with each ring as she gathered her courage to answer. She picked it up just before it went to voicemail. "H-hello?"

"Savannah Robertson Trover, is that really you?"

Tabitha's jovial tone put Savannah at ease. She could practically hear her friend's smile, and could certainly picture it. "It is. Wow — it's been too long. And it's my fault. Tabitha, I am so sorry. So truly, deeply sorry. I hope you can forgive me."

Tabitha made a familiar noise of dismissal. "Water under the bridge. Forgiven and forgotten a long time ago."

"I don't deserve to be let off the hook that easily."

"I could call you a couple names if it would make you feel better."

She laughed, though it made her sad to realize how long she'd gone without the wit and insights and love of the only person, besides Shaun, with whom she'd ever felt a soul connection. "Oh, Tabs. It's so good to hear your voice."

"It's good to hear yours, too. Though I've got to ask — are you alright? Because your message sure sounded concerning."

Savannah gripped the phone tighter and begged the universe for Tabitha's understanding and help. "The very short story is that my faith is … gone."

"Oh. Goodness."

"Yes, you could say that."

"What happened?"

"Well, that's the funny part. I don't know. I mean, I honestly don't know. I had a heart transplant —"

"I heard about that. Could hardly believe it given how healthy you always were."

"I know, right? And ever since, it's like my spirituality has just disappeared. And I don't have anyone I can talk to here who understands. I—I thought you might be able to offer me a little commiseration."

Tabitha's laughter was sympathetic. "Oh, girlfriend. Can I ever. I'll bet you're feeling pretty claustrophobic. Isolated, too."

"Yes, exactly!"

"Why don't you come visit me?"

Savannah gasped. "Are you serious?"

"Absolutely. We've got plenty of room. Fly into Atlanta; I'll give you our address. Just come whenever you want. I'm always here."

Savannah scanned her calendar, which held nothing but two doctor appointments. "Provided I can get a flight with my miles, I can come the day after tomorrow. Wednesday."

"Pot roast night; you'll love it."

Savannah laughed, a feeling of lightness buoying her soul for the first time in months. "I can't wait. And I can't wait to see you."

"Me neither. Listen, I have an appointment in ten, so I need to run. Let me give you my contact info."

Savannah copied the address and phone number into her calendar, and they rang off with a promise to spend many hours catching up. Savannah couldn't stop smiling as she looked up the number of her primary airline to book her flight.

THE SOUND OF SHAUN COMING in took her by surprise. It was only eight-thirty. She briefly wondered if something was wrong, then decided she honestly didn't care.

It was another twenty minutes before he came up to the bedroom and froze in the doorway. "You're leaving?"

She set the sweater she was holding into her suitcase. "Not the way you might think. I'm going to Georgia tomorrow."

"Georgia? *Tomorrow?* What on earth for?"

She set another sweater on the pile. "Believe it or not, I'm going to see Tabitha."

"Tabitha Vaughn?"

"We know any other Tabithas?"

"Well—I'm just surprised."

"I know, me too. Surprised but very excited." She dumped a handful of balled up socks into the suitcase's corner. "And I didn't mean for it to be such a shock; I hadn't planned on going until Wednesday, but I was able to turn in some of my miles for a flight tomorrow, so I figured I might as well. I'm going to leave straight from my clinic visit."

Shaun sat hard on the corner of the bed. "Okay, just—wait a minute. Why are you doing this? What's going on?"

She shrugged. "Let's call it a sabbatical."

"Um ... okay."

She raised her eyebrows as she met his baffled gaze. "You know why I'm going to see *her*, right? You get the connection?"

"Well, yes—I just didn't think, after twenty years ..."

"I know, me neither."

"Where are you staying?"

"With her."

He watched her for another minute as she finished packing away her clothes. "Huh. Well, alright then. Have fun, I guess."

"Thanks."

He stood and wandered into the closet, then came out in his running gear and disappeared into the hall. She heard the door open and shut a few minutes later and frowned. He hadn't seemed particularly broken up about her leaving. She was briefly irritated at his nonchalance. Despite how ugly things had been with them lately, she still would have expected at least a little more interest.

Not that I've been a real joy to live with lately. She forced herself to acknowledge the truth as she folded her sweats. And the more she thought about it, the clearer it became that she wasn't very sad about leaving Shaun, either. Maybe this trip would solve a couple problems at once: help her get her head on straight, and if she was really lucky, the absence would make both Shaun's heart and hers grow fonder.

SHAUN WATCHED SAVANNAH WALK INTO the terminal before pulling away from the curb. He'd never felt so unmoved by her leaving. Actually, unmoved wasn't quite accurate. In truth, he felt relieved.

Back home, he relished the silence of the house, knowing he had the place to himself, even if it was just for a few days. He could think so much better with no interruptions, no need for careful plotting to avoid running into his wife in the hallway. And heaven knew he had a lot of thinking to do.

He'd checked the credit card statements online the night before, looking for the expenses Savannah was raking up on this little jaunt. She had rented a car, at a total of almost three hundred dollars for the four days she'd be gone, and that was before gas. She'd get something to eat at the airport, most likely—possibly at both of them. Another twenty dollars? Luckily she wasn't big on doing touristy things; she preferred to talk to people. Or at least, that's how she used to be. Maybe the new Savannah was a shutterbug who couldn't wait to see the local claim to fame. He wouldn't know.

Either way, these were more expenses he hadn't been expecting. The card Savannah typically used was nearing its limit; he probably should have warned her about that before she left. He'd been avoiding that conversation for a while now, knowing it would inevitably turn into her berating him for answers as to why he had only been paying the minimum balance for so long. But he wasn't ready to have that discussion.

Shaun tried to look on the bright side. With Savannah gone, the part of his brain that focused so much these days on avoiding confrontation would be freed up to figure out how he was going to get out of this financial mess. *And I might as well start right now.* He headed for his office and stood before the white board he used for brainstorming. *What resources can we produce without Savannah having to actually do anything?* He wrote the thought at the top of the board, then stared at it, waiting for inspiration.

Compilation CD? Perhaps a collection of some of her talks.

Women of the Word owned the rights to the presentations she'd done on tour, but A&A had some recordings of independent events, some of them dating back quite a ways. That was definitely a possibility.

The idea sparked another. *Compilation book?* His marker squeaked over the board as he ruminated. Perhaps — a *Complete Savannah Trover Library* or something similar. Maybe he could add the transcripts of a couple of her more popular presentations, to give readers more incentive to buy it if they already had some of the other books.

Worship CD? He shook his head as soon as he was done writing it, knowing it was too soon after the release of the last worship CD they'd compiled. Those were expensive to produce, too, and he wanted to put out as little capital as possible on whatever project they did.

He continued to brainstorm throughout the morning, then stopped for lunch and a run. On his way back to the house he picked up the mail, and seeing the bank statement in the pile squelched his runner's high. Would this be the statement that showed bounced checks? He didn't let himself tear into it on the street like he wanted to, but waited until he was back in his office before ripping open the envelope and facing the unavoidable. Two of them, and no money in savings for overdraft protection. He breathed deeply to keep himself from vomiting.

He took a three-minute shower and came back to his office to brainstorm. An email from her sat in his inbox. He clicked it, numb to whatever it had to say. The message was simple. *You're a day late.* "And a dollar short," he muttered. "Ten thousand of them, in fact. Deal with it, Carlie. You're not getting any blood from this stone. I'm all dried up." He was proud of himself for not letting her email get to him. Obviously she was all bark and no bite.

The phone rang, jarring him from his thoughts. He was surprised to see Marisa's number on the caller ID. "Hey, Marisa. Listen, I'm not going to be going in today —"

"That's fine. I'm not either. Savannah emailed me about her trip and told me to take a vacation."

Shaun chuckled without humor. "How benevolent of her. So what are you going to do with your free time?"

"Well, that's why I'm calling. I think we need to talk."

CHAPTER 11

SAVANNAH PULLED OVER TO THE SIDE OF THE COUNTRY ROAD TO double check the address. This *was* the place. The sprawling antebellum mansion was set back a good two hundred feet from the road, and some kind of orchard stretched for a quarter mile away from either side of it. But it was the sign at the mouth of the gravel driveway that had stunned her: *The Refuge ~ A Christian Recovery Ministry.*

She'd have understood perfectly if it weren't for "ministry" tacked on at the end. That made it sound like ... well, like a Christian ministry. But Tabitha had left the faith twenty years ago. Why would she be working here?

Now Savannah was torn. If Tabitha had changed her mind about Christianity, then talking to her probably wouldn't help like she'd thought it would. But what was she going to do now, just turn around and go home? That was the last place she wanted to be.

Yes, I would rather be at a retreat center apparently full of Christians than to be at home. How sad is that?

She sighed and turned into the driveway, following it to a circle drive in front of the house where she parked. The house was even more impressive up close. The white columns supporting the second-story wraparound porch looked to be freshly painted, and the brick facade gave the structure a stately, solid feel. She could picture Scarlett O'Hara gazing out of the tall windows from behind the purple velvet curtains, and the image made her smile. Her family had all been city folk, most of them residing in Charleston, but her grandmother had lived in a small plantation home in rural South Carolina that had looked like this one's little sister.

Savannah tapped the knocker twice on the door and waited, her breath shallow in her chest. When the door opened, it was like being sucked into a time warp. Tabitha looked just as she had twenty years ago, with only a few laugh lines and a touch of wisdom added to her kind face. Her smile was as welcoming as it had been back then, and before her embarrassment at past foolishness could stop her, Savannah fell into the embrace of her friend's outstretched arms.

"Come on in," Tabitha said after releasing her from the bear hug. "We'll get your bags and park your car later. I've been so excited for you to come, I feel like a kid. I've got spinach dip in the sitting room and all manner of Coke, is that alright?"

Savannah laughed as she followed Tabitha through the warmly decorated foyer. "'All manner of Coke', eh? You certainly have taken to the culture."

Tabitha grinned. "I fell in love with the South. It's got its flaws, but I was blessed to fall in with the folks that I did when I moved out from Colorado." She offered a velvet-backed chair to Savannah beside a table where a tray held a bowl of dip surrounded by crackers. "To drink?"

"Sprite?"

"You've got it. Be right back."

Savannah surveyed the room while she waited for Tabitha to return. The decor was straight from *Southern Living*, and felt like a great big hug from a well-loved aunt. The Southerner in her missed the bright colors and high ceilings and little touches that were hallmarks of the Southern style. She loved her mountain lodge-like home, too, but this place resonated with her roots. It was another remnant of her former self that brought her a grain of comfort.

Tabitha returned, and Savannah accepted the drink she poured for her. "So you've been in this house all this time?"

"Oh, no, we moved here about seven years ago. I was in Savannah before that, believe it or not."

Savannah noticed Tabitha wasn't wearing a wedding ring. "And 'we' would be ..."

"Oh, the ministry I run, The Refuge."

Savannah narrowed her eyes and shook a finger at her, though a smile tugged at her mouth. "You didn't tell me you'd come back to the fold—or that you were in ministry, you sneak."

Tabitha chuckled, her nose wrinkled in the endearing way that had attracted half the boys in college. "I got the impression that it wouldn't go over well. And I knew if you came out it would be good for you. I didn't want anything to change your mind."

"You duped me."

"I'd like to think I saved you from your own misconceptions."

"Ooh, think you know me so well after all this time?"

"Oh, honey," Tabitha said, her words edged with laughter. "Twenty years isn't so long in some ways. And besides, you and I were always like two peas, and I know myself well enough to know that I would have changed my plans, were our roles reversed." She helped herself to some dip and indicated that Savannah should do the same. "Now, I should warn you that in about ten minutes we'll be seeing some more people. Everyone's at the group therapy session at the moment, but after that most everybody will be coming through here on their way to the kitchen."

"Group therapy? What exactly is The Refuge?"

"It's a place for people who have been deeply wounded by the church, or by anyone, really, in the name of Christianity. I started it with a friend about ten years ago. We've had pastors, church and ministry volunteers and staff, missionaries—even people who grew up with spiritually abusive parents who fed them a poisoned view of God. Folks stay here and get counseling, some fellowship, and support as they find their way back to God. The church has a tendency to shoot its wounded—we try to help them heal in the aftermath."

Savannah found it hard to look Tabitha in the eyes, knowing that she had been guilty of 'shooting' Tabitha when she'd begun to question their faith. Instead, she studied the elaborate pattern on the wallpaper. "That's a really beautiful thing to do, Tabitha."

"Thank you."

"How long do folks stay when they come? Is it like Betty Ford, a 28-day program?"

Tabitha chuckled. "No. It's more of a drop-in setup. They stay for as long as they feel necessary, and some people come and go, using us as a supplemental program to the therapy they're already doing in their own hometown. Right now we've got about ten folks staying with us; two more are coming next week, and three are planning to go home." She smiled at Savannah. "And now, of course, there's you, too. But don't worry," she added hastily, "I wasn't expecting you to participate in the program or anything. Though you are welcome to if you want. I'll give you a schedule so you know what's going on when. But now you know why I thought it might be helpful for you to be here—besides the fact that I've been in your shoes."

Savannah sighed and forced herself to meet Tabitha's gaze. "I am sorry, friend. I can't tell you how sorry I am."

Tabitha shook her head. "It's all forgiven, truly. And don't think you were the one that drove me away; I didn't tell you everything that was going on, and you couldn't have known what I was really going through. That was my own fault. I had no reason not to trust you with the details, but I was young and stupid and hurting and knew a lot of it was my own fault, so it was hard to admit everything, even to my closest friend. So, forgive *me* for not being honest with you and giving you a chance to help me when I needed it."

Savannah ached for all the years they'd lost because of pride and hastily-drawn misconceptions. "What was it that you didn't think you could tell me? If you're willing to tell me now, that is. It's alright if you'd rather not."

Tabitha settled deeper into her seat. "No, I don't mind. Remember Professor Hurst? We had him junior year. He was handsome in a Redford kind of way."

Savannah thought for a moment. "Oh—Old Testament, right? Yes, I do remember him."

"Well, we had an affair."

Savannah nearly dropped her glass. "What!" Tabitha chuckled. "I just ... I can't even ..."

"I know, I know. But remember how I started working for the Biblical Studies department senior year? I ended up doing a lot of work for him—research and transcribing and the like. And we were alone together in the department offices quite a lot, because I worked at night and he often stayed late. He was so friendly, and a bit of a flirt, and you remember what I was like back then."

Savannah did indeed. Lithe and beautiful, with serious smarts, but a penchant for free-spirited fun. Savannah often warned her that men would misinterpret her actions as being flirtatious and welcoming in a sexual way, even though she was just vivacious and friendly. She had been a bit of a rule-breaker, too, which only added to the problem. "Let me guess—he thought you were coming on to him."

"Yes. Though he certainly encouraged it and responded with his own flirting; it definitely wasn't one-sided. Anyway, I developed a huge crush on him, and then, because I was heady with hormones and his attention, I fell in love with him."

Tabitha took another cracker and gestured with it as she spoke. "So I worked with him for the whole first semester, and then after I came back from Christmas break he told me he'd missed me and couldn't wait until I'd returned. I read into that all sorts of emotion and affection that probably weren't even there, which I'm sure was his goal, and I admitted that I'd missed him, too, and that I really enjoyed working with him—though I made sure 'really enjoyed' was properly annotated with lots of nonverbal communication that made clear exactly how I felt. After that, things became much more serious. He told me he wanted to marry me, but that we couldn't say anything to anyone because I was still a student and it might look bad. We planned to start publicly dating after graduation and get married at Christmas. But then one night after spring break ..."

"Oh no."

Tabitha nodded. "Yes. And I got pregnant. He freaked out and dumped me, claiming I was a Jezebel, that I'd charmed him—it was all my fault, you know?"

Savannah was heartbroken. "Tabitha, why didn't you tell anyone?"

"Because I was afraid everyone would side with him. You remember how much trouble I got in at that school—no one in administration would have believed me against him. I was afraid they wouldn't graduate me because I'd broken the covenant yet again, and way more seriously."

Savannah was grieved to know it was true. Tabitha was the kind of Christian woman that the school hadn't known what to do with. She hadn't fit the traditional mold, and had challenged every attempt to stuff her into it. She had adhered just barely to the dress code, had both blatantly and secretively bucked the covenant each student signed upon matriculation to the school by drinking (two shots of Bailey's over ice on her 21st birthday), breaking curfew (though she was hardly the only one) and dancing (on the Quad, at noon, with her Sony Walkman plugged into her ears, the day she found out she'd made straight A's for the first time), and often asked the kinds of squabble-inducing questions that professors hated. But she did none of it to try to provoke anyone. She did it because she hated legalism and saw no reason why a liberated woman of the 80's should be constrained by the traditions of the 50's.

Savannah had agreed, but it wasn't her nature to buck the system. It was one of the few ways in which their personalities digressed, and one of the many reasons why Savannah had loved being roommates with Tabitha.

The significance of Tabitha's admission suddenly sank in. Savannah chose her words carefully. "So—you have a child?"

The look of sadness that flashed across her face before she answered made Savannah's heart ache even more. "No. I aborted her."

"Oh Tabs. I am so sorry."

Tabitha shrugged as she took a sip of her soda. "I am too. It was an impulsive decision. I was scared. I didn't know what to do.

I didn't feel like I could tell anyone what was happening — how could I possibly go home to my parents' house pregnant? And by a professor, no less? I just went and did it without letting myself think about it too much. I kept telling myself that it was so early on, it wouldn't really matter. It did, of course, and once it hit me what I'd done I was devastated. That's when everything started falling apart — my faith included."

"And that's when you told me you weren't sure you wanted to be a Christian anymore."

"That's right."

"And like a fool I didn't even push you for an explanation. You understand that I couldn't imagine anything like all of this happening to *you*, right? I mean, it was stupid of me to make any assumptions at all, but I thought it had to do with not getting into the grad school you'd applied to."

Tabitha laughed. "Seriously?"

"Well, your reactions had always been ... big."

She gave a conceding shrug. "That's true; they were."

"And you said something about not believing God cared about your future, or about your pain. I just figured you'd *really* had your heart set on that school." Savannah shook her head. "It didn't occur to me that anything else could be going on. I mean, we lived together. I saw you all the time — when would anything have happened that I wasn't there to see? I never in a thousand years would have thought anything like that was going on."

Tabitha waved a hand. "It's all in the past. And God has used it for good. The Refuge was born out of my desire to help other people who had been hurt like I had been. The family I rented from when I moved out here — they were a true Godsend. They practically adopted me. And over the course of five years or so, they loved me back to faith. They helped me get the ministry started; God laid it on their hearts as well as mine. So how can I complain, you know? He redeemed my lost years and gave me a life with more purpose than I could have imagined." She grinned. "And I'm one of the few people I know actually using my college degree."

"So you're a therapist here?"

"I am. I got my master's in Atlanta, and my PhD, as well."

"Amazing." Savannah shook her head, astonished at the story. "Just amazing. I'm so happy everything turned out so well for you." She chafed a bit at all the God talk, but the serenity and peace and joy she saw in Tabitha's face made her long for the same outcome. She almost didn't want to admit it, but Tabitha might have been right. Maybe Savannah really did need to be here.

THAT EVENING, AFTER THE POT roast dinner that Savannah had to admit was the best she'd ever had, she and Tabitha sat out on the second-story porch cocooned in quilts and continued to catch up on the time they had lost. Tabitha was apparently very skilled at reading people — or at least reading Savannah — because she had yet to ask Savannah what had actually happened. Savannah was relieved to put it off for a little while. She wanted to forget about the reason she'd come out and just focus on regaining the friendship she'd missed so much. Her friends back in the Springs were good people, and she'd enjoyed the time she'd spent with them over the years; but something about her relationship with Tabitha was different, deeper. Tabitha was a Jesus friend, closer than a brother, see-into-your-soul insightful, lavish with both her love and her forgiveness, even in the face of Savannah's foolishneess. She was the sister Savannah had never had, who could read her like a book and didn't buy the facade she tried to erect to save her image or her pride. She knew that, when she did finally tell what had happened, Tabitha wouldn't come back at her with the same empty advice she'd gotten from others — and it wasn't just because she understood what it was like to have your faith ripped away. Tabitha wasn't made uncomfortable by other people's pain.

The sky was black by the time Savannah came to her recent history in the retelling of the last twenty years. "I thought for sure

I was going to die. I never once told Shaun — I didn't tell anyone.
I maintained a brave face and insisted I would be healed, but only
because I thought if I claimed it enough, and got myself to believe
it, that that would be the proof of my faith that God was looking
for. And then, just before the surgery, I had this … this epiphany
about my relationship with God, and I felt like my eyes were finally
opened. Those few days were just … bliss. Mountaintop, day in
and day out. I could feel his presence; I had this clarity of faith and
thought that I hadn't had in a really, really long time. And then I
woke up from the surgery and it was all gone. So much was going
on in those first couple weeks, physically and emotionally and mentally, that it didn't dawn on me until later. It's a serious mind-trip
to know that such an integral part of your body is totally gone, and
someone else's integral part is now in its place — not to mention
that you have it because they're dead." She gave a little shudder,
though the quilt was plenty warm for the mild November night. "I
started noticing little things were different, but I chalked them up
to still recovering from the surgery. I didn't want to go out, but that
was because I didn't want to pick up any germs. I was more clumsy,
but that was because I'd been really weak and sick before the surgery, and my muscles were still rebuilding. That sort of thing. But
other things were happening that I couldn't explain — like, I love
strawberries now. More than chocolate."

Tabitha's eyebrows shot up. "Not really more than chocolate."

"Really."

"Girl, that's weird."

Savannah laughed. "Yes! It is! And I can't account for that at
all. Same with the … God thing." Even saying the word made her
throat hitch a bit, the same way swearing had felt when she'd tried
to do it to look cool in junior high. "I went from being crazy in love
with him, feeling his presence all around me, the Bible just lighting
up when I'd read it, to how I am now."

"Which is?"

She studied the view of the orchard, looking for the right words.

"Feeling like the whole thing is pretty much a crock. Just ... made up. The very concept sounds ridiculous to me. Plus anger sits under the surface all the time, and it flares at the slightest irritation. Especially if it has anything to do with religion. I'd walk into A&A and have a physical reaction—I wanted to just get out of there. The people, the purpose of the place—it all made me sick."

Tabitha said nothing, and Savannah welcomed her unwillingness to jump in with a diagnosis. They sat in silence, their rocking chairs squeaking in unison as their movement fell into sync, until Tabitha offered a simple, "Wow."

"That's an understatement."

"So now what?"

"I don't know. I can't do my work. I can't even fake doing my work. I had a ten-city tour planned and I walked off the stage at the first stop because I couldn't bring myself to even just read the talk I'd written. My marriage is falling apart, my daughter—well, Jessie and I have never had a great relationship in the first place; but this definitely isn't helping."

"I'm so sorry."

Savannah looked at Tabitha and smiled. "Thank you. You know, I don't think anyone has said that. Well—not Marisa or Shaun, and they're the only ones who know what's really going on. They just want to fix it so they can keep A&A from falling to pieces."

"I'm sure they care more about you than the ministry."

"I'm not."

"I'm sorry about that, then, too."

Savannah was ready to get the conversation off of her. "So you never married?"

"No."

"Because of what happened?"

"Because God led me down a different path. But I didn't want anything to do with men for the first couple years after everything, either. And it took me a long time to get over the abortion. I couldn't handle the thought of another pregnancy. I was afraid experiencing those symptoms again would send me into a depression. But now ..." She smiled. "I'm thoroughly content. I love what I do, and I'm good at it, and God has blessed me in so many ways it's almost silly. I have no desire to upset the balance of my life with that kind of relationship. But if God wanted me married, I've no doubt he'd awaken a desire in me for that."

Savannah sighed. "See, all that you just said? In my head, I'm just thinking to myself, 'How pathetic to give God so much credit.'"

Tabitha gave her a look she couldn't read.

"What?"

"Nothing."

"Liar."

Tabitha smiled. "It's hard to turn off the psychologist in me, you know? But you didn't come here to meet with a shrink, you came to meet with a friend who could relate to your pain. So I'm not going to start giving you my professional insights unless you ask."

"But you'll think them in your head, is that it?"

"Probably, yes."

Savannah chuckled. "That's fine with me." She snaked a hand out from beneath the warm quilt to grab her coffee before it got too cold. "So what was it like, leaving the faith?"

"Easy at first. I felt so betrayed — by both God and Richard. That made it a lot easier to walk away. And I'd never quite fit in at the church I grew up in, and was always getting hassled by the admin at Christ College, so that all kind of coalesced in my head with the betrayal. I figured it was all just a sham and I was lucky to get out before I lost my whole life into it. You knew how I'd wanted to get out of Colorado; everything that happened gave me the gumption to actually go. My parents were sad I left, but not all that surprised, I don't think. I didn't tell them about leaving Christianity until a lot later. I didn't really have to tell them; they weren't around to see how I was living."

Savannah raised her brows. "How were you living?"

Tabitha chuckled. "Not as recklessly as you might think. I'd already gotten hurt once; I didn't want to put myself in the position of being hurt again. I got a lame minimum-wage job in Savannah—not what I'd wanted to do with my life, but it got me in a different time zone and I was happy enough for that. I rented a room from the Burlington family, just on the edge of the city, and they were the most welcoming and loving people I think I've ever met. They practically insisted I join them for dinner every night, and Anna always made me breakfast since Trent and I left for work about the same time. They had a daughter a couple years younger than me, and a son in high school. They were this classic Southern old-money family but with so much heart and sincerity and, as I quickly discovered, tremendous faith. They always invited me to church, and were never pushy about it, but I finally told Anna one night why I left Colorado and that I didn't believe in God anymore, just so she wouldn't get her hopes up about me joining them. She started crying—this woman that barely knew me was so broken over my story that she actually cried," Tabitha chuckled. "You know me, I'm not much of a crier myself, but seeing how much she hurt for me really moved me. So I started crying, and that kind of opened the floodgates. I'd never really let myself grieve over everything that had happened—I buried my hurt, especially about the abortion, and made myself buck up and get on with things so I didn't have to think about it."

Savannah grinned. "Reminds me of how doctors always make the worst patients."

Tabitha laughed. "Exactly! If someone else had done that I'd have been warning them about how that kind of stuffed-down pain can come back to bite you. But in myself, I didn't see the problem. I just had to get my life back together.

"Anyway, Anna started praying over me—I mean, not just praying *for* me, but praying over my future and past and my purpose in life.... I'd never heard anyone pray like that before. It was almost scary, how the feeling in the room palpably changed. Like it was charged with spiritual energy. I didn't know it at the time, but she was a serious prayer warrior." Tabitha smiled. "I didn't have a chance staying away from God, living with that family. And of course he knew that, hence the reason I was there. And even though I was a little freaked out by the praying, I didn't want to move out. I didn't exactly want what she had, but I couldn't quite get myself to leave it, either. This all happened after I'd been there about a year and a half. It took almost four more years before I was willing to step foot back in church, but when I did God really grabbed me. I met a woman there, Alanna, who had a slightly similar story to mine, and had gone through a period away from the church as well. We started talking, and God gave us the idea of The Refuge. We started it together with the Burlington's help. That was almost ten years ago now. Alanna ended up getting married and her husband got transferred, so she left about three years ago."

"And here you are."

"Here I am."

"Wow." Savannah snuggled deeper beneath the quilt. "That's a really beautiful story, Tabs."

"All to God's glory, but thanks."

Savannah's cell began to ring in her pocket. She fished it out and saw Marisa's number on the screen. "Sorry—I should probably take this." She answered with trepidation. "Hey Marisa, what's up?"

"Hi, Savannah. Listen, I'm flying out to New York again tomorrow and I've got a layover in Atlanta, around one. My plane for New York doesn't leave until almost 3. Do you think we could meet? I have some stuff from A&A that you need to go through, and I wanted to talk to you about something, in person."

Savannah frowned. "Well, sure, that's fine. Let me find out where we can meet and I'll give you a call back." They hung up and she told Tabitha about the call. "It's never good when someone wants to talk to you 'in person,' is it?"

"Hmmm ... not usually. You never know, though."

"No, I know Marisa. Good news she can't keep under her hat."

"I'll be praying for your meeting."

She gave Tabitha a sidelong look and almost asked her not to. But hearing it from her felt different than it had felt from Shaun and Marisa. More sincere, less threatening. Even if she didn't think it would do any good, it felt good to know her best friend was back at her side.

AT ONE O'CLOCK SAVANNAH ENTERED the Atlanta Bread Company just across the street from the airport. She ordered sweet tea for herself and waited at a table, trying not to feel anxious. Ever since she'd bombed at the book tour gig, her relationship with Marisa had been awkward at best. She'd given up expecting anyone to understand, but Marisa pushed her patience to the limit. Lately Savannah had taken to flat-out lying to get out of seeing her, and had it not been for the "in person" comment she'd have done the same for today.

Savannah grew more nervous as one minute after another passed. She ordered another iced tea and chided herself for her nerves. After all, what was the worst Marisa could have to say?

The more she thought about it the more she wished she hadn't asked herself that.

Marisa finally appeared at half past one. "I'm sorry I'm late; it took longer to get here than I thought it would."

Savannah tapped into her new bitter side to deal with her anxiety. "Never mind. What's one more half hour out of my vacation?" The sarcastic tone was uncomfortable in her mouth, and seeing Marisa become even more flustered made her feel worse. "So," she said, hoping to move things along quickly so she could get back to The Refuge, "what was so important that we had to have this little meeting?"

Marisa pulled a large yellow envelope from her computer bag. "This is some mail that came for you at A&A. I already sent the form replies to the ones that it made sense to, but there were some that I didn't know what to do with."

"Do you want to make replies right now?"

Marisa looked slightly uncomfortable. "Well, no, not really."

Savannah was a little miffed. Wasn't that her job? "Well, alright then. Neither do I, frankly. But couldn't these have waited until I came back?"

"I suppose they could have, but I thought this might be the better way to do it."

She rolled her eyes. "Why?"

Marisa pushed her hair behind her ears, a clear sign she was nervous. "Savannah, I think it's time for me to quit A&A."

Savannah was surprised at how hurt she felt, especially since she had already given Marisa the go-ahead to leave. "I — I didn't think you were ready to go."

"I wasn't. But then all this happened, and I started making my plans to go out to New York, and I realized I just didn't want to come back. Not that I didn't want to come back to *you*," she quickly amended. "I just mean I don't want to leave Jeremy. I'm pretty sure I want to marry him, but I know it would be wiser for us to spend more time together first. He can't leave his job, and my job is … well … precarious."

Savannah told herself she had no right to feel abandoned, but she couldn't deny the emotion. It had been different when she'd been the one telling Marisa to go, especially since Marisa hadn't seemed eager to leave. But to have her officially quit felt like a knife in the gut. "I'm … well, I'm happy for you and Jeremy, of course. I just didn't think you'd be leaving so soon."

"I know, I'm sorry. And I'm sorry that I'm springing this on you while you're on vacation. But I really felt like God was telling me it was the right thing to do. I already turned in my resignation to Shaun."

Savannah was surprised. "You decided that quick. I just told you yesterday you could take some time off."

"Well … I'd already written it. I was just waiting for God to tell me the right time to go."

Savannah bristled at the comment. "Nice of him to ruin my sabbatical."

"Savannah—"

"No, no, never mind. I really am happy for you, Marisa. Was there anything else you wanted to dump on me before you left?"

"Um, no—"

"Alright then, I'm going to get going." Savannah grabbed the envelope from the table and stood. "Have a nice flight. Good luck in New York."

She walked out of the restaurant with tears in her eyes and her emotions in complete confusion. She tried to sort them out as she drove, rather than wallowing and making herself too weepy to drive. She was halfway back to The Refuge before she finally realized the real reason she was so upset. It had nothing to do with Marisa, really, but with A&A. It felt like the beginning of the end. Without Marisa, she had no assistant. But there was no point in hiring someone else, because she wasn't working anymore anyway. And if she wasn't working anymore ...

She decided to push back her return flight when she got back to The Refuge. Suddenly she couldn't bear the thought of going home.

Shaun woke up to the sound of a thud downstairs. He sat up and checked the date on his watch. Savannah wasn't scheduled to come home for another week, now that she'd changed her flight—had she changed it again?

He got out of bed and pulled on a pair of sweats as he called out, "Savannah?"

"Just me, Dad."

He smiled as he finished dressing and went downstairs. "Hey, sweetheart. I didn't know you were coming home this weekend."

"Hey, Mr. Trover." Adam appeared from the dining room. "I was just putting Jessie's school stuff on the table in there for her. Sorry if we woke you up."

"Not a problem. I wouldn't have slept in if I'd known you were coming. What's the occasion?"

Jessie nodded to the pile of books Adam had put on the table.

"I've got a huge project due Monday and wanted to get some more time to work on it. There are just too many distractions on campus, and Adam had to come back anyway for his dad's birthday dinner. He's going to keep me company until he has to meet up with family."

"Ah, well, happy birthday to your dad, Adam. I'm going to get myself some breakfast and have a shower; can I get you two anything?"

"No thanks, Mr. Trover."

"We ate at the dorm," Jessie said.

"Alright then. I'll leave you alone so you can get to work." He went into the kitchen, but could hear Adam and Jessie as they talked in the dining room. He couldn't help but smile at how the two of them sounded together—already like an old married couple who could finish each other's sentences. He and Savannah had been like that once.

His thoughts turned to Jessie and Adam marrying. It wasn't a stretch to imagine it. They'd only been dating since the spring, but sometimes it was just obvious when two people belonged together. He'd been protective of Jessie when she'd told him she and Adam were dating; she'd never had a steady boyfriend, and he wasn't crazy at the idea of some boy trying to get intimate with his daughter. But he'd begrudgingly admitted after seeing them together that, if she *had* to date someone, Adam was the best kind of boy for her to choose. And it was helpful that he and Savannah already knew his family, since his mother worked at A&A. Savannah had chided Shaun for not seeing their relationship in the cards sooner. They'd met when Adam's mother, Ginny, had come on staff with A&A four years ago, and Savannah swore Adam had developed a crush on Jessie the first day they'd met. "I'm surprised it took them this long to get together," she said. "But God was protecting their hearts. Dating at 20 is very different from dating at 16—so much more maturity. I give them a year before they're engaged."

The thought of Jessie getting engaged made Shaun ill. He

couldn't pay for a wedding. He couldn't help them with a down payment on a house, or even co-sign on a loan, given how poor his credit was likely to be at that point. And he knew his daughter's personality—she wouldn't elope. She'd want a giant party, a bash with a band and ten bridesmaids, a guest list of at least two hundred people—probably more since, between the two of them, they knew practically the entire college student body.

No longer hungry, Shaun abandoned the stack of pancakes he'd made and went for a run. When he came back and finished his shower, Adam was gone. Jessie sat at the dining room table, surrounded by notecards and thick books with titles like, *The Psychology of the Child* and *Brain Development and Learning from Birth Through Adolescence*. He was so impressed with her passion for her future family. He'd heard of women going to college to find a husband, but he'd never heard of anyone using their college years to learn how to be a better wife and mother.

"Interesting reading," he said as he pulled out a chair.

"Fascinating, yeah." She smiled at him and he could see the twinkle in her eyes that she always got when Adam had been around. "When Adam saw what they were he asked if he could read them, too, so I'm not the only one who has any idea what's going on with our kids."

Shaun laughed to hide his anguish. "He's already talking kids?"

"I know, can you believe it?" She flashed a self-conscious smile as a blush crept into her cheeks.

"Did they not invite you to lunch?"

"Oh, no, they did. I'm just really desperate to finish this project, and I know how big family lunches at their place can go. Before you know it you've been hanging out and talking with people so long that it's time for dinner. I wouldn't have wanted to leave once I was there, but I would have lost too much work time if I'd stayed."

"Little Miss Responsible."

"I'm a first-born, what can I say?"

"Can I make you some lunch?" he asked.

"Sure, thanks."

He went back to the kitchen and put together soup and sandwiches for both of them. With Savannah gone again, he was determined not to grocery shop until every food in the house was eaten. He'd gone just a few days before she'd left, so he had plenty to work with at the moment. He made grilled cheese sandwiches and tomato soup to counter the chill of the mid-November day and set them up at the kitchen table so nothing spilled on Jessie's project notes. "Thanks, Dad," she said when she came to the table. "So much better than dorm food, even when it's simple."

"Glad you like it. Can Adam cook?" he asked with a wink.

She laughed. "Not really, no. Standard stuff he can handle, but a whole dinner, with sides and everything—not so much."

"Ah, well, you'll have to help him out then." He chuckled when she blushed. "Oh, come on, you know we all think you two will get married."

"You think so?"

"Don't you?"

"Well ..." she smiled. "Yeah."

"Your mom saw it way before even you two did."

"Really? Mom?"

"Oh, yes. She was thrilled when the two of you finally got together. She loves Adam."

"You're kidding. I didn't know that." She let out a snort. "Wish she loved everything else I was into."

"She does, honey. Believe me. She's got high standards, but it's because she wants the best for people."

The sunny look on Jessie's face was gone. She stirred her soup, her eyes focused on her bowl. "Well if she wants me to reach my full potential she should be trying to spend a little more time with me instead of swooping in to criticize me at every turn."

He covered her free hand with his own. "Hey, trust me Jess, I know how it feels to play second fiddle to A&A. But your mom takes her calling very seriously—"

"She was called to be a mother first. Either she forgot about that or God did. Either way, I'm not too happy with either of them in that regard."

She pushed away her half-eaten soup and untouched sandwich. "I'm not really hungry. I'm going to get back to work."

Shaun let her disappear back into the dining room without trying to stop her. He had his way of coping, and she had hers—he wasn't going to push her to be okay with things. It hurt him to see the chasm between her and Savannah, but at this point he wasn't sure it would be wise to encourage healing between the two of them anyway. Who knew who Savannah might be as time went on? And at this rate, there soon wouldn't be an A&A to compete with, anyway.

SAVANNAH SAT IN THE ROCKING chair on the second story porch and watched the peach trees sway in unison with the wind. She pulled the quilt tighter around her shoulders and reluctantly admitted the weather was turning too cool to sit outside. She retreated to her room down the hall, quilt still around her shoulders, and shut herself in the Spartan room before she ran into anyone. She'd talked to a few others since arriving, and everyone was very gracious and kind, even those who recognized her name. But she didn't feel like she could truly relate to them, given she had no real reason for hating God the way she did, and she was reluctant to give them the impression that she empathized completely with their situation. She chose instead to wander the main rooms during the group activities when everyone else was engaged, and kept her interactions with others limited to meals.

Boredom was becoming a problem, however. And boredom eventually led to her thinking, and thinking eventually led her to dwelling on her future, which she was loathe to consider. She was tired of reading, tired of sleeping, tired of staring at the orchard from the porch. What she really wanted to do was cook.

The food at The Refuge had been excellent so far. More than

once Savannah had wanted to venture behind the swinging wood door and talk shop with Aniyah, the Creole woman Tabitha claimed was the best undiscovered treasure in the world of Southern cuisine. Savannah agreed, and had offered her thanks to the cook more than once when she'd brought out another plate of food to the long table where everyone ate together. But she hadn't been ready to risk the possibility of an actual conversation that might turn to spiritual things, which was likely given the nature of The Refuge, especially when talking with people who had gone through the program. Aniyah had done that four years ago. She'd just never left.

Savannah looked around the room once more, just in case something interesting had materialized when she hadn't been looking. No dice. She headed for the kitchen.

Aniyah played Motown girl groups as she worked. The music could be heard through most of the first floor unless multiple doors were closed between you and her. She sang along with a voice that rivaled Diana Ross's and delivered just as much soul. Savannah paused outside the door, reluctant to interrupt the karaoke cooking. She waited for the song to end, her mouth watering at the scent that wafted under the door, and when "Ain't No Mountain" faded to silence she slowly entered.

Three giant steel pots sat on the industrial sized range, steam billowing to the copper hood above them. Four squat rice cookers stood in a line on the counter, and at the island stood Aniyah, her fists punching bread dough in a huge ceramic bowl. "Well, now, looking for a snack? Don't ruin your appetite for dinner, now, or you'll be sorry when the gumbo comes around and you don't have room."

Savannah was six years old again, peeking into her grandmother's kitchen in the hours leading up to a big family meal. It was the place where she first came to love the principles of good cooking—fresh ingredients, combined with skill and attention to detail, to nourish those you loved. Aniyah couldn't have been more than forty, but her stout form conjured memories of Savannah's

Mimi, and she exuded a wisdom and authority that set Savannah back to feeling like a child eager to help and showcase her own budding abilities. But unlike her grandmother, who would shoo her from her workspace with a hand-embroidered tea towel when she spilled the flour or over-mixed the cake batter, Aniyah reached out a hand and said, "My sidekick is out sick, and I'm drowning in the details today. If you're looking for something to do, come on in and lend a hand."

Savannah smiled and let the door swing closed behind her. "It smells amazing in here. Seafood gumbo?"

"Aye-ya. And they need stirring. Spoon's on the counter."

Grateful for the chance to help, she stepped quickly to the range and located the hefty wooden spoon that rested on a coaster. She breathed deeply, savoring the scent of the gumbo as she stirred. Chunks of vegetables and shrimp were visible through the broth. Her stomach rumbled. "I don't suppose I'll get a sneak preview for lending a hand?"

Aniyah laughed as she cut the dough into four sections and spaced them out along the island top. "You dip in there early. I ain't gonna stop you."

"What else can I do when I'm done here?" Savannah asked as she stirred the second pot.

"Grab an apron from the drawer so you don't get messy."

Savannah grinned. "This sounds fun. What am I making?"

"Beignets."

"Oh, I've heard of those! I've always wanted to try one."

Aniyah chuckled. "Aw, you in for a treat then! The dough is in the fridge. Take it out and dust up the island with some of this here flour. Then turn out the dough and roll it. Pin's in the island drawer on the left."

Giddy, Savannah followed Aniyah's instructions, relishing the weight of the hefty wooden rolling pin in her hands and the feeling of usefulness that fed her hungry soul. She rolled out the dough until Aniyah's practiced eye pronounced it thin enough, then hunted down a pizza cutter as her mentor instructed. "Two inch squares. Though I ain't gonna smack ya if you make them a little bigger."

"Only two inches? We're going to have piles of these."

"Oh yes, but they go quick! You'll see when you have 'em." She *tsked* and muttered, "Never had a beignet."

"Well, I'm from Colorado."

"That accent ain't."

Savannah chuckled, pushing the pizza cutter through the dough. "No, that's true. I was born in South Carolina. But my mother wasn't a fan of fried foods."

Aniyah gave her a look. "Was *she* from Colorado?"

"No, just health conscious."

"Mm, mm, mm." Aniyah shook her head. "A shame, that is." She finished greasing the pan and set the French bread loaves on it. "Healthy is important, but enjoying food is underrated. And some foods, you just gotta ignore how bad they are for you so you can have a little enjoyment. Ain't no one I know enjoyed asparagus the way they enjoy a cookie."

Savannah chuckled. "True."

Aniyah slid the pan into the oven, then carried her mixing bowl to the sink and ran the water onto the mountain of dishes. "So how come you in here and not in with the others? You skipping out on therapy?"

Savannah winced inside as she rolled another line into the dough. She hadn't expected to get the third degree from the cook. "I'm not actually ... attending The Refuge. I'm an old friend of Tabitha's."

"Ain't that nice. That woman. Mm." She put a sudsy hand to her heart. "She saved my life, she did. Lord bless her."

"Saved your life? How? If you don't mind me asking, that is."

"Aw no, I's an open book. Nothing to hide, and maybe something I say helps someone else, right?" She scrubbed a pot, her strong arms flexing with the effort. "I's born in the Bayou, see, and my mama be a sorceress."

Savannah gaped. "Seriously?"

"Aw yeah!" She looked at Savannah and laughed. "Not a lot of backwoods witches in Colorado, eh?"

"Well, Wicca is pretty popular, especially up north, but ... you're talking about voodoo, right?"

"That's right. She made up spells for folks, charms and dolls too."

"Like, voodoo dolls? People actually use those?"

"Aye-ya. All the time." She rinsed off the pot and set it on the massive drying rack. "Anyway, she got real sick, and neighbors took her to the hospital one night, even though she didn't want to go, kept saying she'd heal herself. But she'd been getting real bad real quick, and they didn't wanna take the chance of her dying. They asked me later did I want to visit her, and I knew she'd be wanting some of her charms and talismen, so I brought them with. The doctor, he saw them, because I wasn't careful enough — I didn't know that most people thought voodoo was evil. Well, next day, these people show up at my door and take me away!"

"Into foster care?"

"Yup. They put me with an auntie I never knew I had, and she knew about my mama being a sorceress. She insisted I was doing voodoo too, even though I wasn't. She figured I was as evil as my mama just from living under her roof. So she tried to make me holy so's I wouldn't go to hell. Drug me to her church and dunked me in their pool, made me copy out the Bible whenever I did wrong, and whipped me something merciless when I did something real bad. Which wasn't too often, I can tell you, but she thought it was more often than it was."

She shook her head, rinsing off a steel bowl and setting it beside the pot before setting in on another. "I never did see my mama again. I'd never left the Bayou before going to see her at the hospital, and I didn't know where auntie's house was compared to home. Mama had done my school at home, and so did auntie, so I didn't have the chance to run away until I was older. But soon as I could, I did. I was sixteen. Just took off, middle of the night, with my sewing bag full of food and an extra change of clothes. Well, and the money I stole from her — I'd started taking a dollar here, couple quarters there, for two years, knowing I'd need something when I finally had the chance to go.

"I knew how to get to town from her place, so's I just started walking. Got there at dawn and waited at the bus depot 'til it opened. Bought a ticket to New Orleans and told myself I was never going back." She ran her hands beneath the water to rid them of suds, then dried them and nodded to the island in front of Savannah. "You done with those?"

"Oh — yes, sorry. Do we fry them now?"

"Aw no, I do that when y'all are finishing your dinner. Want them to be nice and hot when you eat them or they just aren't as good."

"Can I help you?"

"No need, no need. But thank you for the offer." She dampened a towel, rung it out, and laid it over the dough squares. "You oughtta get cleaned up for dinner. You got flour on your face."

"Is it time for dinner already?" Savannah lifted the apron over her head. "Thanks for letting me help you out. I've been going a little stir crazy lately."

Aniyah raised her brows, giving her a look. "Stir crazy? Here? Aw, you ain't digging deep enough if you be getting bored. This place is touched by God. He changes you here. But you gotta want to be changed, I think, before he does it."

Bristling but not wanting to show it, Savannah hung the apron on the back of the door before backing halfway out of the kitchen in retreat. "I'm looking forward to trying that gumbo."

Aniyah's grin grew wider and she chuckled at her with a shake of her finger. "That's right, you keep running, sister. Run out that door and get yourself spiffed for supper. Just remember God can always run faster than you."

ANIYAH HAD BEEN RIGHT — the beingets were heaven. After having what she justified as a reasonable serving of them, Savannah went back to the kitchen to help with the clean up. It was a quick job with both of them working—Aniyah had cleaned all the baking dishes while the Refugees had been eating, and there were hardly any leftovers. After turning on the dishwasher Aniyah hung up her apron, packed a canvas shopping bag with the remains of dinner, and went home.

Savannah stole back to her room, eyes trained on the floor as though deep in thought to avoid conversation. Once safely alone, she sat heavily on the bed and sighed. Two hours until bedtime at least—what to do until then?

On the small writing desk in the corner sat the yellow envelope she'd gotten from Marisa. She still hadn't opened it. She avoided thinking too much about A&A. But it had to be done eventually, and sorting it would be a decent way to pass the time.

She emptied the contents onto the bed—eight letters altogether, but one in particular caught her eye. The envelope was pink, with an embossed flower in the corner. It smelled faintly of a perfume that seemed familiar, though she couldn't pinpoint why. She ripped it open and slid out the single sheet of paper—pink and embossed liked the envelope—covered in both sides with slanted blue cursive. The scent of the perfume was calming.

Dear Mrs. Trover,

> *This is a very difficult letter to write, mostly because I will be very embarrassed if I am wrong. But I feel in my heart that I'm right, and I'd never forgive myself if I didn't follow that impression.*
>
> *My brother, Charlie, was living in Boulder at the time of his death back in August. As his only living kin, I was notified of his passing by the hospital where he was taken after his car accident. They told me he had chosen to be an organ donor, and I was pleased to hear that—his life had not amounted to much, and I felt like it was a second chance for him, to be able to help someone else to live their life.*

A month after the accident I was at a women's tea at my
church, and your ministry came up in conversation. Someone
mentioned you'd undergone a heart transplant, and I can't explain
why, but I felt compelled to find whatever details were public about
your procedure. I bought your new book, and when I discovered
your surgery occurred the night my brother died, I couldn't help but
think it was more than mere coincidence.

I've done a little bit of research about transplants, and I've
learned that the recipient often wishes he or she could contact the
family of the donor. I don't know if you feel that way or not, but if
you do, I want you to know I would love to meet you. I'm including
my contact information, but please do not feel any pressure to write
or call. I'm just sure you received Charlie's heart, and I'm content
knowing that it went to someone like you; I will not be offended if
you don't want to contact me.

I pray that every day is a blessing, and that Charlie's heart
allows you to live a long, full life in service to the Lord. (It would
be quite the irony if it did, believe me. But with God, all things are
possible!) God bless you and your ministry—I pray for you every day.

Sincerely,

Lori Bates

A torrent of emotions rolled over her. She'd stopped consciously
wondering about her donor weeks ago, but faced with the chance
to learn about him she felt almost desperate for information. And
an inexplicable fondness for this Lori drove her to inhale again the
scent wafting from the stationery.

But this woman believed Savannah to be—well, who everyone
thought she was. She sounded so happy to know Savannah was a
good Christian woman—would Lori be angry if she knew Savannah wasn't? Didn't her life count for something even if she wasn't
speaking to capacity crowds and writing bestsellers? Or even if she
didn't believe in God?

Her hand hovered over her cell phone. She'd have to fake the good Christian woman stuff if she went to meet her — and she definitely wanted to meet her. Could she do it?

Only one way to find out.

Hand trembling, she dialed the number. When a woman answered she knew it was her without even asking. "Lori, this is Savannah Trover."

She heard a gasp, then Lori laughed. "Oh my stars, Savannah, it is so nice of you to call."

"I can't thank you enough for your note. I wish I could explain how much it means to me."

"I'm glad to hear it. Thank you."

"If you were serious about meeting —"

"I was, absolutely."

"What are you doing Friday?"

After hanging up with Lori, she called the airline and arranged her flight, then called the car rental company. She gave them her credit card number, then let her mind wander while she was on hold. She was pulled from her daydream by the customer representative's apology and had to ask her to repeat it.

"I'm sorry, but that card isn't going through."

"It's not?" She read the number off again.

"Still not working, I'm sorry. Do you want to cancel the reservation or try another card?"

Savannah huffed in frustration. "Try another card." She dug out the card she rarely used and read off the number.

"That worked. Thank you."

She finished making the reservation, then hung up and stared at her credit card. "That's just not right," she muttered. She dialed Shaun's number but got his voicemail. "It's me," she said. "I just tried to use the Visa and it wouldn't go through. Any idea what that's about? Did you cancel it for some reason? Let me know."

She'd never had a card denied before. Certainly it was a mistake of some kind. Perhaps Shaun had lost his card and had to cancel them, and had just forgotten to tell her.

She nodded to herself. Yes, that made sense. He probably didn't think she'd need to use the card on the trip, so he hadn't bothered to let her know. That must be it.

Unless it's maxed out.

The thought almost made her laugh aloud. Almost. They had a ridiculously high credit limit on it, there was no way they'd reached it.

Right?

CHAPTER 12

SAVANNAH CHECKED THE ADDRESS ONCE MORE BEFORE PULLING to the curb. Lori's house matched the tone of her voice: small, sweet, and tidy. The suburban Kansas street was lined with tall oaks and prim houses in pastel colors that reminded Savannah of Easter eggs. She had a feeling Lori was either a preschool teacher or a librarian.

She sat in the rental and psyched herself up for the act. *Just keep the conversation on her brother—on Charlie—and off your ministry. You can do this. It's just for a couple hours.* She let herself through the white picket gate and rang the bell. When Lori answered the door, Savannah was overcome with a sense of warmth and affection that melted her apprehension and compelled her to hug the small woman. "It is so wonderful to meet you. Thank you so much for letting me come over."

"Oh of course, of course!" the woman said as she welcomed Savannah in. "I'm so happy you got my note—and that you didn't think I was a loon. I was afraid it would get screened out by an assistant or something and you'd never even see it."

Savannah chuckled. "Actually, my assistant was the one that gave it to me." And now she knew why.

Lori ushered her into a tiny living room with a flower print loveseat and a coffee table set with a tray of cookies and slices of lemon cake. She brought Savannah a mug of coffee, then sat down in a slip-covered chair across from her. "I just can't believe Savannah Trover is sitting in my living room. The ladies at church will never believe me."

The irritation Savannah expected to feel at the comment was nowhere to be found. Instead, she felt a sense of graciousness that she hadn't experienced in a long time. "I'm no one special, believe me. But thank you for thinking I am." She pulled the corner off her slice of bread. "This is really awkward, but I want to say how sorry I am that you lost your brother. Obviously I am tremendously grateful for his willingness to be an organ donor, but as a recipient it's grieving to know you're alive because of someone else's loss."

Lori nodded, her long, mousy brown hair waving over her shoulders. "I can imagine it would be. As Christians, we have such a different understanding of that concept, though, don't we? We are who we are because someone else died so we could live."

Savannah found it easier to fake her agreement with Lori than it had been with anyone else. "That's true. And at least you know you'll see Charlie in heaven." She might not believe in it anymore, but certainly it was what Lori wanted to hear.

But Lori's countenance fell a bit at the comment. "Actually, I don't believe I will. Charlie was an atheist."

Savannah felt like Dorothy opening her front door when she first arrived in Oz. The whole world suddenly looked very different. "Really? Would you mind telling me about him?"

Some of the sun came back into Lori's face. "I'd love to. Charlie was the only family I had left, and we were very close. I miss him, but it helps to talk about him." She settled back with her coffee, but Savannah found herself on the edge of her seat.

"I think I mentioned in my letter that I'd prayed Charlie's life would be somewhat redeemed by his organ donations. I prayed the night I got the call that the people receiving them would go on to do great things for God's kingdom. He was a very wounded person, but never did anything to deal with those wounds, so his life just kept taking more and more tragic turns.

"Our father left us when I was eight and Charlie was four. I was old enough that I had plenty of memories to remind me of why it was good that he was gone, but Charlie didn't. We both suffered for the lack of a father, but Charlie even more so. He sought him out twice, once when he was sixteen, and again when he was twenty-four. Both times our father turned him away, and that made it all the more painful for him.

"Our mom was wounded, too, but she did as best she could by Charlie and me. She was gone a lot, though, working, so Charlie and I grew pretty close from depending on each other so much. He was my best friend until I met my husband. Oh!" Lori stood and crossed the room to the small brick fireplace framed in white wood. She picked up a picture frame from the mantle and handed it to Savannah. "This is him, two years ago on his birthday."

Savannah found herself looking at a man she would have sworn she'd met before. Perhaps it was because of how much he looked like Lori—the same green eyes, the same round face and brown hair. His mouth was different, though, and his expression, despite the happy occasion, looked guarded, even though he was smiling for the camera.

"While we were growing up, we had neighbors that were Christians," Lori continued as she went back to her seat. "Kirk became like a second father to Charlie. They'd go fishing, work on cars together—Kirk fixed up old Mustangs and the like, and Charlie loved to tinker with stuff like that. His wife Pauline was sweet, too, and would let me help her bake. She taught me to sew, too. But Charlie and Kirk were far closer than she and I were, I think because Kirk lost his father when he was young, so he knew how Charlie felt and how badly he needed a strong male role model.

"They'd invite us to church, though Mom wouldn't let us go, and Pauline always had Christian music playing in the house. When I was sixteen she led me to the Lord. Charlie and Kirk didn't talk about faith as much, but I talked with Charlie about it, and when he was about eighteen he started getting real curious and asking me more questions. I really thought he was going to cross the line at one point, but he kept backing away."

Savanna stared at the picture as Lori told her story. She felt a connection with the man in the picture, like they'd spent time together or at least met in person. She'd never actively tried to visualize her donor, yet a mental image had coalesced over time, and it was eerily similar to this.

"But then one day Charlie went over to their house and then came right back. He was absolutely seething. He'd always struggled with anger, but Kirk's easy-going nature had helped him to learn how to calm some of that down. This was the most angry I'd seen him in a long time. He told me that Pauline had answered the door and told him she'd kicked Kirk out. She'd caught him cheating on her. They ended up getting a divorce a couple months later. Kirk never came back, never saw Charlie—the last time Charlie had been there they'd been planning another fishing trip." She shook her head and sipped her coffee again, and Savannah could feel the anger and sadness and betrayal as keenly as though it had happened to her.

"That was it for Charlie, as far as God was concerned. It pushed him over the edge. Between our father abandoning us and Kirk essentially doing the same thing, he was convinced any idea of a Heavenly Father was garbage. For a couple years we didn't speak much—he didn't like that I was a Christian. But our Mom died about eight years ago, and that brought us back together—we were all either of us had. We'd gotten really close again over the last couple years.

"I kept holding out hope that he'd turn to the Lord," she said with a sigh. "He claimed to be an atheist, said God didn't exist, but then other times he'd talk about how much he hated God. I'd point out the irony in hating something that didn't exist, but he could never get over that. I kept thinking, 'Well, maybe he believes God exists more than he realizes he does. That's better than not believing he's there at all!'" She gave Savannah a sad smile. "But he had his chance; he certainly didn't die without hearing the truth."

Savannah was stunned. Not believing God existed, but then hating him, too—it was as though Lori had read her mind. Goosebumps rose on her arms.

"I have an album in the family room with more pictures of Charlie. Would you like to see them?"

Savannah nodded, feeling greedy for whatever information Lori was willing to share. "I'd love to. Thanks."

Lori disappeared into another room and returned with a navy blue album with "Charlie" embossed on the front. The pictures were arranged chronologically, beginning with a hospital-blanket bundle with a baby's face poking out. Savannah flipped the pages slowly, studying each image as though she'd be quizzed.

"What time does your flight leave tonight?" Lori asked.

"Seven forty-five."

"My husband gets home at five and we usually eat dinner around five-thirty. We'd love to have you stay if you think you can still get to the airport on time."

She'd arrived with the plan of darting out as soon as she could, but now she wished she were staying longer. "If it's not an imposition, I would love that."

She and Lori talked about less serious things as Savannah flipped through the album. She chuckled when she came to the more recent pictures—in each one Charlie wore jeans and long-sleeved T-shirts—though by this time she wasn't surprised.

Lori's husband Wayne arrived just before five, and was as pleasant and friendly as his wife. He and Savannah chatted while Lori made dinner—without Savannah's help, though she'd offered—and Lori eventually called them to the table for a dinner of spaghetti and garlic bread. It was almost six when Savannah said she should get going soon.

"Let me bring out dessert before you go," she said. She brought out a cake plate holding a glistening strawberry pie.

Savannah's mouth watered, and she actually let out a groan of happiness. "You'd have no way to know this," she said as she eyed the generous slice Lori cut for her, "but ever since the surgery I have had the most intense craving for strawberries."

Lori handed her the plate with a smile. "That makes total sense," she said. "It was Charlie's favorite food."

SHAUN SHUT DOWN HIS COMPUTER and sat in the quiet of his office. He was beginning to regret signing the lease on an office suite that was so small he'd have to be in a cubicle. It was getting harder and harder to be in the presence of his staff, and being able to hide in his office had become a means of survival for both him and them. They couldn't whisper behind his back if he was right there, and he couldn't pretend that everything was normal when he was stuck in the same depressed atmosphere as them. He could feel that tension every time he entered the room.

His cell rang. He glanced at the screen and groaned inside. He knew what a bad sign it was that he didn't want to talk to his wife whom he hadn't seen in so many days. But there it was: he simply didn't want to. Life at the office might be miserable, but he was strangely, and sadly, happy with the house empty. When she'd been hospitalized it had been a nightmare. Now it was a relief.

He let the call go to voicemail and pulled on his coat. He'd listen to her message in the car.

"See you tomorrow, Brenda," he said with a nod as he passed the receptionist. She didn't even try to smile, just waved and said, "Bye" as he headed out the door. He was going to have to come clean with them soon, or else they'd start abandoning ship. On second thought, maybe he'd just let them do that. It would save him the trouble of having to admit defeat to a roomful of people he once considered family. It would save him from paying severance, too.

He was halfway home when he remembered the voicemail from Savannah. He set the phone on speaker mode and started the message.

"Hi Shaun, it's me. You will never guess where I am. I flew to Kansas this morning to meet the sister of my heart donor. She wrote me a letter that Marisa brought when she came out here the other day. I'm on my way back to the airport now to go back to Georgia, but I wanted to tell you something I discovered. Charlie—that's my donor, Charlie Bates; he was 28 and died in a car crash—he was an atheist. His father left their family when he was little, and a Christian neighbor who took him under his wing ended up cheating on his wife. Between those two events, he was completely soured against God. But what was really crazy was the way his sister, Lori, described it. She said he claimed to be an atheist, but that he also hated God. Shaun, that is exactly how I've been feeling. And it doesn't make sense to hate something that you don't think exists. It's like he knew—just like I knew—that God really was real, but hating him wasn't enough to express how betrayed he felt. He wanted to act like he didn't even exist. But his anger—his *anger*—was so strong that he couldn't bring himself to truly believe God didn't exist, because then where would he direct it all? And guess what else? He practically lived in jeans and long-sleeved T-shirts, and his favorite food was strawberries." She laughed, and Shaun found himself chuckling with her. "Shaun, I don't know how this could be possible, but I think I'm living out Charlie's emotions. Do you know what this means? It means it's not just me! I haven't been able to figure out why I hate God so much because *I* don't—Charlie does! Anyway, I'm going to get on Tabitha's computer when I get back to Georgia and check out my forum to see if anyone else has ever experienced this. But you're much better with all that internet searching—would you be able to look around and see if this phenomenon is documented anywhere? Or better yet, what we can do about it? I can't tell you how happy I am to know this isn't just me. There's a *reason*—"

The voicemail system had cut her off, but he knew she'd said everything she really wanted to say. He started speeding, eager to get online. He found himself actually smiling.

Despite the fact that he'd skipped lunch and barely had breakfast, he didn't even make a pit stop in the kitchen before going straight to his office and booting up his computer. He wrote down a list of search terms as he waited for the system to finish starting up. *Memories stored in organs, transplanting memories, organ donor memories.* He opened a browser window and typed the first phrase in. He expected to get something about sentimental views of musical instruments, but instead hit pay dirt with the very first result. He read the brief article which gave little scientific information, but confirmed the likely existence of a phenomenon called cellular memories. Armed with an exact phrase, he searched again. 'Cellular memories' brought up more than enough information to start with. He spent the next two hours reading and making notes to share with Savannah.

- *Cellular memories: hypothesis that personal memories, tastes, personality traits, etc. are stored in cells throughout the body, not just the brain*
- *Some anecdotal support for the theory, but no peer-reviewed studies have been done*
- *Dr. Pearsall, an expert in the field (the only one, apparently)*
- *how to make it stop — can't find anything on this*

It was this last bit that frustrated Shaun the most. He read everything he could find online that seemed a legitimate description of the phenomenon, and in none of the articles was there any mention of how the recipients got those memories "turned off." Certainly there had to be some way.

He finally stopped when a sudden wave of nausea reminded him of how long it had been since his last meal. As he threw together a hasty dinner, he tried not to let himself get too excited at this new discovery. If they could identify Savannah's struggles as really being cellular memories, then at least they had a cause, a documented — albeit not completely accepted — type of event that others had also experienced.

Perhaps he'd try to contact Dr. Pearsall. It couldn't hurt. Shaun hadn't read any stories that seemed exactly like Savannah's — none of them seemed to involve changes in spirituality. Musical and food preferences, yes. From one religion to another — or to none — not so much. Leave it to Savannah to be the exception to the rule.

There had to be a fix, a cure. There had to be. He held on to that as he ate and surfed the web some more, praying there was an article he hadn't read yet that touched on how to stop cellular memories. He couldn't let himself think about what was in store if there wasn't.

SAVANNAH'S CELL RANG HER AWAKE. Shaun's number was on the screen. "Hi there."

"Hi — did I wake you? I thought for sure you'd be up by now."

"I should be, don't worry about it. I was up late."

"Me too. Reading about cellular memories."

She sat up, fully awake at the phrase. "Yes! Me too! You got my message then."

"And got on the computer as soon as I got home. Fascinating."

"Sure — until it's happening to you."

"So did you see that an organ recipient wrote a book about her cellular memory experience?"

"I did. Tabitha is going to get it from the library for me today."

"And Dr. Pearsall —"

"Yes, I saw him, too. I want to read his book as well. Maybe it tells how to get off this train."

She heard Shaun sigh. "That was the one thing I couldn't find anything on. Did you?"

She sank back against the pillow. "No. For a minute there I was hoping you were going to have found the missing piece. I do have to admit, though — I feel a lot better knowing I'm not going crazy."

"So — does it make it easier for you to think past it all, to fake it better, now that you know it's not really you thinking those thoughts? I don't suppose you've changed your mind about the book tour ..."

She slammed her hand down on the bed beside her. "You've got to be kidding me."

"I just thought—"

"No, it doesn't change that. I'm sorry that's such an inconvenience for you."

"Savannah—"

"Look, I'm not happy about all this either, remember? And it doesn't make it any easier on me when you try to goad me into going along with your plans and pour on the guilt. I need support, not a constant reminder of how I'm failing everyone."

"So you want me to lie about how I'm feeling?"

"No, I want you to say, 'Wow, Savannah, I'm sorry, that really sucks, this must be really hard for you.' Not 'You're ruining my life.'"

"I never said that."

"You didn't have to."

The silence that ensued made her ears ring. "I need some breakfast. I'll talk to you later." She hung up without waiting for a response. *Well, that was a lousy way to start my morning.* She chose her clothing and took a shower, all the while feeling like someone was watching her. Knowing now that the new Savannah was really the old Charlie, as though his soul were still hanging around trying to get her attention, was disconcerting. Creepy, actually. She hurried down to the main floor where there was more activity, suddenly uncomfortable being alone.

Tabitha greeted her as she entered the therapy room. "Just on my way to group. Want to join us?"

Savannah chuckled. "Only if you think you can help Charlie."

"Sorry, I don't think my theology allows for psychoanalyzing the deceased."

"Mine didn't either, but now I'm not so sure. Listen, can I use your computer again? I want to order that other book we saw, the one that isn't at the library."

"Sure, go ahead. I'll be done at eleven, if you want to talk."

Savannah looked up the book again, then attempted her first-ever online purchase. She filled out the plethora of fields to create an account, then hit 'submit,' hoping she'd done everything right. When the error screen came up, she groaned. What had she done wrong?"

Please review your credit card information and try again.

"*That* was the other thing I wanted to talk to Shaun about!" She cursed herself as she pulled out the other credit card and entered its information. This time the order went through. It was at that point that she realized she'd listed her home as the destination for the book. Who knew how long it would be before she actually got to read it? She cursed herself again and began a new internet search with the terms "stop cellular memories."

It was the only piece of information that didn't seem to exist.

SAVANNAH WAS STARTLED WHEN TABITHA appeared. "My gosh, it is already eleven?"

"Eleven-thirty, actually. Did you want lunch?"

Savannah rubbed her eyes; they burned from staring so long at the screen. "Yes, I should."

Tabitha gave her one of her looks that meant she knew more about how you felt than you probably wanted her to. "Didn't find what you were looking for?"

"It's the one thing no one writes about. Either that or I'm just not searching for the right thing."

They walked to the dining room where everyone else was already eating. "I had so much hope last night. The whole way home on that flight, I just kept thinking this was the beginning of the end of all of this. Now that I had an idea of what was going on, I'd be able to put a stop to it. But now I feel like I'm just doomed to live like this forever." She didn't tell Tabitha how the chill had left her chest when she'd visited Lori, and how this morning, when faced with the absence of the information she desperately needed, it had once again returned.

Tabitha wrapped an arm around Savannah's shoulders. "God has a plan."

Savannah shuddered Tabitha's arm away. "Don't even say that."

She regretted the words instantly, but only because she knew how they must hurt Tabitha. It was an apt reflection of the fears that gripped her, however — that this was who she was now, a cold-hearted witch, in more ways than one.

CHAPTER 13

SHAUN LET OUT A GROWL AND SLAMMED THE PHONE BACK INTO its cradle with a curse before leaving his office. He was jumpy with anger at how Savannah turned his words back on him, how they couldn't have a civil conversation anymore. He needed a run to clear his head.

Jessie was in the hallway, moving with quiet steps away from his office. "When did you get here?"

She stopped and slowly turned. He could read her expression loud and clear. "A little while ago."

"You heard it all."

"Yeah."

He blew out a breath and shrugged. "I'm sorry you had to hear that."

She cocked her head slightly, and her expression became unreadable. "Are you and Mom getting a divorce?"

"No, honey, we're not." He hoped his face wasn't as clear to her as hers often was to him. He wasn't sure how well he could hide his doubt about the statement he'd just made. He put his arm around her and led her to the kitchen. "All married couples have their rough patches; it doesn't mean they're going to split up. Your mom and I agreed a long time ago divorce would never be an option."

She sat on a barstool as he started the coffeepot. "But that was before she turned into ... whoever she is now," she said. "She's not the same person. She doesn't even believe in God anymore, does she? So what reason does *she* have to keep divorce off the table?"

He was getting uncomfortable with this conversation. He wasn't ready to talk with Jessie about something he himself hadn't figured out yet. *I should never have told her everything Savannah was going through.* "We're not getting a divorce, Jess. Trust me. Now, what brings you home? You're a college student. You should be sleeping in until noon, not driving home before breakfast. I didn't think I'd see you again before Thanksgiving."

"I left some stuff in my closet that I wanted to bring back to campus. I meant to get it when I was here last but I forgot. The rest of my weekend is really packed, so I wanted to come now while I had the time." She swiveled on the seat, eyes concentrated on the marble countertop. "Is Mom coming home for Thanksgiving?"

Shaun tried not to show his irritation. "I don't know, we haven't talked about it."

"What if she doesn't come home?"

He chuckled. "What, and relocates to Georgia? I don't think she could handle the humidity."

"I'm serious, Dad. What if she decides she's done with us and just stays there? What if the new Savannah *likes* humidity?"

He rolled his eyes at her. "You're getting melodramatic, Jessie. Trust me, she's not staying there forever."

"Well, when is she coming back then?"

He shrugged and took down two mugs from the cabinet. "I don't know. When she's gotten herself together, I guess. Did you hear the first part of the conversation, about cellular memory?"

"No, I came in when you started getting angry."

He winced. "Well, your mom met with the sister of her heart donor and found out some very interesting information." He outlined Savannah's conversation with Lori and the discovery they'd both made of the theory. "So we feel like we're going in the right direction. We just have to do more research."

"That sounds ... weird. Did you find anything that said how to stop the cellular memories from interfering with the recipient?"

"Unfortunately, that's the one thing nobody mentions. From what I gather they may fade with time, but it's not like you can just switch them off, or speed up the fading process."

"So she's like this indefinitely?"

"I guess so, yes."

She frowned at him. "But what about A&A? It *can't* last like this indefinitely, can it? She's not speaking or traveling—where will the income come from?"

"Her new book is still selling, and so are her past books— whenever a new one comes out it always revives the sales of the others, even if it's just for a little while. It's not like there's no money coming in at all. You have plenty of things in your own life to worry about, Jessie, don't dwell on this one."

"How can't I, Dad? Adam's family would be in dire straits if A&A went down. I can't *not* worry about it."

He squeezed her shoulder. "I know, honey. But we just have to trust that God will take care of everything."

She shrugged off his hand and slipped from the barstool to open the fridge and pull out the milk. "I haven't been real thrilled with how God has handled things lately. I don't know how willing I am to trust that he's going to snap his fingers and make all this okay."

He wished he could admit he felt the same way, but he wasn't about to feed into her own struggle and doubt with his own. Though hearing her speak like that made him sad—and even more stressed. If she were to find out what was going on—if A&A really did collapse—he'd be just as much to blame for her walking away from God as Savannah would be.

He responded with something lame, hoping it didn't sound as phony to her. He poured them both coffee, but she excused her- self, taking her mug to her bedroom and shutting the door. Shaun slumped onto the couch and prayed for what he realized was the first time in weeks. *You've got to show me how to fix this. I've got to fix this. Tell me what to do.*

He stared at the trees, waiting for an answer, and tried not to assume the ever-stronger impression that closing A&A was actu- ally from God. Surely that was his own fear talking. Why would God want to shut down such an important ministry? *Regardless, nothing is going to get fixed if we're not talking to each other.* He had to go to Georgia. He had to get face-to-face with Savannah and talk all this through. It had been less than a week since she'd been gone, but already it felt like a month. The distance between them grew exponentially with every day that passed. They needed to reconnect, fast.

He took his coffee to his office and looked up their frequent flyer miles, only to discover Savannah had dipped into them for both her flight to Georgia and to Kansas. There weren't enough left for him to book a round-trip ticket. He cursed under his breath and debated the importance of the trip for just a moment, then looked up a flight and tried to book it.

I'm sorry, your purchase did not go through. Please check your credit card account number and try again.

Shaun's stomach sank. *Please Jesus, help me.*

TABITHA APPEARED AT THE KITCHEN door. "Shaun's here."

Savannah nearly chopped her knuckles into the onions. "Okay, thanks. I'll be out in a minute."

Tabitha shut the door and Savannah groaned.

"Who's this Shaun?" Aniyah asked, eyebrows arched.

"My husband."

"He come to visit you? Aw, that's sweet."

A snort escaped. "It's not a visit. More like a business meeting."

Aniyah *tsked*. "Don't be assuming the worst, now."

"It's not an assumption, trust me." She slid a finger down the side of the knife, knocking minced vegetables to the cutting board. "Into the pot?"

"Yeah. Thanks for helping. You spoiling me. Gonna miss you when you go."

"Well, hopefully that won't happen for a while." She hadn't admitted that to Tabitha yet, fearing she'd be given a deadline. But the thought of returning to Colorado put a knot in her chest that made it hard to breathe.

Being in Georgia was so lovely. It was easy to forget about Colorado, about A&A, about her family, when she was surrounded by such warm and loving people who didn't press her to be anyone other than who she felt she was right then. The others at The Refuge understood how wounds of the soul could change you on a deep level. They didn't expect you to fake it or try to deny your pain. Not that the pain she felt was actually hers. None of them knew that, though. And knowing it didn't make anything any easier for her.

But with Shaun here, she couldn't live in her pretty Georgia world of denial. She had to face what was going on back home because of her. And since she couldn't do anything about any of it, she didn't really want to face it.

She dawdled as much as she dared, then went to the sitting room where she and Tabitha had talked the first day she'd arrived. He was sitting in one of the corner seats by the window, staring out at the orchard of leafless trees. It had been only a week— how was it that he already felt like a stranger?

"Hi."

He looked up at her. For a moment she could have sworn he didn't recognize her. "Hey."

They didn't touch. She sat down in the chair diagonal from him and tried to muster some affection, or even a feeling of friendliness. It didn't work. "I've been meaning to ask you. I tried to use the Visa the other day and it was denied. What's that about?"

He waved a hand. "Just a glitch. It happened to me, too. Use the Mastercard until I get it sorted out."

She thought about that for a moment, but couldn't get it to make sense. "What is there to sort out?"

"I don't know. They're looking into it."

She narrowed her eyes. "I don't think you're being honest with me."

He sighed, and his expression aged him ten years. "Look, Savannah, I was hoping we'd be able to ... to think through some things a little more level-headedly if I came out here. I don't want to get into any arguments."

She worked to keep her tone even. "I'm not trying to get into an argument. I'm trying to get a straight answer."

"We need to talk about more important things."

"More important than why you're evading my questions?"

"A&A is going under." She shut her mouth, eyes wide as Shaun continued. "We're barely making ends meet. We have no way to budget for the future because we have no idea what our income will be next month, much less for the next quarter. Your book is selling, and numbers have gone up for your backlist, but none are as high as we'd hoped. We don't have the book tour income we'd been counting on, and in fact lost money when we canceled—"

"You don't have to remind me, I know what happened," she snapped.

"I'm not trying to make you feel guilty—"

"Oh no? Look, I know I cost the ministry money, I know I'm to blame—"

"Look I'm not trying to blame you." He stopped, took a deep breath, started again with his tone lowered. "I'm just trying to lay everything out on the table. This is what we're dealing with, and I don't know how much longer I can keep things together over there. The fact is we're falling apart, and without you at the helm we're doomed."

She swallowed hard. The joy at the thought of not having that weight on her shoulders anymore was buried by the horror of costing her staff their jobs and casting such a shameful light on her family. "So what are you saying?"

"I'm saying I think we need to shut it down."

"What? No."

"Then tell me how to keep it open."

"I don't know. That's not my department."

Shaun scoffed. "No, your department is writing books and speaking about them, and you're not doing either one."

Savannah blinked back tears. "Well, I'm sorry."

"Sorry doesn't pay the bills. We need to close, the sooner the better."

Savannah hugged herself, the cold in her chest seeming to course through every vein of her body. "I can't believe it's coming to this."

Surprise joined frustration in his face. "*I* can't believe you're not jumping at the chance to shut it down. You don't even believe in the ministry's mission anymore, what do you care if it thrives or dies?"

"Because that ministry is the culmination of my blood, sweat, and tears! It's not like I've forgotten who I was before all this happened, Shaun. We both gave the last ten years of our lives to that place. How can you think I'd be happy to close it?"

"You may not have forgotten who you were, but it doesn't change the fact that you're not that person anymore. The new Savannah is making it pretty clear that the priorities from her old life are out the window."

She couldn't deny it, much as she wanted to. And she couldn't deny that he was right about the ministry—it had to be closed. Keeping it open was impossible—and at this point, not even reasonable. She wiped tears from her cheeks with her sleeves. "Fine. Shut it down then. Just tell them ... tell them I'm not strong enough to keep working." She let out a snort. "Oh, what do I care—you can tell them the truth if you want. It doesn't matter anymore anyway."

She stood and turned toward the stairs, but Shaun sprang from his seat and grabbed her arm. "Wait, where are you going?"

"Back to my room. I have books on cellular memory I'm reading."

"Well—can I at least come up with you? Bring up my bag?"

She was confused. "What—are you staying here?"

"Of course. I'm staying with you—aren't I? I mean, I assumed ..."

His words died off as they blinked at each other in awkward surprise. The thought of sharing her bed with him made her skin crawl. "Um, that's fine ... I guess. I just thought ..." She sighed. "Never mind. Bring your bag."

Maybe Tabitha had a cot he could sleep on.

SHAUN THREW HIS BAG INTO the back of the taxi. "So you're coming back Wednesday, right?"

She cringed. "Actually, I changed my flight again."

Great. Another $75 down the drain. "But you'll be back for Thanksgiving at least, right?"

"I — well — you know, that's two weeks away, we can talk about it later."

He shook his head but said nothing. She kept her mouth shut so nothing snarky could slip out. He slid into the back seat of the cab and shut the door without saying goodbye.

Savannah watched the cab kick up dust down the long driveway, and willed the tension in her shoulders to finally release. It had been the most awkward two days of her life, having Shaun here; but even though she was glad it was over, she wasn't glad to see him go. Not because she missed him, or for any reasons at all affectionate or intimate, but because of what he was going to do once he got home.

She went back up to her room and crawled under the covers of her bed to continue reading her book. It was an autobiography about a heart and lung transplant recipient who had experienced drastic changes in her personality after her surgery. It was one of the most well-known and well-documented instances of cellular memory, and Savannah found comfort in the author's familiar struggles. She was making a list of things the woman had done to cope with the bizarre experience, hoping to create a roadmap to follow as she tried to figure out life while sharing Charlie's heart. When she'd first found the book she'd researched the author, hoping they might be able to connect and Savannah might glean some wisdom from her. But the first article she'd found had been the woman's obituary.

She read through lunch, not feeling up to socializing with the other Refugees or Aniyah, and only stopped when her cell phone rang in the early afternoon. Marisa's name came up on the screen, which was the only reason she answered. "Hi, Marisa."

"Savannah, hi. Is Shaun still there?"

"No, he left a few hours ago. How did you know he was here?"

"Brenda told me. I talked to her earlier. That's actually why I'm calling. She phoned me this morning because she wanted to know if I knew anything about A&A shutting down."

Savannah sat up, confused. "What? Why was she asking about that?"

Marisa's stalling sigh made Savannah ill. "Apparently a couple people's paychecks bounced over the last couple days. She tried calling Shaun about it, but he never answered his cell."

She thought back to his visit and realized she'd never even heard his phone ring. Would he really have turned it off? Or not even brought it? He never did that. *He knew before he came out that A&A was going to close.*

"Anyway, people over there are in a panic and no one knows what to do or what's going on. That's why Brenda called me; she was hoping I'd heard something from you, or could at least get some information for them."

Savannah hung her head and rubbed a hand over her eyes. "Oh, Marisa ... yes, we actually are closing A&A. But we just decided that yesterday. Shaun didn't tell me how desperate things were right now; I thought we were closing it because the future was so uncertain. I had no idea things were already as bleak as they are. I feel awful. Listen — tell me whose checks bounced and I'll pay them out of our personal account."

Marisa gave her the names, and Savannah swallowed back her tears as she wrote them down. The guilt and depression she'd managed to keep at bay while on her sabbatical came crashing down on her as she stared at the names of people she'd worked with for years.

"There's something else," Marisa said. Savannah could hear the delicate note in her voice that told her how uncomfortable she was bringing this up. "I never told you about this because ... well, I figured there was a reasonable explanation and I didn't want to make any assumptions. But now ..." She sighed. "Months ago, when I'd given Shaun your receipts from the tour, I ended up finding a few more that had fallen out of the pile in my car. I brought them back in and he was already gone, but the other receipts and a reimbursement form were sitting on his desk. I figured I'd make it easy on him and list them on the form myself, and when I did I saw items on the form that weren't from the tour. I had never seen the charges before, they didn't ring any bells."

Savannah remembered doing the same thing, and how she'd held on to the information to use as a weapon should she need it. She'd forgotten about it. But she wasn't about to admit she already knew and hadn't done anything about it. "Thanks for telling me, Marisa. I'll ask Shaun about that." She made an excuse for leaving and hung up as quickly as she could.

Messing around with receipts ... She couldn't think of any reasons for doing such a thing that didn't involve some sort of financial scheming. But that made her consider something else. What if closing A&A wasn't entirely her fault? The thought gave her a brief shot of relief, until it sank in that Shaun was then guilty of something that was likely to be unethical, possibly even illegal.

Oh, Shaun. What have you done?

SHAUN'S WORLD CRUMBLED A LITTLE more when he came home from the office two days later. Jessie's car was in the driveway, and that wasn't a good thing in the middle of the week. He didn't have to see the bank statement to know why she was there.

He hated himself. He'd been hating himself for a while, but just not dwelling on it. He'd redirected the brunt of his loathing to Savannah, though she didn't know it—mostly the hating was done in his head. But the inevitable had finally happened, and now his daughter was caught in the net. What kind of father was he? What kind of husband, what kind of business manager?

The walls were closing in. It made it hard to breathe.

He snuck in quietly, hoping to establish a defense before facing

Jessie. He prepared his speech, then walked the house in search of her. The sooner he got this over with, the better.

She was crying in her room. He knocked gently on the door, then opened it. "Sweetheart, I'm so sorry."

His sympathy brought on a fresh round of tears. She buried her head in his chest, which surprised him—he'd expected her anger. After a few minutes the sobs died down and she said, "Adam broke up with me."

It wasn't what he'd been expecting. "Wh-what? Why, what happened?" He began plotting Adam's demise.

"Because of A&A shutting down. He said he couldn't imagine marrying into the family that screwed his over so bad."

She began to cry again. Shaun flagellated himself in his head. "Jessie, I'm so sorry. We wouldn't have done it if we didn't have to; I hope you know that. We just couldn't keep it afloat."

"I know, Dad, I know. I'm not blaming you." She sniffed and disengaged herself from his embrace to flop onto the bed. "It's not your fault Mom went off the deep end. If she'd just get her act together, this wouldn't have happened."

"She can't help it either, Jess. I don't think we can fully understand what she's going through. This whole cellular memories phenomenon—"

"I don't buy it." She shook her head emphatically. "I asked one of our professors about it. He said it's pretty much all a crock. People just hear things being talked about in the OR while they're anesthetized, it gets into their subconscious, that sort of thing. She's just using it as an excuse. Don't let her dupe you, Dad."

Shaun sat beside Jessie, scrambling for a response. He hadn't expected her to lay all the blame on Savannah. It was tempting to let her take the fall. *Let Jessie hate her from afar—at least I won't lose my daughter, too.* But as he watched her mop her tears, he knew she needed a mother, and to drive a wedge even further between them would eventually hurt Jessie as well. He didn't want to be the one that caused that if he could help it. "Look, sweetheart ... I know you're upset, and you have every right to be. But your mother doesn't deserve all the blame. Other issues were at play here."

"Like what?"

He hadn't thought that far. "Well, confidentiality restricts me from saying anything," he said quickly. "But I just wanted you to know that. It's not entirely her fault."

"But if she hadn't gone crazy, it could have stayed open, right? Even if there were other issues — that's the main one."

He sighed. "She hasn't gone crazy, Jess. But yes, I guess you're right, it could have stayed open."

She rolled her eyes. "Oh, and on top of this, guess what I got in the mail today? A letter from the registrar, saying my tuition isn't paid. So now I get to deal with that mix-up. Like I have the time."

Shaun closed his eyes. He'd been right. "Actually — I had a feeling that might happen."

"What? Why?"

"Because your tuition *isn't* paid."

Incredulity seized her expression. "You knew? You knew this might happen and you didn't tell me?"

"I was hoping to get it all sorted out before it came to this. I didn't want you to lose sleep over something that might not even happen."

Her features were pinched with bitterness. "Unbelievable. The ministry *and* your personal finances are shot. How can you keep defending her?"

"Because it's not all her fault."

"How do you figure?" She threw down the soggy tissue. "It doesn't matter, I'm a pariah at school now anyway. I probably would have dropped out after finals were over."

"No, Jessie, you can't — "

"I can't stay, Dad, not if we can't pay for me to be there. I don't qualify for any of the scholarships, and financial aid doesn't just kick in like that. We'd have to fill out paperwork and applications and all that stuff. And they're not going to let me back if I don't have it all in place before the semester starts. Fat chance of that right now. So what choice do I have?" She shook her head, then speared him with an angry stare. "Dad, I think we need to cut and run."

"I beg your pardon?"

"You need to leave Mom—before she completely ruins you and drags us both down."

Shaun was astounded. "Jessica Faith, how can you say that? She's my wife, I made a promise. I can't just leave her."

"You're not leaving her, Dad! She left you already. Is she coming back for Thanksgiving? She's not, right? She's already run away; and even if she hadn't, she's not who she was. You didn't make a promise to her, not to this Savannah."

Shaun stood, needing to distance himself before she actually talked him into it, and headed for the door. "This is ridiculous. I'm not going to have this conversation. For the last time, I'm not leaving her. If she leaves me, then so be it; but I won't have the failure of our marriage be on me."

"So what, you're just walking away from me?"

"I'm walking away from this conversation. You're entitled to your own thoughts and emotions, but I don't have to be party to them."

"See? She's pulling us apart even when she's not here. It used to always be you and me, Dad. And now I don't have you either."

He groaned. "Jessie—"

"Forget it." She grabbed her keys from the dresser and stormed past him and down the stairs. He heard the door slam a moment later.

Anger and frustration and self-loathing drove his fist into the wall beside her door. The drywall caved beneath his knuckles. He let out a howl that did little to relieve the pressure inside. He hated himself. He hated Savannah, too, and, if he was honest, God.

But mostly he just hated himself.

JESSIE POWER-WALKED, HEAD DOWN, FROM her car to the dorm. The rational side of her brain didn't really believe everyone was staring and talking behind her back the way the rest of her suspected, but it didn't make her feel any better. Someone, somewhere was likely talking about her, or at least her family, and everyone who saw her likely knew who she was—and what had happened. For once she hated being at such a small school. The grapevine was lightning fast, and she had nowhere to hide.

She should have been in her child psych lecture right now. The second midterm was in two days. Next week she had a presentation due for her 21st Century issues class. She'd actually been looking forward to both of them. She'd always enjoyed tests and speeches and projects—she loved school, loved learning, loved showing off what she'd learned. Never in a million years would she ever have dreamed she would drop out of college. But she couldn't stay now. Even if her Dad did come up with the money, she didn't want to keep running into Adam, or deal with people talking about her family.

I'll come back, she thought as she taped together a box from the back of her closet. *No, scrap that—I'll go somewhere else. I can't come back here.* At least not until everyone she knew had graduated. And she didn't want to wait that long. Maybe she'd try one of their extension campuses—she thought there might be one in Denver. She could move out, go find a job and an apartment up in the city somewhere. *Because I'm not living at home. Even if Mom is in Georgia.*

A knock on the door made her hands twitch and drop the sweater she was folding. "Who's there?"

"Angie."

"What!?" Jessie flung open the door. "Oh my gosh, what are you doing here?"

They threw their arms around each other. "My afternoon class got canceled and I knew you were having a hard time. Thought I'd drive down."

"What if I'd been in class?"

Angie let her loaded backpack fall to the floor. "I'd have had plenty to keep me busy."

Jessie shut the door and cleared a space off her bed. "Excuse the mess. I'm packing."

"You're leaving?"

"Yup."

"This is all because of Adam?"

"No—you haven't heard the latest." Jessie told her about the letter she'd received, and about her conversation with Shaun the day before. "I swear I'm in the Twilight Zone. My life is completely upside down. And it's so … claustrophobic here. Everyone knows about A&A, everyone knows about Adam and me, and give it long enough and everyone will know that I was getting kicked out for not paying tuition. I can't wait to get out of here."

"You can't let them drive you away like that, Jess. They should be ashamed of themselves, gossiping like that. How un-Christianly of them."

"Tell me about it—but I'm not about to subject myself to that kind of torture just so they can learn a lesson. Besides, I can't stay. My tuition isn't paid up."

"Oh, right." Angie took a box from the stack and began to tape it together. "So wait a minute. Tell me again what your mom thinks she has?"

"The cellular memory thing, you mean?"

"Yeah."

Jessie let out a scoff. "Yeah, get this: she thinks she's, like, becoming her donor or something like that."

"What?"

"Supposedly there's this thing that happens to some people when they get a transplant. They start taking on the characteristics of their donor. So she thinks all this weird stuff that's been happening to her, all these changes in her personality and everything, are because of her heart donor." She wiggled her fingers and rolled her eyes. "Like she's in some episode of *Star Trek* or something."

"You don't think it's possible?"

"Possible? I don't know—maybe. Anything is possible, right?

But I went onto this transplant forum that she joined so I could look around and see what other people said about this sort of thing." She left out the fact that she'd originally joined to snoop on her mother, which had backfired since Savannah turned out to be more of a lurker than a poster. What few things she'd written hadn't provided Jessie with the insights she'd hoped for. "And no one else mentions it. I mean, this is an international forum, you'd think there'd be some big discussions if it were common — or even credible. But there's nothing there. So personally, I think she's using it as an excuse. She's drained their savings, she's run away from her family, she's destroyed the ministry — I think she's just looking for something she can blame it on."

"But doing all those things wouldn't be like your mom, right? *Something* has to be driving her to do this stuff."

Jessie's hands went to her hips. "Seriously? You're defending her?"

"I'm just saying there has to be some reason, because the Savannah Trover I know wouldn't have done all those things."

"Yeah, see, that's the thing." Jessie dropped a stack of books into a box. "Everyone thinks they know what Savannah Trover is like. They think she's some spiritual powerhouse, all goodness and light. I've told you a million times how rotten our relationship is, how critical she is, how selfish — and she still managed to pull the wool over your eyes. I feel like I'm the only person on the planet who sees her for what she is. Even after all the crap she's pulled and the ways she's screwed up our family, Dad's still defending her and insisting it's not all her fault. Whatever." She swiped at the tears that had formed in her eyes and pulled another handful of books from the shelves. "As far as *why* she's doing this stuff — I don't know. But I'm not surprised."

Angie gave her a sympathetic look. "I'm sorry, Jess. I don't know what to say."

Jessie rubbed her eyes with the end of her sleeve. "That's alright. Just ... don't cross over to the dark side and start trying to convince me she's not at fault here. I don't have anyone I can lean on anymore — not my dad, not Adam ..." The mention of Adam crumbled her already fragile emotional state. "I still can't believe he broke up with me. I thought he loved me."

Angie's arm went around her shoulder as she began to cry. "I'm so sorry, Jess. I really am."

"And oh my gosh — how glad am I that we never slept together!"

Angie chuckled. "No kidding."

Jessie accepted the tissue Angie pulled from the box on her desk and mopped her tears. "Thanks. I appreciate it. I'm glad you came down — though I'm sorry I'm such a mess."

"That's why I came, duh."

Jessie sniffed and chuckled through her tears. "True. Well, just a couple more days and I'll be out of here. And who knows, maybe I'll join you up in Denver someday soon."

"You're gonna transfer?"

"I don't know." Jessie shrugged. "But I'm not living at home for long. That's for sure."

SAVANNAH'S CELL RANG AS SHE was taking another bite of the strawberry cheesecake she'd made for that night's dessert. Seeing Shaun's name made her groan aloud. Definitely not someone she wanted to talk to right now. She tried to hit a button to send it to voicemail, but her finger slipped and hit the talk button instead.

"Oh crap," she muttered, picking it up. "Hello?"

"Savannah, we need to talk."

"Look, Shaun, I'm just getting ready for bed, how about — "

"Adam broke up with Jessie because we're closing A&A."

"What? That little fink! That's ridiculous!"

"Well, I agree, but he did it anyway. Jessie is in a really bad place, and I think you need to talk to her."

"Me?" She laughed "Shaun, I'm sure I'm the last person she wants to hear from."

"She needs to know you're on her side."

"If she needs to know that, then why hasn't she called? I find it hard to believe she actually wants to talk to me. She never does."

"That's because she's learned she's not as important to you as other things are."

"That's also ridiculous."

"Is it? Ever since you started A&A she's been a second priority at best. She knows it and she's tired of it. She ... she actually asked me to leave you."

"Leave me—like, *divorce* me? You've got to be kidding."

"The way she sees it, you've left us already—emotionally before, and physically now."

Savannah couldn't believe it was really that bad. Yes, she and Jessie had trouble connecting, but certainly she knew Savannah loved her. "Well, I hope you set her straight."

"I tried, yes. But honestly, Savannah, I don't know what to think anymore. You're avoiding us, you haven't said a thing about coming home any time soon, even though Thanksgiving is in a week—"

"Wait a minute. Are you actually siding with her?"

"I'm just saying I don't see how we can keep up our marriage through this trial when you're running away and you aren't even *you* anymore."

The air disappeared from her lungs. She slumped against the wall, thoughts spinning, until she grabbed onto one that gave her a rebuttal. "Well, since we're just laying it all out there—explain what you were doing with the reimbursement forms from the last tour."

His response came a beat too late. "I don't know what you're talking about."

"You listed receipts on my form that weren't from our trip."

"No, I didn't. Maybe that's a cellular memory, too. Was Charlie an accountant?"

"That's bunk, Shaun, and you know it. Marisa witnessed it, too."

"Obviously she was mistaken—and why was she snooping around in my office? That alone would make me question whatever it was she told you. Obviously she was bitter about something and trying to make trouble for me."

"Shaun Michael Trover, you are a bald-faced liar."

"Enough of this. I need to go find Jessie and try to help her deal with the fact that her almost-fiance dumped her—something her *mother* should be doing." The line went dead before Savannah could cry foul.

She was too shocked for tears. Her daughter wanted her out of her life. Her husband was lying, obviously, about something. Both of them were blaming her for the collapse of their worlds.

But could she really blame them?

She sat, frozen on the bed, until a wind kicked up outside and sent something flying into the window. The sharp sound scared her; she jumped and clutched a hand to her chest, where her heart galloped in fear. The adrenaline wouldn't back down, though. She had too much to be afraid of.

IT WAS JUST AN EXCUSE, really. Shaun wasn't going after Jessie. She needed her space, and he didn't want to keep putting himself in a position to have to defend Savannah. He'd just wanted to get off the phone.

He retreated to his office and shut the door, then turned the ringer off on his phone in case Savannah called again. He shut down his computer as well, and when the screen went black, the room went completely dark. No distraction, no input, no stimulation. This was what he needed right now.

It was time to face the fact that he was a failure. It didn't matter what Savannah had done, it didn't change the truth about Shaun. Her shortcomings had contributed to the disaster that now lay at his feet; but had he not stolen from A&A's savings, had he not squandered their own personal assets, things would look very different right now. He had ruined everything, and if several thousand dollars didn't fall into his lap very soon, everyone was going to know about it.

He tried to think rationally about every facet of the situation. Likely outcomes: He would go to jail. His daughter would hate him, and she would need some serious therapy to sort out all the ways she had been hurt by both her parents and God. His wife would hate him, and given her position in the ministry, it was possible she could be implicated.

Despite what he'd told Jessie, his opinion of divorce was beginning to change. He was starting to think that leaving both Savannah and Jessie might be the most compassionate thing he could do. And once he'd put as much emotional and physical distance between himself and them as he could, then he could kill himself so he could get out from under the mountain he had created. He could leave a letter explaining everything so Savannah wasn't blamed for the ministry's financial ruin. His death might even pull Savannah and Jessie together. At least they'd have their disgust for him in common.

He nodded to himself as he rocked in his desk chair. It was a decent plan. Not one he was quite ready to implement, but knowing he had it in his back pocket gave him a sense of control for the first time in months.

He turned his computer back on. He needed to start getting the details sorted. First he'd figure out the divorce, then he'd figure out the death. For a moment he began to miss them, as though the plan had already been set in motion, but he reassured himself as he brought up an internet browser. At least he'd see them again in heaven.

Savannah pulled the coat tighter around her shoulders and dodged a peach tree branch she'd veered too close to on her unsteady feet. The sun was setting, and the sky was awash in watercolors that she knew must look brighter to others. Everything today had been cast in gray to her.

She was such a mess of emotions she couldn't even sort out what exactly she was feeling. Depression was one of them, she was pretty sure. Probably some hard-core anxiety, too. And, of course, the ever-present anger. She thought it ironic that she was living in a place that housed two full-time counselors and yet she had no one to talk to. She didn't want to bring all this up to Tabitha; she didn't think she'd earned the right to go to her with such deep troubles, not when Savannah had basically told Tabitha to take a hike when she'd tried to do the very same thing. She'd also gotten a call that morning from Rose, the therapist she'd talked to back in Colorado, that had brought her even lower. "Just checking in," she'd said in her message. "I haven't gotten very much help yet on your situation, but I didn't want you to think I'd forgotten about you." Savannah was tempted to tell her to give up. If there was any help to be found, someone would have by now. And despite the friendliness and empathy of the others staying there, none of them had any idea what she was going through.

She'd never been so alone. At least in the past she'd always had God to talk to. But now she had no one.

The wind picked up and she squinted against the dirt that flew into her face. A storm was rolling in from the north; she could see the massive black clouds in the distance. Part of her wondered if she should even be out here—how much stress would her heart take? Would she be okay if she started shivering? *Maybe it wouldn't be the end of the world if this heart went out too.* Her next check-up at the cardiology clinic was coming up; maybe they'd see her heart was getting too stressed and they'd give her a new one. Maybe if she got someone else's heart she'd go back to being who she was. Maybe she could request a Christian this time. It would limit her odds of getting one before she died, but even then she'd at least be done with this nightmare.

She stopped in her tracks. "Am I suicidal?" She spoke aloud to the trees, really not sure if she was or not. She didn't *think* so, but maybe she was close. How else could she escape Charlie's hold on her? Apparently she could do nothing, and his thoughts were ruining everything. How bad an idea was it really?

When you can't, God can. It was one of her tag-lines, one of the things she'd always worked into her books and talks. She'd lived by it, and then life had started clicking along just fine and she hadn't needed to test its truth anymore. She'd gotten good at doing on her own whatever needed to be done. Her transplant had been the first thing she'd had to rely on God for in a long time. Now it seemed like her life was one giant "can't", but there wasn't anyone she could turn to who could.

Over the last twenty-four hours, the weight of the anger in her heart and the chaos in her head had grown tenfold. She was so close to a fix, and yet completely stymied as to how to get it. She felt like she was on the edge of a cliff, teetering, waiting for an outstretched hand to reach just a little further, grab her jacket and yank her back to safety. But the hand just hovered there, a couple inches short.

The wind picked up again. She was beginning to regret coming out here. The orchard was barren without a place to shelter from the wind—or from herself. No bedclothes to hide beneath, no armchair to curl up in to escape to her latest book. The orchard had no distractions, and she realized she'd been living the last week from one distraction to the next because she didn't know how else to cope. How do you look reality in the face when it's so despairing? Why even bother?

The house was a hundred yards away now, and as the force of her emotions and fear began a cascade through her system, she found herself without any protection or defense.

Jessie, Shaun, A&A, Adam, Marisa, her reputation, her family, her marriage, her *self*... the loss and potential loss of so many things dear to her began to cave in on her. It was all because of this stupid heart, this heart that didn't seem to realize Charlie was gone and Savannah was its home.

She had to get rid of this heart. But how?

She began to run down the aisles between the bare peach trees, their naked limbs bending with the wind like arms reaching out to grab her. She swerved to avoid a rock in the path and her jacket snagged on a low branch. She'd been an avid jogger before her illness, but the months since had atrophied her muscles to mush. She ignored their burn, the complaints of tendons challenged without a warm-up, and pushed herself farther and farther, the house receding behind her like a movie finale. She thought only of her heart, of taxing it beyond its capacity, of punishing it for destroying her life. She wanted it to burst. *And if they don't find me in time, maybe that's okay.*

Her eyes streamed, her lungs burned, her heart slammed in her chest—until a hole in the path caught her foot and sent her flying face-down into the dirt. She burst into tears and screamed without thinking. *"Jesus!"*

The name was like a key in the lock of the floodgates that held back the fullness of Charlie's pain. They swung open, pouring a tidal wave of grief and anger and desperation over Savannah's soul. Her fingers dug into the ground as she sobbed, seeking an anchor lest the emotion sweep her away. Her heart kicked in her chest as though trying to literally pound its way out.

Fear surfaced through the waves. What was she thinking, pushing herself that way? She didn't really want to die, did she?

She couldn't tell anymore what was her pain and what was Charlie's. He was already dead, but his heart didn't know it. If she didn't get it under control, it might kill her, too.

She sucked in deep breaths, trying to slow the beat and rein in the overwhelming feelings. "Slow down, relax, be calm," she panted. And then—because what did she have to lose?—"You're mine. Charlie is gone, and you're mine now. That anger is dead. That pain is done. Let it go. Just let it go already."

Like flotsam from a shipwreck, thoughts swirled through her head that she knew instinctively were not hers, thoughts that told her life was a waste and love was a myth and God was a fairy tale. She pounded her fists to the ground and yelled. "No! Lies, lies, lies!" And then, grasping onto new thoughts that floated in the current like life preservers, she begged, "Be real, God. Be real again. I can't do this anymore. Make this stop. This has to stop! Charlie is gone—you're gone, Charlie, you're dead, and this heart is *mine!*"

Her voice escalated with every sentence, her fists punctuating them on the dirt, until she dropped her head to the ground and waited for something to carry her away.

She had nothing left. No thoughts, no emotions. All were gone, like an ocean squall that disappears as quickly as it came, leaving you clinging to your raft and unsure if you can really trust it's over. Her heart began to slow, her breath to regulate. She released the ground and slowly pushed herself up to her feet, standing cautiously as though the earth might tip and send her crashing down again. She felt different. She couldn't identify the reason, but with each slow step that brought her closer to the house the difference became more pronounced.

Limping, she mounted the stairs to the front door. She headed for her room, ignoring the looks of concern from the others as she bypassed the flow of people leaving the dining room from dinner. She washed the earth from her face and hands, stripped off her stained clothes, and crawled beneath the blankets as exhaustion overtook her.

In the seconds before she fell into a hard sleep, she realized the difference was peace.

CHAPTER 14

Sunlight bathed the room when Savannah awoke. Every muscle ached when she rolled from the bed, but she relished the sensation as she sat on the floor to stretch. It felt good to have awakened her body again, beat it into submission, shown it who was boss. She smiled, her body responding to the wake-up call of a few pilates poses.

She was still not her old self. Foreign feelings still coursed through her veins, but the strange peace that had enveloped her before falling asleep the night before was still there. She noted with great pleasure that the simmering anger had cooled as well. Not completely, but enough to give her hope.

She had new feelings as well, ones that she could claim as her own. Empowerment. Ambition. *No more hiding, no more distractions. Time to stare it all in the face and deal with it head on.* It was time to find healing instead of despairing that it would ever come.

Her resources at The Refuge were too good to pass up. She found Tabitha and told her what had happened the night before. "I'm ready to try the group therapy, if you're still alright with that. I don't know if it's going to help, but I might as well try—and if nothing else it'll give me something else to do with my time."

Tabitha hugged her. "You've gone through the fire and come out the other side."

"That's about how I felt."

"Group is at ten."

"I'll be there."

She had half an hour, and she spent it on the porch with a notebook. She labeled a page *Shaun* and began to list the issues she could identify, trying to bring order to all the confusion that had reigned in her head lately. After that she listed the steps she could think of that might help resolve things, or at least slow their descent into total catastrophe.

A little before ten she left the rocking chair and made her way to the group therapy room, where a circle of chairs awaited the Refugees. She was greeted with warm smiles that bolstered her courage. If they could do it, so could she. Even though she wasn't sure what "it" was.

After everyone was seated, Tabitha announced Savannah to the group. "I know you've all met her already, but I wanted to give her an official introduction as a Refugee member. Welcome to the group, Savannah."

Savannah gave a nod and tried not to look as nervous as she felt. After a brief murmur of welcome from the others, Tabitha kicked off the session with a statement-structured prayer that lacked any sense of a prayer at all. "God can heal us, and we ask him to do that today," she said with eyes open, locking gazes with each person in turn as she spoke. "God can soften our hearts toward those who have wounded us, and can bring us out of the pain we've been living in. Do you agree?"

Some—though not all, Savannah noticed—echoed their agreement. She wondered if her own prayer for a softened heart would do any good, since her heart wasn't exactly *her* heart. *Maybe it's like praying for someone else.* Though that would require that she actually pray, and while she had called out to Jesus the night before, it hadn't exactly been in a reverent and prayerful way. She wasn't sure if she was ready to take that step, especially if uttering that one name had brought on such a tempest. What kind of storm would a whole prayer unleash? She decided she would open herself to the prayers of others, but not attempt her own quite yet. *Baby steps.*

Tabitha began talking about the subject of the day's meeting: what forgiveness looked like and how it would help them, versus what it did, if anything, for the person that wounded them. She listened to

Tabitha's teaching, and to the honest and sometimes gut-wrenching admissions of the Refugees who were willing to share with the group. Her mind wandered a bit as she listened, attempting to determine how her own situation could be helped by this, but by the time lunch rolled around and they all filed out together she found she was energized and encouraged by the meeting. Tabitha stopped her before they entered the dining room and asked, "So, what did you think?"

"It was … it was good, I think. I'm really glad I did it. I'm still not sure how this is going to help me, but I'm willing to try it."

Tabitha wrapped an arm around her shoulder. "I'm so glad."

Savannah was struck with an idea. "Listen. Would you be willing to pray for me? Not out loud, necessarily, just … while we're standing here."

Tabitha's smile was electric. "Absolutely." She led Savannah to the windows, and they each took a seat and stared out to the land that stretched along the front of the house. She found herself almost cheering Tabitha on in her mind, as though this one prayer might actually change anything. After a moment Tabitha turned to her and smiled. "Done."

"Painless. Thanks. Baby steps are good, right?"

"They're crucial, yes."

"Okay, good." She inhaled deeply, relishing the peace that was still hanging around. "Baby steps I think I can do."

SHAUN WANDERED THE EMPTY GROCERY store aisle without really seeing the items on the shelves. He didn't actually need anything—he still had a decent amount of food to finish off—but he'd been desperate to escape the prison of the empty house where he felt compelled to hide during the day. Midnight was the perfect time to venture out without the likelihood of running into someone who now hated him.

He turned the corner, eyes snagged by a bright display of soda cases arranged in a pattern, and walked right into a customer ticking items off a list. "I'm sorry—"

"Oh."

Shaun and Marisa stared at each other as a blanket of awkwardness settled over them. "I wasn't looking where I was going; forgive me," Shaun finally said, stepping out of her way.

Her look of surprise morphed to irritation as she pocketed the list. "Slinking around in the dark," she said, her tone sardonic. "That's fitting."

He stared at her in frank shock. This was the woman who had shared their table at countless holidays and casual get-togethers, whom he'd seen nearly every day for years. She'd been like a sister to Savannah and, in turn, like family to him. He never would have expected so much venom. "Well ... so are you," was all he could manage to come up with in retort.

She rolled her eyes. "Taking a break from a night of packing so I can get to New York by Thanksgiving. I needed a break and a meal."

"New York — that's great."

"Yeah — at least I have somewhere to go to. Unlike the other people you left in the lurch."

"Marisa, I didn't — "

"Look. I know you were doing something with the reimbursement forms. I should have followed my gut but I just couldn't bring myself to believe that you would steal from the ministry. And don't think I don't know that's the root of the ministry's financial issues. If I could prove it I would."

Panic began to rise. How much did she know? How had she figured it out? "I ... I don't know what you're talking about."

"Whatever." She pushed past him, then turned and skewered him with her eyes. "I just pray more people don't get hurt by your selfishness. Six people who lived and breathed that ministry and looked up to you and Savannah is enough of a body count." She spun and walked away, leaving Shaun speechless with fear. He abandoned his empty basket in the middle of the aisle and left the store, walking quickly and keeping an eye out for Marisa lest he run into her again. He was gripped by the irrational thought that she'd be able to read his mind the longer they were in the same vicinity. He had to get out, *now*.

He jumped into the car and fought not to speed the whole way home. Even back in the confines of his depressing house he didn't feel any safer. Marisa knew something, and even though it wasn't much, it was enough to ruin him and Savannah if she went public with it. Even without solid proof people would believe whatever accusation she leveled against him, given the abrupt shuttering of the ministry.

How much evidence of suspicion would the police need? The IRS? What if others knew, too, but had never said anything? He'd been so careful, but obviously not careful enough. What other slip-ups had he made that he was unaware of? Who else was sitting at home, stewing at the meager severance they'd been doled out at the ministry's closing, plotting out their revenge?

He had a timeline for how things were supposed to go. He had the information he needed, he was just trying to figure out how to go about starting things off. It was taking longer than he'd expected to ramp up the courage to tell Savannah he wanted a divorce. But after that, assuming she cooperated, things could go quickly. And then he could finish things, up in the mountains, somewhere where he'd be eventually found. Then it would all be over and Savannah and Jessie could get on with their lives.

But knowing that Marisa was on to him, even with what little evidence she had, changed things entirely. The plan needed to go more quickly.

Either that, or he had to skip to the end.

SAVANNAH WASHED THE RAW HAMBURGER from her hands. "Can't wait for lunch, Aniyah. Thanks again."

"Naw, thank you, 'Vannah. It's nice to work a little slower and not have to rush. The three of us make a good team. Gonna miss you when you go." Her eyes glinted when Savannah glanced at her. "And just when is that, anyhow?"

"Trying not to think about it." She made room for Tim, the quiet young man who worked as Aniyah's assistant, as he passed behind her with a sack of potatoes. "Who knows what might happen. Maybe I'll just move here for good." *If only.*

Aniyah let out one of her deep chuckles. "Aw, 'Vanna, stop that now."

Savannah dried her hands. "It's about time to go. Are you ready?"

Aniyah slid the green onions she'd been dicing into a bowl and covered it with plastic. "Just about. Now Tim, you watch them fries and make sure they don't burn. You get overwhelmed, you just holler. I'll hear you."

Tim looked up from the pile of fries he'd made. "I'll be fine, Aniyah."

"Let the boy be," Savannah said with a grin. "He's plenty competent."

Aniyah pulled off her apron. "I just don't like leaving my kitchen."

The two women walked out together and Savannah said quietly, "You think Tim even knows how to holler?" Aniyah's laugh echoed through the foyer.

With the scent of hamburger and spices still in her nose, Savannah followed Aniyah into the group therapy room where nearly everyone else was already present. As much as she'd begun to enjoy meeting with the others, she hated leaving the kitchen just as much as Aniyah did. It was where she felt most in touch with her old self. The act of service, not just to Aniyah and Tim, but for the Refugees and Tabitha as well, gave her a sense of purpose and served as her way to thank them for letting her hide among them while she sorted out her life. Even the thought of her family wasn't enough to stir a desire to leave. She tried not to dwell on that uncomfortable truth.

Tabitha saw them enter and smiled. "Alright folks, I think we're ready to start." The group settled into their seats and gave Tabitha their attention. "Every once in a while a former Refugee comes back to share his or her story with us, as a way to encourage and support those who are struggling the same way they did. And today Aniyah is going to do that for us. She's been here for a few years now, cooking up the world-class fare we get to eat every day, and now she would like to share her experience. Aniyah—whenever you're ready."

Aniyah had everyone's full attention. Savannah had only heard a small sliver of the story, the first day she'd stepped into the kitchen to lend a hand. Aniyah had never continued the tale, and Savannah hadn't felt comfortable asking. Now, with the others, she waited with anticipation to hear how the feisty woman had come to stay at The Refuge.

"Sometimes folks think I's telling tales when I tell them about my life. But I think I can trust y'all to know I ain't lying. And hopefully it'll speak to you, somehow. God's been good about redeeming my lost years that way.

"My mama was a voodoo priestess. We lived out in the Bayou, in a shack you couldn't reach but by boat. I learned cooking from her, though it wasn't just food we cooked, but charms and spells, too—though mostly I just watched when she did those."

She told her story without hyperbole to the riveted audience, repeating the details Savannah had heard while cutting beignets.

"So's I got to New Orleans and couldn't get a job. Didn't know my social security number, and didn't want to bring attention to myself trying to find it. I took to the street, turning tricks to make money, but then this guy finds me and gives me my first crack. It was all downhill from there. Had to keep selling myself to buy the crack, and because of the crack I couldn't do nothing else but keep turning tricks.

"Sometimes when I wasn't high—which wasn't very often—I would think about my mama, and my auntie, and about spirits and God and all that. I'd grown up surrounded by talk about the *loa*, the spirits and souls, and when I got to Auntie's she talked about the spirit and soul all the time, too, but in a different way. Mama's way had been mysterious and beautiful, and a little creepy some-times—but Auntie's way had been all mean and depressing. I was never good enough. I was always bad, always sinful and evil, didn't matter if I really did something wrong or not.

"This street preacher used to come down to the tent city and talk about God. Most folks didn't like him, thought he was gonna rat on them to the police or something. But all he ever did was talk about God loving people, even when they was all messed up. One day he saw me watching him, and he came right over to me and said, 'Sister, he was bruised for your transgressions and crushed for your iniquities because he loves you.' I didn't know what he was talking about, but it sounded like a lot to go through just to love someone like me."

She tugged at a thread on her sleeve. "But then I'd think about Auntie and what she said about God, and I figured Street Preacher didn't know enough about me, 'cause if he did he'd know God could never love someone like me. And besides, why would I want him to? What had he done for me? I was a homeless druggie prostitute—a whole Bible worth of sins rolled into one, and ain't nothing lovable about that."

She looked to Tabitha and smiled. "But then one day this white woman comes walking down by the tent city, looking all pulled together and nice. I saw her and thought she'd be done for, but it was like nobody saw her but me. I was on the corner, looking for customers, and she stopped and said, 'God told me to help you. Can I please help you?'"

All eyes turned to Tabitha, who shrugged and grinned. "Well, he did."

"That was the first time I thought maybe Street Preacher was right. Maybe God was trying to look out for me. Maybe this white lady was an angel. So's I didn't even let myself think about it, I just said okay. She walked me to her car, and it was like we was invisible, nobody was looking at us like they shoulda been—this cleaned-up white woman and this dirty black lady that looked like a skeleton. She took me to a rehab place and checked me in and come to visit me every day. And when I was finally clean, she brought me here."

Tabitha shrugged again at the faces that looked to her in awe. "Nothing like that had ever happened to me before, but truly, I felt like God told me to find her and help her. I was on the other side of town, meeting with a psychologist that had been working with spiritual abuse cases, and when I left I got this impression to turn right at this one street, so I did. Then left at another, then right again, and then I saw an open parking spot on the street and just grabbed it. And then it was like God said, 'Just start walking.' I figured I'd know what I was supposed to do when I came to it, but I will admit I was nervous—that was not a good part of town. But when I saw her, I just ... *knew*. Knew she was the one God meant for me to find, knew she needed to get clean. Some good friends of mine—they're like my adoptive parents, actually—paid for her rehab."

"But you weren't a believer before, right, Aniyah?" Savannah asked. "Why did you come here?"

Tabitha answered. "I told her about The Refuge and we figured together that, if nothing else, this would be a safe place for her to be. Alanna—she helped me start The Refuge—she was the one in charge of the kitchen, but her husband was being relocated and we knew we had to find someone else. I asked Aniyah if she wanted to try her hand at cooking, in exchange for free room and board and, if she wanted, therapy."

"I wasn't gonna say no, not to a roof over my head and decent food. Plus, how could I say no to the woman who saved my life?"

Aniyah pulled one sneakered foot beneath herself and continued. "So Alanna taught me some basic cooking stuff, and when I wasn't working I would sit in group therapy or just talk with folks. I didn't tell no one why I was really there; they all just thought I was the new cook. And after a while I started thinking about how different these God people was from my auntie. For a while I was real confused—I mean, if one person says God loves you, and another says God hates you because you're a sinner, then who do you believe? People like Tabitha here was making me want to believe God was real and really did love me, but then I'd remember Auntie, and I didn't wanna get involved with him if she was the one who was right.

"So one day I told Tabitha I needed to figure God out once and for all. Was he good like she said, or just waiting to zap me like Auntie said? So she gave me a Bible and said, 'Just start reading, and we'll talk.' Now, I'd read the Bible before; Auntie made me write it out word for word sometimes, when she thought I was being bad. But I'd never just read it straight, you know? And I didn't get a lot of it, but Tabitha and I, we talked about the parts I got stuck on, and after a while I started thinking Auntie must have got it all real wrong. God seemed mighty patient with his stupid children. And then when Jesus came—whooee, that was love like I've never seen! I read through those gospels in just a couple nights. And when I was done, I thought, this is what I want. I want this Jesus. And I knew Jesus and God was like a package deal, and I decided that was okay. Because that God, in the Bible, was nothing like the God Auntie tried to teach me about. This one loved me, and was sad I had to go through such a rotten life."

The room was silent as Aniyah paused, her lip trembling and tears glistening in her eyes. She pushed a corner of her sleeve to her eyes, then said, "Anyways, that's why I'm here, and that's why I stay. 'Cause I love God and I love to take care of the people who're trying to find him again. Now, you gotta excuse me while I go finish up making your lunch." She stood and hurried out, head bowed, while the Refugees showered her with applause.

Tabitha began to talk, but Savannah didn't hear her. Her mind was churning, not just in shock from her friend's story, but with the frenzied pinballing of ideas on the verge of breaking through. As soon as the session was over Savannah skipped lunch and went to her room to think.

Legs folded beneath her on the bed, she sat with her notebook and pen, staring out the window at the orchard as she worked on the knot of thoughts in her head. After a few minutes she began to write. *Charlie was mad at God because of the betrayal he experienced of both his father and his neighbor. He projected the unloving, unprincipled characters of these two men onto God. He heard God was loving, but didn't understand why a loving God would let happen the things that he experienced. Charlie believed God had abandoned him just as his father had abandoned him. He was unwilling to believe anything that might paint God in a better light, because he couldn't get past his own hurt.*

It wasn't identical to Aniyah's story, but the parallels were there. Both had made assumptions about God based on the very ungodly actions of other people. But, unlike Charlie, Aniyah had gone to the source to figure out once and for all who God really was. It was then Savannah realized she'd allowed her thoughts and feelings—or, more accurately, Charlie's—to dictate what she thought about God, rather than going back to the source and reminding herself what was really true.

She flipped the page and began writing again, her words scrawled with haste. *WHAT I KNOW TO BE TRUE ABOUT GOD:*

She concentrated on the view again as she fought to recall the things she'd once believed about God. These she wrote slowly, wanting to make sure she was getting them right, as she forced herself not to analyze whether or not she actually agreed with them.

- *God's ways are not man's ways/when we don't understand why he's doing or not doing something, it's because of our own lack of knowledge*
- *The existence of evil does not disprove the existence of God*
- *Just because we* <u>think</u> *God has abandoned us does not mean he actually has*
- *God does not leave his children*
- *God can use our pain and painful circumstances for good*
- *God can heal us if we let him*

She stared at what she had written. It didn't take up a lot of room, it wasn't full of epiphanies or revolutionary thoughts, but it embodied a radical retooling of her thought process from how it had been over the last three months. She didn't actually believe all those statements about God, but that didn't matter. What was more important was the lesson that emotion and experience didn't always tell the truth.

She picked up her pen again and wrote, *Do I believe God is real?* She paused, thinking before writing. *My heart does not. Not sure about my head— hard to isolate those thoughts apart from my emotions. Do I want him to be real?* She paused again, though she knew the answer already. She just wasn't sure what to do with it. *I think my head does. My heart does not.*

So how do I get my heart on the same page as my head?

She set down her pen and picked up her jacket. The sun was shining. It was time to head back to the orchard.

There was no wind today, no storm on the horizon. She walked the same path she had run down just a couple days before, the memory of that evening vivid in her mind. The anger she usually felt had diminished significantly since then, though it was still there, manifesting itself more as a feeling of disgruntled annoyance than real anger. The peace that had bloomed after her catharsis was also still there. Changes were definitely happening, and moving her in the right direction, but that last hurdle still seemed impossible to jump. The open expanse of the orchard gave her the space she needed to think about how to attack it.

She thought back to what she had written in her room. *Fact: Charlie's heart was hardened because of the pain people put him through, not because of God. He had projected those people's actions onto God and aimed his anger at him.* Maybe if she tried to address the hurts that he had been subjected to, validate his pain, and separate the anger from the fact of the situations, she'd be able to ease some of the negative emotions.

But how?

She took a quick look around, then spoke before she could convince herself she was crazy. "I know you were hurt. But you shouldn't dwell on your pain to the exclusion of the good things that happened in your life." She laughed aloud in nervous embarrassment, the sound swallowed by the silence that surrounded her in the hibernating orchard. Shaun would have her committed if he heard her talking to herself this way. Tabitha, on the other hand, would probably applaud her. She felt utterly foolish doing it, but in the absence of any other ideas, it certainly wouldn't hurt. "I think it's time to let go of that pain and get on with your life already. Well—not *your* life, since you're dead, but let me get on with *my* life at least." She rubbed a hand across her forehead, as though that might dislodge some better ideas. She wasn't messing with spirits or anything, was she? That was the last thing she needed to deal with now—possession by Charlie's hell-bound soul.

She tried a different approach. If the hurt were actually hers, what would she want to hear? It dawned on her that the things that came to mind to say—*get over it, move on*—weren't exactly empathetic. No wonder she and Jessie had a hard time communicating. Affirmation and encouragement had never come easily to her when it came to her own family. To a stranger, a woman pouring out her soul at a book signing or in the meet-and-greet after a speaking event, she could effuse gentle and inspiring advice without a problem. Why not for those she was closest to?

Another problem for another day. Let's focus on getting back to normal first, then we can go to Rose for some therapy. She tried again, picturing herself in her mind as wounded, hurting. What would she need to hear?

"You were hurt. Your father should have been there for you, he should have provided you with the love and knowledge and positive example that fathers are supposed to give their children. He robbed you of the security and love that you needed to thrive in your childhood. That wasn't your fault. He was wrong for leaving."

She let the words sink in, imagined them flowing through her veins and into her heart, absorbing into the tissue and soothing the cells. "Kirk was not a perfect human being. You idolized him because he was everything you needed—a strong man who shared your interests and took you under his wing, who taught you the things fathers are supposed to teach. He took a real interest in you, and invested himself in you. He even made you think twice about the conclusions you'd come to about religion. But he wasn't perfect, despite how you thought he was. He was a broken, fallen man, like all of us are, and he made a very big mistake.

"But he didn't do it to hurt you. He didn't do it to hurt anyone. He had a problem, and he tried to solve it the wrong way; it backfired and ruined his marriage. That doesn't mean that everything he told you was wrong."

She stopped walking and stared down the row of trees that stretched beyond her vision. She almost expected Charlie to materialize in the distance, like a peach tree orchard version of *Field of Dreams*. As nutty as it felt to talk to herself, she had to admit it felt like a step in the right direction. She wasn't any less disgruntled, any more willing to believe in God, but she did feel more open to thinking about him and possibly even reaching out to him, just as an experiment, to see what might happen. It struck her that praying for a release from the emotions might be the next thing she needed to do.

She wasn't sure if screaming at Jesus counted as praying to him. If it didn't, then it had been three months since she'd uttered anything to God. She wasn't sure she was ready to try yet.

Savannah turned back toward the house. Tabitha would be finishing up lunch, the rest of the Refugees heading out to do whatever they chose to do while waiting for their individual therapy appointments. Maybe she and Tabitha could hide away somewhere and Tabitha could try praying for her again. Maybe even aloud.

The thought was not repulsive. That was a good sign.

SAVANNAH WAS IN A GOOD mood. It felt almost foreign, but she wasn't one to deny a gift the universe (or, dare she consider it—

God) had given her. Dinner had been eaten, Tabitha had prayed over her and she had lived to tell, and she was feeling cautiously hopeful that things might eventually turn out okay.

She decided to call Shaun. It was hard talking to him these days without feeling defensive, but she was feeling more amiable than she had in months, and maybe that would make all the difference. She sat out on the patio in her favorite rocking chair and hoped he was home.

"Hello?"

Savannah was surprised. "Jessie, hi honey. It's Mom."

"What do you want?"

She stopped rocking. "Well, I'm fine, thanks. How are you?"

"Oh, just peachy. The entire campus is ostracizing me and they're threatening to kick me out for unpaid tuition. So I saved them all the trouble and just moved home."

The pain in Jessie's voice was loud and clear. Savannah ached with every word. "Oh sweetheart, I'm so sorry."

"Whatever. If you were sorry you wouldn't have done all this."

"Jessie, I know it's hard to understand what's going on —"

"I'm not six, Mother, don't talk to me like this is some big grown-up problem that little me can't understand. You bailed on every commitment you had and left everyone to clean up after you."

"Jessica, please understand. There's more going on here than my issues. Your dad —"

"Don't try to drag Dad down with you. You two are so dysfunctional, I swear! You're trying to implicate him, he's trying to defend you —"

"Defend me?"

"— it makes me sick."

The line went dead. Savannah gaped at the cell, head spinning. Things were apparently worse than she'd believed them to be, that much was clear. And with her daughter practically disowning her, Savannah knew it was time to go home. She had to get to the bottom of Shaun's role in all this, and do whatever she could to salvage her relationship with Jessie.

She went in and began packing, but stopped when she realized she was picking and choosing what to bring back. *This isn't home. You can't assume Tabitha can or will hold this room for you. Who knows when you'll be back. Or if.*

But was she ready to move on? She didn't feel ready. *Though, as you've already discovered, emotions can lie.* But what would Tabitha say about her using the place like a hotel, just coming and going as she pleased?

She debated, frozen in the middle of the room with a pair of cargo pants in her hands, then slowly folded them and placed them into the duffel. *I can always bring it all back.* She stuffed the last shirt into the bag and zipped her books into the side pockets, then brought the bag downstairs and sought out Tabitha.

"I have to go home. Jessie left school and something's going on with Shaun."

Tabitha gave her a hug. "I'll cancel my therapy sessions and drive you to the airport. When's your flight?"

"I didn't even make one. I'm just going to find the first plane I can get on."

Tabitha tracked down Jim, the other resident therapist, and told him her plans, then ushered Savannah to the passenger van that sat in the barn-like garage. "May I pray aloud?" she asked as they turned onto the main road.

"Um ... yes."

Savannah gazed out the window at the scenery they passed as Tabitha kept up her spiritual assault on the plans of the enemy to destroy Savannah and her family. She was trying not to listen, but even though Tabitha kept her voice low, every word seemed to seep in. She didn't feel uncomfortable, though. Oddly, the prayers made her feel safe. Maybe she had truly reached a turning point. Maybe she *was* ready to leave.

SAVANNAH ENTERED HER HOME JUST before ten p.m. No one called out; she heard no sounds at all. She'd been gone less than two weeks but she felt like an intruder.

She stood in the foyer, determining her next move. She checked the garage and neither Shaun's nor Jessie's cars were there. No point trying to track down Jessie; who knew where she might be, and she'd come home eventually. So would Shaun—and if she wanted to do any snooping, she'd best do it before then.

She left her bag by the door and went into Shaun's office. She had never cased someone's private space before. She walked around the room, eyes peeled for anything suspicious, though she didn't know what that might be. Finally she sat down at his desk and began to open drawers. Now she really felt like an intruder.

Office supplies, software, files for the bills and insurance papers. Nothing looked out of the ordinary. She tried the drawers on the other side of the desk. The top one was empty. The bottom one was locked.

She searched for a key but found none. She opened the empty drawer again and examined the rails on which it slid, looking for a way to remove it. With some jiggling it finally came free, and she was able to peer down into the drawer below. A manila file, a binder, and a CD sat inside.

She pulled them out and opened the folder. Inside were four letters from the IRS, dated six years back. The first notified him that A&A was being audited because of suspicious tax filings their first two years in business. The second informed him of the amount due. The last two were late notices for those payments.

Savannah didn't know A&A had ever been audited. How could Shaun have kept that from her? And *how* did he keep it from her?

She looked again at the letter stating the amount owed. It was larger than she would have expected. Had Shaun not paid *any* of their taxes those years?

Next she opened the binder. It turned out to be an executive checkbook, where only a few of the checks seemed to be missing. The stubs were all blank, there was nothing indicating what the checks had been made out for. The address was A&A's.

Her hands went clammy. She'd seen the kinds of paychecks the staff got. They didn't look like these. Neither did the reimbursement checks. What were these used for—and why were there apparently two sets of checkbooks?

Then she took the CD out of its case. There was nothing indicating what had been burned to it. She turned on his computer, then inserted the disc and waited for it to boot up. When she brought up the list of drives, the CD was listed as *A&A Financials*. She opened it, which launched the budgeting program Shaun used for the ministry. Spreadsheets and pie charts popped up on the screen. She didn't know what she was looking for, but she clicked around anyway, hoping something would stand out.

It did.

Here and there on the spreadsheet were amounts highlighted in blue. They were unlabeled, and did nothing when she clicked on them. All were fairly small; the largest was only $12.53. She counted them, flipping from one worksheet to another, until the total was over fifty and the amount equaled just over $450. *What on earth?*

She glanced back into the drawer, hoping she'd missed something that might give her more information. She saw it in the back. Another checkbook.

The checks inside contained only Shaun's name, and their home address. The next check number was 118. Didn't they usually start at 101? Seventeen checks missing, most likely, and no duplicates. Shaun had never told her he had a separate checking account.

She picked up the checkbooks to put them back in the drawer, and a loose check slipped out of the back of the smaller book. It had been partially filled out, then scribbled over as though to void it; the written-out version of the amount had been botched. The payee was listed as Carlie Stone. The amount in the box was $4000. The date was from last July.

Carlie Stone. Why do I know that name? She searched her memory, repeating it aloud, waiting for it to trigger something. Someone she met through A&A? No—someone who worked there. A short-lived administrative assistant, less than six months if she remembered correctly. They'd hired Brenda after that, three years ago.

Savannah put the check back into place and returned it, along with the other items, to the drawer. She shoved the top drawer in, then launched Shaun's email client, hoping it was still what he used. The inbox contained messages from yesterday. *Still in use!* She entered *Carlie Stone* into the search box. A page's worth of emails filed onto the screen. She scrolled down and opened the first one, dated September of 2006.

Don't think I don't know why I was fired. You are a liar, Shaun Trover. I'm plenty stable and I'm plenty competent. You're the one who is sick in the head.

I want a thousand dollars by the end of the day on Friday. If it's not here by then I'm going to tell Savannah we had an affair and tell her what you're doing with A&A's bank accounts.

Savannah's hand trembled as she clicked the message that Shaun had written in reply.

This is blackmail, Carlie. This is illegal. And it's not even true. We gave you a decent severance that you didn't even technically qualify for, just be happy you have that and leave me alone.

Carlie's next reply was a single sentence. *You really want to test me?*

Savannah opened each of the emails, which came at uneven intervals over the last few years. Sometimes months would go by, sometimes less than six weeks. At first she asked for the same amount every time, then starting last year the amount increased, until the most recent email asked for $10,000. Shaun's response had been simple. *I don't have any money!!!*

She hadn't replied yet. He'd written her three weeks ago.

Savannah jumped when the front door closed. She'd spaced out, staring at the computer, feeling completely undone and not knowing what to do next. She scrambled to close the email client and was shutting the computer down when she heard Jessie call, "Mom?"

Relief flooded her. She went out to the foyer and saw her daughter looking as though she hadn't slept in a week. Her cheeks were red, her hair damp at the temples. "I saw your bag." Jessie nodded to the carry-on leaning against the wall. "I didn't know you were coming home."

"I just got in a bit ago. Last minute decision. Where were you so late at night?"

"Went for a run at the church's gym."

Savannah smiled. They actually did share something in common. "I didn't know you ran."

"Big surprise."

Jessie turned to go upstairs. Savannah followed her. "Listen, Jessie, can we talk? I've had some revelations the last couple days, and one of them pertains to you."

"Whatever."

She followed her to her room and sat on the bed while Jessie sat on the floor and began to stretch. She didn't make eye contact with Savannah at all, acted as though she wasn't even in the room. Savannah decided to just forge ahead and see what happened. "I realized the other day I have a tendency to brush your troubles aside and not be very sympathetic. I tell you to buck up and get over it and don't really give you the space you might need to deal with things the way you want to. And I don't often give you a lot of encouragement or support. I guess ... I guess I just wanted to make sure you knew how to take care of yourself, that you wouldn't be one of those girls always looking for some boy's shoulder to cry on. I wanted you to be independent and strong—and you *are* strong, but ..." Savannah sighed. "Anyway, I hope you know what I'm trying to say."

Jessie snorted. "And?"

"And?"

"All that and no apology. That's pathetic, Mom."

"Didn't I just apologize?"

"No. There was nothing apologetic there but your tone, and after the last ten years I deserve a lot more than that."

Savannah was wounded, but knew she'd earned that comment. "You're right. I'm sorry."

"Real heartfelt."

"No, Jessica, listen: I'm really, *really* sorry. I'm sorry I wasn't more attentive to your frustrations, I'm sorry I wasn't there for you the way you needed me to be, and … I'm sorry if you felt like you weren't as important to me as A&A was."

Jessie finally looked her in the eye, but her expression was anything but forgiving. "Buzz words. You've been talking to Dad."

"Well … yes. But that doesn't mean I'm not being honest. I know this doesn't excuse it, but in my head, I was justifying the time I spent away from you because I thought the work I was doing at A&A would help make the world a better place for *you*. I was trying to reshape what it meant to be a Christian woman, trying to make it a better experience for women now and women in the future, like you. But I didn't think about how your womanhood would be shaped by your childhood, and by how absent I was from it. I'm sorry."

Jessie's stare locked on Savannah's for a moment more before she finally broke the connection and stood. "Shocker. You finally figured it out."

"Yes, I did. And I'm here now and I want to do what I can to help. I know you don't necessarily trust me right now, and I understand why. I won't push you to share with me what's going on, but I *do* want to know, and I do want to help if I can."

Jessie eyed her warily. "Let me think about it. I'm going to go take a shower."

"Go right ahead. Are you hungry? I'll make us something to eat. Do you know when your father will be home?"

"No. I don't even know where he is."

"Alright then. Come on down when you're ready; I'll go cook something up."

Savannah went downstairs, pride still smarting but feeling far more confident in the restoration of their relationship than she'd expected to be. She opened the cupboards, searching for comfort food, and was pleasantly surprised when she found what she was looking for.

Jessie appeared half an hour later, her hair still wet. "Waffles?"

"I always find carbs comforting."

Savannah put a plate of two waffles in front of Jessie, along with a glass of milk. "So."

"So."

"Dad told me about Adam."

Jessie's eyes went to her plate and stayed there. "Yeah."

"That was incredibly shallow of him."

"I don't know ... I don't feel like I can really blame him."

"Why not?"

"Because it makes sense he'd be so hurt. And what if our roles had been reversed — would I really want to go see his parents, spend Christmas day with them, knowing they'd put you out of a job?"

Savannah was encouraged by how little judgment was in Jessie's tone. "I understand his loyalty to his family, and what a tight spot this has put them in. Ministries operate very differently from businesses. The knowledge of a higher purpose involved and a shared belief system breaks down those formal, business-like walls that people tend to erect between themselves and their superiors. We were all like family at A&A; which was good. But when life happens and businesses fail, people need to realize it wasn't done intentionally. Nothing personal was meant by it. Mistakes have been made that I'm just now finding out about, and those mistakes are part of what led to A&A's demise. I don't want to go into details," she added when she saw Jessie look up with curiosity, "because I want to make sure I've got all my facts straight — and I need to talk to your father to do that. But point being — Adam should have known our family better than to think we'd ever hurt his family — or anyone — on purpose. We didn't 'screw them over.' The money ran out and we had to close down."

Jessie nodded a little as she cut her waffle across the gridlines.

"I guess that makes some sense. I'm just ... I'm mad at God that all this happened. I don't see how any of this can turn out well."

Savannah brought her own plate to the bar and sat beside her daughter. "I know how that feels, believe me. At least your anger is *yours*."

"Yeah ... Dad told me about the whole cellular memories thing." She looked sideways at Savannah. "I'm having a hard time believing it. Sounds a little kooky to me."

"It sounds kooky to me, too. But what other theories are there to explain it all?" She poured maple syrup over the waffles, wishing she had some strawberries. "But the good news is that I had started therapy back in Georgia, and I think it's helping."

"Really?"

"Yes. The folks at The Refuge are pretty remarkable. I hope you get to meet Tabitha someday. And Aniyah. The cooking this woman does, let me tell you ..."

They continued to talk after dinner about Savannah's experiences in Georgia and Jessie's trials at school, until the clock on the mantel struck 2:30 and Jessie decided to turn in. Savannah sat in the living room with the remains of her coffee, longing for Aniyah's sweet tea and reflecting on the last three hours she'd spent with her daughter. She couldn't remember the last time they'd talked that long. She wasn't actually sure they ever had.

But as the night settled around her, the warmth from their conversation gave way to a chill at the memory of what she'd found in Shaun's office. She was getting anxious to hear the whole story. When would Shaun get home?

By 3:30, she was worried that he wouldn't.

CHAPTER 15

THE SOUND OF THE GARAGE DOOR OPENING STARTLED SAVANnah awake. She pushed herself upright on the couch where she'd fallen asleep and checked her watch. 4:15 a.m. *What on earth has he been doing all this time?*

She stood and straightened her clothes as she psyched herself up for the confrontation. When he walked in and saw her, she knew things would not go well. She tried not to sound as angry as she felt. "Where have you been all night? I was really starting to worry."

"Honestly? I came home three hours ago and saw you through the window. I didn't feel like talking. What are you doing home?"

"It sounded like things were getting desperate here. I thought it wise to come back and do what I could to keep them from falling apart."

He snorted, not even bothering to look her in the eyes. "A day late and a dollar short, darling."

"Not when it comes to Jessie. Just in time, actually."

He said nothing and walked away toward his office. She steeled her courage and said, "So what's the story with Carlie Stone?"

He froze, his back still turned to her. "What did you say?"

"I know everything, Shaun. Carlie, the audit, the fact that you're doing something with the ministry's money."

He said nothing, and a rock took up residence in Savannah's chest. What if she'd been horribly wrong? But then his shoulders slumped. His entire frame seemed to deflate. He turned, and his face was filled with grief, his eyes imploring her not to hate him. "I'm sorry, Savannah. God, I am so sorry. I can't even—" His voice broke; he covered his eyes with a trembling hand. "I thought I could get everything worked out. I did everything I could think of to shore up A&A and replenish our savings. But everything I tried backfired on me. I never meant to ruin us, I swear."

He sank into a chair and Savannah followed suit, stunned silent at hearing their personal savings had been affected too. In a trembling voice, Shaun laid out everything that had happened.

It had all started with the letter from the IRS. The first two years A&A had been an official entity, Shaun had done the accounting, teaching himself along the way. Unfortunately, he'd made some very large mistakes on their taxes, and when the government came calling three years later the ministry owed twice as much money as he'd thought they did. Too embarrassed to admit his mistake, he decided not to tell the new accountant, who would have paid the back taxes out of A&A's savings, which at the time were so meager they wouldn't have been sufficient anyway. Instead, he had paid the taxes with their personal savings, depositing it into A&A and then pulling it out so it was an official A&A payment.

His plan had been to skim a little here, a little there, and pay back to their savings what he'd used to pay the taxes. He made sure to always maintain some level of access to A&A's financials, and to keep the amounts small so they wouldn't be detected. He hired accountants who were green, who were star-stuck with Savannah and had no problem rubber-stamping anything that came from her. He began submitting personal receipts for reimbursement on her forms as a way to collect back what the ministry owed him.

It had worked fine for a while — until they'd hired Carlie Stone. She had been zealous about her job and about the ministry, always looking for ways to help the other staffers when she had free time. She was a hard worker, but there was something off about her — her manic-like energy, the way she violated others' personal space, her seeming lack of understanding of social cues. She would walk into someone's cubicle and offer to help, then began doing whatever she thought they wanted done without waiting for their response, even if it meant reading their reports or shuffling through the info cards they were trying to enter. People appreciated the offer of help, but not the way it was executed.

Shaun had left some receipts and a reimbursement form labeled as Savannah's on his desk before leaving for a meeting. She'd gone in and decided to finish the form for him, and in doing so had noticed some of the receipts were for things Savannah hadn't purchased—lunch from fast food restaurants (she never ate fast food), office supplies (it was Carlie's job to order those), magazines and subscriptions (Carlie was pretty sure Savannah didn't read Forbes Magazine or subscribe to Lebed's stock picks). She'd gotten suspicious and confronted Shaun, who had denied any wrongdoing and had refused to explain himself to her. He'd let her go soon after citing "personality conflicts" as the reason. A few months later she'd sent her first threat and demand for money.

"I thought if I gave her what she wanted, she'd just go away. I didn't think she'd keep coming back. But by the time I realized she wasn't going to stop, I was afraid of what she might say to people, and of whom she might decide to talk to. It would have sounded bad enough had she followed through with her original threat, but then to add to it that I'd been paying her not to talk?"

"So, let me guess," Savannah said, fighting to keep her voice neutral. "Nick figured out what was going on, too, and that's why you fired him."

"He was close. He hadn't figured it out yet, no; but I was afraid he would. He was more conscientious with your forms than I thought he'd be. I couldn't take any chances."

"And then I got sick—"

"And the bills started pouring in." He reached out a hand to her, a gesture of surrender. "Don't hate me, Savannah. I was a fool and I know it. Please forgive me."

Her heart was in turmoil. The anger she'd been happily living without had erupted again during Shaun's confession. Ten years of her life down the drain because he hadn't been man enough to admit his mistake. And now they were buried under debt and had no way to pay it off, had no way to pay their mortgage or the electric bill or their daughter's tuition.

"I ... I can't even begin to talk to you about this right now. It's so much more than I ..." Savannah wanted to punch out a window, she was so angry. "Never mind. I'm going to bed." She turned to head up the stairs and saw a shadow move in the hall. *Oh no.* "Jessie?" The shadow stopped. Shaun's head dropped into his hands. "Jessie, honey, I know you're there. Come out where I can see you."

Jessie stepped out of the dark. Savannah could see the tears on her cheeks. Savannah tried to keep her tone even, to not let her anger spill into her conversation with her daughter. "You heard everything, didn't you?"

"I can't believe you." Jessie was looking not back at Savannah, but at Shaun. "You lied to me. You let me think it was all Mom's fault." She disappeared down the back stairwell, and a moment later they heard the door to the garage open and slam shut and Jessie's car rev to life.

Shaun moaned. "I can't believe she heard me."

"Well, you'd better go chase her down. I'm not doing your reconciliation for you." She left and went into the guest bedroom, unwilling to sleep in the space that reminded her so much of him. She shut the door, waited until she saw Shaun's car swing into the early morning in pursuit of Jessie, then let herself fall apart.

JESSIE POUNDED A FIST ON the steering wheel as another sob broke from her throat. If she'd felt betrayed before by her father's support of Savannah, hearing that it was actually he who was responsible for A&A's downfall and their family's descent into near-bankruptcy made her feel like she'd been knifed in the chest. He was a coward, a liar, a thief. Her family tree was rotten to the core. She felt doomed.

Driving on autopilot, she soon found herself on the empty lanes of I–25, the major highway that bisected the state. She took it north, deciding to go to Angie's, then almost immediately changing her mind as she realized what time it was. Angie was in the throes of midterms just as she would be if she were still in school; to wake her before dawn with Jessie's family drama would be unfair. She couldn't do anything to help anyway. Instead, she took the exit for the 105 into Monument and drove to Angie's parents' house.

Angie's parents — her mother, especially — had always treated Jessie like she was part of the family. It had been a long time since she'd seen them, given how infrequently she and Angie were able to get together these days. But their home was the safest place Jessie could think of, and as exhaustion threatened to put her asleep at the wheel, she knew she had to stop somewhere. It was the most logical place to go.

But once she was in the driveway of their stone ranch, she was overwhelmed with embarrassment. It was just past five a.m., the eastern sky glowing with the impending sunrise. She couldn't just knock on their door now. Instead, she wrote *Sleeping in the backseat ~Jessie* on a napkin and gently closed their screen door on it, then climbed into the back of her car and proceeded once more to weep.

It was like finding out she was adopted, that the people she'd called Mom and Dad her whole life were just stand-ins for the people who held the titles by biology. No one was who they said they were. The anchors of her life were gone.

No, not true. What about God?

An excellent question. And one she didn't feel emotionally prepared to answer right now.

But plenty of other questions needed to be answered instead. What now? Where to go? What to do? Who to trust? Each was daunting, but vital. Without answers she was adrift and alone, when what she really needed was someone to wrap their arms around her and let her know her life could be salvaged.

Through her tears she spied the slim leather-bound Bible she'd kept in her car since high school. She pulled it from the seat-back pocket and held it to her face. Its smell brought back memories of youth group meetings and after-school Bible studies, back in the days when she was embarrassed by her mother's rising fame and struggling to come to terms with the Savannah she knew and the Savannah everyone assumed her mother was. Through it all, she'd never doubted God, never confused her frustration toward her mother with what she believed. Somewhere along the years she'd learned not to blame God for the actions of his followers, and the realization that these new revelations about her parents did nothing to alter God's character or promises brought on a wave of relief. She opened the book to the Psalms and began to read, searching for the verses where David's struggles and pain drove him to beg for God's mercy and compassion. She could certainly relate to him tonight.

A TAPPING ON THE GLASS startled Jessie awake. The kind face of Angie's mother, Gayle, almost brought on her tears again, and she rolled down the window as she felt the flush of self-consciousness warm her face.

"That can't be comfortable." Gayle smiled. "You know we have a perfectly serviceable guest room you could have slept in."

"I didn't get here until five."

"Ah, then I understand. Hungry?"

Jessie gave her a sheepish nod. "A little."

"Come on in. Lyle is out of town and I'd love some company."

Jessie climbed out of the backseat and tried in vain to smooth out her rumpled pajamas. Gayle eyed her as she held open the door for her. "You actually changed into your pajamas to sleep in your car?"

Jessie gave an embarrassed chuckle. "I was already in them when I left the house."

"Ah. Gotcha." She pulled out a chair at the kitchen table. "Coffee?"

"Thanks."

Gayle placed a steaming mug in front of Jessie, then pulled a box of pancake mix from the pantry. "I'm going to guess that whatever sent you driving around town in the middle of the night is serious enough to warrant pancakes, but if you're really in the mood for cereal I've got Cheerios, too."

"Pancakes would be great." A small smile tugged at her lips. "I always find carbs comforting. But," she added quickly, "you don't have to go to all that trouble."

"Nonsense, I'm happy to do it." She glanced at Jessie with eyebrows arched as she poured the mix into a bowl. "So what happened?"

Jessie stirred milk and sugar into her coffee as she recounted the last few weeks in flat narrative. Her emotions felt turned off now, as though they'd gotten used up over the last twenty-four hours. When she reached the end she gave a little shrug. "So I'm out of school now, and just ... I don't know. I don't know what comes next. You know, my mom and I had an almost decent conversation last night, although I'm still not at all prepared to let bygones be bygones and pretend like everything's fine now. But now, knowing what really happened with A&A, feeling like the rug got pulled out from under me ... I don't have the energy to try to work on things with her. And it sucks, because I feel like we might have had a chance, like she was starting to come around. But all this *stuff* ... I'm just so overwhelmed by it. I want to just lump her and Dad and Adam and everything into one giant ball and throw the whole thing out, even if they don't all deserve it. And I know that's stupid, but ..."

Gayle set a short stack of pancakes in front of Jessie. "It's not stupid at all. Of course you're overwhelmed. I'm not surprised. I wouldn't expect you to jump up and start sorting things out; sometimes it takes a while after the dust has settled before you can really start working on things, untangling them and fixing them. But I have to say I think you're handling things very well."

Jessie rolled her eyes and smiled. "I ran away in the middle of the night."

"A very honest response, believe me. You needed space to think. Perfectly acceptable. Although," her tone changed as she raised a brow, "please tell me your parents aren't wandering Colorado Springs looking for you."

Jessie squeezed her eyes shut and slumped in her seat. "Um ..."

"Can you at least text them?"

"I didn't bring my phone."

"Alright then. Why don't you use mine, or get on our computer and email them. I can understand not wanting to call, but if it were Angie at your parents' place I'd be mad if they didn't make her tell me she was okay."

Jessie sighed. "You're right. Okay. Can I use your phone?"

Gayle gave Jessie her cell, and she tapped in a quick message. *J here. I'm ok. Be home later.* "If they call back, I don't want to talk to them."

"Fair enough. "

Gayle let Jessie eat in silence, refilling her coffee and adding pancakes to the plate as she finished. Eventually Jessie held up a hand. "I'm stuffed. That was really good. Thank you."

"Sometimes crises make you ravenous."

Jessie chuckled. "Yeah."

"So now what? You're more than welcome to stay here for the day. I promise to leave you alone, unless you want something to do, in which case I'll commandeer your help in organizing my sewing room."

Jessie smiled. "Thanks for the offer. But, as much as I don't want to, I should probably go home. I'm sorry for crashing your breakfast."

Gayle laughed. "Hardly, sweetheart. I'm glad you came." She laid a kind hand on Jessie's arm. "And listen. I want you to know that we'll never judge you based on what your parents do. And honestly, I don't think many people will. And those that do — well, they're not the kinds of people you need to be associating with anyway." She smiled. "Your parents are human. They've made huge mistakes, just like the vast majority of people on this planet. But you're not your parents. You can learn from this, and I'm sure it will affect you, but it doesn't have to define you. God's plan for you hasn't changed in the light of all this — nor has his plan for your parents changed. God knew it all was coming. It's a lie from Satan that your life is ruined because of their decisions. It's not ruined. It's just unfolding."

Jessie sniffed as a fresh wave of tears welled in her eyes. "Thanks, Gayle."

"Of course, sweetheart. Drive safely, okay? You're sure you're alright?"

"Yeah, I'm fine."

"Alright then. And listen, you can crash my breakfast anytime." Jessie gave her another hug. "I'll remember that."

Gayle's eyes twinkled. "Just, you know, wear some real clothes next time."

SAVANNAH AWOKE TO THE NEIGHBOR'S dog barking. The clock on the nightstand read 7:04. Her mind began to churn, and she knew there was no point in attempting more sleep. She pulled the down comforter over her head, burrowing beneath the sheets. She wanted to hide and never come out—or, even better, to just go back to Georgia. She was done—with her marriage, with everything. She was beginning to feel a lot more empathy with Charlie. And now she had something to share in group therapy at The Refuge. Lucky her.

Then she realized she'd never heard Jessie come in. She'd heard Shaun come home, heard him shuffle down the hall to their bedroom and shut the door without even trying to do it quietly. But Jessie, whose room was next door to the guest bedroom where Savannah had slept, had either been extremely quiet or else had never come home.

She got up and tiptoed out, hoping to avoid Shaun until she figured out what her response to him was going to be. Jessie's door was still open. She searched the room briefly, looking for the pajamas she'd been wearing when she'd left. They weren't there.

It didn't matter how done she was with Shaun, she couldn't leave and risk losing the tenuous connection she had to Jessie. She had to go find her.

She went downstairs and made coffee while inhaling a bowl of cereal. The problem was, she didn't actually know where to go to find her daughter. Not the college, obviously, but other than that she could be anywhere. Who were her friends outside of Adam and people on campus? She didn't know. Where did she hang out when she was home? Again, she had no idea.

She poured the coffee in a travel mug and went to the car. Her brain felt muddled. She longed for the orchard, to walk between the trees and have so much space to think.

She pulled out of the garage and headed to the northbound freeway. She'd gone running at a state-protected open space north of the city once a few years back; that would have to do.

It was close to eight by the time she found her way to a parking spot in a gravel lot beside a stone sign proclaiming *Greenland Open Space*. More cars were there than she'd expected. She got out and saw a group not too far up the path, comprised mostly of children and a few women. As she neared them she noticed the children—probably between 8 and 10 years old—had notebooks in hand and were writing things down as they saw them along the path. One of the mothers was talking about the kinds of animals that lived in the open space. Savannah deduced it was a homeschooling group.

She skirted them, moving quickly so no one would notice the tears on her cheeks. She had homeschooled Jessie for a couple years. But then A&A had come into existence and she'd put her in school so she could work. How different would things be now had she not made that sacrifice? Even if she'd pursued A&A, but had made a way to school Jessie as well, would they have butted heads all the time, made each other crazy? Or would they have grown together, learning about each other, how to relate to each other, to talk together. Savannah had a feeling she'd at least know now where to look for her daughter.

Thoughts of the other sacrifices she'd made began to fill her mind. Quality time with her husband. Anonymity. Closer friendships with her girlfriends. She'd never considered herself a go-getter, the kind of person who would stop at nothing to achieve what she wanted. And yet she had. Not with the ruthless, heartless ambition of the corporate world, but with passion and conviction to the exclusion of all else, which she easily justified because in the end it was all for God.

Her anger began to take on a new form. It was aimed at herself. Why hadn't she counted the cost to her family? Why hadn't she given herself more margin, insisted on more boundaries? Had she really thought the two people most precious to her would escape unscathed?

Her anger needed an outlet. She walked faster, not with the same intent that had driven her in the orchard, but simply to burn off the energy that fueled her anger. Her thoughts formed themselves as conversation as she picked up speed.

Why didn't you stop me? Why didn't you open my eyes? What kind of God lets people do such stupid things in his name? And the last couple years, when it wasn't about you anymore, but all about me, you should have stopped me. If you're real, that is.

Then it dawned on her: He had. The days before the surgery came back to her — the mourning, the remorse, the repentance.

Okay, so maybe you did. Maybe. *I'm not entirely convinced that wasn't just my own guilt preying on my weakened emotional state. But then why did all the rest of this happen?*

Well, I guess Shaun's actions are his own, and A&A just got caught in the crossfire. Along with me. And Jessie. So what does that mean, exactly? That A&A wasn't doing a good job? That the ministry was pointless — or that it was actually offensive to you? And I have serious issues with the fact that you let this happen to all the great people we worked with. None of this was their fault. How could you do this to them?

Her feet pounded the pavement, slower than their old jogging rhythm, but steady. Her body still felt awkward in exercise, but the effect it had on her mind was the same. Her next clinic appointment was in two days. She wondered what the stress test would show, what they'd say if they knew she was exerting herself so much.

And what's the deal with all this cellular memory stuff? Is that what it really is? Or am I out of my mind? After reading Dr. Pearsall's book, I have to admit I'm a believer. I just wish more people were so I didn't sound like a lunatic. And if you designed our bodies to work this way, then you really should have designed an off switch.

She slowed herself when the path curved, not wanting to go too far in case something happened to her heart. She turned around and started to walk back, squinting into the sun.

Look, wherever Jessie is, can you please take care of her? I have a hard time believing she'd do something stupid and get herself in trouble, but she was upset and not thinking clearly. Get her home safely. Or help me find her.

She stopped walking as the impact of her words caught up with her. Had she actually been praying? She took a mental inventory. She was still angry with herself, but toward God the feeling had faded from disgruntled irritation to simple doubt — Was he real? Was he listening? Did he care?

She never would have guessed that doubt could make her so happy.

SAVANNAH SNUCK INTO THE HOUSE, easing the door shut and grabbing her carry-on that was still leaning against the wall. She brought it up to the guest bedroom, alert for signs that Shaun was around. His car was still in the garage, but perhaps he was out for a run. She slipped into the guest bathroom and showered, enjoying the ache of her muscles from the exercise. Just one more piece of the old Savannah coming back into focus. Hopefully it wouldn't be the last.

When she was dressed, she went back downstairs and ran smack into Shaun as he came out of the kitchen. She glowered at him, then sidestepped him without a word and went to the kitchen for some lunch.

"Jessie came in just after you got in the shower," he said.

Relief washed over her. "Good. She texted me just before I came home, saying she was alright. Hadn't said when she'd be home, though. Thank you for telling me." She pulled out the ingredients for a stir fry, ignoring the sounds that told her Shaun had followed her.

"Savannah, I just want to say again how sorry I am."

"Save it. I'm not ready to talk about this again with you."

Zucchini, broccoli, carrots, cabbage. She chopped with vigor, keeping her back to him and trying to fill the silence with her cooking. She could have made something less labor-intensive, but it gave her something else to think about and an outlet for her antsy energy.

Shaun, however, wasn't ready to give up. "So what now?"

Chop, julienne, shred. "I don't know, Shaun." And she didn't. She felt betrayed. Shaun was like a stranger to her. What could she realistically expect of herself in such a situation? Leaving the marriage certainly felt like a justifiable option, even if she wasn't ready to admit it.

But as she dropped the vegetables into the wok, it dawned on her that Shaun had likely felt the same way after she'd changed so much. And he hadn't left.

"I'm just … not ready to forgive you yet." She hoped he would catch the fact that she wasn't ruling it out entirely.

"I understand," he said quickly. "I wouldn't expect you to be."

She whisked soy sauce and cornstarch in a bowl, set it aside. "I had an idea while I was out. I'd like to bring Jessie to Georgia with me, if she's willing, and if Tabitha can spare the room. I think she'd benefit from being at The Refuge, and it would give the two of us the chance to bond some more."

"That makes sense." He spoke slowly, and she knew he was trying to decide if those reasons were the real ones or decoys.

"It's not like we'll be gone forever." She finally turned to look him in the eyes, then tried to soften her tone. "I still need some time, too. But I want to do what I can to help us get untangled from our … financial issues. If you want, I can pack away the things I really want to keep, and you can try to sell the house and whatever furnishings people want. There's very little in the way of stuff that I'm attached to. And we've got some nice things; I'm sure you could sell or consign them for a good price."

He managed a smile. "That's a good idea."

She stirred the vegetables and chose her words carefully. "You *are* going to come clean with everyone, right?"

His response took a few seconds to come. "Come clean?"

"With the staff."

"With — wait, you mean, tell them everything?"

She breathed deeply, trying not to let her anger build up the wall they were trying to tear down. "Yes. Everything. Don't you think that's the right thing to do? Apologize — to Nick, to Carlie —"

"Carlie! Are you nuts?"

"She's doing what she's doing because of what *you* did, Shaun. Admit your mistake to everyone and you take away her power. Plus, you really do owe her an apology if you fired her, even partly, because of what she found out. And it would be better to do it before she made good on her threats."

Shaun ran a hand over his face and wandered out of the kitchen. Savannah turned back to her stir fry, astounded at who her husband had turned out to be. She never would have believed his story if it hadn't come straight from him.

She plated the food and ate as she tried to envision their future. *Was* there a future for them? The life they'd been living — more business partners than lovers — was not appealing. She didn't want that life back. And now that she knew who Shaun really was, she wasn't so sure she wanted him, anyway. If he did what he needed to do, showed he was willing to change — maybe she'd concede to giving it another try. But would they ever be able to go back to how they had been before A&A had transformed them from lovers to coworkers?

The longer she pondered, the clearer things became, and after she finished eating she made a stop at Shaun's office before calling Tabitha about her idea.

"Just to put your mind at ease — I don't want a divorce."

The fact that he looked so shocked broke her heart. "You don't? Why not?"

"I don't think it's what God would want."

The look intensified. "You actually care what God wants?"

"Well, not exactly — but I don't want to make any decisions I might regret. And I think I would regret that."

He smiled. "I'm glad to hear that."

She smiled back. "Yeah. Me too."

JESSIE TOOK A BITE OF her apple and keyed in the URL of the *Colorado Springs Gazette*'s website, then clicked on their job listings. She couldn't handle the bookstore for much longer, not with all the comments she heard from customers when they saw Savannah's books on the shelves. The other staff hadn't been too bad, though Torrie had been standoffish for the last week or so. Jessie tried not to care, but it wasn't working. She needed a change.

She still hadn't seen her mother since coming home from Angie's house. She'd run into her father, to whom she had refused to talk before locking herself in her bedroom and falling asleep. She'd woken just an hour later, but the nap had done her good. She hadn't been ready to take on all the questions of her future, but she had felt ready to take a small step. The job search felt doable.

A knock, then a call of "Jessie?" broke her concentration. Her mother. The walls went up once again around her heart. "Come in."

Savannah's face held a look of cautiousness, of apprehension. Not expressions she was used to seeing on her mother. "I'm sorry to interrupt you," she said, sounding truly concerned that Jessie may have been in the middle of something important. "I just wanted to talk to you for a minute. That alright?"

"Um — yeah, sure."

Savannah sat on the edge of the bed. "I'm really sorry about last night. I'm sorry you had to find out that way. Thanks for letting us know you were alright; we were getting worried."

Jessie felt a twinge of guilt. "Yeah ... I'm sorry I ran out like that."

"That's alright; you needed your space."

Jessie smiled a bit at the echo of Gayle's words. "Yeah, I did."

Savannah pulled the ends of her sweater over her hands as her demeanor seemed to shift to one of almost nervousness. "Listen, I wanted to propose something. It—it might sound sort of weird, but just hear me out, okay?"

"Okay." She was curious despite herself.

"Okay, so ... I told you about the Refuge, and Tabitha and Aniyah, and all that ... they've really helped me, and Tabitha has a really amazing program there. I know we haven't talked a ton about everything that's happened lately, or about the things your dad did, so for all I know you're handling things really well. But, even though you're an incredibly strong and smart young woman, I know you've been hit with a lot of big stuff lately, and I thought it might be helpful for you—if you wanted to, that is—to come to The Refuge with me for a while."

Jessie hadn't known what to expect, but this wouldn't have even been on the list. "What? Seriously?"

"You wouldn't have to go to the sessions if you didn't want to— if it just didn't seem like something that was going to be helpful, no one would make you participate. So, if nothing else, it would be a vacation, and heaven knows you need one."

She had to smile at that. "Yeah, that would be nice."

"No expectations, no pressure—just an opportunity to commiserate with some people who can relate to what you're going through, in their own way, and who might be able to give you some insights. And I promise you'll have your privacy. I won't go to the sessions that you go to, so you don't feel like you have to censor yourself. Heck, we don't even have to talk while we're there; you'll have your own room and everything. I talked it over with Tabitha and she's totally fine with it all."

Jessie slowly tilted her chair back, thinking. "Wow. That's ... that's quite an offer."

"You don't have to answer right now, either." Savannah stood, her hands popping out of the sleeves. "Let me know what you decide. And like I said, no pressure." She gave Jessie a quick hug, then left her to her thoughts.

Jessie watched the door close, feeling like she was in a dream. Had her mother really just apologized, affirmed Jessie's fragile emotional state, and then actually managed to offer help without making it sound condescending? If that was the result of her time at The Refuge, then that alone was a reason to go.

But even if it wasn't, she had to admit the opportunity sounded amazing. The vacation aspect alone was enough to make her want to pack her bags. But to be able to finally dump all her frustrations and anger and grief over the events of the last few years and get some help in sorting through and dealing with it—it was almost too good to be true.

So what do you think? She stared at the computer and took another bite of her apple. A warmth grew in her heart as she imagined the place her mother had told her about the night before. She finished her apple, closed out the classifieds, and picked up her cell phone and dialed. "Hey Torrie, it's Jess. Look, I'm really sorry to spring this on you, but it looks like I'm going to have to resign. I can probably give you another week, but then I'm … well, I'm going away for a while."

She couldn't help the smile that stretched across her face.

THE HOUSE WAS SILENT, BUT for the first time in months, the silence didn't weigh on Shaun like a suffocating blanket. With his secrets spilled, he could breathe more easily, stand up a little straighter, even though the future was a gaping hole of uncertainty. All that was left now was to apologize.

He wasn't so naïve as to think that would then be the end of it. He knew serious consequences still lay ahead of him. But the hopelessness that had clawed at his soul and driven him to consider suicide was gone, and even the worst-case scenarios didn't scare him as much as they once had. It was hard to believe he'd been that desperate. He thanked God for the hundredth time for saving him from himself.

Before him on the desk laid a list of names. Each of the A&A staff was there, as were Nick and Pastor John. He picked up his pen and hesitated a moment before adding Carlie to the end. His eyes narrowed as he put down the pen, but he didn't scratch her name out like he wanted to. He knew in his heart Savannah was right.

He turned to his computer and began to type. He knew he ought to apologize to everyone face-to-face, and he still planned to do that, but not without some assistance. He outlined what his apology would cover, then began to write the script which would keep him from babbling and trying to defend himself. This wasn't a way for him to justify his actions, as much as he wanted to. This was a way to try to mend the bridges he'd burned the day he'd locked the door on A&A's office for the last time.

Rough draft complete, he stood to distance himself from the fallout of his pride and took a moment to wander the small space of his office. Soon he'd need to start paring down to the essentials, sacrificing the tokens of success that lined his bookshelves and walls for the sake of his family. They'd put the house on the market next month and sell what possessions they could to knock down some of the medical debt that still hung over them. It felt good to have a plan, even if the plan meant giving up so many of the things that had fed his sense of self-worth and security—or required him to place himself at the feet of those he had wronged and ask for their forgiveness. That part of the plan hurt. But with God's help—and only because of God's help—he'd do it.

A sudden throb in his head made him wince. He looked at the clock and groaned. More time had passed than he had realized. He took one last look at the computer screen, replaced a vague statement of wrongdoing with a flat-out, unadorned, stark admission of guilt, then shut down the machine and went to bed.

SHAUN, JESSIE, AND SAVANNAH SPENT the next few days packing up their most prized possessions and stashing the boxes in the garage. They filled their cars with whatever didn't make the cut and brought the donations to the Springs Rescue Mission. Shaun made an appointment with a Realtor to have the house listed as soon as possible. Then, three days after Thanksgiving, Savannah and Jessie boarded a plane for Georgia.

Jessie stared out the window at the vast stretches of farmland that filled her view out the plane's window. "I can't believe I'm finally flying somewhere."

"Someday we'll make sure to fly over the Rockies. There's a view for you."

"I can't believe you did this all the time."

Savannah chuckled. "Me neither."

She began to flip through her magazine, though her mind was elsewhere. The next few months would bring chaos and uncertainty as the house hopefully sold and they tried to determine where to settle down. She wasn't tied to Colorado, and Jessie had confided that she was happy to be getting out as well. Shaun hadn't spoken much on the subject. He didn't think it appropriate to express an opinion since it was his fault they didn't have much choice. She had tried to reassure him that selling their home of twenty years and moving on to new things was an exciting adventure, but he hadn't bought it. Surely once their debts were paid off he'd be in a better frame of mind.

When they arrived at The Refuge, Jessie's first words were, "Oh wow, look at the orchard."

Savannah slowed as they neared the house, giving Jessie a longer look. "It's a great place to go for a good think. Just don't run through there. Lots of rocks and holes for your foot to catch."

Jessie grinned. "Do you speak from experience?"

"Sadly, yes."

She pulled the rental car to the back of the building, parking it alongside the passenger van. "I volunteered you as manual labor to Tabitha in exchange for room and board. You'll be painting the garage."

Jessie laughed. "Yeah, right."

"Okay, maybe not. She did say plenty of things needed to be done, so you could either help me in the kitchen or tackle her To Do list."

"I don't have your cooking skills."

"I'm sure if you really tried—" Savannah stopped herself as Jessie's face clouded. "I mean, if you were interested, I'm sure you'd do great. I'd love to teach you what I know. But if you don't want to, that's okay, too."

Jessie raised an eyebrow, looking wary. "Do you mean that?"

"Yes."

Jessie nodded. "Okay. I'll think about it."

They brought their bags into the house. The doors to the group therapy room were closed, a meeting likely in session. "Wait here," she said. "I'll see if I can find Tabitha."

She went to Tabitha's office, but she wasn't there. An envelope with her name on it sat in the middle of the empty desk, however.

Welcome back! You and Jessie are in rooms 3 and 5. I'm off campus until 3, but will come find you when I'm back. I have a proposition for you.

Tabs

Savannah folded the letter and put it in her pocket. A proposition? That sounded intriguing.

She led Jessie upstairs, then took possession of her old room. She unpacked, then went to Jessie's room to see if she needed anything. She'd put her things away already and was sitting at the window seat with a ball of green yarn and a few inches of a project hanging off the end of a red crochet hook. Savannah gaped. "You crochet? Since when?"

Jessie looked sheepish. "Adam's mom taught me."

Savannah took a breath. "Ah." Then she smiled. "Will you teach me?"

Jessie grinned. "Seriously?"

"I've never tried anything like that. But I'd like to learn."

"I thought you hated doing crafty stuff like this."

"Well, yes, I did. I think because that kind of thing was always foisted on me by my mother, as though I couldn't possibly be a proper woman if I didn't know how to make things by hand. But I'll bet it's relaxing."

"When I don't forget how to do a stitch, yes."

Savannah nodded. "Yes, I definitely want to try."

"I'm not that good," Jessie said. "I only know how to do a few stitches."

"That's more than I can do."

"I have a hook you can use, but we'll have to get you some yarn. Think there's a store around here?"

"We'll ask Tabitha. I'm sure she'll know."

"My ears are burning." Tabitha poked her head into the room. "Did I just hear my name?"

"You did. We need yarn."

"There's a great place twenty minutes from here. We'll take a field trip." She extended a hand to Jessie. "I'm Tabitha. I'm so happy to finally get to meet you, Jessie."

"Thanks, Tabitha. And thanks for letting me come."

"Of course, of course. Folks are hanging out in the common room at the moment. Feel free to stay here or go down and mingle. I'd like to talk to your mother for a minute, though, if that's alright."

Jessie nodded, picking up her yarn. "I'll go down and see what people are up to. Anyone else down there do anything like this?"

"Actually, yes — look for Anne, long curly red hair. I've seen her knitting a few times."

Jessie's eyes lit up. "Great, thanks."

They all went downstairs, and Tabitha took Savannah to her office.

"Oh, a private talk. This must be serious."

Tabitha chuckled. "Not so much serious as official." She sat back in her chair and regarded Savannah with a smile. "But first of all, how are you?"

"You know, I feel pretty okay."

"That's an improvement."

"A huge one, yes. I feel ... peace, about selling the house and moving. Still no clue where we'll move to, but I think it'll all work out in the end."

"You were *this close* to saying something that sounded decidedly Christian."

She laughed. "Yeah, I know. I very nearly did, to be honest."

"So ..."

"Still doubting. But not angry. And not closed off to the idea. More ... curious and confused."

Tabitha beamed. "That's fantastic. And it makes me even more sure that this is a God thing."

"What's 'this'?" Savannah grinned. "Do I get to hear your proposition?"

"Yes. So here's the thing. Aniyah is leaving."

Savannah gasped. "What? No!"

"She's been looking for her auntie lately. Just 'felt like she needed to.' And she found her—and she's dying. She has no one, so Aniyah is going to go to her."

"But—to go back there—"

Tabitha shrugged. "She thinks she's ready to face her again. And she thinks God is telling her to go, so she's not willing to say no."

"So what's going to happen to your kitchen? You going to start catering Chick-Fil-A or something?"

Tabitha laughed. "No. I was hoping to hire you."

Savannah's jaw fell. "You're kidding me."

"Not at all. When you called to say you wanted to come back with Jessie, and you told me about selling the house ... it was like God wrote it on the wall."

"But—but what happens if we move somewhere else?"

"I'll keep you for as long as you're willing to stay. If it's a month, it's a month. If it's a year, it's a year. I'm not too concerned about that. God has it figured out, so I'll just sit back and let it unfold."

"This is ... this is amazing."

"I think we'll be able to work it so you can come to the therapy sessions, too, if you want to."

"I'd love that."

"Well, then, it's official. I'll get the employee paperwork together and get you on the payroll. Aniyah leaves next week, so you'll have a few days of overlap for her to help you transition into the position."

Savannah shook her head. "This is just incredible, Tabitha. Thank you, God." Her eyes went wide and she slapped a hand over her mouth in surprise.

Tabitha gasped. "Savannah! Did you mean that?"

Savannah nodded. "You know," she said, grinning, "I think I did."

EPILOGUE

Savannah's cell jangled in her pocket. She gave the gumbo one more stir, then set the lid onto the pot and pulled out the phone. Shaun's number showed on the screen. "Hi, Shaun."

"Hey, Savannah. I just accepted an offer on the house."

She let out a whoop. "That's fantastic! How much?"

"Only ten thousand under asking price."

"Oh, Shaun, that's incredible! What a relief."

"We close January 25th, though, so we need to figure out where we—I mean, where I'm going after that."

"Well ..." Savannah brushed egg white over the top of the French bread dough. "I don't know if you're interested, but I've been keeping an eye on places out here; there are a couple really nice places not far from The Refuge. If you wanted to look at them when you come out, I'll find a Realtor and get some appointments set up. When will you be out again?"

"I've got a ticket for the 23rd—but I may not be able to come out."

"What? Why not?"

He paused; she could hear the deep intake of breath that always signaled unwelcome news. "I got a call from the *Denver Post* today."

Her heart sank. "Oh no."

"Yeah. She did it."

"Oh Shaun—"

"It's okay. I mean—it's not at all okay, but I'm not surprised it happened, and I deserve pretty much anything they throw at me now."

"Well—so now what?"

"I'm going to contact the lawyer we had for A&A and consult with him. I don't know what to expect. I just ..." His voice broke and Savannah's eyes misted in empathy.

"I don't know what to say, Shaun. I'm so sorry. I wish there was something I could do."

"I know, I know." He cleared his throat, and sounded stronger when he continued. "I'm not going to dwell on it right now. There's no point. I'm doing the best I can right now to make amends and that's all I can think to do. Maybe it'll count for something if—when—I go to court. Anyway, I'll let you know what the lawyer says. But it wouldn't surprise me if he advised me to stay in Colorado."

"That makes sense." She rubbed her wrist over her forehead. "I'm ... I'm just so sorry, Shaun."

"Don't be, Van. I have no one to blame but myself. Maybe this is just God's way of making sure I do the right thing. I'm not sure I'd have had the strength to turn myself in otherwise. It's been hard enough facing everyone and telling them the truth."

She ached for him, knowing the embarrassment and self-loathing he was struggling with, and found herself wishing she could be there to comfort him. Another step forward. It was a slow process, but their marriage really was on the mend. "I wish I could be there right now. I—I miss you."

"Really?"

She smiled. "Yeah, really."

"I wish you could be here too. Tell me how things are going. Tell me how Jessie is."

She gave him an update until the timer went off on the gumbo and she had to focus on finishing dinner. She gave the pots a final stir after hanging up, then slid the loaves into the oven and went in search of Jessie to tell her the news.

She found her with three other Refugees, all of whom held yarn projects of one kind or another. The multitalented Anne was taking a break from knitting to tutor Jessie in crocheting circles. Savannah watched Jessie and felt a warmth spread through her at the look on her daughter's face. She had fallen in quickly with the others and had begun going to therapy, though she never told Savannah what she shared. Savannah didn't mind, though. She was just thankful for Tabitha's generosity, and for the fact that Jessie had somewhere to go to heal.

Jessie glanced up at her and smiled as she held up her crochet. "Hey Mom. Check out this flower. Isn't it cool?"

"Very impressive. You're really good at that."

Jessie beamed. "Thanks. So what's up?"

"I can tell you later; I didn't know you were in the middle of a lesson."

"That's alright," Anne said. "Group starts in five so we should break anyway."

The others began to pack away their things. Savannah took a seat beside Jessie, but waited until the others had left before telling Jessie about the phone call. "I just talked to your dad. He sold the house."

Jessie's face betrayed conflicting emotions. "Oh—oh wow."

"There's something else, too." She broke the news about the reporter from the *Denver Post*, and Jessie's face belied fear. "So I don't know if he'll be coming out or not. He'll let us know once he's talked to the lawyer."

Jessie stuffed her yarn in her messenger bag, avoiding Savannah's eyes. "Okay. Thanks for telling me."

"You okay, sweetheart?"

"Yeah, fine." Jessie stood, still not meeting Savannah's gaze. "You coming to therapy today?"

"Yes. In a minute."

"Okay. See you in there."

"Alright, honey." She watched her daughter disappear into the powder room, then saw Tabitha come out of her office and head for the therapy room. "Hey, Tabs?"

She stopped and turned. "Oh, hey, Savannah. You ready?"

"Just about. I'm going to check dinner one more time. Just ... do me a favor and pray for Jessie? And Shaun, too. I'll tell you about it all later, but ... life is catching up with us and the unknown is scary."

Tabitha nodded, instantly sober. "Of course, Van. I'm honored to pray for your family." She gave Savannah a hug. "See you in a few?"

"Yes. I'll be right there."

She returned to the kitchen and went over her checklist one more time. Then, after setting a timer for the bread and clipping it to her jeans pocket, she joined the others in the therapy room.

Tabitha had already started and was giving them the background story on Savannah's heart transplant. " ... which occurred about five months ago, right Savannah?"

"My transplant? Yes. End of August."

"After the surgery her heart worked fine in the physical sense, but other things were not as they had been before. Savannah has agreed to share that story with us today. Savannah?"

She couldn't believe she used to make a living standing in front of hundreds of people, sometimes thousands, and talking to them as though it was just her and one person having coffee. She rubbed her damp palms on her jeans and gave them all a nervous smile, then began to recount her story.

It was only the second time she'd strung it all together and told it, beginning to end, and the first time she'd told a bunch of strangers. To her own ears it sounded incredulous, and she'd worried they'd all think she was a head case, but the faces of the Refugees told her they were at least willing to believe it had all happened the way she claimed it did.

She gave them an embarrassed smile as her story came to a close. "The bottom line is that God is becoming more real and more relational to me every day, so I'm going to keep working the same way I've been working and just hope—and pray, when I can—that I'm able to get back to the relationship he and I once had."

She shrugged a little, signaling the end of her testimony, and received a round of applause. She ducked her head as she felt her face heat, and when the applause died down Tabitha began to lead them in a discussion. Keeping the promise she'd made to Jessie, Savannah slipped out and eventually sat in the foyer. Her mind was wandering, thinking about the feeling she'd had as she'd spoken to their little group. She truly couldn't imagine going back to those huge auditoriums and women's retreats, but she could imagine talking with small groups like she just had, trying to share some hope with people who were struggling to find some. It was the same way she felt about her job at The Refuge, serving people by filling their stomachs with the fortifying meals Aniyah had taught her to make. Providing someone with a meal was more than just providing them with their daily allotment of calories. It was a chance to show them love, to comfort them, to soothe them. To be able to sit at the long, rough-hewn dining room table after an emotional therapy session and enjoy a home-cooked meal could fill the soul as well as the stomach.

The timer went off, and Savannah returned to the kitchen. The scent of the gumbo and fresh bread made her mouth water and reminded her of Aniyah, who had written twice to assuage their concerns for her. After removing the loaves from the oven, she opened the pass-through between the kitchen and the dining room. The heavenly aromas wafted from one space to the other as she set the dishes and silverware, buffet-style, on the pass-through counter. She had just finished laying out the napkins and side plates on the table when the door opened and the first of the Refugees entered. "Oh, my gosh," an ex-pastor said. "That has got to be the best thing I've ever smelled."

"It'll be the best thing you've ever tasted in about five minutes," she said with a grin.

The others were close behind, and soon the hall was filled with the community she had come to love. Ever changing as people left and arrived, but bound by a shared experience of pain and disappointment and the shared hope of recovery, the community had come to be more than just a recovery group to Savannah. It represented a new chapter in her life. Before, she had maintained a certain distance, kept herself from getting too emotionally involved, even with one-on-one encounters. Now she labored to supply people with something that would nourish them for the journey ahead, getting her hands dirty and her clothes stained, and then sitting with them, eating with them, sharing with them.

She went through the line last, then took a seat beside Jessie as Tabitha stood and held a slice of French bread aloft. "Friends," she said, "let us give thanks, and eat."

ACKNOWLEDGMENTS

Many thanks and much gratitude to:

My ever-amazing husband, Daniel, for all the ways he makes it possible for me to write. It never goes unnoticed and I'll never take it for granted. I love you so much, babe.

My generous parents, Lee and Leslie, for the myriad ways they support and encourage not just me, but my whole family.

Meagan Casimir, Jim Gleason, Eric Goberman, and Don Peshek, for sharing their heart transplant stories and helping me with the accuracy of the medical side of the story.

Dr. Kate Hrach, for sharing her time and knowledge and reading my manuscript to make sure my medical ignorance didn't show.

Dudley Delffs, for getting me such amazing book covers!

Sarah Fields, for providing Marisa with the perfect name.

Miriam, April, Jessica, Ruth, Heather, Linda, Debbie, and Maggie, for stepping in when my creativity cut out. (Thank heavens for Facebook!)

My Lord and Savior, Jesus Christ, for showing me His heart and redeeming my own.

The Weight of Shadows

A Novel

Alison Strobel

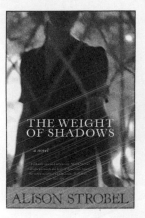

In *The Weight of Shadows*, by Alison Strobel, after a difficult childhood, Kim has built a successful life for herself ... but she'd leave it all if it meant being rid of the guilt she harbors over a tragic mistake she made years ago.

When she meets Rick, she finds everything she needs—including a way to pay for her sins every time he hits her. Kim and Rick's new neighbor, Joshua, knows more than Kim realizes about Rick, but Joshua has battles of his own to fight. Soon to intersect Kim and Rick's lives is Debbie, who has saved countless women from abuse through the shelter she runs, but Debbie might be as desperate for love as the women she serves.

Meanwhile, as Rick's wrath extends to their baby, Kim must decide if her penance is more important than protecting that innocent life— and if she should dare leave Rick when he has the power to bring her hidden crime to light.

Available in stores and online!

Share Your Thoughts

With the Author: Your comments will be forwarded to the author when you send them to *zauthor@zondervan.com*.

With Zondervan: Submit your review of this book by writing to *zreview@zondervan.com*.

Free Online Resources at
www.zondervan.com

Zondervan AuthorTracker: Be notified whenever your favorite authors publish new books, go on tour, or post an update about what's happening in their lives at www.zondervan.com/authortracker.

Daily Bible Verses and Devotions: Enrich your life with daily Bible verses or devotions that help you start every morning focused on God. Visit www.zondervan.com/newsletters.

Free Email Publications: Sign up for newsletters on Christian living, academic resources, church ministry, fiction, children's resources, and more. Visit www.zondervan.com/newsletters.

Zondervan Bible Search: Find and compare Bible passages in a variety of translations at www.zondervanbiblesearch.com.

Other Benefits: Register yourself to receive online benefits like coupons and special offers, or to participate in research.